I0670363

Deal with the Devil

by
J. Gunnar Grey

Second Edition

δ

Dingbat Publishing

Second Edition September 2013:
    Dingbat Publishing
    Humble, Texas
    www.DingbatPublishing.Weebly.com
    ISBN 978-1-940520-06-3
    Cover Art by Dingbat Publishing and J. Gunnar Grey
    Inset by Elaina Lee

First Edition May 2011:
    Astraea Press (www.AstraeaPress.com)
    ISBN 1466426306
    ISBN-13 978-1466426306
    Cover Art by Elaina Lee

So many amazing people had a hand in the recreation of me as a writer—Patrick Picciarelli and Barbara Miller at Seton Hill University, the entire Writing Popular Fiction department and all the supportive alumni online, and three of the best critique partners imaginable, Melanie Card, Alexa Grave, and Kay Springsteen.

But this first one must be dedicated to my mother and sister Debra, who always believed, and to my wonderful husband, John. Garfield and teddy bear rolled into one, you've always been my Campaspe.

Cupid and my Campaspe

Cupid and my Campaspe played
At cards for kisses;
Cupid paid.
He stakes his quiver, bow, and arrows,
His mother's doves and team of sparrows,
Loses them too; then down he throws
The coral of his lip, the rose
Growing on's cheek (but none knows how),
With these the crystal of his brow,
And then the dimple of his chin:
All these did my Campaspe win.
At last he set her both his eyes;
She won, and Cupid blind did rise.
O Love! has she done this to thee?
What shall, alas, become of me?

John Lyly (c. 1553 or 1554 – November 1606)

Prologue

28 May 1940
seven kilometers east of the Aa Canal, France

Fear squeezed the prisoners in an iron and icy grip. Clarke could smell it, more pungent than stale uniforms and fresh sweat, taste it in the dust caking his face and lips. The other British officers, sitting in a huddle around him, stared at the dry turf between their knees or off into some unknowable vacuum. None would meet his gaze.

"How many of us are there?"

Beside him, Brownell shrugged and swiped at his brow with one sleeve. With his hands bound, it looked as if he shielded his face from a blow. It grated on Clarke's nerves, revved his rumbling temper.

"Does it matter?" Brownell asked.

"It does to me."

Brownell shot him a look, not so much baffled as vexed. Good; a fight was better than collapse. They'd argued often in the last weeks, as their steady school-age friendship underwent some sort of relational twist while the British Expeditionary Force retreated across France. But for now Brownell held his peace. He half-rose, dark eyes scanning the small crowd and lips moving. Clarke's temper twisted, bitterness rising at the sight: Brownell had a well-deserved Oxford first in mathematics, but he still counted like a five-year-old.

He didn't deserve to be murdered.

Not far from Brownell, in the midst of a small emptiness left by the lower ranks, a light colonel with tired eyes slumped over his lap, epaulettes drooping to match his mustaches. He was the senior officer in the group. He should take command, organize a fight. All they had to do was get one man outside the guards' field of fire, and they'd have a chance. A suicidal chance, but better than being murdered without a struggle.

But he just sat there, staring into space. Around him, none of the many second lieutenants lifted their chins. One young subaltern wept. All huddled together, as if needing warmth even in the direct sunlight.

Beyond their circle, two grey-clad soldiers lounged on ammunition crates behind a tripod-mounted machine gun. They weren't typical German Army soldiers, although the uniforms and weapons were the same. These were something new the Germans had invented, something called the *Waffen SS*, whatever that meant.

Clarke lit his last cigarette, the binding cord cutting into his wrists. They weren't soldiers. They were criminals— murderers dressed up and playing soldier, like a bunch of teenaged hoodlums wearing Dad's collar and tie whilst robbing the corner sweet shop. It was ludicrous. Obscene.

"Do you want to use my fingers, too?"

Brownell's cautious settling back ended with a thump and one savage word. "There's twenty-two of us."

Clarke's swearing was whole-hearted and much lengthier. "Wonder who's going to dig our graves. Think the bastards will make us dig them ourselves?"

"Shut up, Clarke. We don't know anything for certain." Brownell crossed his legs again. His shoulders and bound hands drooped, as if the knowledge he denied was heavier than he could support.

"The hell we don't." Clarke took a long drag, yanking the smoke into his lungs until he choked. "Wonder how our kids have grown."

Brownell peered up at him without turning his head.

Clarke flicked ash. "The last photo Cezanne sent, Bobby looked as if he's almost too big for her lap. I tried to figure out how tall that would make him. But it wouldn't matter if she'd taken his photograph against a yardstick. I have to measure my son against my leg or it means nothing."

"You should have taken the leave."

In February, with the invasion season in cold storage, the 48th (South Midland) Division had offered its staff and line officers a brief visit home. None of them had seen their families since the previous September. Brownell had gone and now his wife was expecting their second baby. Clarke had made a point of staying with the troops, who hadn't been offered the option.

Now Cezanne would never have his second child, never have the daughter she wanted so terribly—unless she remarried. And that thought, more than his impending death, made Clarke squeeze his eyes shut and swallow the tightness in his throat.

"I know." He glanced from his cigarette to the turf. Maybe starting a grass fire would help them escape. More likely the Germans would let them burn.

"Clarke, you've always been a bloody fool."

"I know that, too."

Angry voices rose, climbing over each other, not close but loud. Clarke stared past the machine-gun emplacement to the command tent, camouflaged beneath wispy trees. The Germans inside had to be shouting toe to toe.

"What do you think the row's about?" Brownell asked.

"I hope it's about us, and I hope that German Army chap wins."

Brownell lifted his head. "You think so?"

Clarke shrugged. "Don't recall much German from school, and I can't make out their words even if I did. They could be arguing about us, their orders, or a skirt, for all I know."

Brownell's head sank again.

The voices fell silent. The tent flap whipped aside and two German officers emerged. The Army officer, a non-com's sidecap replacing the usual peaked cap, stalked toward the huddled prisoners, his riding boots raising puffs of dust. The *Waffen SS* officer, Greis, followed more slowly, a little smile curving the corners of his narrow lips.

Clarke's heart sank. It was only too obvious who had won.

Near the edge of their huddle, the Army officer stopped, legs spraddled, hands on hips, staring in a slow sweep as if he wanted to impress every man on his memory. His face was pale, with scorching blotches of color in his tanned cheeks. He breathed as if he'd been running.

"What do you think?" Clarke glanced at Brownell. He froze.

Brownell's staring eyes were huge. His mouth hung open for a long moment. Then he snapped his jaw shut and wet his lips. "Clarke, that's—"

But the Army officer was issuing orders, German words stuttering in a staccato rhythm like a machine gun, and Brownell swallowed the rest of his sentence. Automatically, Clarke turned to see what the fuss was about—and smashed into the German officer's smoking glare, aimed right at him.

"You," he said in English. "Come on, I don't have all day."

9

Two of the *Waffen SS* soldiers waded into the sitting Englishmen, grabbed Clarke by the arms, and heaved him to his feet. So this was it; he'd go first. His legs were asleep, but damned if he'd take any help from these murderers. He shook off their arms, dropped his cigarette butt, and forced his tingling legs to carry his weight as they escorted him, one on either side, to the German officer.

Halfway there, he glanced back at Brownell. Brownell's mouth was open again and he was half on his feet, legs beneath him as if for a sudden push. Clarke shook his head—Brownell needed to save his major effort for his own life, not waste it on a fool's attempt at gallantry—and mouthed *goodbye*. Without waiting for a response, he turned away.

It was a ruddy awful way to part.

When Clarke turned, he was eye to eye with the German officer. Although they weren't close and sunshine blazed between them, there seemed barely room between their bodies to breathe. The heat of the German's anger smoldered still, like a flare not quite burned out. But his brown eyes were clear and even a trifle desperate as he gazed into Clarke's, as if he awaited some response and they were all running out of time.

Clarke sniffed in his face.

The German turned away. Was it Clarke's imagination, or was the tinge of color in those cheeks even darker? He could only hope.

"Right," the German said over his shoulder, "come on." He led the way to his open staff car, on the far side of the tent.

The SS guards crowded Clarke on either side, forcing him along. He passed close enough to Greis—the murderer—to punch him. He nearly did.

The guards put Clarke into the front passenger seat of the staff car. A layer of dust coated the faded interior. The officer slid behind the steering wheel. Greis sauntered to the driver's side and leaned one gloved hand against the door panel as the officer started the engine.

"Are you certain you can handle the prisoner alone?" A mocking half-smile still adorned Greis' lips, the smile of the winner. He adjusted his black leather gloves, never glancing at Clarke. Despite the smile, there was no humor in his narrow hatchet face, only contempt. "Perhaps I should have one of my soldiers accompany you."

Clarke seethed. He should have chanced that punch.

The officer shifted gears. "He's welcome to run along behind."

The smile slipped by a hair, then resumed. Only now it seemed fixed.

The officer released the clutch and gunned the engine. A spurt of dust slewed over Greis' polished boots and up to his squenched eyes.

Clarke stared back at Brownell's strangely hopeful face until the encampment was cut off by rising ground. Then he swung about. The dusty road rolled toward the staff car then vanished beneath it. Strong sunlight baked the interior, and he smelled fresh sweat along with the mechanical blend of oil and petrol. The engine vibrated up his spine, tapped against his eardrums.

One man. One pistol. No rifle, no tommy gun. No guard.

After that wisecrack at Greis, he'd regret killing this man. But he'd do it. A single pistol wasn't much firepower, but with it he could take this one, then return to the encampment for the prisoners. They didn't have to die today.

The *Wehrmacht* officer took the road over the crest of a small ridge and down into a grove of trees. To their left, the land dipped into a shallow valley, matted with brush and low trees that swarmed up the slope to the road. To their right, the trees thickened into a forest toward the ridge's crest.

Under the midday twilight of that canopy, the *Wehrmacht* officer steered the staff car onto the verge and killed the engine. In the silence, Clarke listened to his heart beating and knew, with cold certainty, that he didn't want to die for the hopeless defense of France. He twisted his wrists, trying to break the cords, but they only cut more sharply. The silence was so deep he thought he could hear the German's heart, too; then Clarke wondered if the man even had one.

He turned to face the German as he, too, slewed in his seat. Again they stared at each other, and Clarke took stock of his new captor. This was the man he had to defeat if he and the others were to live.

They seemed the same height, an inch or so beneath six feet. But while Clarke was solid, the German was more slender, shoulders tapering to hips that needed suspenders. His face echoed that line in a wedge shape, broad at the forehead and narrowing through well-defined cheekbones to a pointed chin. His brown hair was dark, the color of cocoa, and combed back from his high forehead in the Continental fashion. A formidable reserve of energy fired his eyes from within; even sitting motionless behind the wheel of the car, he seemed to vibrate like a tuning fork, and Clarke wondered how he kept his hands still.

Like most modern German officers, he was clean-shaven, his uniform tailored although not of the highest quality. The Iron Cross ribbon, red and white and black, decorated his left breast pocket; the knotted silver cords on his shoulders were bare of insignia, in the manner of a major. His earlier anger had drained, leaving his brown eyes clear, and Clarke knew he wasn't imagining the touch of derision now in their depths.

For one crazy moment, Clarke believed he had known this man at some point in their past, that he had only to sweep away the agitation to remember a more innocent age. But of course that was impossible. His subconscious thoughts were returning—to Sandhurst, University College, Eton, or even his father's estate, this German officer symbolizing someone haunting his memory. One thing for certain: this man didn't have the polish of rank. There was an earthy edge beneath his combat-hardened sophistication.

Clarke pushed the thought aside and cleared his throat. "Is this it, then? Shot while attempting to escape?"

The German produced a pack of cigarettes and shook one halfway out. "Do you use these things?"

Clarke fought his pride—he didn't want to accept any-thing from a German—but his sudden nicotine craving was stronger. He took the fag and the light that followed, and cradled it in his bound hands for a drag. "A last cigarette?"

"Every condemned man deserves one." But the German's tone was light.

"It's not a joking matter."

This time the German's stare was considering. "You're right," he finally said. "It's not."

"I know what happened at Guise."

"So do I." The German seemed to reach a decision and opened his door. "Step out. I want to show you something."

Clarke hesitated. The German shrugged, drew his pistol, snapped the magazine from its butt and pocketed it, and tossed the gun itself onto the dashboard. "We don't have much time. Come on." He closed the driver's door softly and stepped to the opposite verge of the road.

For a moment Clarke stared, flabbergasted. But he wasn't hallucinating. His only guard truly had unloaded his only weapon and turned his back. The shelter of the trees was on his side of the road and temptingly near. But his curiosity won the brief struggle. There had to be a reason for this otherwise senseless behavior, and Clarke wanted to know what it was. He followed the German to the opposite side of the road and stood beside his enemy.

The German cupped his cigarette in his left hand, glowing edge toward his palm, and gestured to the shallow valley at their feet. Neither hand left the deepest shadows spread by the trees overhead.

"See them?"

It took a moment. Then a motion caught Clarke's eye. The valley was alive with almost-hidden yet shifting forms. He peered closer and made out camouflage netting, a half-track, machine-gun nests, hammocks.

"On the left," the German continued, "those are Greis' *Waffen SS* troops, from the *Leibstandarte Adolf Hitler*." He paused for a drag. "Undoubtedly some of the best soldiers I've ever seen."

"Murdering bastards."

"That, too." He pointed with his chin. "On the right, those are elements of my own division, the First Panzer." He peered sideways at Clarke through the gloom, smoke drifting from his mouth. "A *Wehrmacht* unit."

Clarke peered back, blankly.

The German sighed. His gaze dropped openly to Clarke's upper-sleeve regimental insignia for the Royal Warwickshires. He straightened and grunted. "Infantry: oh, frag. I'll try using small words."

Heat climbed Clarke's neck. "Was that an insult?"

He got another sideways stare. "If you're in any doubt—" The German took another drag, eyes slitted against the smoke. "We're all tired, you know. The campaign hasn't been long—"

"Six frigging weeks."

"About right—but we haven't stopped until today. Are you catching on?"

"No," Clarke snapped, "I am not catching on. What are you getting at?"

The German closed his eyes. "The two units haven't joined up all that well, have they? You could march a brass band through there at full volume and nobody would notice." Again the sideways glance. "Especially if the brass band in question kept to the *Wehrmacht* side."

Clarke got it. "Did you have any particular brass band in mind?"

"Progress." The German nodded once. He ground the butt of his cigarette underfoot without ever showing the fire edge to the valley. "Three days ago, Greis—that pig back there—"

"I know who he is."

"—murdered thirty British officers at Guise. He didn't have facilities to hold them; he didn't want to spare the troops to guard them. He claimed he had orders, that it was in retaliation for the officers he'd lost in combat. So he ordered them shot."

"I know." An admission of knowledge seemed to be the only intelligent thing he'd said all day. He dropped his own cigarette and asked the question that mattered most to him.

"Did he make them dig their own graves?"

"French privates," the German said, his tone cool but not as cool as it sounded. "The mass grave was multinational. I heard him give the order, I saw the massacre, and I saw the grave filled. Well, the situation hasn't changed. He's amassed British officer prisoners, whom he particularly hates because you didn't flock en masse to the Anglo-Saxon banner Hitler waved. He doesn't have facilities prepared for you, and he doesn't want to spare the troops to guard you or move you to the rear. He still claims he's under orders, although I let him know I couldn't find any reference to them at headquarters. And nothing else I said made any difference, either."

Clarke fought his mulishness. His decency won. "Thank you for trying."

The German spared him a puzzled glance, then pulled a penknife from his pocket and sliced through the cord binding Clarke's wrists. As he folded the blade away, he nodded toward the distant glint of water. "That's the Aa Canal."

"I know what it is."

"Just checking. We have orders to stop there."

Clarke stared. "Can't imagine why."

"Neither can I." The German shrugged. "It's a mistake, of course. If we truly wanted to destroy you, we should keep going all the way to the beach and drive you into the water." His sideways glance this time was a curious mixture of pride, shame, and defiance. "You and I both know the B.E.F. doesn't have the firepower left to stop us."

Just another German bastard after all. "That's your opinion and not any sort of fact."

The German grinned. In the shadows and gloom beneath the trees, his face lightened as if by magic. They had to be close in age. A vague tremor of unease made Clarke's fingers tingle; he refused to call it envy. While he had frittered away his—and his wife's—youth in an all-out assault upon law-court silks, this German had learned how to live. While he had developed a career, this man had developed his character.

"I expected no less from you," the German said. "Our orders come from the highest. They say stop at the Aa Canal— so no matter what we think, we'll stop at the Aa Canal. And that means—"

"—that means," Clarke interrupted, "anyone down on the beach will be out of range of your artillery."

The German nodded. "So long as that brass band reaches the canal before, oh, five o'clock tomorrow morning. That's about how long it will take us."

So there it was. This German major offered life and

freedom—for him. Not for Brownell, nor the colonel with the drooping shoulders, nor the weeping subaltern or anonymous lieutenants squatting on the scuffed turf. Clarke tried to harden his heart. He couldn't.

He cleared his throat. "Why are you doing this?"

This time, the German's sideways stare was compounded of equal parts derision and hilarity. He shook out two more cigarettes, passed one to Clarke, and lit both behind the cover of his turned shoulder. As an afterthought he handed over the remainder of the pack and the matches.

"Do you remember the cricket match against Cambridge?" he asked.

Clarke forgot the landscape and even the doomed prisoners. He stared at the German officer and it was as if a spotlight slowly illuminated the man within his memory.

"Of course," the German continued, "I couldn't follow cricket in those days. For that matter, I still can't. But even I knew we were in deep trouble. We were so far behind we could barely see daylight."

The face in Clarke's memory wasn't sophisticated or battle-hardened. It was a younger face, uncertain, wide-eyed, softer about the edges, but nevertheless the same. The body was more slender, bulked out by a cheap, rusty-black academical robe, the thinner arms juggling an armload of used poetry textbooks. Even the memory made Clarke sneer. And in a heartbeat he was ashamed of the sneer and of himself.

"But then the coach sent you in to bat," the German rambled on, oblivious, "and it was as if the whole field came alive, the spectators, the team, everyone. You strode onto the pitch with your head in the air, the bat in your hand, a swagger in your step, and for one shining moment there was no doubt within the entire of Oxfordshire that you could do it." He shrugged and flicked ash. "We still lost the match, of course, but I have to admit you looked magnificent just walking onto the field." No sideways stare this time; the German turned to face him squarely. "Do you recognize me yet?"

"You're—"

"—yes, that grubby foreign exchange student, the one who was too poor to buy a sweater for the winter." He dropped his half-smoked cigarette onto the verge and stepped on it. "I never forgot you, Clarke. Of course, there's a world of difference between the upper classes laughing, and the lower- and middle-class sources of their amusement."

"Look—"

"Don't bother." The German strode back to his car.

Clarke thrashed his memory and dredged up a name.

"Faust—your name's Faust."

"Really." Major Faust retrieved his pistol from the dashboard of the staff car and handed it butt-first to Clarke, his left hand hurling the loaded magazine into the deepest grass within the forest shadows. "I don't have anything heavier with me, so that's the best I can do for you. The evacuating British troops are massing on the beach outside Dunkirk. I suggest you get down there as soon as it's dark. There should be enough soldiers who haven't lost their Lee Enfields to make up a raiding party to rescue the encampment. Who knows, they might even have some ammunition."

Clarke ignored the pistol in his hand and stared at Faust. It was an insane risk, the sort taken by the legendary Dr. Faustus—a practitioner of dark, mysterious metaphysical arts, someone who commanded the sun and the moon, the winds and tides, the forces of Mars, with utter disregard for his own future safety.

Clarke shuddered.

Still oblivious, Faust opened the car door and paused, one foot on the running board. "At Guise, Greis waited until dawn before opening fire. But there's no guarantee he'll be so patient this time. He thinks I'm taking you to headquarters for interrogation, so they won't expect you back and they won't wait. Wear something over your face, and I might get away with this." He stepped into the staff car. "Good luck, Clarke. My regards to Brownell after you rescue him."

"Wait." Clarke didn't recognize his own throttled voice. "Why are you doing this?" Even as he said it, he knew that wasn't the best way of asking his question, it wasn't even the proper question and in his current agitation he didn't know how to rephrase it. But Faust was pressing the starter and his moment was over.

Faust rolled his eyes. "You don't have time for this. Oh, and if you get a chance, put a bullet through Greis for me, will you?" He shifted gears and the car rolled forward. "Pigs like him give all us Germans a bad name."

The staff car disappeared around the next bend, leaving Clarke standing in the middle of the shadowy road. He desperately wanted the answer to his question. He'd never hear it now, and that bothered him most of all.

He fell to his knees in the long grass, scrabbling for the loaded magazine.

1

late evening, Saturday, 24 August 1940
over the village of Patchbourne, England

Something soft and annoying whooshed past his face. Faust brushed at it, but it was already gone and he was too damn sleepy to care. He dropped his arm to the bed.

There was no bed.

There wasn't anything. His arm was dangling out in space. So was the rest of him. Faust snapped his eyes open. A strong wind pummeled him, tumbled him arse over head. The ground was a long way down. He was falling and it was real, not some stupid nightmare.

Panic leapt like a predator through his veins. He twisted, fighting against gravity. An icicle of light from the distant ground stabbed at his eyes, swept past him, and far below, several red flashes popped in quick succession. A rumbling vibrated the air around him, something that sounded like an artillery round exploded nearby, and sharp chemical smoke scoured his nostrils.

Then tight cords wrapped about his body, between his legs, jerking him upright and throwing him higher, dangling him across the light-slashed night sky. The rumbling intensified. His head snapped back. Above him, a parachute canopy blazed white in the spotlight from below. Beyond it loomed a huge dark beast, moving past in impossible slow motion. It towered over him. The parachute danced closer, second by drawn-out second; then it bowed, canted, and slid away, laying Faust on his back as it hauled him aside.

He gripped the harness shroudlines, his chest and belly flinching. It was the bomber, the one he'd been riding in. The belly hatch framed Erhard's laughing face, lit from below by a spotlight. With one hand, Erhard clutched the rubber coaming, cupping the other about his mouth. He yelled something—something short—that was overwhelmed by the racket and growing distance.

Maybe the plane was having mechanical problems—but Faust, Erhard, and the mechanics had tuned the Heinkel's twin engines all afternoon. No one else was bailing out.

Erhard had thrown him overboard.

It didn't matter how much schnapps he'd slugged nor how drunk he remained. When Faust hit the ground, Erhard was toast.

The spotlight's cone slid from the front half of the bomber to the tail fin, the glare flashing across the metal and leaving a dark, mysterious line at the tailfin's hinge. The line and the glare slid across the matte metal, twisting and writhing, finally falling off the back edge. The bomber was turning from the light. It pirouetted in a slow, graceful curtsy like a prancing war horse and plowed into the side of the neighboring plane. Metal screeched and crumpled. The two bombers hung motionless, pinned to the night sky by the fingers of light from below. Then Erhard's plane rolled the other one over. Flames spiraled from the mass of cartwheeling metal.

From between the bombers fell a squirming, thrashing human. Another white canopy blossomed above it. But within moments the parachute silk convulsed in scarlet flames, melted to flaring sparks of gold and orange, and crumpled to nothingness. In a clear, bizarre second, Faust again glimpsed Erhard's face, no longer laughing but mouth open in a scream not drowned by the clamor as he fell beyond the spotlight's reach.

The entwined bombers exploded. Faust twisted, wrapping his elbows about his face, hands clutching the shroudlines. Something sharp and hot punched his right shoulder. Heat flared across his back. But when he twisted back around, the night sky was empty. The droning engines ebbed away and the searchlights vanished one by one. A final, embarrassingly late flak round exploded well behind the departing squadron and black smoke drifted through the lone remaining searchlight finger.

The light fastened onto him and his slaloming parachute, tracking his descent. He exhaled, one relieved whoosh. He'd been trained on parachutes before the invasion of Norway, months ago, but this was his first real jump. Okay, it wasn't that bad. But he couldn't wait for the ground crews to find him so he could scramble back to Paris, and if he never flew again, it would be too soon.

His breath caught. German groundfire had no reason to shoot at German planes.

Where the hell was he?

The spotlight vanished, leaving him blind upon his stage. He glanced down just as his feet slammed into something solid. His knees buckled, tumbling him backward into stubbly stalks. The scent of fresh-mown grass was overlaid with the acrid tang of burning metal. Clouds lowered the night sky almost within reach. Shoot, he didn't want to deal with Erhard's mess tonight, no matter where he was. Faust lay on his back and closed his eyes, letting the alcohol fuzz take over again. The klaxon of the air-raid alarm seemed to fade, not to silence but to an incomprehensible distance, like waves creaming over a remote Dover beach. Matthew Arnold wrote that one, about pebbles being drawn back then flung ashore by waves on the Sea of Faith. *Ah, love, let us be true to one another...*

But the unpoetical parachute harness tugged at his torso and groin, jerking him awake and dragging him prone across the field. The canopy billowed about. Sharp stubble poked his shoulders and back. He grunted, eyes jolting open.

There was a quick release snap somewhere. He fumbled with the harness, found something, and pressed it. It clicked and the pressure about his chest released, letting him twist from the harness. Any possibility of carefully gathering the miles of cloth into a manageable bundle was swept away when the rousing breeze yanked the 'chute right out of his hands. Crouched on his knees, he watched the white silk sail away, like some demented specter, toward a distant stand of dark waving trees, and tried to decide if it mattered a damn. Parachutes were reusable, weren't they? Should he try to chase the thing down? He closed his eyes and rubbed his face. Nope, he was still drunk, worrying about a frigging parachute when he should be worrying about himself.

A quivering voice blew with the breeze across the dark void surrounding him. "Jake, you sure he came down out here? I thought he was heading nearer town."

Faust's eyes flew open. The wind gusting over his exposed skin, face and hands, was suddenly chill. He shivered and hugged himself. The twisting in the pit of his stomach was more than just alcohol coming back to haunt him. Some deep part of his soul, something as primeval as the night itself, quaked beneath his skin. But his conscious mind hadn't yet figured out why.

A second voice spoke, more quietly than the first, and steadier. "Be quiet, you daft bugger."

Another gust of cold air splashed across his face, reaching through his skin into his heart and brain and being. Faust heard his breath rasping in the night's quiet and tried to still it. But the beating of his heart was just as loud and would not be calmed.

They spoke in English.

He wanted to be still so his unseen visitors wouldn't detect his presence, but he had to admit he froze because he was too scared to move. It took long moments before he could convince his body to curl over and duck his head down between his shoulders to hide his face. And no matter what he did, his lungs demanded oxygen and sounded like a bellows working it.

"Jake, there's something moving over by the trees."

He was beginning to sympathize with poor Jake: that daft bugger really wouldn't shut up.

"Yeah, I see it. Let's work our way over there, *quietly*, now."

Faust tensed every muscle he possessed, ready to run or fight for it. But he wasn't near any trees. His nerves quivered as the wind danced over his skin. It might be a small animal, shaking the branches at the far end of the field—then he remembered how his parachute had billowed about like a live thing and blown away toward those trees. He stuffed his hand into his mouth, stifling a giggle.

He held himself still, breathing more easily, until the discreet footfalls waned in the night. Then he scrambled up, balanced a moment to make certain he'd stay that way, and staggered in the opposite direction. A hedgerow bordered the field at the foot of a small hill, and a white-painted gate partway along glowed like a beacon. He scuttled toward it. There had to be somewhere he could hide.

2

the same evening
near Patchbourne

The gate emptied onto a rutted dirt lane, barely wide
enough for a team or small tractor. Faust hid behind the
hedgerow, listening until he was certain the lane was deserted,
then he clambered over the gate. He stumbled across the ruts,
missed his step at the edge, and rolled down a steep bank,
flailing and scrabbling at passing bushes, until he fetched up
with a grunt against something harder and much more stable
than himself.

Through the pounding of his heart he listened without
moving. Water chattered nearby. The freshening breeze gossiped
through leaves. But no human voices spoke, in English or any
other language. The ground beneath his aching body was hard
and knobbly, sharp rocks and pebbles that shifted when he
flexed his legs. His racing pulse eased and he lifted his head.

He'd rolled down a slope too steep to be plowed and
fetched up against the scattered scree of a rockslide. Just
below his landing site, a lively stream danced in rills down a
gentler slope. Bracken and juvenile beeches crowded both
banks, imparting a musky, heathery scent to the gusting wind.
Overhead, the clouds were lifting; soon he'd have the moon to
guide him.

Ignoring the growing pain in his right arm, he used the
rocks to push himself up, then leaned over the stream. Into its
dancing midst he deposited the remains of his dinner, hanging
onto the slender trunk of a young beech and retching until his

stomach ached. Cripes, how much had he drunk?

He remembered wine with dinner—in the beachfront café with Erhard, that had been. Then there'd been brandy afterwards, and then schnapps on the flightline, the two of them sitting on folding chairs beneath the bomber's wing and passing a bottle, maybe two, back and forth, just talking. They'd been there for hours before the *Staffel* had flown out. What the hell had they found to talk about for so long? If Erhard, too, had been drunk, that could explain what he'd done and how he'd crashed the bomber.

The mess he'd made smelled like vinegar, bitter and rancid, as it flowed downstream. No wonder his stomach had wanted to be rid of it. He stumbled into the night, beside the stream down this gentler slope, and took inventory.

He knew he hadn't imagined what he'd heard: those two men, Jake and the daft bugger, had spoken English. Their accents had been rough, working class—farmers or laborers, probably—which made it highly unlikely they'd been practicing a foreign language while out scouring the fields for his parachuted self during a wartime bombing mission. And the places in mainland Europe over which said bombing mission might be flown, where the working-class inhabitants might casually converse in the English language, were few to none. The conclusion was inescapable.

He was in England.

In a way, the conclusion was a relief. Granted, the situation was bad to disastrous—he was lost in enemy territory, without supplies, food, a compass, or a map, and the enemy were alerted to his unwanted presence. But he had attended university here, he spoke the language, and he knew the general customs and geography. And he liked the English; the year he'd spent at Oxford was easily the best of his life. Right now, what he liked best about them was, they were not as a rule murderous. Even though he was in uniform, if he could keep his head and avoid capture, he had a good chance of locating the coast, swimming the Channel, and getting back to the mainland.

As opposed to, say, running into someone like that pig Greis and getting shot just for being in the wrong place at the wrong time.

The fear eased its stranglehold. Faust's shoulders sagged and he rotated them in stiff circles. But the movement started more aches, dozens of them, scattered across his back, stabbing into the fleshy rear of his right arm, and burning among his ribs beneath. It felt like more than just bruises—his back and arm felt damp beneath his clothing—and he remembered the scorching metal from the exploding planes that had flashed across his back while he'd swung beneath the parachute.

Add injured to his list of disasters.

He stumbled on, beneath the young beeches and along the bank of the stream, picking his way by what little light reflected from the water. No, he wasn't worried about the English shooting him out of hand. But the thought of sitting in a prisoner-of-war camp for the remainder of the war—and unlike everyone else he knew, he expected another long war— that caused him to wipe cold sweat from his face.

He'd only gone along with Erhard for the damn ride because the man had insisted, that much Faust remembered. But there his memory quit. If Erhard really had thrown him out over England—well, he'd paid for it. His parachute had burned and he had to be dead.

Surely bailing out over England hadn't been Faust's idea. Surely, as a staff officer in training, with the complexities of operations and the thrilling terror of his own command before him, with a real career finally at hand, surely he'd have to be more than just drunk—crazy, at the very least—

He wanted a career. More than anything. Didn't he?

Come on, Erhard had said, come for a ride with papa.

Faust dragged his sleeve across his forehead, streaking it with more cold sweat.

He managed not to swear. Aloud.

3

dawn Sunday, 25 August 1940
Woodrow, outside the hamlet of Patchley Abbey

Faust stepped from the shelter of the birches as suddenly as if he'd exited a building. Before he'd recovered from the surprise, he took that next step. A small bluff gaped beneath his descending foot. The world tumbled, then deposited him on his hands and knees in plain sight. The misty light of sunrise spilled around him, splashed from a wineglass full of dawn.

His few glimpses last night of the crescent moon, glancing through slashes in the cloud cover, had confirmed his southeast course along the bank of the chattering little stream. Good; if he really was in England—and it sure looked, and sounded, and smelled, and felt like it—then that was the direction he wanted to go. The southeastern-most tip of England was the point closest to the mainland, and if he was going to swim or sail his way across, that was the best jumping-off place. The less time he spent in the water, the better.

But then the stream curved off due east and the moon vanished, leaving him stumbling in a dark and unknown world. He tripped his way across interminable fields, getting to know them on a face-to-face basis, and little bits of each dirtied his hands and uniform. Pain pounded an insistent rhythm in his right arm, his shoulder, his back, his head, and most deafeningly in his side. Each breath stabbed around his ribcage all the way to his left shoulder blade. If he could manage one deep breath, fill his lungs without that slicing pain, perhaps he could clear his head and sort himself out. But he could only gasp in shallow draughts that made the landscape spin about him and left the fog in his mind as thick as an old-fashioned London pea-souper. Every time he tripped, it became harder to force himself back up.

About an hour ago he'd struck the northern edge of a line of trees. He'd cut south beneath their shelter and relaxed with his first satisfaction when the ragged line widened about him into a small sheltering forest. Soon he'd stop for the day and rest in the comfort of the trees' cover. He'd walked all night and driven all the previous night, and he'd earned a rest. But maybe he could manage another mile first.

And then he stumbled from cover and fell down a little slope into a pool of dawnlight that splashed across his hands as if he was the pebble tossed into the pond, and when he raised his head to look about, he found himself staring across a kitchen garden into the eyes of the most beautiful girl in the world.

He couldn't move. He crouched on hands and knees, gasping for breath, and measured the depth of surprise in those incredible eyes. Everything around him faded into insignificance, even the pain pounding its insistent rumba rhythm. Confused thoughts stumbled through his brain, each just showing itself for a moment as if afraid to break cover, and he wondered who she could possibly be. Had Sir Thomas Wyatt seen such a look in Anne Boleyn's fine dark eyes? *Whoso list to hunt, I know where is an hind, But as for me, alas—*

"Alcock?" she called. Her voice was English, of course, cultured and measured like a poetry reading. "Alcock, is that you?"

Faust shook his head. Nope, not Alcock. *And with a beck ye shall me call—*

She grabbed a shotgun and rose from the farmhouse stoop. "Who are you?"

Whatever answer Wyatt had received no longer mattered. Poetry vanished like a season past. Damn, was he *still* drunk? Mooning away while she shot his prat off? Faust scrambled up and spun back to the little rampart.

But the farmyard, and his head, spun tighter. His feet tried to follow, then the horizon and the rest of the world joined the dance. He hit the ground full-length and cried out as pain ricocheted through his body. For a moment he could only lie still while the echoes faded like ghosts into the depths of his brain. If he could escape back into the forest while she went for help—

He scrabbled up, grabbed for a handhold on the little rampart, glanced over his shoulder. And froze.

A pair of dark brogues were planted among the rows of staked tomatoes, beyond his reach. A pair of shapely, naked legs rose above them and disappeared into the depths of a tweed skirt. Above the skirt rose a body—the most beautiful body in the world—but then he saw the bore of the shotgun aimed at him, a finger curled about the trigger, and his fingers dug into the dirt of the bank. He raised his gaze to meet hers.

Not Anne Boleyn; Campaspe. *Cupid and my Campaspe played at cards for kisses; Cupid paid—*

—and he'd pay if he moved. The bore of the shotgun never wavered from his center of mass. He couldn't bring himself to look down, though, because that would mean looking away from her face, a heart-shape framed by a dark auburn bob, the short ends whipped across her mouth and jutting chin. Her fiery hazel eyes, her coral lips, the roses in her flushed face, were mesmerizing. At that range, she couldn't miss if she were blind—

—*At last he set her both his eyes; She won, and Cupid blind did rise—*

—and the pellets would rip his guts out.

Maybe he wasn't drunk. Maybe he was crazy.

"Dad!" she called. "Dad!"

She was calling for help; she wasn't going to fire; he wasn't going to die. He dropped his head beneath the edge of the rampart as if onto a pillow, never looking away from her face. *Oh Love! has she done this to thee? What shall, alas, become of me?*

A voice came from a distance. "Jennifer? What is it?"

Her name was Jennifer. It didn't fit. It sounded too tame, too unpoetical—what the hell rhymed with Jennifer?—too backwater English village lane-ish. She was ferocious. She should have a name like—

"I've caught a German." Her eyes never left his, and the warmth that seeped through him at the thought was more intoxicating than anything Erhard had served.

Me. Faust smiled. *She's caught me.* She should have a name like—

A man appeared beside her. Faust barely noticed him. Like—

"Well done," the old man said. The barrel of a second shotgun aligned beside the one she aimed at him. That didn't seem important, either. "Run up to the Hall and fetch Sergeant Tanyon. We'll wait here."

He spoke like a professor. Like—

But she turned and ran before Faust could complete the thought, and her spell was broken. Cold reality flooded his soul, routing the warmth she'd provided. He'd been captured. His muscles shuddered. He hadn't been so tired since the French campaign and he'd never hurt so much in his life. He let his eyes drift closed. His position, sprawled across the base of the rampart, wasn't particularly comfortable, but it was too much work to shift.

"*Sind Sie verletzen?*" It was the old man's tenor again, gentle and genteel.

Educated. Scholarly. Not military.

Faust opened his eyes at the thought. But while the old man's voice was gentle, his lean ascetic face was stern; his frame was slight, but he held himself straight as a soldier. And the lined hands cradling the shotgun were steady. Faust shuddered again. Now that he was still, the early morning air seemed chilly. His right arm spasmed with pain and he gasped.

"Yes," he said without thinking, "but I don't think it's bad."

The old man's pause was momentary. "We'll have our doctor look at you when he returns," he said, also in English. "He's at a nearby town right now. It was bombed last night."

"Yes, I know." For some reason he giggled, ending in another gasp. His fingers dug deeper into the dirt.

"Of course." This time the elegant tenor was only a murmur.

There seemed nothing else to say. Faust cradled his head on his folded left arm, curled his legs into a tangle, and waited under the watchful old man's shotgun, too numb to feel anything beyond exhaustion.

4

the same morning
Woodrow, outside the hamlet of Patchley Abbey

No matter what rhymed with Jennifer, she didn't reappear. But within minutes, the old man she'd addressed as "Dad" was joined by two teenaged youths in khaki uniforms, who seemed content to hang back and stare at Faust with their jaws and Lee Enfield rifles dangling. He barely glanced at them, but unfortunately they were followed by a middle-aged sergeant whose square face seemed devoid of any expression beyond cynical experience. With this sergeant's arrival, Faust felt his last immediate chance of escape slip away. His left fist clenched. Okay, he'd spend a few days in English custody. Only long enough to find out what was wrong with him and get it treated, no longer. Jennifer he'd have to forget, no matter how beautiful she was.

The sergeant and the old man escorted him into the farmhouse of honey-colored stone, the kids in uniform straggling behind. They trooped through a modernized kitchen into a low sitting room with surprisingly elegant furniture: a small sofa with carved feet protruding beneath its flowered slipcover, easy chairs, table lamps that looked like cut crystal, and a polished oak dining table and sideboard. A door on one wall was closed but not bolted, blackout drapes imperfectly drawn over the windows on either side. Through a doorway in an adjacent wall, just beyond a staircase, he spotted shelves piled with books and a layer of dust, the corner of a desk jutting into view. That would be the old scholar's retreat. The more he thought about it, the more he wondered what this old man, and his furniture, were doing in such a place, so far from the halls of academe.

While the young soldiers opened the blackout drapes and lit the fire in the old-fashioned hearth, the sergeant took charge of Faust. He was patted down; stripped of his tunic, wallet, and papers; handed a blue woolly blanket; then pointed toward a bare wooden chair the old man placed before the fire. Faust glanced at the sofa, but after his intimate association with all that dirt, he supposed he should be grateful they allowed him indoors at all. He sagged against the chair's ladder back, then grimaced and shifted his weight off his miserable right side.

The sergeant stood on the other side of the hearth, out of reach, right hand resting on his holstered revolver. The old man spread Faust's grey uniform tunic across the table and stared at it, then reached for his wallet.

Footsteps clattered on the kitchen's hardwood floor, then through the entryway strode a lieutenant not much older than the teenaged soldiers. But this kid's uniform, although rumpled and stained with mud at the knees, was more sharply cut and of higher quality cloth; it hadn't come off some government-stores rack. The lieutenant paused at the kitchen door, the firelight flashing off his white-blond hair, his equally pale eyes glancing about the room. His gaze fastened onto Faust, sitting on his schoolboy's chair before the fire. Faust's blood stirred at the implicit challenge. Then the lieutenant strode past and joined the old man at the table. Their heads bent together, and their murmurs were so low Faust could not overhear their words.

The fire was of apple wood and the aroma filled the paneled room to its shadowy corners. The sweet earthiness was soothing, almost as good as a cigarette. Now that he was sitting down he seemed to be getting a second wind, the pain perhaps arousing him, but it could also be nerves. No matter how often he reminded himself that he wasn't in danger, that he wouldn't stay in English custody a moment longer than he could manage, his breathing had quickened and his stomach tightened since he had entered the farmhouse with that sergeant and his revolver behind him. It seemed there was something inherently unnerving about being a captive, something amplified by being trapped indoors, and he couldn't shake the memory of the disheartened English prisoners he had seen in France—one group in particular.

But he didn't want to think about that. To distract himself, he twisted like a pretzel and managed a look at the blackened stain across the ripped right shoulder of his mouse-grey shirt, his once-white undervest, and his equally ripped flesh beneath. No wonder he hurt. But it didn't seem all that life-threatening, even to his own biased view, and a few days of first aid should see him through. Then he could escape.

Idly, he wondered why the two Englishmen at the table found his tunic so fascinating. It was just an ordinary field-grey service tunic, worn as part of his walking-out dress, nothing more. At least he hadn't completed training as a staff officer; if he'd been captured with those two bright red stripes down each side of his trousers, then he'd really have attracted some attention. And they would have kept a much closer eye on him. As it was, perhaps he could claim to be someone unimportant and slip away during an unguarded moment.

He waited for twenty minutes by the ormolu clock atop the mantel while the two Englishmen fingered his tunic and ransacked his wallet and *Soldbuch*. Watching them made him feel strangely self-conscious and violated, as if it were his soul being passed from hand to hand rather than his papers, while the sergeant eyed him, it seemed without blinking. If only he'd stopped in the shelter of that little forest and waited out the day—he had the uneasy feeling he'd blame himself for that rashness for a long time.

Finally the old man looked up and stared at him across the table. Their gazes meshed and the intensity in the old man's eyes raised another prickle of defiance within Faust. This, then, was the man in command, despite his country tweed suit and civilized lined face, and not the uniformed blond lieutenant who, despite his lack of years, seemed fairly competent. This was the man he'd have to get past if he wanted to get home.

The old man broke eye contact, murmured something to the lieutenant, then strode past Faust through the study doorway and out of sight. He returned a moment later carrying a balloon glass with amber liquid sloshing about its base.

"My name is Stoner," he said. "I know your right arm is injured; can you manage this alone?"

"Yes, thank you." He accepted the glass with his left hand. He would have preferred tea or coffee, to assist the final stages of his sobering-up process, but when he took a sip he discovered it wasn't whiskey but brandy, elegant and mellow. He took a second, deeper drink, emptying the glass as the warmth washed through him rather like an orgasm. "That helps." He decided to push his luck. "You know, I thought I had some cigarettes when I arrived here."

"Of course. Excuse me." Stoner produced a silver case

from the inside pocket of his tweed jacket and opened it atop the coffee table near Faust's elbow. "Help yourself." He took one himself then lit both with a matching silver lighter.

"Again, thank you." He'd been wrong; the wood smoke wasn't nearly as good. The cigarette was as cultured and elegant as the furniture, the books, the brandy, the old man himself, and again Faust wondered what such a professorial type was doing out here in the boondocks. Perhaps he'd retired to the country to write. A lot of dons did that when they'd had enough of teaching boneheaded students.

Stoner took a companionable drag then let his cigarette burn untouched. "You know, you must answer a few questions for us."

Faust let smoke drift through his parted lips. The idea of baring himself further made his skin crawl, but international law required his cooperation. Besides, if he didn't talk, he'd attract more attention than he wanted. He trawled in as deep a breath as he could manage. "Yes, I know."

The lieutenant sat at the table and opened a notepad, pencil in hand.

"Your name?" Stoner asked.

He glanced at the table, where his *Soldbuch* lay in plain sight.

"Oh, yes, I've seen your identification," Stoner said. "But I should hear it from you, as well."

He would have shrugged but knew in advance it would hurt. "Hans-Joachim Faust."

"Rank?"

"Major."

"Branch of service?"

"Army."

"Not *Luftwaffe*?"

He jerked awake. Set against the crackling of the fire and scratching of the pencil, the conversation had quickly reached a lulling rhythm, question-answer-question-answer, and he had fallen headfirst into it. There was no telling what he might have said in such a half-hypnotized state. He sat up straighter, deliberately making himself uncomfortable.

"No, not *Luftwaffe*."

"Date of birth?"

"November fifteen of nineteen-thirteen."

"Next of kin?"

Again he wanted to shrug but instead took a long drag. "None."

"None?" Stoner seemed surprised. "There's no wife, no girlfriend, no one we should inform of your safety?"

31

Of course; he still had Ritzi's photograph in his wallet. He hadn't thought of her all night, not even to compare her to Jennifer. Would he ever see either woman again? Ritzi, he realized, didn't matter, no matter what she could do between the sheets; but the thought of not seeing Jennifer again, even just to stare at, made his stomach feel as if he'd swallowed a brick without chewing. "She threw me over a few hours before I boarded the plane."

"Oh, dear, and such a lovely girl." Stoner stared, the intensity in his blue eyes fading in the firelight, and when he spoke his voice had softened from its businesslike tones to match. "So you've no one?"

Faust paused at the shift in tone and words. "That's right." To change the subject—and he didn't care if the old man realized it or not, that was too personal even for a legalized rape—he closed the lid of the silver cigarette case and admired the etched design. "Handsome case."

"Yes, isn't it?" As if he too welcomed the change of subject, Stoner's voice returned to its previous efficiency. "I must admit I'm dreadfully proud of it. It was a gift from the senior common room upon the occasion of my retirement."

He closed his eyes and thought hard, his index finger gently tracing the etched outline of stylized lilies. During his year at Oxford, he'd had his hands full with his own coursework, but even so, he'd heard some of the gossip around the university, and the collection of literature professors at Magdalen College had been far too famous for even him to have missed. "You tutored poetry at Magdalen, right?"

Stoner nodded and pierced him with one side-slanted blue eye, his head tilted away. "And you read Elizabethan poetry for a year at University College."

It was as if something inside Faust moved. For one horrible moment he stared at that shrewd blue eye, glittering in the firelight, and believed every fantastic story he'd ever heard about English cleverness.

"No, I'm not psychic." There was an edge of humor to Stoner's voice, but he didn't release Faust from his stare. "But the tutor at Univ is a friend of mine."

Irritated, Faust jerked his gaze away and tossed the butt of his cigarette into the fire. He should have figured that out for himself. "Mr. Wurlitzer, you mean." Damn it, it was just his awful luck to run into someone who knew of him as soon as he landed. He helped himself to a second cigarette—hopefully they were rationed and he was costing the old geezer—and Stoner lit it for him without comment.

"Yes, Timothy Wurlitzer. I clearly recall a conversation we

had back in, oh, it must have been nineteen thirty or thirty-one, when he told me of his most dedicated and promising student, who just happened to be from Germany and only at Oxford for the single year. A soft-spoken young man, Wurlitzer said, but with some hard-line views to his politics."

For a second, Faust let the warmth of the second-hand compliment flow through him. Then he remembered a debate on the absolute power of medieval and Renaissance monarchs which included some of his own unflattering references to the Nazis, and managed a self-conscious laugh. "I don't suppose it would do me any good to claim to be someone else."

"Not in the slightest."

The outer door burst open and Jennifer erupted into the room. "Dad—" Her glance froze on Faust, sitting before the fire still fingering the cigarette case, and she stopped so short her hair swung across her chin.

He stared back for another of those horrible moments. It was the same young woman he had seen guarding Woodrow's back porch with a shotgun, that was obvious. But at the same time, it wasn't the same woman at all. There was nothing of Anne Boleyn here, much less Campaspe, and images of coral lips and roses in her cheeks seemed suddenly sophomoric and embarrassing. This was a practical, unpoetical female in brogues and country tweeds, with her hair unbrushed and a smudge of dirt on her nose, and even Shakespeare couldn't make more of her than that.

And she wasn't even good-looking, much less beautiful. Too many of her facial features argued with each other. Her eyes were generously separated and glowed hazel in her clear skin, but her mouth was too wide and her nose too small, as if they belonged on different faces entirely. Her figure and legs were worth the look, but her prettiest feature was easily her glorious auburn hair, although the bob did little for her heart-shaped face except frame it. Even for a second, even all the way across the garden, even during the agony of that moment, how could he have considered her the most beautiful girl in the world?

As if she read his thoughts on his face, Jennifer visibly composed herself. She lifted her pointy chin until it aimed right at him like another form of shotgun. The effect was devastating; she didn't have much nose for looking down, but Faust had to admit she made the most of what nose she did have. The heat in his face had nothing to do with the fire, the blanket, or the brandy, and he turned hastily back to the hearth.

But he couldn't help overhearing her words with Stoner.

"I've just spoken with Sally, and Harriet didn't return with her. Do you know if she came back earlier?"

"No," Stoner said, "I don't believe so. But you might check upstairs."

Faust expected that, with her energy, Jennifer would thunder up the wooden staircase. But he didn't hear her footsteps at all. Surprised, he glanced about the room, but she truly had left, and he imagined he caught a glimpse of her tweed skirt disappearing from view at the top of the stairs.

"My granddaughter," Stoner said, and there was an edge to his voice.

That, too, was a clear enough message. Well, it was only to be expected—he was an enemy officer, after all. "A beautiful lady, sir."

"She'll do." Stoner rested one hip atop the table and folded his hands in his lap. On the surface his expression was neutral, but some powerful emotion bubbled just beneath those still waters. "So you are Hans-Joachim Faust."

Surely they had gotten beyond that point by now. "Yes, the last time I checked in the mirror."

Stoner's smile was brief. "Tell me, *Herr Major*, why should one of Adolf Hitler's bright young Panzer officers participate in the bombing of such a military backwater as Patchbourne's airfield?"

"Would you believe I treated myself to a forbidden joyride?" he said, then could have kicked himself.

Stoner's expression softened and his mouth relaxed. But his eyes sharpened, and the contradiction fueled Faust's turn back toward the hearth. "And why would such a joyride, as you call it, be *verboten*?"

For once, Faust had no trouble holding his tongue. He'd said more than enough already. From the corner of his eye, he saw the edge of the tweed skirt reappear at the top of the stairs and remain there motionless. His feet twitched on the hardwood floor. For some reason, he didn't want her to hear the rest of this. He didn't want to hear it himself, but he couldn't stop Stoner's mouth and the helplessness was infuriating.

"Might it be so because the *Oberkommando der Wehrmacht* anticipates the necessity of your skilled services at some not-too-distant point in the future, and did not want to risk losing those services for what you term a joyride?"

The smoke from the cigarette twined about him like a chain. Again his face burned, as if Jennifer—and the lieutenant busily scribbling notes, and the sergeant with one hand on his revolver, and Stoner with his lined ascetic face and carnivore's smile—as if all of them saw him, not discomfited, but naked. The edge of the tweed skirt seemed frozen in place.

Stoner's voice hammered at him as if from a distance, merciless and insistent. "We are discussing the incipient German invasion of England, are we not? Is it possible this was not a joyride at all, but a reconnaissance mission to evaluate potential invasion routes?"

Intelligence. Faust closed his eyes as something alive twisted in his guts. The old don hadn't retired to the country to write a book; he'd moved here from the halls of academe to run some intelligence-related operation. Bad enough to land in the neighborhood of someone who knew of him; but to walk right into the hands of a government agent was beyond even his usual bad luck. If Erhard wasn't already dead—

Come to think of it, the town the old man had mentioned, Patchbourne—there had been a market town not twenty miles from Oxford by that name. Erhard hadn't just thrown him out of a plane over England; he'd deliberately aimed for Faust's old territory, where he'd be recognized and captured most easily.

For the first time in his life, murder seemed perfectly logical.

"*Herr Major*, in the intervening years since your education, have you come to consider yourself a Nazi?"

Enough. He jerked the cigarette butt into the fire and glanced openly at the head of the stairs. "No."

"Oh, very well," Stoner said. "My dear?"

The remainder of the skirt moved into view. Jennifer paused at the foot of the stairs, staring at him, her fists clenched. This time, he couldn't bring himself to return the compliment. Just looking at her was embarrassing, after his earlier silly thoughts, and if he never saw her again, it would be too soon.

"Is Harriet upstairs?" Stoner asked.

"No." Jennifer's stare never left Faust; he could feel it almost like a physical touch, but kept his own gaze on the dancing flames. "I'll go ask the Alcocks if they've seen her."

In contrast to the abruptness of her entrance into the house, her exit was as soft as if the floor were made of glass. He barely heard the click of the door closing behind her.

Stoner's glance touched the crumpled field-grey tunic on the table before returning to Faust. "I'm certain, *Herr Major*, you could tell me some interesting facts about the Panzer armies currently training in France."

But Jennifer's vanishing, again, broke the spell. He cleared his throat. "Hans-Joachim Faust. Major, *Wehrmacht*.

Serial number—"

"We've already gone over that, you know. It's time to move on."

He stared into the fire and wondered, for no sane reason he could imagine, what Jennifer Stoner, with her uncontrolled energy and her stupendous grace, would be like in bed. He was certain she was a virgin. "I have nothing further to say."

5

afternoon
the Main Quad, University College, Oxford

The two men stepped from beneath the gateway arch, their black academical robes gusting about them in the breeze off the High Street. The sudden blaze of sunlight, glaring full into his face after the walk along the High's shady side, made Stoner squench his eyes closed for a few steps. But with the long, wide, and deserted central walkway of University's Main Quad opening before them, marigolds and greensward on either hand and no one within sight, a few steps taken blindly weren't likely to trip him up.

Unlike walking blind within his present assignment.

The surrounding buildings, three stories of warm honey-toned oolite, encircled them, and the massive crenellated tower reared behind. Sunlight glittered from the rows of windows beneath the decorative risers and touched the ridiculous statue of James II, in Roman toga and armor, in its niche above the gate. Stoner paused, facing back the way they'd come, and let the warmth melt his cold fear. He'd taught at Magdalen, not University, so this wasn't precisely where he belonged; but he had to admit merely walking onto the campus felt like coming home, which didn't bode well for his theory that he was as comfortable in the Army as the University.

"Now," Timothy Wurlitzer said from behind, breaking into his reverie, "what is so secretive it couldn't be discussed in the pub?"

Stoner paused and glanced about a final time as if

admiring the splendid Jacobean architecture, ignoring Wurlitzer's snort. Only when he was certain they were truly alone did he speak. "Do you recall a foreign exchange student you tutored back in nineteen thirty or so?"

"Hans-Joachim Faust? Of course I remember him. Charming lad."

"He came calling this morning."

Wurlitzer's smile died. As if on cue, the sun vanished behind a band of brewing clouds, racing before the west wind. The men's black robes billowed about them in a sudden gust, surely not an omen.

"Did he, now."

"In the uniform of a major in the Panzer Corps."

"So it's true." Wurlitzer sighed. "I'd heard stories. Who would have thought it, after his disparaging remarks about the Nazis? Certainly not I."

"His tone hasn't changed," Stoner said. "I presume he was conscripted and preferred not to face a firing squad. So beyond a neat summary of his political viewpoints, what can you tell me of him?"

Wurlitzer absently tugged his briar pipe and tobacco pouch from the sleeve of his robe. "You realize I knew him close to ten years ago? He wasn't twenty at the time."

Of course he knew that. But Wurlitzer continued before Stoner could produce a suitably caustic remark.

"He's a difficult man to classify. At the time, I would have compared him to a monk."

"A monk?" Stoner recalled Faust's gaze lingering on Jennifer's body and his protective rage surged anew. "He's outgrown that, at least."

"I don't mean to imply a lack of interest." Wurlitzer struck a match and held its spurting edge to his pipe, pausing until smoke spiraled from the bowl. "For that matter, I'm not certain true monks can be honestly accused thereof. But Faust was raised in a Catholic orphanage and he learned all his mannerisms from the Benedictines. At the time I found him a remarkably clever young man, but just as remarkably unworldly."

Stoner humphed. "A summary of his religious affiliation joins his political views. Progress is made."

Wurlitzer treated him to a dry look. "He attended services on campus rather than seek out a Catholic community within the area. Does that assist?"

The sideways stare was a Wurlitzer classic. Stoner had retired and moved from Oxford over a year ago, but in that time Wurlitzer hadn't changed a whit that mattered. Perhaps his hair was a shade greyer and he'd definitely lost a few pounds on wartime rationing. But his blue eyes still lit from within like a lighthouse of intellect, and Stoner didn't doubt that undergraduates still quailed at their twinkling challenge.

"By birth and background, Faust belonged to the lowest of the working class and supported himself while in school by cooking in a *gasthaus*." Wurlitzer struck another match and sucked flame into his pipe, gaze darting about the quad. "However, I could easily picture him as a secretary or a gentleman's gentleman, one of that superior sort who handles his principal's affairs with verve." His gaze stopped on Stoner and his old twinkle flamed, brighter than the match. "Rather like Bunter or Jeeves."

Stoner smiled. "And what have you been reading lately?" But he wouldn't force that embarrassing admission from an old friend. "How did such a man as you describe gain admittance to the hidebound Prussian officer corps?"

Wurlitzer shoved the tobacco pouch into his sleeve. "By earning admission to the technical university of Munich."

Stoner paused. All those years ago, when Wurlitzer had told him the promising young German was only in Oxford for the year, he'd assumed Faust had been a non-degree student rather than a special transfer student. Obviously he'd been wrong. "That's rather a grand achievement for an orphan with neither prospects nor sponsorship."

The brawling clouds parted. The sun came out, drenching them in light and warmth. In silent mutual agreement they strolled further down the path between the riotous marigolds, their shadows stretching left across the greenery like oversized bats.

"My point is, Cedric, Faust never truly outgrew his humble beginnings, at least not while I knew him." Wurlitzer stopped and again glanced about. "He always seemed a bit surprised at finding himself in the exalted company of our undergraduates, such as they are. He had a thorough grounding in Elizabethan poetry before he arrived, mainly self-taught, but he always seemed worried he was missing something, some arcane or culturally-based point which everyone else understood, and he hesitated to speak up in debates. He had no prospects beyond those he made for himself, so the predatory females at St. Hilda's and Somerville wouldn't even glance at him—" Wurlitzer's teeth flashed about the stem of his pipe "—although he certainly watched them. He didn't try to fit in. But he tried hard not to give offense."

"What on earth does that mean?"

"Let me tell you about the sweater incident. Here, let's

pause a bit; this brier wants tending."

They stopped on the cobblestones between the flowerbeds. While Wurlitzer busied himself with the brier, Stoner pulled his own pouch and traveling clay from his sleeve and began packing it, more for something to do with his hands than from any nicotine yearning. Ahead, the panes in the tall oriel window glittered in the hot August sunshine and the black-and-white face of the clock above flashed sun sparks, while the lower quarters of the arched windows and the doors into the Hall and Chapel remained in shadow. Memories of his years at Magdalen tugged at him, and he knew his smile was wistful. It was impossible to live and teach for thirty years in one location without feeling wretchedly strong ties.

"The sweater incident." If he didn't prompt, Wurlitzer would keep him there all day while he fussed with that impossible brier.

"Yes." Wurlitzer gripped the pipe between his teeth. "Yes, that's better. I believe I mentioned Faust was poor as the proverbial church mouse. He once confided to me that his entire life savings amounted to something like ten pounds sterling, and he was spending all of it for one year's study here. As part of his economizing, rather than purchase a sweater for winter, he made one."

Stoner paused with a pinch of tobacco between his fingers. "Beg pardon?"

"It seems the sisters at the orphanage taught him—not knitting, what's the other homely handicraft?"

"Do you mean crochet?"

"That's it," Wurlitzer said, "one hook, not two needles. Actually, it was rather a nice sweater and nothing of which he need be ashamed—a pleasant light blue with a few bands of white about the chest, and it fit him well. But some of our more snobbish students ragged him over it. After that incident he never wore it outside his rooms."

"Presumably he didn't wish to be ragged?"

"Faust didn't give a damn whether he was ragged or not. In fact, he seemed to expect it, and perhaps it was such preparation that enabled him to allow even the cruelest hazing to roll off. His friends were far more upset by it than he and there were some bitter words in his absence. But to the end of his time here, he never responded in kind."

Glancing down at his tobacco pouch, Stoner found he still held a pinch of weed between his fingers, forgotten as he listened. "Mannerisms from the Benedictines. I see what you mean; he's an interesting study."

"Even more interesting, when he finally did take his

degree at Munich, it was in engineering."

Stoner glanced up. "Are you saying he spent his entire life savings, not on his career—"

"The scholarship fund, of course, paid his university expenditures here. But when it came time to spend his own money, he put it toward the love of his life—English sixteenth-century poetry." Wurlitzer's teeth flashed again. "Granted, for as long as we kept in touch, he had difficulty putting together a career of any sort."

The tobacco was still between his thumb and index finger. Stoner dropped it back into the pouch and returned it and the clay to his sleeve. He felt as if he dangled on the verge of a momentous discovery, and one incautious move would send him either tumbling headfirst into understanding or rolling away from that edge to safety. It was a disquieting sensation.

"Are you saying he's an Anglophile or just a bloody idealist?"

Wurlitzer shrugged, his robe swaying about him. "Perhaps both." At Stoner's sniff, he relented. "I'm saying you two have much in common."

The sun played among the clouds, throwing their lonely pathway into deeper shadow, and cold fear again encased Stoner. If that were true, the coming experience would not be pleasant, should Brigadier Marone confirm the assignment. He sucked in a deep breath and tried to keep his voice light. "That should make the cheese rather more binding. I must break him."

The sparkle faded from Wurlitzer's face. He removed the brier from his teeth.

"We are at war." The reminder was unnecessary and Stoner hated himself for saying it. But he was always more secure in an argument if he built an invincible wall of logic to defend his position. "It's possible he has information of value. His weaknesses, Timmy; tell me his weaknesses."

Wurlitzer puffed for a moment in silence. His pipe was finally drawing and smoke billowed as if from a steam engine.

Stoner held his patience, examining the tracery of the arched windows before him line by line. His growing sense of comprehension confirmed which way he'd tumbled. Well, war was no time to consider personal safety, nor emotional comfort.

"Should you feel the need to drive him," Wurlitzer said into their silence, "you might prey on his insecurities, particularly his naiveté, presuming it's still the driving force it once was, and also the nagging doubt that tells him he's missing something important. That, and keeping him locked up in prison so he can't ramble about as he's wont to do, will upset his equilibrium more than anything else I could suggest." He paused. "Should you be able to lead him, which would be more in keeping with an honorably retired professor, you might offer him the one thing he's never known."

That sounded like a Wurlitzer word game of the sort they'd played for thirty years. But when Stoner faced his friend, instead of the twinkle he expected, he found ice instead. A sudden gust billowed their robes.

"And what might that be?"

"A home." Wurlitzer stared at the battlements of the massive tower, giving Stoner a good view of his sturdy shoulder.

If the sod meant Jennifer, he could think again. Stoner turned his own shoulder, aware that their silence this time was not so companionable.

But the cold silence didn't last long. "You're right. We are at war, aren't we?" Wurlitzer said. "Cedric, there's one further action you should take."

Stoner didn't turn even though the clouds thinned and the air glowed about them. "Yes?"

"I recently heard from another former student of the same vintage as Faust, by the name of Grandon Brownell. What he told me was in the strictest confidence."

If so, Wurlitzer wouldn't have mentioned it unless it was also of the utmost importance. Intrigued, Stoner glanced over his shoulder and met his friend's earnest gaze head-on.

"Grandon Brownell, you say?"

"And Robert Trenton Clarke." Wurlitzer looked up as the sun broke free, flooding the decorative risers and upper windows of the northern-facing Hall and Chapel. The lower windows and doors remained in shadow. "Presumably they filed reports of their adventures when they disembarked in Brighton after the evacuation from Dunkirk. I believe they serve with the Royal Warwickshires." He sighed. "This is such an imposing quadrangle. I hope that's enough for you to locate them."

In contrast to the Hall and Chapel, the stones of the southern-facing battlement were lit and each pane shimmered, clear and unhidden. "Rather like yourself, Timmy, old man: stalwart and dignified. Yes, that should be quite enough."

6

the same afternoon
Patchley Abbey, Woodrow, and Margeaux Hall

The sun was westering in a pale sky as Stoner strode east along the lane, not fast enough to kick up a real angina attack but enough to give him some exercise. The summer had been a hot one, cool mornings and evenings with blazing days, interspersed with terrific thunderstorms, and the wildflowers were in roaring bloom at the feet of the drystone walls on either side of the road. As he left Pamela Alcock's chicken farm and Jerome Owen's graceful rows of turnips behind, the lane surged up one last rise into the little forest the locals called the Dark, and his heart was starting to tighten as he paused atop the crest in the shade of the massive beeches.

Below his resting point, the lane continued down the rise and escaped the forest's reach into the glaring sunlight. Just beyond that demarcation, the old Roman rampart and another drystone wall contained Caspar Wynant's pedigreed Jerseys in their lush meadow. On the north side, his little farmhouse, Woodrow, nestled in its hollow below the rampart, with Jennifer's kitchen garden occupying every sunny spot not already claimed by the dilapidated barn, the apple trees, or the rutted drive. Beneath the apple trees snaked the mortared stone wall, with the final hill rising beyond and, halfway to its crest, the looming Renaissance bulk of Margeaux Hall.

Ivy trailed along the base of Caspar's drystone wall. Stoner plucked some, fleshing out the hothouse carnations he'd purchased in the Oxford market; otherwise there wouldn't

43

be enough for Jennifer's vase and Harriet's hair, if she'd returned.

He'd been flabbergasted speechless when Brigadier Marone, in command of an experimental project to make use of captured German spies rather than seek their execution, had activated Stoner's long-moribund Reserve commission and placed him in charge of the operation at Margeaux Hall. Once past the surprise, he'd been pleased; his years in a German prisoner of war camp during the first war, his enforced knowledge of the language, lifestyle, and mannerisms, could finally be of service to England. But the longer he managed the Wildflower base, enslaving men trapped between treason to their homeland and the English hangman's noose, the deeper grew that cold fear. As much as he yearned to protect his nation and family against the looming German invasion, this was a long, slippery slope that threatened to spill him into something worse.

He paused on Woodrow's porch, arranging the greenery about the carnations. He'd now have to place young Faust within the same trap. Faust wasn't so young, of course; if the birthdate he'd given was accurate, he had lived the better part of twenty-seven years and was entering what was so blandly called the prime of life. And full of that life he was, with his active face that didn't seem capable of keeping secrets, expressive dark eyes, restless hands and feet. If they'd met a few years earlier, Stoner would have tutored him in poetry and perhaps grown as fond of him as Wurlitzer.

But with England's back to the proverbial wall and the German Army poised on the shore of France, ready to invade, Stoner's job was to destroy him.

He straightened and entered the farmhouse. "My dear?"

Jennifer appeared from the kitchen, apron over her flowered housedress and soapsuds to her elbows, a damp smudge plastering a lock of auburn hair across her cheek. "Dad, you shouldn't." She kissed his cheek.

He returned her salute, her quick smile awakening his. "I know you like them."

"I do at that." She wiped her hands on the apron and vanished into the kitchen. Her voice trailed behind. "Any word on our bad girl?"

"Nothing." He heard the disappointment in his own voice; if she'd heard anything, she'd have said so at once. And while the drained, earnest-faced flight lieutenants at RAF Patchbourne had remembered dancing with Harriet at the pub last night, none of them recalled seeing her after the air raid klaxon had sounded.

Jennifer reappeared with the carnations and ivy in a vase, setting it on the oak dining table they'd brought from Oxford. She lingered over it, draping the vines in patterns, tucking them close then stretching them out along the polished wood. "Where on earth can she be?" Suddenly she was angry. "What is she thinking?"

Her hands were quick and delicate, sorting the flowers by height. The tug at Stoner's heart had nothing to do with his health. The war was maturing her too soon and there was nothing to be done about it. She looked after her sister, typed reports, cultivated the garden, managed the house, and never had time for herself. She hadn't even painted her nails lately. At nineteen, she should be at University or off on a grand tour of the continent—getting bronzed in Italy or philosophical in Greece, or laid in Paris, for all he cared. So long as she didn't become Teutonized in England...

Finally he said, "I suppose she's just being young."

Jennifer's sideways glance was ironic. "I was young once, you know. I never ran off." She cocked her head, just as her mother used to do. "Did you?"

She was enchanting and his smile appeared at her command. "No. I cannot say I ever did."

She smiled in return, her hazel eyes lighting up her face. Stoner wondered if Faust had seen her delightful inner beauty during the few moments he'd spent in her presence—with or without the shotgun. He'd seemed puzzled when she'd burst in on them, no matter how his eyes had lingered on her and no matter how efficiently she'd put him in his place. Stoner treasured the memory; like Jennifer herself, it was a keeper.

"Have you eaten?" she asked.

"I was going to ask Mrs. Alcock for something up at the Hall." He glanced at the clock on the mantel. "I have a briefing with Jack and Sergeant Tanyon in five minutes." He paused. He hated asking, but there was no one else. "Can you be spared?"

"Of course." Her hands vanished behind her back and the apron fell off. "Do I look all right?"

"Ravishing."

"Which means I need to brush." She balled the apron and threw it into the kitchen, ducking for the stairs. "Give me one minute."

It took her three, of course, but he didn't mention it as they entered the inner keep of Margeaux Hall through the postern gate and crossed the lawn in silence. Only when they neared the military wing's entrance did Jennifer speak. "Is this about the new man—the one I caught?"

45

"It is indeed." He shifted his briefcase to his left hand and opened the door for her, eyeing her as she stepped past him. "You catch interesting men, my dear."

"Did you expect otherwise?" Her voice and eyebrows were arch.

The vestibule of Margeaux Hall's modern wing was of glass, after the fashion of the Crystal Palace, and the afternoon sun blazed in like a searchlight. The reception desk had been placed sideways, so the man at the switchboard could see out without having the sun fully in his eyes. Norris, currently on duty, noted their entry and the time into the log.

"Any word on Miss Harriet?" he asked, his sharp Geordie accent for once gentle.

Stoner shook his head. "Nothing, Norris, thank you for asking. Are there any messages?"

"Awfully pretty girl," Norris said. "Brigadier Marone rang up, sir. Lieutenant Bruckmann took the call, and he and Sergeant Tanyon are waiting in your office."

"No dispatches?"

"Not tonight, sir."

"Thank you, Norris."

In the airy modern sitting room he'd appropriated for his office, Tanyon and Bruckmann rose from the two wing chairs before the desk as the door opened. Stoner entered, but Jennifer hung on the threshold.

"Is it a report you need typed? I can get right on it."

"It is, my dear, but I'd like you to sit in on this meeting first. You should be aware of what this operation entails."

"Goodness." She smoothed her dress, her face not quite straight, either. "My first briefing."

Stoner hadn't changed from his uniform, so Lieutenant Bruckmann came to attention, his white-blond hair gleaming in the sunshine streaming through the French windows. Sergeant Tanyon, barrel-chested and Regular Army, held the pose longer.

"I've an initial report for you, sir," Bruckmann said.

"Thank you, Jack." Stoner gestured the two men from his work area to the sitting room proper, where sofas and more wing chairs congregated between one French window and the fireplace. "Before you begin, has Brigadier Marone reached a decision? I presume that's why he rang."

"Yes, sir." Bruckmann sat back on the sofa, sat forward, shifted away. "He confirms you are to undertake Faust's interrogation yourself."

"Damn." Stoner closed his eyes. He rarely swore, but such a disappointment deserved an indulgence. "He knows I have little experience in this field, and Faust is the biggest fish we've caught. I do wish he'd give the task to the London Cage."

Sergeant Tanyon sat in the farthest wing chair, his arms crossed and blue jaw tight. Without speaking, he stared at the fireplace, as if images of all the extra work this new project entailed weighed on his mind.

Bruckmann retrieved Stoner's briefcase, settled it on his knees, and twirled the combination. "He seemed to think the mutual Oxford experience—between you and Faust, I mean—might establish some rapport."

Stoner scoffed. "If Brigadier Marone believes reliving school-day memories with a tough, front-line combat soldier will break him, then he's ready to retire. And he's younger than I."

"You are retired," Jennifer said.

"Was, my dear. Reactivated for the duration."

Bruckmann's lips curved in a small smile. "I don't think that's what he meant." He cracked the briefcase open without looking inside and set it on the coffee table between them. "I think he meant something more along the lines of a professor-student relationship."

"That's even—" but before Stoner could continue, he remembered Wurlitzer's comments regarding Faust's in-security. Most students outgrew the need for mentoring relationships, but a man uncertain of his position, locked in a tiny bedroom, deprived of stimulus and exercise, and under the intense pressures of interrogation, might be forced back into such a role. "Well. Perhaps." He rubbed his tired eyes. "All right, we're saddled with it. What do you have for me?"

Bruckmann dragged a canvas sack from beside his chair and produced Faust's field-grey uniform tunic. Stoner hitched closer.

"The chap at the London Cage confirmed most of what we guessed." Bruckmann spread the tunic across his knees. "Faust's promotion to major came in the field and he hasn't taken the time to visit a tailor for a full refit." He pointed to the top of the sleeve. "Here, you can see where the old shoulder board was ripped out and the new one sewn in poorly. And he's not wearing the white piping of a staff officer but the pink of a Panzerman, so he's still in training. Also, as you noticed this morning, he didn't wear a staff officer's breeches with red stripes down the legs."

"And that ribbon is the Iron Cross?" Stoner asked.

"Yes, sir. According to his paybook, Faust was awarded the medal Second Class in Poland and First Class in Norway."

Bruckmann draped the tunic across his knee so the

shoulder strap faced up. At the fold, Stoner glimpsed the charred and bloody edges where shrapnel from an exploding aircraft had ripped into cloth and the human flesh beneath. In the first war, his own khaki trousers had looked the same after German machine-gun bullets slammed through them. The memory of his combat injuries, a war ago and a lifetime away, reminded him of the agony of hot sharp metal and what Faust endured. Stoner didn't try to quell his sympathy. It was better to recognize such softer emotions as they occurred so he could prevent them from interfering with his judgment, and also allow a human face to show through the pressure he would apply to Faust. The deception was distasteful, but necessary.

Bruckmann pointed to the silver pin, a curly Germanic letter A, attached to Faust's shoulder board. "This means he's on the staff of Field Marshal von Rundstedt's Army Group A. And he's actual staff, not some general's adjutant or aide; there's no aiguillette here." He folded the tunic and set it on the coffee table beside the briefcase. "So he's not just a simple Panzerman, no matter what he might claim."

"What is he, then?" Jennifer asked.

"At the least," Stoner said, "he's a brave tank commander who was so successful at his trade that he was promoted to general staff training. It's the highest compliment the *Wehrmacht* could offer him. As to what he's doing here in England, I can see several possibilities. It is conceivable he told the unguarded truth this morning when he blurted out he'd been joyriding. He certainly clammed up quickly enough when he realized he'd said more than he'd intended.

"But it's also possible he's here to evaluate potential invasion routes. His knowledge of the area and the language would tend to support that theory."

"That would make him a spy," Bruckmann said.

"And there is another, rather ugly possibility." Stoner paused. The more he considered the implications, the uglier it seemed and the less he liked it. "Eduard Best."

Bruckmann, Tanyon, and Jennifer all stared at him. Stoner pictured three students, nonplussed by a tricky debate question—*"Discuss the differences between the burlesque and the mock heroic using examples from Butler and Pope"*—and smiled despite the ugliness of those possibilities.

Tanyon cleared his throat. "Eduard Best is locked up on the third floor."

"Yes," Stoner said, "but the Germans don't know that, or so we hope. They believe he's still lecturing economics at Wadham, gathering information and rumors from the staff and students. After all, he's still making radio contact with them on schedule."

"So you think German intelligence sent Faust to work with Best?" Bruckmann blew out his cheeks. "That would definitely make him a spy."

"Blindfold for one, on order," Tanyon said. "Why would he wear uniform? You'd think he'd wear civilian clothing and try to blend in."

"I don't know," Stoner said. "His person and entire situation are enigmas. But this means that, until we know where we stand, we must be very careful with him." He turned to Tanyon. "Sergeant, I must ask you to take him on as a personal project."

Tanyon froze. "Sir—"

Stoner waved him to silence. "I know you are overworked—we all are—but this is a job no one else here is qualified to perform." He leaned forward and touched the red, white, and black ribbon notched about the tunic's second button. "The Iron Cross is specifically a decoration for valor in combat at the risk of one's own life. Faust won this honor twice."

He paused, letting that sink in. Tanyon's Regular Army shoulders sank.

"You and I both know," Stoner continued, "there is a tremendous difference between a rear-echelon soldier and a warrior. Our young squad are good material but at this stage of their training, Faust can easily dominate them, even with his right arm injured. You and I, sergeant, are the only soldiers in this establishment with combat experience, and I am too old and worn to handle him myself. To you must fall this particular honor."

"Yes, sir." Tanyon didn't appear flattered. "No offense, sir, and I don't mean to grumble, but I'm also personally handling Best, and Lemelsen, and the squad hasn't settled in proper, and the recordkeeping is falling behind—"

"I believe we can turn Ruhnke and possibly Lemelsen over to Corporal Pym. He's learned a lot, hasn't he?"

"Well, yes, sir, but as for experience—" He stopped on his own this time and rubbed his eyes. "Yes, sir."

"Would Faust and Best know each other?" Jennifer asked.

"Oh, yes, I believe they might. Did I not mention that? Prior to his 'escape' from Nazi Germany, Best taught at the Munich University, during the same years when Faust earned a degree at the Munich Technical University."

Tanyon and Bruckmann exchanged glances, but Jennifer watched him with her glorious hazel eyes opened wide. Stoner's heart melted again. Some perceptive man soon was going to see past her surface plainness and sweep her away, and what would he do then?

"So. Here is the plan." Stoner rose and crossed to the cold fireplace, hands clasped behind his back as he marshaled his thoughts. "We must assume the worst of Major Faust."

"Meaning espionage," Bruckmann said.

"Meaning mayhem, rape, and murder, if necessary. Whatever pressure can be brought to bear on him, we must bring it, true or otherwise." Stoner turned to Tanyon. "He's to remain within his quarters, allowed no exercise, no conversations with anyone except myself or Lieutenant Bruckmann, and no diversions or entertainment of any sort."

"What about Dr. Harris?" Tanyon asked.

"Well, we mustn't interfere with the good doctor's treatment of his patient. Medical visits to the infirmary are allowed. I believe Dr. Harris also intends to send Faust to the Patchbourne hospital for X-rays, and I'm afraid, sergeant, you must see to that personally, as well."

"Do me best, sir."

"Of course you will. We must also look to our defenses."

Tanyon grunted assent. "That Faust is trouble in trousers."

"As you say." Stoner returned to the sitting area and pulled the notebook from his briefcase, untangling it from his academicals. He'd written out everything Wurlitzer had told him, using the spiky jagged scrawl that allowed his hand to move almost as swiftly as his mind. No one but Jennifer would be able to read it. "Should an officer be so unfortunate as to be captured in wartime, it is his duty to attempt escape. Never mind the chances of actual success are virtually nil, nor that he must risk his life in the process. It's his sworn duty."

"Nice to be warned in advance, I suppose," Jennifer said.

"Precisely. We know he's going to try something. Considering our doubts as to his mission and intentions, we cannot permit it."

"That won't be easy, sir," Bruckmann said.

"It certainly won't." He handed the pad to Jennifer. When she took it, he laid a hand on her arm to keep her in the discussion. "And once the interrogation process is well forward, he's going to be under tremendous pressure. I do not authorize brutality, sergeant; however, you may find threats are necessary to control him."

"Understood, sir."

He turned to Jennifer and squeezed her arm. "My dear, I must ask you to speak with the ladies in our little garrison. I don't want Faust to obtain a hostage and therefore all of you are to keep clear of him."

"Well." She looked away and smoothed her dress on the sofa. "Of course not." She glanced back up, startled. "Oh, blimey, Harriet—"

"—when she returns, must be kept as far from him as possible. I have no doubt he can be a charming devil, with those soft dark eyes and Continental manners, should the mood strike him or the situation warrant." He turned to Bruckmann, whose notepad and pencil were ready. "For you, Jack, I have three rather special assignments. Firstly, try to learn something regarding the wreckage of the German plane that came down near Patchbourne Saturday night."

"Anything specific, sir?"

"We're trying to ascertain if that aircraft is the one that transported Faust. If it's a bomber, then it's possible he is after all telling the truth when he claims he was shot down. But if it's a fighter, with only room for one man aboard, then Faust must have been a passenger on another plane, one he perhaps left willingly."

"Which would give his joyride story the lie." Bruckmann scribbled without pausing, even as he spoke. "Got it."

"The salvage people should also be able to ascertain, from the plane's wreckage, to what squadron it belonged and at which airfield it was based, which may help us understand something of Faust's movements prior to the initiation of his adventure. We do know Army Group A is headquartered in Paris, so that is his presumed starting point."

"Got it."

"The second job is a tad more complicated." Stoner waited until Bruckmann glanced up from his notes. "According to Wurlitzer, Faust had two close friends during his time at University College, Peter Munting and George Barrington, the Viscount Godwin. I want you to track them down."

Bruckmann resumed his shorthand. "What am I looking for?"

"Here we're fishing, Jack, which is why it's complicated and I'm putting the assignment into your imaginative hands. Sound them out and learn what you can."

"Got it, sir. Third job?"

Stoner glanced down at his hands. They seemed steady enough, although he sensed this was the most valuable and exciting information Wurlitzer had given him. "Two more names for you to track down are Robert Trenton Clarke and Grandon Brownell. I can give you a lead on them: they are officers of the Royal Warwickshires who served with the B.E.F.

in France and escaped during the debacle at Dunkirk."

"Got it." Bruckmann flipped the page over. "What have they to do with Faust?"

Stoner ignored the question. Bruckmann, he knew, would be neither presumptuous nor indiscreet enough to ask again. "I'm certain they filed reports with their regimental intelligence officers. I want copies of those reports."

Bruckmann's glance was confused. "I understand."

"And of course," Stoner said, allowing a touch of irony to creep into his voice, "I need it all tomorrow."

The lead of the flying pencil snapped. "Sir—"

"Prioritize, Jack, giving preference to the third and first assignments. And after Jennifer finishes typing my notes and report, if she has time, perhaps she can assist you."

She lifted her chin. "Of course I shall."

"I'll have an addendum to attach to the end of that report, my dear, to outline our strategy. We should receive multiple dispatches tomorrow, and we'll send this to Brigadier Marone by return trip."

She glanced through his pages of spidery scrawl. "It's getting rather busy around here, Dad."

"If we hadn't lost half our qualified intelligence officers in France—" He sighed. "I believe it will be worse before it's better."

7

early evening
Margeaux Hall

Typing Stoner's report, including the hastily scrawled addendum, took Jennifer three quarters of an hour. Stoner insisted only typed reports be sent to London; with the scratchy handwriting he employed for staff communications, the why was only too obvious. She'd taken to typing most of his reports herself, because anyone else would have to interrupt him every few moments with another question, while she'd only had to do so twice. For a two-page report, well, that wasn't so bad. He never complained when she barged in, always smiling at her with his winsome little-boy eyes, but he was hugely busy, planning the details of his attack upon that man Faust. Best let him alone to get on with it.

She separated the carbons, collated the original and four copies, stapled each, two-hole punched two copies, three-hole punched the others, then ran all five through the date-time stamp on the corner of Steven Wainwright's desk. He didn't look up from his scrutiny of the invoices on his blotter, although Maggie Wainwright, typing quartermaster's orders at the next desk, paused her steady rhythm until Jennifer finished. As if she'd be interested in a married man, or an unmarried one, until her work was caught up.

The three-holed copies were for Stoner's personal use and files, for writing his memoirs at some future date, and those copies she'd put away later. For now she tucked them beneath the blotter on her desk.

The two-holed copies were for the official archives of the goings-on within Margeaux Hall, for the analytical tome to be written by some googly four-eyed historian at some other future date, and those copies she placed in the in-box on Jack Bruckmann's desk for him to deal with.

He glanced up at her, momentarily distracted, twirling the telephone cord about his fingers. But within seconds his eyes glazed as his focus returned to that nether world of inner thought that seemed to exist only for the duration of calls to government departments. He moved aside so she could nip open the drawer beneath his elbow and snag the dispatch key, and never missed a word of his conversation. "Look, Miss Diddington—very well, Dagmar—all right, but you do have a lovely voice—"

No secretary in any official department in this woman's Army was going to fall for that line, meaning it wouldn't be long before he brought up the big bad wolf of Brigadier Marone of MI5, trying vinegar instead of honey. That was the story of their working lives: no one had ever heard of Cedric Stoner, or Margeaux Hall, and he was only a major, and a reactivated one at that, and there were so many little intelligence bureaus out there and everyone had to check with security before they could release anything. They just had to do the best they could with minimal patronage.

The original report she took to the sunset-drenched vestibule where Norris still sat, now reading a comic book since everyone knew the officers were busy. The active dispatch case was kept in the top drawer of the filing cabinet behind the duty desk, and she had to stand mere inches from him as she unlocked the case and slid the report inside. But although she monitored her sensations intimately, she felt nothing unusual despite his proximity, and couldn't stifle a sigh.

When told a squad of eligible young soldiers very near their age would be attached to Margeaux Hall, she'd been as excited as Harriet—well, perhaps not as giddy, but certainly as intrigued. After all, it wasn't as if she hadn't felt such stirrings before; she had, she liked them, and wouldn't mind experiencing them again. And it wasn't as if she didn't know how to handle men who wanted to force her to feel them against her will; just ask that Faust fellow. But so far, none of the squad had aroused any such sensations within her, certainly not Norris with his comic books, darting eyes, and sharp angles. He was only a few months her junior, but she couldn't help considering him a boy, not a man.

She relocked the dispatch case, slid the filing cabinet drawer to, and turned in time to see Norris' eyes dart aside.

She froze, but he didn't look again, instead too casually turning a page and leaning over it.

At least when Faust stared at her, it was frank, candid, and, well, professional. But this was low and made her skin crawl. She huffed, spun, and returned to the grand ballroom just as Bruckmann hung up the phone.

"Any luck?" she asked.

He leaned back in his chair, tilting it, and stretched. "I had to promise to take her for a drink next time I'm in Brighton. But yes, she said she'd send those reports."

"Brighton." Jennifer perched on the corner of his desk. "Must be nice. How often do you get down there?"

"Never, heavens. She has a voice like a dragon and probably the face to match."

She laughed, and his lips curved in a shy smile. If any of these men was going to move her, it was likely to be Jack Bruckmann. With his education, his background was closest to hers, and while not really handsome—not in her opinion, at least—he didn't make her want to run for the shower. But still... nothing.

Perhaps she was just working too hard.

"You know, I was planning on attending Sunday services tonight," he said.

She nodded. "Me, too. It's not going to happen, though, is it?"

Bruckmann thumped the chair back down, and again Jennifer congratulated herself for placing scatter rugs beneath the desks and chairs. Otherwise the ballroom's wonderful hardwood floor would have been hopelessly scarred months ago.

"Look, if you'll type up the notes on that downed plane, I'll get started tracking down these two chaps." Bruckmann grabbed his notepad and read aloud. "Peter Munting and George Barrington, the Viscount Godwin."

"Can you imagine hobnobbing with a viscount?"

He shrugged. "Godwin's one of the old marcher lords." He ripped some pages from the pad. "It's not like John of Gaunt or the Duke of Gloucester, or anyone truly powerful."

"Oh, you mean a Welshman? One of those lovely lads with liquid eyes and a singing voice like a meadowlark?" She shrugged in her turn as his pale blue eyes widened with glee. Whether she was attracted to Bruckmann or not, it couldn't hurt to keep him wondering. "Can't be bothered. Goodness, how much can one say about a crash? You've got five pages here."

"Believe me, I had no idea myself."

The two downed German planes, she learned as she typed, had been identified by the wreckage as Heinkel 111 P-4 twin-engine bombers. The markings (5J + LN) on what little remained of one plane's fuselage identified it as attached to the fifth *Staffel* or wing of squadron KGr 4, "General Wever," based in Le Havre and currently employed in the medium-altitude bombing of RAF airfields in central England. The two planes had apparently collided in midair over Patchbourne, prior to reaching their intended target, and their bomb payloads had exploded, scattering debris from the runway to the hospital. The charred remains of nine crew members—

They were at war. She forced her fingers to keep typing.

—nine crew members were recovered from the debris, beyond possible identification. A tenth had been thrown clear prior to the explosion but without benefit of a parachute, and his remains had been recovered near the hospital. His documents identified him as *Hauptmann* Erhard Bohnes of Munich.

Heinkels normally carried a crew of five, Bruckmann's notes continued. However, it was possible one of the planes had carried a sixth man, as implied by the parachute sighted, either as supernumerary or as additional crew, as some Heinkels currently in medium-altitude bombing roles were beginning to carry additional machine guns and gunners for protection against RAF fighters.

The Red Cross had been notified of the recovery of the bodies and of plans for their interment, et cetera.

Again she separated, collated, stapled, punched, stamped, and distributed. Again she held her breath until Maggie Wainwright resumed typing. And again she caught Norris staring and huffed at him before returning to the ballroom. If he wasn't going to be honest enough to let her stare him down, she'd communicate her displeasure in another manner.

Bruckmann covered the receiver. "He's waiting for that. Do you mind?"

Jennifer smiled, grabbed both reports, and crossed the ballroom to Stoner's door. She knocked and slipped inside.

A scramble of papers covered the desk. Stoner glanced up, at first blankly, as if he couldn't remember who she was. Then he propped his chin on one fist, on top of the carnage, and smiled impishly at her. "And you're bringing me even more."

She could never help smiling back at him. Oh, if only she could find a man like him—cultured, intelligent, witty, and brave. A man, please, not a boy. "I wouldn't except Jack said you were waiting for this. It's his airplane report."

"Oh, good." He sat up straight. "Another piece for the puzzle."

She gave him his copies, then slid behind his desk and dropped to the floor by his chair, facing the secretarial station behind him. The shelf beneath held a row of binders, and she tugged out the second one and inserted the other set of copies into its innards, chronologically by date and time.

The report just ahead was one Bruckmann had typed, discussing some preliminary results from their Wildflower operation. The four turned enemy spies they handled, it seemed, were accepted by the German intelligence bureau without question, and on at least one occasion the *Luftwaffe* had initiated a bombing raid based upon the bogus information they'd submitted. Well, that had to be good news.

"My dear, did you type this?" Stoner gestured with the aircraft report.

She closed the binder and hefted it back onto the shelf. "You don't have to be so protective of me. I'm made of sterner stuff than that implies."

"I don't—"

"And don't scold Jack." It didn't take much effort to keep her voice level; she could never really become angry at her grandfather. "He's as overworked as the rest of us and looking for help wherever he can find it. I mean, don't you use Homer Owen to relay messages for you?" They'd received a call from the Abbey Arms pub earlier, alerting them of Stoner's return.

He sighed. "And the poor man has taken to keeping a pad and pencil beneath the bar. You're right, of course. I'm sorry you had to see such things, just the same."

She scrambled up. "Jack has convinced a dragon lady in Brighton to send us copies of those officers' reports, and he's tracking Faust's two friends now." She shook out her twisted skirt. "Instead of going to evening service."

Stoner placed the airplane report atop one of the stacks scattered across his desk. He didn't answer. Jennifer supposed there was nothing he could say, and the vicar could think of them as he pleased.

"Dad."

He glanced up. His eyes, his face, his entire mien seemed tired.

But her mouth and mind would not produce the question that terrified her. Instead, she blurted out, "Where is Harriet?"

"If she's gotten herself married, I assure you, it shall be annulled." His eyes were gentle.

Her smile would not be repressed. "Consummated or otherwise?"

This time he didn't smile in return. "Precisely."

So he knew she was being cowardly, and that would never do. She found air from somewhere and forced out the question that controlled all their futures. "Are the Germans coming?"

His expression softened. "I don't know." He reached up and took her hand. "It took their Panzers, with Faust assisting, a mere six weeks to conquer France, utterly decimate the combined British and French armies, and drive their remnants into the North Sea. I cannot imagine what could possibly stop them from repeating that procedure on this side of the Channel." He smiled thinly. "Certainly not Harry Oldfield's Home Guard troop. Nor you and I with our little shotguns."

Strangely, his brutal assessment calmed her. She breathed more easily. "Does Faust know about it? Or how to stop them?"

"He may. Perhaps he even assisted drawing up their battle plans. And if he doesn't know the actual date of their invasion, as a staff officer for a major German combat unit, it's possible he knows much of the means intended."

"Then he's just got to tell us, that's all." She kissed his cheek and lingered over it—he did like it so—before heading for the door. Surely there was more she could do to assist.

8

early morning, Monday, 26 August 1940
Margeaux Hall

Stoner called Bruckmann and Jennifer to his office for a final briefing the next morning. Mrs. Alcock insisted on serving their coffee, rather than entrusting the errand to Sally, and after an examination of their tired faces she poured the first cup for Stoner.

"Oh, lovely," he said. "There's milk." Not much, of course. Wartime rationing gave priority to soldiers and children, leaving little for stodgy retired professors playing intelligence games. But he'd be justified using enough to lighten the color in his cup by two shades. After all, Bruckmann preferred his coffee straight and he only had to share with Jennifer.

Tiredness dragged at him in a weighty undertow. But above it his body felt light, his confidence buoyed by their intense preparations. Unless Faust proved to be more sophisticated in intelligence-related matters than the captured Germans Stoner had previously met, their detailed plan of attack had good chance of bearing much fruit.

Mrs. Alcock tilted her grizzled head as she poured for Bruckmann. "Any word on Miss Harriet, now?"

Stoner sighed, his heart instantly heavier. Constable Mercer had rung the previous evening to report in a dispirited voice. He heard the same emotion in his own as he said, "Nothing."

"Well." She poured for Jennifer, set the pot on the tray atop the desk, and stared at them again, her hands folded beneath her apron. Her eyes were tired, as if she too had analyzed data, sorted reports, and typed notes half the night. "Well, she'll show up when she's good and ready, I suppose."

Stoner waited until the door closed behind her before turning to Bruckmann, sitting beside Jennifer in the two wing chairs before his desk. "Do you have anything new for me?"

"Yes, sir, but I'm not certain what to make of it." Bruckmann held his cup beneath his nose and inhaled, as if the aroma was sufficient to arouse him, but then he set it down untasted. He looked at the tray, his cup, the floor—anywhere except into Stoner's eyes.

Stoner straightened. His old heart picked up speed and set his cup down.

"Go ahead, Jack."

"It's those two friends of Faust's." Bruckmann picked up his cup again and this time sipped. "I didn't contact them, not after I realized—" He stopped short. Down went the cup again and this time the saucer rattled.

Jennifer's eyes widened.

When Stoner spoke, he kept his voice quiet. "Tell me of Peter Munting."

"Major Munting is attached to MI5 in London."

Jennifer gasped, coffee sloshing. "He's one of us."

"Is he?" Bruckmann's voice was surprisingly sharp.

She started to speak again. But Stoner held up a hand.

"And the Viscount Godwin?" he asked.

"—is a Spitfire squadron leader stationed at RAF Patchbourne." Finally Bruckmann looked up. He wet his lips. "I was thinking, if Faust had come to England to gather information for the German invasion, well—"

Stoner maintained his calm and finished the thought Bruckmann couldn't. "—he could contact his old friend, the squadron leader, who is stationed a half mile from where Faust's parachute touched down. The squadron leader, in turn, could get all the information required from their mutual friend, the military intelligence officer in London. Assuming, of course, that neither gentleman minds committing treason."

"Exactly."

It made a horrible sort of sense. In the quiet, broken only by the ticking of the carriage clock on the mantel, Stoner stared into his coffee cup and felt his heart give a strange sort of double jump. If this was tea, now, he could read the leaves and tell Faust's fortune, perhaps learn what that enigmatic young man was up to. He rubbed his eyes and wished again that Brigadier Marone had sent Faust to the London Cage, where all other captured German officers were interrogated and where the staff were much more experienced at this sort of thing than he and his tired, brave, overworked team.

But then his mind took the next step and his heart chilled. If Brigadier Marone suspected one of his staff of duplicity, he'd want Faust kept far from there. After all, an officer attached to MI5 would have easy access to a prisoner at the Cage.

These suspicions he'd keep to himself. If they had stumbled into something big and ugly, intended to tumble and defeat England from within, he had the relative comfort of knowing that the most cold-blooded intelligence general available was monitoring the situation.

"You did well, Jack," he said.

There was a knock on the door and Tanyon leaned into the office sitting room. "The sleeper's awake, sir. I'll have him down for you in an hour."

"Thank you, Sergeant."

"Sir." He exited, closing the door behind him.

"Dad, what do we do?" Jennifer's voice trembled.

For a moment, Stoner only allowed himself to consider how much he loved her. When he smiled, letting all that love show, she managed a shaky one in return.

"Nothing has changed, my dear. We must break Faust."

"Do you think we have a chance?" Bruckmann asked.

"Oh, yes, I do at that." He sipped his coffee. Their carefully laid plan still seemed sound. It was too late for nerves; battle was about to be joined, and he had a nation and family to defend. "Now, if you lovely young people will allow me thirty minutes, I shall scratch out a few more notes for Brigadier Marone. Jennifer, I hope you won't mind typing them for me?"

9

the same morning
Margeaux Hall

His batman forgot to wake him again. Faust stirred, the sheet coarse against his skin, sunlight warming his face, and knew he was late without opening his eyes: a staff officer, even one in training, should never sleep past dawn. His throat was dry and sore, with a sour and dirty taste as if he'd drunk way too much, but without his usual morning-after headache. Left-handed, he scrubbed the grit from his eyes and scratched his chin. Astonishment flooded him at the stubble. Just what had happened last night? And why couldn't he remember any of it? He was a heavy sleeper, but this empty memory and scratchy face seemed excessive.

He opened his eyes to a small and unfamiliar bedroom, containing the bare minimum to qualify for the term—bed, small table, wooden chair, low dresser, bars on the closed window, no drapes, and not one single ornament. It was stark. It couldn't be a new billet; it was far too bare and drab for a staff officer's room; he'd been sleeping in a swank hotel in Paris. Besides, Brandt might forget to wake him once or twice—for which he would now be boiled in vitriol and returned to his previous duties—but he'd at least set out a shaving kit and Ritzi's picture, Faust's books and Agfa camera. So this wasn't a billet, new or otherwise, but he still couldn't remember it.

Erhard; he'd driven to Le Havre to see Erhard. An image of the flightline, lumbering Heinkel bombers trundling toward takeoff, shimmering in a haze of petrol and heat, seemed to be the last memory in his head. So he must have spent the night and this was a *Luftwaffe* billet, borrowed for the occasion, which would explain why Brandt wasn't handy. But that had been a stupid thing to do, after *Oberst* von Maacht had ordered him to remain near headquarters, and he could only imagine how drunk he must have been for Erhard to suggest it and for him to agree. He had to telephone Paris and explain.

Faust pushed himself erect.

Pain sliced from his right triceps into his shoulder and all the way to his fingers, sudden and excruciating. His arm collapsed beneath him. He fell back onto the pillow, reeling, and cradled his arm as a flood of memories poured in behind the pain: falling, an explosion, stumbling through the unnerving English night. A woman's ferocious and intriguing face over a capably-held but unpoetical shotgun. Searched; guarded; questioned. Captured.

It was too much to take lying down. He fought through the shock and the memories, rolled onto his left arm, and pushed himself upright. The cold wooden floor beneath his feet and the chill air on his naked limbs woke him further, but fuzz and fog still clouded his head. Pain chewed at his triceps, nipped across his shoulder blade, and something burned, deep and insistent, among the ribs beneath his arm.

It was true. It was all true. *Our en'mies now are masters of the walls*, and even now he couldn't stop himself from playing his favorite stupid game and finding a line of poetry to fit his circumstances. But even Surrey couldn't help him out of Erhard's mess.

Vaguely he recalled an infirmary, white and comfortingly warm, where a doctor had removed bits of shrapnel from his back and right arm then stitched him up; where a male nurse, slender and kind, had applied bandages and teased some liquid down his throat. He'd been drugged. How long had he slept? That was oblique sunlight; it was the following morning or another, even later one. At least a full day, then.

Three campaigns—Poland, Norway, western Europe— and never a scratch, barely a serious scare. One frigging joyride over the English Channel and here he sat, taking stock of shrapnel damage while liquid warmth dampened his undervest beneath his arm. He'd told everybody who'd listen that the English weren't going to be pushovers, no matter how poorly prepared the B.E.F. had seemed in France. He just hadn't intended to prove it himself.

Come on, Erhard had said, *come for a ride with papa. We'll be back before dawn. No one will ever know.*

63

Damn you, Erhard, whether you're in heaven or hell. And Faust had his own theory regarding that particular current address.

Although it was August, the air was uncomfortably cool against his bare skin. He'd last seen his uniform as his English captors pawed it. It wasn't anywhere he could see. He leaned over and, left-handed, opened each dresser drawer far enough for a glance. But they were empty. His uniform, like his cigarettes and *Soldbuch* and wallet, could be gone for good. The old geezer, Stoner, hadn't left anything unravaged, despite his cultured charm.

He shouldn't have thought of those cigarettes.

He shook out the faded patchwork quilt and slung it one-handed about his shoulders. He'd worn a blanket when first captured, too, in the sitting room of the farmhouse—Woodrow, Stoner had called it. But it didn't seem likely he was still there; he'd have been taken someplace more secure than a simple, unfenced farmhouse. There had been a manor on the hill rising beside Woodrow, with a high mortared-stone wall about it. The depths of his consciousness released another vague memory of a postern gate in a wall and a path across a lawn to a glass-fronted vestibule—yes, that had been before the infirmary—but after that he drew another blank. Had he staggered upstairs, or was that only part of some exhausted nightmare?

He took the two steps to the window. Yes, there was the wall, encircling a lawn at least three stories below and extending not quite half a mile distant. Lines of apple trees on the wall's far side rested ancient branches atop it and draped them over like a skirt. Beyond the apple trees stood a Georgian farmhouse that could be Woodrow, eaves and spiraling chimneys and grey slate roof peering through the branches that dipped almost to the ground. A man could probably lean out of the upper windows and pick breakfast from the trees, which sounded like a silly line from Marlowe's *Passionate Shepherd*.

Beyond the farmhouse loomed another dark mass of trees—the oaks, beeches, and birches he'd traveled that nerve-wracking night, so close they seemed to beckon. If only he'd heeded his instincts and stopped in their shelter before dawn, rather than trying to fight it out for another mile.

The view to the right was blocked by another wing of the building he was in, great worked blocks of the famous Oxfordshire honey-hued stone forming what seemed to be a massively built baroque mansion with mullioned windows. The wall encircled it. Below, the lawn was bisected by a single macadam lane, likely a wartime construction considering its disregard of aesthetics, slicing without mercy between formal beds of roses where a grizzled gardener knelt, hands busy. Other than the atrocious road, it was such an English vista, exactly the sort he loved, like the Oxford quads when he'd stayed overlong at the Bodleian or the Bird and Baby with Barrington and Munting, and ran for a lecture with his gown flapping. Faust smiled; those had been the best of times.

And with apologies to Dickens, these promised to be the worst. He collapsed onto the chair beside the table, clutching the blanket about his body as if it could contain his rising nerves. Vividly he remembered those defeated English officers, sitting in the scuffed French turf, encircled by *Waffen SS* soldiers with machine guns trained—the sick fear in their eyes, their hunched shoulders, the collapse that almost stank. If this bedroom contained a mirror, he might see that expression in his own eyes.

Keys rattled outside the door. Faust jerked around, his muscles tightening. Pain spasmed across his right side. The walls seemed to close in around him and he yearned to scramble for cover. The lock groaned then snapped. He rose to his feet—he couldn't help it, he wanted to seem cool and collected but his body wasn't listening—and the door opened.

It was the sergeant from the morning of his capture, the one conspicuous by his competent silence. Black hair framed a face that probably came in handy while playing cards, for the dark eyes, measuring and assessing, gave nothing away. He was solid and barrel-chested without being stout and would require more than one punch to go down, filling the doorway with his body as he filled Faust's vision with his stare. "*Guten morgen.*"

Hah. A weakness. His accent was lousy. Not that it would help.

"Good morning," Faust said.

"Sit down."

At least he said it politely, sort of. Faust sat, the quilt blooming about him on the chair. Suddenly he felt ridiculous, a welcome flush of anger trailing behind. Of all the crazy things that had happened in his life, this had to be the worst.

The sergeant stepped back from the doorway. His place was taken by a slim kid in uniform—maybe one of those in the background at his capture, although Faust hadn't paid enough attention to them to remember their faces. This one had drab dark blond hair, cut so close to his bullet head he looked shorn at first glance, and his blue eyes seemed to be focused upon some inner space that refused admittance to the rest of the world. He set a tray on the table and left again. Faust smelled cereal and realized he was famished.

The sergeant reappeared. "You feeling suicidal this morning?"

There were slices of tomato and apple as well as a bowl of oatmeal, and what looked like strong tea as well as a tin of warm water. But that question was even more intriguing. "What?"

The sergeant's lips thinned, the first sign of emotion he'd yet displayed. "It's a simple question. Do you feel like slitting your wrists this morning?"

"Not while breakfast is getting cold."

"It's a cold breakfast," the sergeant said.

He would either learn to like this man, or find out how many punches it did take to put him down. There wasn't going to be any middle ground here.

"Snap to it, Ellington," the sergeant said over his shoulder. "It's going to be a busy day even without your lollygagging."

Ellington returned, shaking his head with his lips parted. He draped Faust's uniform across the foot of the bed and dropped his boots on the floor. He then produced a safety razor, a tiny square of unmounted mirror, a ragged sponge, and a small cake of soap from his pocket, set them on the tray by the tin of water, and left.

"I'll be back in forty minutes. Be ready." The sergeant closed the door.

The lock snapped home with a thud that climbed Faust's spine. He didn't like that sound. He didn't like being ordered around, he didn't like being a prisoner, and he really didn't like that rude, bossy sergeant. Especially since he was pretty certain Stoner, *perfidious Albion* personified, awaited him at the end of those forty minutes.

The oatmeal was cold, but a tiny dollop of molasses made it palatable and the fresh stuff was great. The tea was black and lukewarm but stronger than a mule's kick. He ate everything, yearned again for a cigarette, then washed and shaved left-handed, only cutting himself once. Pointedly, he avoided examining his expression in that mirror. He'd take Clarke's defiance as his example, not the whipped ones who'd sat in the turf and stared at nothing.

But when he wriggled into his trousers, he realized his suspenders and brown gunbelt weren't there. It made him pause. The only reason the English had for withholding anything was to prevent him from using it. As it didn't make sense for them to want his pants to fall down, maybe they did expect him to be suicidal and hang himself with his braces. Or maybe they were worried he might use them as a rope, to tie up a guard or escape out a window. Maybe there was a window without bars. That was something to watch for.

He would have to think further about escaping, as soon as he figured out how to keep his pants up during the process. And as soon as he knew how badly he was injured.

His mouse-grey shirt was unmended and unwashed, ripped across the back shoulder and sliced through at the arm, dark stains spreading from the collar to the waist and from the spine to the right cuff. The size of the tears and the extent of the stain made him pause; perhaps his injury was more serious than he'd realized. His undervest, he knew, had to look the same, although his neck was too swollen to button his collar and he couldn't twist his head far enough to see his back. Great; now he needed new clothes, too, and had no idea where they'd come from. Surely the English had higher priorities than a prisoner's wardrobe.

Wriggling into his shirt and tunic without moving his right arm from his side was a challenge, but he twisted like a Bavarian pretzel rather than wait for help. He had to pull his heel into his crotch to tie his ankle boots, so at least he had one thrill to look forward to until his arm healed. Thankfully he hadn't worn his high field boots; he could never have pulled those on one-handed.

Every nerve in his body screamed for a cigarette. If he was taken to Stoner, he'd ask. Pride had its limits.

He was lacing his second boot when keys rattled outside the door.

"I told you to be ready," the sergeant said.

He didn't glance up, just kept lacing. "I left my watch at home."

"I'm not lending you mine."

He tied the last lace. Wait—his hair. "Do you have a comb?"

"Not for you."

Jerk. Faust dampened his hair with the sponge and dirty water, and fingered it back from his face. It would have to do. "Okay. Ready."

The sergeant, his lips thinned, stepped back from the door. "Come on, then."

The hall he stepped into was dim despite its pale walls and molding. A soft glow from the eastern end was overpowered by a blaze from the western one, and by the uneven light he counted more than a dozen closed doors alternating along its length, the ones on the northern wall bolted; his own door was one of those. Another youngster in uniform, one with such a lousy haircut that Faust was certain he hadn't seen him before, stood waiting partly along the eastern end of the hallway; when Faust exited the room, the kid turned and walked toward the far end, his khaki uniform a dark silhouette against the dim glow. As the sergeant blocked the brighter western end, Faust had no choice but to turn left and follow, cradling his right arm at his waist.

At the end of the hall opened a stairwell, lit only by a skylight in the roof above. The soldier led him down two narrow flights, the sergeant's footsteps clumping behind.

The ground floor opened on the right into a grand ballroom, now a combination sitting room and typists' pool. On the near end crowded several mismatched sofas and a half-dozen assorted armchairs, arranged around coffee tables littered with ash trays, magazines, and tattered decks of cards. Garnet swags were drawn from the bank of floor-to-ceiling windows stretching along the southern-facing wall. A large old-fashioned console radio droned a gardening show for the lone teenaged soldier smoking in splendid isolation.

They'd probably notice if Faust ran over and yanked the cigarette from the kid's hand. Damn it.

At the other end of the ballroom were a half-dozen scuffed metal desks, two facing rows with room in between. At three of them, typists plied their trade: a wispy-thin man between thirty and forty, a sullen-faced lady of the same age, and Jennifer Stoner. His feet stumbled to a stop when he saw her—she really was plain, even the auburn hair he remembered so vividly wasn't all that great—but she merely glanced up for a brief, distracted moment and her fingers never stopped flying. He felt himself redden. That woman was murder on a man's ego, and nothing like Campaspe. Her name suited, after all.

The north side of the long ballroom, opposite the windows, was paneled in oak. The young soldier led Faust past an open door—a billiard and darts room, he learned in passing—past a closed one, and knocked on the last door. Beyond, at the corridor's end, a final door stood partly open, a wash of daylight spilling through. It had to be the entryway. Guarded, surely, but again, something to remember.

The soldier opened the door and leaned in. "The new one, sir."

From within, a professorial voice answered. "Thank you, Carmichael."

That voice he had no trouble remembering.

Carmichael's dark curly hair was cut so unevenly, his

ears seemed lopsided. He gestured Faust forward. Faust straightened his shoulders and entered the lists. Saint George awaited.

10

the same morning
Margeaux Hall

At first glance, Faust's heart sank to somewhere near his boots.

Stoner stood behind an unbearably tidy desk, his aged frame straight as a soldier's. He wore a soft dove grey suit, white shirt, regimental tie, and he returned Faust's stare without blinking. The edges of Stoner's thin lips turned up and those keen blue eyes were gentle. But it was the sort of look a delighted dog gave a morsel of steak before snapping it up, and Faust just knew he was about to be eaten alive.

Without thinking he brought his heels together when he halted before the desk, giving Stoner the same heel-click he'd give to a senior German officer. When Stoner's eyes crinkled at the corners, Faust gritted his teeth. The way this was going, Stoner might not even bother to chew first.

"*Guten Morgen, Herr Major.*" Stoner didn't stumble over the German syllables. His voice was gentle as his gaze and just as encouraging. "I hope you slept well?"

"Thank you." Faust matched his tone to Stoner's. He could at least show grace while going down. "I seem to have slept for a long time?"

Stoner gestured toward the two wing chairs positioned before the desk, an occasional table between them. Faust chose the nearest one, on the left, and sat cradling his injured arm in his lap. The sergeant took up a silent post behind him and to the right, out of reach and with one of the French windows, rather than Stoner, in the line of fire. The old man settled behind the desk.

Stoner's inner sanctum was a sweeping, airy sitting room. Shades of blue dominated: pastel on the walls interspersed with stretches of pine paneling that lanced up to the high wainscoted ceiling; navy for the mantelpiece, trellis rug, and the drapes drawn back from the French windows; darkest delft for the two sofas and additional wing chairs arranged on the left side of the room. This sitting area faced a white-brick hearth and was bordered by a low sideboard holding crystal decanters and overturned glasses. The desk and secretarial station near the wall, between the French windows, and the cot in the corner seemed afterthoughts among the décor.

"You've slept for just over a day, which seems to be Dr. Harris' favorite remedy for whatever ails one." In the gentle morning light, the lines of the old man's face congregated about the corners of his eyes and lips, the skin beneath his eyes and chin barely beginning to sag. He didn't seem quite as old as Faust had originally thought, perhaps sixty at most. "When I first brought my family here from Oxford, Jennifer had the unfortunate idea of cleaning the outside of her bedroom windows from the bough of the nearest apple tree."

Faust couldn't restrain a wince. "I sense an ouch coming."

"Yes, one window would not open as the branches were in the way, but unfortunately the other would and out she climbed. But bruises only, and frankly, I believe her dignity suffered far worse than her anatomy. Nevertheless, Dr. Harris poured the same anodyne concoction down her throat, she slept for the prescribed twenty-four hours, and was fine the next day."

Behind Faust, the door opened. He swiveled. The young blond lieutenant entered, natty in his well-cut walking-out uniform. He crossed the room, passing the silent sergeant, and placed an unopened ten-pack of Players Navy Cut and a book of matches on the table beside Faust. "These are for you."

He hadn't even had to ask. Maybe this wasn't going to be the complete disaster he expected. "That's what I call real kindness. Thank you." Very much: his first cigarette of the day was long overdue. He tore into the pack. "You know, with your coloring, you could be a poster boy for the Nazis."

"Bastards." The lieutenant's tone was conversational. He settled at the oak secretary's desk behind Stoner's and grabbed a sharpened pencil. A notepad was already set out, blank and ready.

Stoner cleared his throat. "You remember my assistant, Lieutenant Bruckmann?"

"How could I forget." He held up the Players. "May I?"

"Certainly."

He lit up like a starving man, inhaled as deeply as his injured side permitted, held it until he choked, exhaled slowly. The sudden nicotine surge was exquisite, like an old friend he hadn't seen for too long, and worth the brief spin the room took about him. He closed his eyes, feeling his muscles relax and the pain in his arm and side diminish. At such a moment, it was easy to believe the world was at peace, too, and full of magic and poetry. *Stand still, you ever-moving spheres of heaven, that time may cease and midnight never come...*

But when he opened his eyes, Stoner was right there, hands folded on the blotter, that small smile still in place. He didn't seem quite as carnivorous as he had a moment ago, and Faust smiled back.

"Herr Major, are you ready?"

His smile twisted into something wry. Here he was, holding up the entire war for a moment with Marlowe and a cigarette. Granted, he needed it badly. "Thank you for your patience, Mr. Stoner. Yes, I'm ready."

"Then I must ask you what series of events brought you to these shores."

At the secretarial station, Bruckmann began writing.

Faust glanced down at the glowing tip of his cigarette. His muscles had relaxed until his body curved back into the chair, and the pain had receded to a distant murmur, like voices whispering in another room. Everything felt better. He inhaled until his injured side fired a warning salvo across his ribs. Oxygen joined the nicotine soaking through his system, and he was as prepared for battle as he was going to be. "I'm sorry, Mr. Stoner, but I really can't discuss that with you."

Stoner tilted his chin. Foreboding shot through Faust; he didn't trust that tilt.

"Are you saying there is a military reason for your presence here?"

He dragged again, hard. "I didn't say anything of the sort."

"It's implied in your statement. After all, we've been sitting here pleasantly discussing various topics of general interest. Presumably, therefore, it's only military matters that you are unwilling to discuss."

Another drag, and he wondered how long that pack had to last him. Still, there were worse forms of interrogation than chatting with an old man, albeit a damned clever one. "No, there is no military reason for my presence here. However, that series of events touches on several military topics and I'm not comfortable discussing those with you. As you have just proven for the second time in our acquaintance, you are far too adept at drawing inferences from whatever I do say for me to feel comfortable discussing anything more sensitive than the weather."

Stoner withdrew his silver cigarette case from his breast pocket and lit up, too, leaving the case open on the desk. "Well. Let us review your situation, shall we? First, you have readily admitted that you serve in the *Wehrmacht*, not the *Luftwaffe*."

Faust paused, uncertain where Stoner was leading him. "That's right."

Stoner again tilted his head. "I was not aware German Army officers crewed Air Force warplanes."

He winced. Should he try to bluff something here? No, the intelligence lectures he had mostly slept through had repeatedly emphasized never lie to an interrogator, and although he couldn't recall why, there had to be a good reason. "We don't."

"So we have immediately established that you are not here for a legitimate military purpose, which leaves two possibilities: either you are here as the result of an accident—"

"Which is the case."

"—or you are here for an illegitimate purpose."

"An illegitimate purpose?" He dragged again, thinking through the implications of that phrase. "You mean espionage?"

"Indeed."

He let smoke drift from his mouth. Him as a spy—now there was a novel concept. "You know, Mr. Stoner, I was starting to like you—"

"I'm touched." The irony was light.

"—but you play rough."

Stoner tapped ash and continued as if he hadn't spoken. "Your German military intelligence service, the *Abwehr*, has experienced difficulty obtaining information regarding our defenses in these islands."

He took a long last drag and stubbed the quarter-inch butt out in the glass ashtray on the table at his elbow. "I didn't know that."

"The Royal Air Force, on the other hand, has had remarkable success against *Luftwaffe* reconnaissance aircraft, which has denied the *Abwehr* aerial photographs of those defenses."

"I didn't know that, either."

"As it would be criminal folly for the German high command to attempt an invasion without first fully analyzing the defenses of their intended target, the *Abwehr* has little option but to infiltrate agents within England."

Faust cradled his injured arm against his side. He could see where the conversation was going now and Stoner's relentless logic left him cold. Oh, if he'd brought his camera along for the ride, that would really have given Stoner a reason for suspicion.

"*Herr Major,* if the *Abwehr* selected an agent to infiltrate the Oxford area, it would be someone with your precise qualifications."

Even knowing it was coming, the blow was a knockout. "You mean, I know the area—"

"—and you speak the language flawlessly, although with more of an American accent than an English one. You are a clever and resourceful field officer and therefore know what information would be of value and what would be dross. You have the social skills to fit into all but the highest levels of society, and perhaps you even know people who would not be averse to supplying you with the information you would require. Finally, I believe you earned an engineering degree from Munich's technical university, which would also qualify you to learn the fine art of sabotage prior to your exportation by the *Abwehr.*"

Come on, Erhard had said, *come for a ride with papa. It'll be just like going home for you.*

"You're forgetting, Mr. Stoner, that I'm a military officer in uniform. Doesn't that protect me against allegations of espionage?"

"It does nothing of the sort." Stoner stubbed out his cigarette. "The Geneva Convention does exempt soldiers in uniform on reconnaissance missions from charges of espionage. However, its otherwise specific language does not define the term employed, the 'zone of operations of the hostile army,' and my own powers-that-be boggle at applying that term to these islands."

Faust rubbed his neck and forced himself to breathe. "I don't know what to say."

"Then allow me to conclude." Stoner folded his hands atop his spotless blotter. "We know there is a German intelligence network in place within Oxford."

"You know more than I do."

"We know that because we've broken it."

"Then it wasn't so hot, was it?"

"And they told us another agent was coming."

Faust quit breathing again.

"Under these circumstances, *Herr Major,* surely you understand we must verify your position before accepting you as an honorable prisoner of war."

He realized he was chewing his lower lip and made himself stop. Again he cursed Erhard: *why here, you cretin, of all the places on the planet?* "I see."

"You should also understand that I am not the person you must convince of your innocence. I am only the case-worker, so to speak, gathering information to forward to my superiors. The decision of whether to accept you into the prisoner of war system within this country, or to charge you with espionage and seek your execution, will be made at a higher level within the chain of command." Stoner paused. "I do hope this is clear."

"Devastatingly so." He glanced at the packet of Players, temptingly near beside the ashtray at his right elbow. "Excuse me for a temporary change of subject, but are cigarettes rationed?"

"Of course. One pack per month."

A welcome surge of anger warmed his chilled skin. "Ten cigarettes for thirty days is cruel and unusual punishment, Mr. Stoner. I guarantee I won't survive it."

"Such a pity." Stoner's smile was brief. "I must ask you again to explain your presence here," he paused, as if for emphasis, "even if only in general terms."

Faust stared out the left-hand French window at the line of apple trees bordering the outer wall, with Woodrow's upper storey, spiraling chimneys, and slate roof rising above. Seen from that angle, Jennifer's idea of cleaning the upper windows from the apple trees didn't seem all that silly; the lower branches dangled almost to the ground, the middle ones were at the same level as the windows, and it would require neither a remarkably agile person nor a long reach for the task. It would take balance more than anything else, to know how far one could stretch before toppling off.

Stoner's charges were horrifyingly plausible, and beneath Faust's fading flush of anger his fear remained, colder than ever. If he said nothing, he faced possible execution, which would help no one, least of all himself. If he said too much, he became a traitor. Somewhere in between those extremes, he had to find a point of compromise, as close to quiescence as he could persuade Stoner to accept. It was balance again, with a long way to fall.

"Okay," he said, "in general terms—on Saturday I visited an acquaintance who was a *Luftwaffe* pilot. He suggested I ride along on his next bombing run and see what it was like. Like an idiot, I agreed, and here I am."

Stoner kept staring at him, eyebrows slightly up as if awaiting more. The pause stretched until even the background scratching of Bruckmann's pencil stopped. Faust forced himself to hold Stoner's unwavering stare but he reddened beneath its weight, and finally he admitted defeat and looked back out the French window.

"You didn't expect my entire life history, did you?"

"Granted, it's a start. And granted, it's in general terms." Stoner tapped his fingers on the blotter. "I must have more detail, you know, enough to convince the chain of command above me that you are speaking the truth."

"Mr. Stoner, I don't have a good face for poker. If I'm telling a lie, you'll know it."

Stoner's eyebrows crept higher. "I'm afraid that's not evidence which will convince those powers-that-be of your innocence. Perhaps we should try this another way." He pulled a small sheaf of papers from the top drawer of his desk, the first indication that this was more than a show office. "I am going to ask you a series of questions concerning the details of the aircraft and the flight, things we already know, and we'll judge how well your answers correspond to these unassailable facts."

Faust looked away again. It would be easy for Stoner to lead him on, query after query, until he said more than he'd intended. They'd done that dance before Woodrow's apple-wood fire. "I don't know much about flying."

"Do you know what type of plane it was?" Stoner took a blank sheet of paper and wrote on it, then flipped it over. "There's my answer, based upon the wreckage we recovered."

He cradled his injured arm closer to his side. This seemed so harmless that there had to be a catch. "Mr. Stoner, do you have any idea how difficult this is for me?"

"Oh, yes, *Herr Major,* I'm afraid I do."

Faust glanced up, surprised. There was only one way Stoner could know—by personal experience.

"To explain that," Stoner said, "I'm going to tell you a story. In the Great War, I was a major commanding the Fourth Battalion of the Oxfordshire and Buckinghamshire Light Infantry. At that time, the Fourth was composed of volunteers from the university, and I had served as their commander in a reserve capacity for seven years prior to nineteen-fifteen, when we took part in the attack at Neuve Chapelle, in the Pas-de-Calais, on the tenth of March. We were attached to General Henry Rawlinson's Fourth Corps and were assigned a position in the center of the attack against the village itself." Stoner riveted Faust with a keen stare. "Notice, *Herr Major,* the amount of detail I am giving you. Should you need to confirm my story, it would not be difficult."

Faust reddened at the urbane rebuke.

"By nightfall, we had captured the village but had received no further orders. Communication with headquarters was not good and we weren't certain of the location of the Gharwal Brigade on our right, so we dug in and waited for morning rather than push forward and perhaps allow ourselves to be flanked."

"I would have done the same," Faust said, intrigued despite himself.

"I believe any sane commander would have done so." Stoner tapped his already neat papers into a squared stack and aligned them on the blotter's center. "However, during the night, the German units reinforced their new line before the Bois de Biez. Specifically, they brought up machine guns and positioned them behind steel plating, so that they fired just above a man's knees. Our follow-up attack the next day—the eleventh of March, that was—ran into those machine guns and ground to an abrupt halt. During the final retreat from no man's land, I was struck in both thighs and fainted into one of the wide drainage ditches common to the area.

"It was dusk before I came to my senses. I heard my name being called, again and again, and when I peered over the edge of the ditch I saw a line of my men searching for me through the shell holes and debris. Unfortunately, I was nearer the German lines than my own and to rescue me, my men would have had to run the gauntlet of those machine guns." Stoner shrugged. "Sometimes the Germans honored a cease-fire to rescue the wounded from the field; sometimes they didn't. I decided not to chance it and remained quiet. After midnight, my men gave up and returned to their trenches. I crawled from the ditch and began dragging myself back to our lines, but the German sentries spotted me within minutes and I was taken captive."

Faust fought a shudder. Stoner's calm description of an ordeal that could only be described as brutal was more horrifying than anything he had experienced in combat himself. His own capture, at the hands of a young lady—beautiful or not—seemed tame, even trivial, by comparison. The chill climbed his spine as Stoner kept speaking in the same steady voice.

"I spent two years as a guest of the Kaiser, as we termed it, including a week of intense interrogation from a hospital bed in Douai." He leaned forward and folded his hands atop the irritatingly neat stack of papers. The intensity of his stare softened, but only at the edges. "So when I say I understand your current confusion and trepidation, *Herr Major,* you may believe what I say."

The shudder won. Faust measured the depth of Stoner's poise and contrasted it to the shattered stumps of humanity that were the Great War veterans he had known as a boy—gas victims with wet sucking coughs, amputees in wheeled chairs or with flapping sleeves. For the first time, he realized his greatest fear in combat was not death.

"Mr. Stoner, may I ask: do your wounds still bother you? I mean, after all these years—" The question suddenly seemed invasive and personal. Faust fell silent.

But Stoner didn't even shift in his chair. "No, not for years. I used to have a weather leg, and knew when it would rain or when to expect the first snows, and everyone laughed at me—"

Faust laughed.

"—but that's mostly passed off." The intensity faded further from Stoner's gaze and his eyes softened. "No, the medical care I received as a prisoner was rather good. It was the overall treatment that was bad."

"Bad?"

"Rather dreadful must be the most accurate description." Stoner leaned back again. "The Germans didn't seem to know what to do with us once the interrogations were complete. Their solution was to herd us together in old factory buildings with barbed-wire fences about them, and post guards with dogs on the outside."

"Isn't that what a prison is supposed to be?" The way Stoner kept mentioning "the Germans," as if there wasn't one sitting across from him, was both annoying and disquieting. Faust refused to squirm.

"No, it was actually an inhumane arrangement. It omitted such creature comforts as private space, activities to consume time, and room for exercise. Food became scarce, especially beginning the winter of nineteen-seventeen, and what was available was both inadequate and mediocre. Many of us would have starved were it not for parcels from home. And the German general staff rather naturally tended to place their most capable officers on the front lines, leaving the dregs of the corps to tend for us."

Stoner fixed Faust with a professorial eye, and he realized he was being lectured. Amusement routed his nervousness; it was impossible not to like the old geezer, despite the situation and despite his incessant tidiness.

"In all armies, there is a sort of officer who doesn't know how to wield his authority. He's not necessarily sadistic, but the sensation of power goes to his head and he tends to lord it over anyone unfortunate enough to fall beneath his rule, such as prisoners of war. These officers referred to me as 'truculent' because I refused to tolerate their petty abuses."

"I know the sort you mean," Faust said. "In basic training, I ran into a lot of career corporals. They particularly enjoyed making trouble for those of us who'd attended gymnasium or university. Mr. Stoner, is my math off?"

Stoner's eyebrows lifted into question marks.

"You said you were captured in March of nineteen-fifteen and you were a prisoner for two years. But the war lasted until November of nineteen-eighteen."

Stoner shook his head. "No error, *Herr Major*. I was also called 'unruly' because I refused to settle down and enjoy life in the camps, such as it was. My fifth escape attempt bore much fruit and I returned safely to the Allied lines, where I was almost shot by a nervous French sentry for my pains."

"I'm impressed." He felt comfortable enough to risk the obvious question. "How did you escape?"

Stoner chuckled. "I am not here to give you ideas, young man."

"Perhaps not." Despite this second rebuke, Faust still felt confidence in their growing relationship. Stoner wasn't such a bad old codger, after all. "May I ask a rather personal question? Do you dream about these events?"

Stoner's eyebrows arched again. "Why do you ask?"

He chose his words carefully. "Because a friend of mine who died in Poland—well, in his last letter, he said he'd seen some things he'd rather forget. But he kept dreaming about them."

Again Stoner fixed him with that relentless stare. "You say your friend died in Poland, not that he was killed in battle."

With a shock, Faust realized how much he had relaxed and how off-guard he'd become. Stoner's perceptivity shot through him like a cold enema: with his decades of managing students, the old man could read him like a posted sign. It was Faust's third warning and it was embarrassing that he'd needed it. He looked away from that keen gaze, out the window at the apple boughs heavy with green fruit, but heard himself answering even though he hadn't intended to. "He was found in his quarters. It might have been an accident while cleaning his pistol."

"And then again, it might not?" Stoner's voice was gentle.

"If, as you say, he was a sensitive man."

Faust spoke the simple truth. "Siegi should have been a monk. He had no business in the army."

Stoner silently closed his silver cigarette case and slipped it into his inner pocket. He didn't seem to want to answer, any more than Faust had, but when he looked back up his expression was frank. "I don't dream of those events, but rather of similar ones that evoke the same ugly, searing emotions."

Again words were dragged from him and this time he could taste them. "Ugly emotions." The bitter flavor roused memories of his own, quick repulsive flashes. He quelled them. But once awakened they refused to leave, and his heart began beating faster.

The old man's gaze was kindly, as if he spoke to a child, and his voice sank to a murmur. "The initial fury of the assault. The utter helplessness of finding myself and my men beneath those German machine guns, and panic when the bullets ripped into my legs. Horror and despair when I realized I would not be rescued." He paused. "And of course, as you know, the bitter pill of surrender."

The gentle voice reached into Faust's soul and ripped it open, showing him emotions he hadn't known what to call, hadn't even known he'd experienced. It aroused a gut-wrenching echo within him. This time, he couldn't look away from Stoner's stare. He wasn't certain he understood Stoner, but he now knew the old man understood him to his core and his heart thumped at the thought.

But before he could digest that, Stoner leaned forward. He rapped one finger on the sheet of paper, shattering the brittle moment like a pane of glass. "Come, *Herr Major*, your answer. What type of plane was it?"

For a moment longer he agonized. What to say? Stoner's logic was so relentless, so damned *logical*, that he could think of no rebuttal and no reason not to comply. To say nothing was to risk execution as a spy—and his only certainty at that moment was, he didn't want to die. But if he made one admission, it would be easier to make the second and harder not to continue.

On impulse, he reached across the desk, grabbed the sheet of paper, and tugged it from beneath Stoner's unresisting fingers. No one stopped him. Stoner sat still, complacent hands clasped atop the blotter. Faust flipped the paper over and read *Heinkel 111 P-4,* written in a beautiful flowing script, and slumped in his chair.

"Did I lie to you?" Stoner's voice was even gentler.

He leaned against the desk and let relief wash through him. But the position stretched his right side and the injury fired a warning salvo across his ribs. He settled back.

"No, sir, you did not." He rubbed his neck. Tension had ironed his muscles into ridges. "It was a Heinkel."

Stoner leaned back in his chair and crossed his legs, as if nothing important had just happened. "You say you visited an acquaintance. Did you go to the airfield where he was based?"

His neck tightened again. "Yes."

"What airfield was that?" When Faust again hesitated, Stoner took another sheet of paper, wrote on it, then flipped it over. "And this time, you first."

He sighed. "All right, Mr. Stoner, I'm going to trust you. It was Le Havre."

Stoner displayed his answer, *Le Havre,* then removed both sheets from the desk, leaving only the small sheaf of papers in their neat stack. Otherwise the desk held a glass ashtray, now with a few scatterings of ash and one butt in its geographic center, an old and battered pen-and-ink stand, the spotless blotter, and a reading lamp with a wide decorative brass base off to Stoner's right. Faust wondered what the old man's bedroom looked like. Were his shoes aligned on the floor? Shirts and suits arranged by color with ties pre-knotted?

"Did you say your acquaintance was the pilot?" Stoner asked.

"Yes, Erhard Bohnes. We've known each other since we were kids." There was nothing he needed to add to that; Stoner wasn't interested in his personal history; but again he found himself rambling. "There were four of us the same age at the orphanage, and we all joined the military. Siegi died in Poland in January, Tomas was killed in France in June, and now Erhard."

Stoner leaned forward abruptly. "Are you saying all of your friends died this year?"

He stared out the French window at the apple trees. Why had he brought up this subject? Surely Stoner couldn't care less, and his ears warmed. "I don't know about the English ones. The last letter I received from them, a farewell until the end of hostilities, was dated September first of last year."

He looked back into Stoner's gaze in time to see a flash of something, understanding, perhaps, quickly stilled behind the old man's usual steady intensity. So that had hit home. Good; reciprocal emotion could only help.

But before they could continue, there was a knock on the door. Without prompting, Bruckmann set down his pencil and went to answer, walking as silently past Faust as he'd sat in his chair taking notes all morning. Stoner folded his hands and watched his lieutenant without speaking.

After the usual murmurs, Bruckmann said, "Constable Mercer to see you, sir."

Stoner's face tightened and the lines about his eyes deepened. "Perhaps he's found my missing granddaughter. *Herr Major,* I must ask you to excuse me while I handle a personal matter."

He rose. "Of course." Was the mysterious Harriet still missing? He wanted to ask but didn't want to pry further.

Stoner rose, as well. "Sergeant Tanyon, please return the prisoner to his quarters."

11

the same morning
Margeaux Hall

Stoner rose behind his desk, strangely giddy as he watched Faust stride for the door, Sergeant Tanyon behind him. Constable Mercer would not report personally unless he had momentous news to impart—in short, unless he had found Harriet. But as to why he hadn't simply telephoned or sent the girl home, well, that set his old heart to double-thumping again.

A general pile-up ensued at the door as Constable Mercer didn't wait to be announced. Stoner stiffened; if Faust felt threatened and wanted a hostage, it was a dangerous opportunity. Mercer had been constable of Patchley Abbey all his life, and like Stoner had been recalled to service for the duration when his replacement went off to war. At his age he'd be no match for a trained combat soldier, even an injured one, although he wasn't precisely frail with his stout dumpy build and shovel-shaped hands. Stoner was certain that, in his day, he could have emptied a brawling pub without breaking sweat.

But Faust stepped aside for the older man, even bowing slightly from the waist. Mercer gave the German uniform a quick glance but it seemed his mind was on other things, and with barely an acknowledging nod he rolled past Faust and into Stoner's office. After one horrified glance, Tanyon closed the door behind them.

"Blimey," Bruckmann whispered, barely breathing. "That was close."

Mercer glanced at him, eyes alert. Although it felt false, Stoner let himself smile. Perhaps there was snow on that chimney; fire remained in the boiler.

"Is that the German caused all the fuss Saturday night?" Mercer asked.

"That's the man," Stoner said.

To his surprise, the constable thinned his lips and shook his head. "Never can tell with foreigners. Seems a gentleman, don't he?"

"Constable, have you found my granddaughter?"

But Mercer merely stared at him, indignation draining away like beer from an overturned bottle. His mouth opened but no words came forth, and when it closed again it was with finality.

"I see." Stoner sat down and leaned back in his chair. He forced himself to breathe deeply. It would do her no good for him to have a heart attack. "I take it the news is not good?"

"No, sir. I'm afraid it isn't."

He knew, without hearing the words he knew. But he had to be certain. "How bad is it?"

Mercer's big shoulders drooped. "As bad as it gets. I'm sorry."

He'd been so certain she was fine, simply run away for a bit—for pique, for romance, even for fun or spite. But he'd been so certain she'd reappear when her mood changed. This, the worst news of all, he'd never expected.

He found himself staring at his cot, in the far corner of the room, and at the little table he used as a nightstand. He walked to it, suddenly aware of how difficult it could be for an old man to walk, and lifted one of the silver frames nestled there. Jennifer and Harriet, aged eleven and nine, grinned out at him from the profusion of flowers in the garden of his old Oxford home. There were carnations in Jennifer's slender hands, daisies in Harriet's two tails, and Asiatic lilies hemmed them in on both sides, wavering behind their hair, bright and dark.

Harriet in her long white nightgown, eight years old and first arrived in his quiet home, sitting in his lap, beating her fists against his chest and howling for her mother who would never return. Harriet at ten, again dressed for sleep, climbing into his and Daphne's bed for her bedtime story, no, she wasn't too old for that and she wasn't going to sleep until she had her way. At fourteen, wildflowers in her hair, swinging with the big bands on the radio all around the living room until he'd give ten years off his life for a bit of the quiet he used to know. Just two days ago, in her bright yellow dress and with her dark hair fluffed about her face, resplendent in pink lipstick and nail polish, no, she wasn't too young to go to the village dance and help entertain the pilots who were defending England, it was her civic duty and she wasn't going to be quiet until she had her way.

As usual, she'd had her way. He had given in; he hadn't supervised nor protected her; he had let her go off with Sally who wasn't two years older. And now he'd have all the quiet he'd ever wanted, which was much more than he could bear.

He hugged the frame to his chest as if he could still shelter her there, as if she could still beat against him with her fists, not for her dead mother but for her dead self. Was he crying? If it brought his littlest girl back to him, he'd bawl without shame.

He turned. The two men stood, staring. Bruckmann's eyes were huge, shocked and disbelieving. Constable Mercer, the bearer of bad news, huddled before the desk like an errant and aging schoolboy.

"Please tell me whatever you can," Stoner said.

Mercer drew a deep breath. "We found her in the Dark."

"Was it an accident?"

"No, sir."

"Some wild beast?"

"A male one."

Bruckmann made a wordless noise. He sounded sick.

"My poor little girl." Stoner returned to his desk, still cradling the framed photograph. He maintained enough self-control to sit carefully, rather than collapse, for the way his old heart ached that would have been a collapse indeed. "There's one thing I must know, constable: when did she die?"

Mercer hesitated. "I need Dr. Harris to make certain." Before Stoner could speak, he rushed on. "But I think she died the night she vanished."

"Of course. The night of the dance, when every off-duty pilot from RAF Patchbourne crowded our little village."

"Sir." Bruckmann hesitated.

Stoner said it for him. "It was also the night of the air raid, when a German officer ran loose across the countryside and was captured exiting the Dark."

"Exactly." Mercer squared his shoulders. "Major Stoner, please understand—I've never had to investigate a murder before."

"Which of us has?" Stoner arranged the frame on his desk, angling it to keep the picture hidden from anyone across from him, jealously guarding her image from prying eyes. If only he'd been as protective Saturday night.

"I have to call the Metropolitan Police for help."

Granted, asking a village bobby to investigate a murder was rather like asking Stoner himself to break a trained German intelligence agent. A welcome core of rage grew within him. Neither he nor Mercer was disabled yet. "Of course, constable. I'll cooperate in any way I can."

After Mercer left, Bruckmann stepped forward. "Sir, I am so sorry. Is there anything I can do?"

"Yes, Jack. Please send Jennifer in. And leave us alone for a bit."

12

the same morning
Margeaux Hall

The third-floor bedroom door closed behind him. Faust again shivered when the bolt snapped home, then listened to the footsteps of Tanyon and his young assistant with the lousy haircut, Carmichael, as they clumped down the corridor and away. It was a lonely sound. *And wilt thou leave me thus?* Wyatt had asked, as usual phrasing Faust's emotions almost four hundred years before he felt them. Like Stoner, Wyatt was so perceptive he should have been outlawed. Granted, he nearly had been.

Faust usually didn't mind being alone, but with the burden of Stoner's interview weighing on him, a discussion with Barrington or Wurlitzer, those gentle souls, would have helped him sort out his thoughts. Even Munting, the original ass, would go down a treat just then—anyone would help, rather than sitting and staring at that cold, stark room with the barred window.

But he shouldn't have thought of them, either. He missed them too much, and the hole left in his life by the absence of his two closest friends was heavier than Stoner's allegations and more painful than his arm and side. Munting would laugh at him and pick a sly argument, but Barrington would lean his chin on a fist, that little smile lifting his lips, and talk him through the problem. If, of course, he could be heard through Munting.

The tray of dirty dishes and shaving gear was gone;

otherwise the room was just as he'd left it, with the bed rumpled and the faded patchwork quilt tossed over the chair. He sighed, hissing when his side complained. Brother Harmonious had raised him better than this. Left-handed, he straightened the sheets and hoped to straighten himself out at the same time.

Stoner's war story bothered him. Such treatment of a captured enemy officer was immoral, and while he didn't expect reality to obey his own poetical views, the confirmation of how low Germany had sunk was too similar to that pig Greis.

He stilled, bent over the bed. Surely Clarke had reported his adventure, meaning the name of Faust was not unknown in certain English military intelligence circles. Another chill, a big one, climbed his spine. He'd have to be certain to say nothing of that affair to Stoner. No matter how intriguing he found the old codger, he fully expected the man to do his duty and the Clarke affair was blackmail bait of the worst magnitude. If he was sent to a prisoner of war camp full of Nazis and that story was leaked, the English guards would find him dangling from the rafters some morning. At best.

The allegations of espionage were no more comforting and he didn't find that aspect of Stoner charming at all. It was a disquieting thought. Having survived Erhard's outrageous misadventure, it would be unthinkable to die now, executed for something as stupid as this. Did they shoot spies or hang them? He paused with the quilt in his hand. Did he really want to know?

Not a chance he could fold the quilt one-handed. He draped it as neatly as he could manage across the foot of the bed. Then, chores done, he dragged the chair around the table so he could watch out the window, easing his left shoulder against the ladder back and cradling his right arm in his lap.

A horse and rider trotted across the distant expanse of lawn, beyond the rose beds and near the hanging boughs loaded with green apples. The horse, a chestnut hunter with a glossy coat and powerful haunches, held his attention for the first glance. There was an escape attempt right there if he could find an unguarded gate; the wall was too high for even a nice beast like that. But then he realized the rider was a woman and the horse faded to the background.

She rode astride, her legs long in high boots and gently flaring breeches, wrapped about the horse's barrel as if molded there. Even across the distance, he could trace the elegant tear drops of her breasts and her narrow hips. Her face at least wasn't ugly although the shadow of her derby hid her eyes, and her hair shone brilliantly golden in the sunlight. It rippled about her shoulders as her body pulsed with the horse's motion, following the trot like an echo. It required no stretch of his imagination to picture a man there instead of a saddle and his blood warmed.

Somewhere in the quiet building, someone shouted.

Moments later a woman ran stumbling across the lawn, auburn hair and tweed skirt flying. Faust sat up straight, squinting through the bright sunlight, as the horse shied and the rider stilled it, and Jennifer ran past them as if they didn't exist. She collided with the wrought-iron postern gate camouflaged beneath the overhanging branches, then slammed it with her open palms and slumped against it. For a long moment she hung there, her body shaking visibly even over that distance. Then she dug a keyring from her pocket, fumbled about, and unlocked the gate. She charged through, leaving it open behind her. The sumptuous rider kicked the horse back into a trot, rounded the corner, and vanished from view.

If Constable Mercer had found Stoner's missing granddaughter, the news was not good. Poor Jennifer, so upset; perhaps her missing sister had snuck off to visit a friend and been caught in the air raid. No matter how disappointed he'd been when he'd realized she wasn't the most beautiful girl in the world, he was sorry for her.

Nevertheless, he eyed the gaping postern gate. If they left it open, he'd found the first chink in their security. But a soldier followed Jennifer's path to the gate, glancing over his shoulder as he scurried across the lawn. It was Carmichael of the bad haircut. Still stealing glances back the way he'd come, Carmichael pulled the postern closed and locked it with his own set of keys, then returned at a trot to Margeaux Hall.

So there was an entry to the Hall on the west end of this wing. If Carmichael had been alone on duty at the front door, he'd left his post to seal the breach in the Hall's defenses. Or perhaps someone else had been on duty and had called Carmichael to go lock the gate. But then there was no reason for the furtive glances toward the windows of the Hall, where officers and sergeants might lurk. No, that had been the mien of a soldier away from his post. Faust filed the information away: Carmichael could be lured.

Now nothing moved on the green expanse of lawn; not even a breath of wind shifted the apple leaves nor the yellow and pink roses in their formal beds. He rested his elbow on the sill and his chin on his fist, feeling his shoulders sag. Out in the corridor, men's voices rose, one shrill and excited, the other subdued. Before he could make out their words, a door closed and cut them off.

Why had he ever left Paris? So Ritzi broke up with him. So Oberst von Maacht chewed him out. Again. So what? He'd lost girlfriends before. He'd been reamed before. That was just the way women, and the Army, worked. But he had suddenly needed room—all the room between Paris and Le Havre. He couldn't even advance the pitiful excuse of needing a brotherly hug from Erhard; he regretted the man's death, of course, but hell, if ever somebody asked for it, it was Erhard. Besides, Faust hadn't set out for Le Havre; he'd just started driving and wound up there. It was still astonishing he and Erhard had found enough to discuss for an entire day, morning, afternoon, and evening. Whatever it had been, he still couldn't remember it. Or, as Wyatt phrased it, *The stars be hid that led me to this pain.*

No, something had changed him during the French campaign, rubbing his normally prosaic nerves raw. And he didn't need even one guess to know what that something had been.

Damn Greis. Damn Clarke. Damn himself, for being so thin-skinned that he could be rattled so deeply.

Behind him, keys rattled and the lock snapped. Faust twisted on the chair, gasping and flinching as his unconsidered motion sent a spasm of pain wrapping about his ribcage.

Sergeant Tanyon filled the doorway, legs spraddled. His poker face had cracked; his eyes were narrowed, nostrils flared, teeth clenched. Rage pulsed from him like steam from a locomotive.

"What's wrong?"

The sergeant stepped back into the corridor. "Come on, snap to it. Don't have all day."

Everyone was upset, not just Jennifer. He eased into the corridor. Maybe he could take advantage of a general distraction. A swift glance about showed that, this time, Tanyon was alone. Faust turned west into the corridor, toward the blaze of sunlight and toward Tanyon, who moved to block his path.

"Not that way."

They were close—too close. It was a chance: Tanyon alone here, Carmichael at the entry, then the keys to the postern and away.

But just as the thought crossed his mind, Tanyon dropped his hand to his holster. Before Faust could react, he heard the snap, and then he stared down the barrel of the sergeant's Webley .455 revolver. He froze, their gazes locked, and he knew the moment was past. He forced himself to relax despite the barrel aimed at him.

Tanyon's smile was cruel. "Your eyes give you away."

More than ever he wanted to have it out with the jerk. "And yours glow in the dark." Before Tanyon could respond, he turned around and trudged down the corridor toward the eastern staircase and the skylight's dim glow.

Behind him, Tanyon grunted. Although he listened for it, Faust never heard the snap of a closing holster, although it was perhaps lost in the sergeant's clumping tread. The knowledge left an odd, tense sensation between Faust's shoulder blades, as if a target had been painted there. It didn't cool his temper.

Tanyon clearly was the lynchpin of Stoner's staff. Bruckmann was a junior lieutenant, clever but inexperienced, and he'd seen no other officers so far. All of the soldiers he'd seen—what very English names, Carmichael, Ellington, who knew what else—they were all teenagers and seemed frightened of both him and the war.

But Tanyon was a different matter. He was a career soldier and had seen action somewhere, perhaps in France with the B.E.F. His experience handling aggressive prisoners seemed limited; otherwise, he'd never have let Faust get so close. Unfortunately, he wouldn't get that particular opportunity again, and he had the sneaking suspicion he'd have to fight for his next one.

"To the right here," Tanyon said. "Down to the infirmary and go straight in."

They had only descended one flight and were in a narrow hallway on the second floor—the English first floor, Faust reminded himself. He followed directions and passed several closed doors before he came to an open one on the left. His swift glance swept over a guardroom, with rifles standing in a vertical case, a transmitter-receiver on a stout table, a radioman wearing headphones, an empty prison cell with its door hanging open, and several youngsters in British Army uniforms bent over clipboards but eyeing him as he passed. Good; now he knew what part of the building to avoid. The rifles he'd ignore unless his situation became desperate; the English would go after him with a vengeance if he grabbed a weapon and it wouldn't be worth it for a short-term advantage.

"Who left the bleeding door open?" The voice was loud enough to still be heard, even though he was several steps past. "Riff-raff out in the hall—oh, sorry, sergeant. Didn't know it was you."

Faust turned as Tanyon reached out and closed the door on the explosion of laughter.

Maybe humor would help. "I think soldiers are the same the world over, no matter what language they speak."

Behind him, Tanyon's sniff was loud. "Ours aren't murderers."

After France, that stung. Faust walked in hot silence to the next door on the right, also open. The room beyond, painted hospital white, tugged at his memories. He paused in the doorway.

"You've suddenly got a real attitude, sergeant. What have I done to you?"

The Webley was level at waist height. Tanyon fingered the trigger. "Go on, inside."

Something had definitely happened, causing that smoldering anger deep in Tanyon's eyes. The sergeant hadn't behaved like this before. He'd been rude, yes, but otherwise capable and quiet to the point of invisibility. Now he seemed to be itching for a fight.

Well, Tanyon would find he wasn't shy when the time came. But they'd have to wait for it, at least until Faust knew what was wrong with his arm and side. He eased through the doorway, hearing Tanyon close, but not too close, behind. Yep, he'd wasted that opportunity.

His sweeping glance over the infirmary stopped at the windows, wide open and quite without bars. Yearning stirred within him. The second floor wasn't so high; he could jump from a window without killing himself. The wall, though; escaping was going to boil down to that wall, and how he'd get over it with one functional arm, he didn't know.

A small, wiry young man, wearing a white smock unbuttoned over British Army Medical Corps khaki, glanced up from the instrument table in the corner, where he was packing a black bag. It was the kind nurse who had bandaged his wounds Sunday morning.

"Good morning," Faust said. "I remember you, sort of."

"Hello to you, too." The nurse raised his voice. "Dr. Harris!"

A tall man of about forty pushed through an inner door and stopped short. His brown hair was already greying, concentration lines clustering at the corners of his green eyes, and his unbuttoned white smock covered a rumpled brown flannel suit. His movements were swift and intense, and his mouth was pinched tight.

"Right, good to see you awake. Cavanaugh, we'll do this one first." Dr. Harris ducked back through the door.

Cavanaugh left the bag and led Faust to the examination table before those wonderful windows. Tanyon stayed near the entry.

"We're in a bit of a hurry here." Cavanaugh's voice was

apologetic. "Can you manage those buttons alone?"

"In the interest of speed, no." He let Cavanaugh open his tunic and slide it down his arms behind him, although twisting his right arm back made him gasp.

"I suppose that wasn't the best idea I've ever had," Cavanaugh said. "The shirt and undervest, too."

Those had to be peeled off, stiff with dried blood, and it stung.

"I thought it bled this morning," Faust said.

"You've been using the arm." Cavanaugh unwound the bandage. "Doctor?"

Dr. Harris was suddenly beside them. "You've torn the stitches."

"I didn't remember where I was this morning until I tried to sit up." The breeze sighing through the casement windows caressed his bare skin—O *happy dames, that may embrace the fruit of your delight,* Surrey again—but when he peered down, his side and arm were splotched with oceans of black bruises, the continents between swollen and red. He looked back out the window.

"Bet that hurt." The doctor's touch on the back of his arm was light. "Can you lift the elbow at all?"

"Not really." He tried; his arm shuddered, collapsed against his side, and the pain flashed like a flame. He managed to keep his voice level. "Ouch."

"How about this inflamed spot beneath your arm?"

"That burns."

"Badly?"

"Fairly. And consistently."

"Right," Dr. Harris said again. "We missed some shrapnel. Cavanaugh, tighten the stitches, clean him up, rebandage using acriflavine and zinc ointment. Then get on the horn to Patchbourne hospital and make an appointment with the X-ray machine for this afternoon. I'll want anterior and lateral views of the chest." He paused. "Then meet me on the scene. Is the bag ready?"

"Yes, I think so."

Dr. Harris poked among the black bag's innards then closed it and swiveled back to Faust. "We'll have to get that shrapnel out of you fast or it will become infected. In that location, we could kiss you goodbye."

"I'd rather you didn't," Faust said.

Dr. Harris stared at him. After a moment, his chin drooped.

"Nothing personal, but you're just not my type."

"Yes, well, I'll try to restrain myself. And I'm not willing to operate blind."

"Why not?"

"Because you've got lungs in there," Dr. Harris said bluntly, "and I'd rather not meet them on a first-name basis. I'm only a country doctor, you know. Later, Cavanaugh." He shot a last glance at Faust, then pushed past Tanyon and was gone.

After ten agonizing minutes, Cavanaugh let him refasten his own tunic and was lifting the telephone receiver as Faust turned to Tanyon.

"Thank you for your patience, sergeant."

Without answering, Tanyon stepped into the corridor and blocked its western end. "Back to the stairs and down."

Faust rolled his eyes and obeyed, again cradling his right arm in his left.

The implied advice from both Cavanaugh and Dr. Harris was not to use the arm or the stitches would tear again. The pain was bad enough for him to believe the worst, especially now that the wounds had been well handled, and neither medical man had offered so much as an aspirin. Not for a prisoner?

He sighed. Whatever means he used to escape—through the window, on horseback, over the wall, down the toilet—he'd need two arms. He imagined swimming the Strait of Dover with one arm, salt water soaking through the bandages. He quailed. A small boat couldn't be all that difficult to manage. After all, he'd survived his first parachute jump.

Which meant he had no business pushing his lousy luck any further. Stowing away was sounding more attractive by the moment. There was still commerce between neutral countries and England, and he'd always wanted to visit Spain and Portugal.

Downstairs in the grand ballroom, only the middle-aged wispy clerk still slumped over his typewriter. His face was buried in his hands and he was so still, Faust wondered if he slept where he sat.

The console radio, like the typewriters, was silent. The soldier who'd been listening to the gardening show now stood at Stoner's closed door. As Faust and Tanyon approached, he knocked and stuck his head within.

"He's here, sir."

Stoner's voice carried despite its softness. "Thank you, Corporal Pym."

Lance corporal, Faust thought, glad for a distraction from the throbbing pain and noting the single chevron on this youngster's sleeve. This, then, was Tanyon's assistant, although a quick glance showed no obvious superiority. Pym seemed no older, no smarter, no more experienced than Ellington or Carmichael, although his mouth was at least closed and his haircut didn't make his head look lopsided. There was some difference, then, that couldn't be seen with the naked eye and this would be the other man to watch.

He at least met Faust's stare without flinching, grey eyes level beneath thick blond hair, as he pushed Stoner's door open and stood aside.

13

the same morning
Margeaux Hall

Halfway through the door, Faust checked on his heel. Stoner looked terrible. He stood behind his tidy desk with only the same small sheaf of papers before him, and he seemed old and tired and worn. Earlier, everything about him had been raised: his eyebrows, his chin, the corners of his mouth. But now he drooped, as if claimed by gravity. Only his eyes, although tired, still showed the morning's determination, and his keen stare fastened onto Faust as he crossed the wide room as if to read his soul through his skull.

At the secretarial desk between the French windows, Bruckmann seemed tense, his lean face taut and pulled back by the ears. He shot quick keen glances at his boss but otherwise kept his head down. His pencil was ready in his hand.

Without thinking, Faust again brought his heels together in an audible click. Irritation at himself flashed then as quickly vanished. Showing respect for an old man, enemy or no, was not weakness.

"Mr. Stoner," he said, "are you all right?"

Stoner just stared at him. The ice in his scrutiny solidified into steel. The difference, Faust realized, was rage. A cold hollow sensation began in his chest and spread to his fingertips, leaving them tingling. The missing granddaughter. She hadn't been hurt in that damned bombing raid; she'd been killed. And he was the closest available German target.

"Be seated," Stoner finally said.

He eased into the same wing chair as before, not watching as Tanyon took up his post. Listening to Stoner's silence, bearing the weight of his fury, was intolerable after the almost pleasant morning they'd spent together, the freedom he'd started to feel within this imprisoned relationship. "Look, if your granddaughter was hurt, I'm sorry."

Unfortunately his attempt at frankness struck a raw nerve. Stoner straightened as if bitten and his glare flashed. "Is this a confession?"

"What?" He shook his head. "I don't understand what you're talking about."

The grey lips thinned and paled further. "And I do not understand you. Explain yourself."

Those were the words and tone of an irritated professor. But the rage was much deeper and more personal. He should take offense. But what Faust had mistaken for tiredness in Stoner's eyes he now knew was pain, and resentment for his own dignity was a non-starter.

"I'm sorry." Words tumbled from him; caught between confusion and some crazy version of insecurity, he didn't know what to say first. "I assumed—I mean, everyone is angry. Seems to be angry. At me. You said earlier your granddaughter was missing. I assumed she'd been hurt in the air raid." He paused. "For what it's worth, I don't believe in bombing civilians."

Bruckmann glanced his way for the first time, expression cynical, then returned to his shorthand.

Stoner stared at him, as if measuring the depth of his apology. Faust forced himself to hold that stare, although he thought the weight of it would flatten him. But if he was going to talk his way out of trouble with the British government, he needed the old man, if not on his side, then at least not antagonistic. He forced himself not to look away. At least his face, as usual, would betray his honesty.

Stoner finally broke their stare, lowering his gaze to his notes. But his shoulders, usually so straight, bowed over the desk.

"Then we shall continue where we left off." He tidied the already tidy papers. "Please tell me again the events leading to your presence here, with considerably more detail than you gave the first time."

Faust hesitated. They were past the first round of anger. But it hadn't dissipated. It still lurked in the corners of the room, beneath the furniture, up the chimney, in the background of Stoner's iron control. He wouldn't be surprised if it leaked forth later and assaulted him again. Grief was like that, and Stoner had said nothing to indicate whether the anger was directed at him personally or merely at Germans in general.

Stoner stirred. Faust's stomach tightened. He didn't want to seem truculent and spur that anger accidentally.

"It's okay, Mr. Stoner, you've established your credibility. I'm just trying to decide where to begin, and please don't tell me at the beginning."

"That would appear to be the logical starting point." Stoner's voice was dry and brittle. But his color seemed better.

Faust leaned back and closed his eyes. When he quit tracking Stoner's anger and sat still, he realized the pain in his arm was getting worse. Sharp stabs in his side reduced his breathing to quick shallow panting, just like Saturday night, and his head was starting to spin. He cradled his arm more closely and wondered if he could spare a cigarette from his precious pack; the nicotine would soothe him. He had to be careful. In this condition, it would be easy for Stoner to trick him into saying more than he'd intended.

Whether he liked it or not, he had to explain the reason he'd accepted Erhard's invitation. For that explanation to make sense, he had to put the story in context, which meant he had to start in Paris. If he left the details out, words like *Paris* and *Army Corps,* then not even Stoner could divine that he was a staff officer and maybe he could continue to keep that secret to himself. The only location Stoner needed to know was the one he already had—Le Havre.

"In the Army, I haven't been in my current assignment long." He opened his eyes and found Stoner's stare, still measuring him to an indecent degree, right where he'd left it. "I've held similar positions in the recent past, but not at such a high level." He caught himself; he was getting too close to the full truth. "It's been a sort of apprenticeship, an intended learning experience, and I frankly don't believe I've been all that successful although I've worked hard and learned a lot."

"This is clear."

"Last Sunday—no, the Sunday prior, my batman got drunk and overslept. I didn't wake on my own, so I was late to the office Monday morning and the first assistant adjutant assigned me a week of typing duties as punishment." Faust rubbed his neck. *Oberst* von Maacht had been delighted to reduce the holder of a university degree to a common clerk. "And the week went downhill from there. Something happened every single day to make me look incompetent.

"The senior officers were working eighteen to twenty hours straight and I had to work with them. I can be a fast typist or an accurate one, but not both, so they must have considered me pretty useless. The smart plan would have been to put my head down, do my work, and keep my mouth shut, so of course that's not what I did."

"What did you do, *Herr Major?*" Stoner's color was still improving, the grey melting into a more vibrant tone. Well, that wouldn't hurt anyone, not even Faust.

"On Thursday I tried to discuss the—the meaning of what I was typing with the first assistant adjutant. There were some points that didn't seem to make a lot of sense. I was trying to learn something and I thought that was the purpose of the assignment." He couldn't stifle a sigh even though it shot fire across his ribs. Von Maacht's eyes had popped at such effrontery. "I was told I was there to learn how the work was done, not what or why, and I had to learn a hell of a lot more before I earned the right to ask such questions."

"Your first assistant adjutant sounds a most unpleasant individual."

"I don't think I ever saw that man smile without looking like a stalking predator." The pain stabbed even deeper. He leaned back, shifted in the seat, pulled his right arm further into his lap, supported it above then below the elbow. Nothing eased the pounding. "Anyway, by Friday evening I was fed up and ready for a break. I managed to get out of the office at a decent hour, so I called my girlfriend and arranged to meet her at a nice restaurant."

Stoner stirred again. "Tell me about her."

"Ritzi Schröder is a nightclub singer." When Stoner's eyebrows shot to an alarming altitude, Faust expanded. "Maybe she's not what you'd call suitable material for an officer's wife. But she's a beautiful woman, witty and sophisticated and a great dancer, and I loved doing the town with her. I'd connived the permits for her to come to France, because she has the perfect deep throaty voice for that American swing music that's banned at home. She'd been in France just over a week by then but hadn't yet found a position, so she agreed to meet me."

"I see." Stoner's eyebrows hadn't descended far. His color was almost back to normal, though, even if his stare had suddenly sharpened. "Please continue."

"All I wanted was a relaxing evening. I had arranged for Saturday off duty but had to be back in the office on Sunday, thankfully no longer typing, so I intended to stay out late, drink a bit too much, and find some place romantic to walk with a gorgeous lady." Faust rubbed his neck again. "She met me at the restaurant. As soon as she walked in, I knew I was in trouble."

She had worn his favorite dress, black shimmery stuff draped off the shoulders, and her marcelled hair had gleamed golden about her neck in an invitation for his fingers. But her body had been so stiff with angry determination that even her hips hadn't swayed when she'd stalked toward him, chin lowered ready for battle, and his heart sank again at the memory.

"It wasn't much of a fight because I was tired, already angry, and not willing to play her game. It wasn't about marriage or anything like that, but it was about something I wasn't willing to do, not even for her, and I'd already told her my answer so I wasn't patient when I repeated it. She raised her voice—I shushed her—she stood up—of course I rose, too—she threw her chardonnay in my face and all over my best uniform—then she walked out and everyone in the restaurant started laughing."

Bruckmann shot him another look. But his pencil didn't pause.

Stoner's eyebrows had regained their former altitude. "Somewhat melodramatic."

Faust remembered not to shrug in time. "That's what you get, dating a singer. I paid the bill, left, and walked back to my billet. I was changing into civilian clothes to go out for a quiet dinner somewhere else when a messenger from headquarters arrived, so instead I put on my second-best uniform—" he waved a sardonic hand to indicate he still wore it "—and reported to the first assistant adjutant. It seems that when Ritzi raised her voice, someone overheard our conversation, recognized me, and reported the incident."

Stoner grimaced. "I imagine that rounded off a most pleasant evening."

"He was thorough." Finally, a sign of sympathy. Faust looked aside, toward the cold fireplace with its navy blue mantelpiece, where a carriage clock chimed noon. "He ended by ordering me to remain close to headquarters until further notice. So of course I went straight to the motorpool, requisitioned a car, and drove to Le Havre."

Stoner paused until the last chime died away. "Why?"

"I was angry, Mr. Stoner. I needed to calm down and sort myself out, and I do that best by driving, even with wartime petrol rationing. Actually, I didn't set out for Le Havre. I just started driving, found a nice twisty road that would hold my attention, and followed it."

"You mean, of course, the road along the Seine."

Faust quit breathing. If he'd been hoisted that easily— "I

never mentioned my starting point, Mr. Stoner."

"And very careful you were not to do so." Stoner leaned back in his chair and crossed his legs, again as if it didn't matter. "However, my wife and I lived in Paris for some years after the first war and I've driven the road between there and Le Havre many times. Besides, if a German cabaret singer wished to perform in France, naturally her first choice of venue would be Paris."

Yep, he had. Faust couldn't stop himself from swallowing. He was on dangerous ground now and Stoner held the heights. If only he could take a deep breath, maybe he could concentrate. But each breath hurt worse than the last.

"I see your point. Anyway, after a while I ran into a roadblock crew who weren't impressed by my rank and demanded to know where I was going. I remembered Erhard was at Le Havre and told them that, then decided what the hell and went there after all. I didn't really like him all that much." Why he'd said that, he couldn't imagine. But again he found himself expanding. "Actually, we didn't like each other. But we understood each other because we'd been acquainted so long. And nobody in Paris would be looking for me before Sunday, in any case.

"So Erhard and I ate breakfast, and talked, and worked with the mechanics for a while, and talked, and went to a café on shore for lunch, and talked some more. And I got senseless drunk. Erhard suggested I ride along on his bombing run. He said we'd be back before dawn, I'd have plenty of time to return to Paris, and no one would ever know." He caught his breath as fire shot from his underarm into his fingertips and shoulder. "And here I am, Mr. Stoner, and everyone's going to know."

For the first time Stoner glanced aside. Faust traced his gaze to a silver photograph frame on his desk, just beyond the blotter. It hadn't been there in the morning. Harriet? More than ever, he was certain she was dead.

"A frustrating week," the old man finally said.

"With a frustrating ending."

Stoner picked up his sheaf of papers and settled them in his lap. "We shall temporarily leave the topic of your adventures and turn to subjects which should be familiar to a general staff officer in training."

The world lurched as if the ground had been kicked from beneath him, leaving him dangling in space without a parachute. The pleasant room faded around him. "I beg your pardon?"

Stoner merely raised his eyebrows. "Your shoulder

boards and *Soldbuch* detail your position, you know."

He should have figured that out for himself.

"Granted, you still wear the pink *Waffenfarbe* of an armored unit on your shoulder boards rather than the more appropriate white of Army Group command staff." He tapped the papers together. "Unless both are lies, of course."

He reddened and craned his neck to peer at his shoulder boards. The silver insignia for Army Group A gleamed. "You know, I've worn those things for so long I'd forgotten they were there."

Stoner waved a hand. "Perfectly understandable. However, perhaps you've noticed I've not asked any questions concerning your career as an officer?"

He closed his eyes and thunked his head against the chair back. He felt so stupid it even outweighed the pain. "Of course not. Every detail is spelled out in my paybook."

"So I know that when you speak of your first assistant adjutant, you mean *Oberst* Bruno von Maacht."

He glanced up, shaken to his boots. "I neither confirm nor deny that."

Stoner riffled the papers in his hands. "As I intimated earlier this morning, *Herr Major,* these facts are already known to us. I am not attempting to obtain military secrets from you and this is not—at least, not yet—an interrogation. We are working to ascertain your status."

"I understand, but I'm not comfortable with this." He cocked his head; at least that didn't hurt. "Are you telling me you know the general staff composition for the entire Army Group? How?"

"Asking questions is my bailiwick, *Herr Major,* not yours."

Stoner again ran his thumb along the sheaf's edge and an unchewed brick invaded Faust's stomach. So much paper would detail more than the Army Group command staff; it would include the entire order of battle, the name of every important officer within the chain of command. There were typist corporals sleeping within the headquarters building, under armed guard at all times, to prevent just such information leaving the premises.

He felt sick. "I'm starting to believe those horror stories I've heard about British military intelligence."

"Thank you." Stoner's voice was grave, without a trace of sarcasm. "Perhaps I can explain my current intention best by example. When our troops evacuated France, they brought with them certain items of German weaponry, which I had the opportunity to examine and operate during my last visit to

London. One of these items was a tripod-mounted machine gun which I believe was designated an MG34." He paused. "Are you familiar with this weapon?"

"Well." There seemed little point in denying it; the MG34 was widely used, in tanks, in aircraft, and by infantry. And as Stoner had just pointed out, military hardware was so easily captured it was hardly a state secret. Again he wished he could catch his breath and clear his mind. "Yes, I am."

"So if I tell you the weapon I operated in London was air-cooled and fired 7.92 Mauser ammunition, either from a drum magazine or belt-fed, and was equipped with a periscope to allow it to be fired remotely, without exposing the gunner's head to enemy fire, would you believe that I too am familiar with this weapon?"

"I guess I have to."

"And therefore if I ask you to tell me how many rounds that magazine holds, you will also understand I am not pumping you for military secrets, but rather asking you to confirm what I already know?"

"I suppose."

Stoner lifted his chin. It was his first positive movement, and illogically Faust's heart lifted in response.

"How many rounds, *Herr Major?*"

He hesitated only a moment more. "The smaller drum holds fifty rounds, the larger one seventy-five."

"Does this machine gun ever jam?"

"When it gets dirty, it can be temperamental."

"As a number of other interested officers fired ahead of me and it jammed several times while I emptied one small drum of fifty rounds, I must therefore agree you are equally familiar with the MG34." Stoner placed the papers atop the blotter. "Do you see my intention here, *Herr Major?*"

"Yes, I see where you're going." He let himself relax and the pain eased slightly. Stoner had endured this from a hospital bed? He blanched at the thought.

"Therefore, when I say *Generalfeldmarschall* Gerd von Rundstedt's chief of staff is *General der Infanterie* Georg von Sonderstern, his chief of operations is *Oberst* Günther Blumentritt, his first assistant adjutant—as we have already discussed—is *Oberst* von Maacht—" Stoner glanced up from his perusal of the top sheet "—do you believe I am familiar with the composition of Army Group A's general staff?"

It was infuriating. But inarguable. "Better than me, I think."

"Then I am going to ask you to name the third assistant

adjutant."

He only paused for a moment. "*Hauptmann* Erich Heller."

"That confirms my information. The quartermaster?"

It lasted for an hour. After finishing with the Army Group, Stoner took him line by line through the staffs of its two component armies, the 9th and the 16th, and then each of their twelve individual corps, where Faust's knowledge was much skimpier. Several times his information didn't tally with Stoner's, but only when the officer in question had been reassigned, wounded, or killed during or after the French campaign; when that happened, Stoner made a note of the discrepancy and moved on. And each time Faust became suspicious, Stoner rattled off three or four names without missing a beat. For the last quarter hour, Stoner spoke only to ask questions.

The little clock chimed one as he flipped over the last page and sat back. "Thank you, *Herr Major*. We are finished for today."

"Wait a minute." Faust pushed through the pain and sat forward. "I've done what you wanted. Isn't this over?"

"How can it be?" Stoner's eyebrows lifted again. "All we've done is ascertain that you are either telling the truth when you claim to be a staff officer in training, or you are a particularly well-briefed espionage agent pretending to be one, which would be a decidedly clever cover, by the way." He straightened the stack of papers and inserted them into the top drawer of his desk. "It is still possible you are both, you know."

He sagged but recoiled when his right shoulder hit the chair back. This time, he couldn't restrain a wordless cry.

"*Herr Major*, are you in pain? You should have said so; I would have sent for medical assistance."

"Yes, Mr. Stoner, I am in pain. But it's nothing to the aggravation I feel." He spoke through his teeth. "I assumed this was a one-step process."

"Hopefully I gave you no reason for such an assumption. You should expect this investigation to take a number of weeks."

"Weeks?" He shook his head, quick sharp jerks that radiated pain down his side. "I can't do it. I know you under-stand: sooner or later I'm going to say more than I intend. I can't risk it."

Stoner stared at him. His eyes, glancing across Faust's cradled right arm, seemed concerned. Otherwise not a flicker of emotion rearranged his face. "If this is your final answer, then I will submit my report and you will shortly leave this establishment."

He blinked. "Going where?"

"Probably the Tower of London." Stoner tilted his head.

Where Wyatt, Raleigh, and so many other poets and courtiers had been imprisoned. And died. Again his heart beat faster. "Well, the Tower is on my list of places to see, just not from the inside."

"You must make the decision."

He rubbed his eyes. It was impossible to think through the pain and there was little sense in trying. "Since my options are limited, I'll try to work with you for a while."

"An equitable solution." Stoner glanced aside. "And do not hesitate to request medical attention. It will not be denied you."

"Thank you." He followed Stoner's gaze to the frame and focused himself enough to say the civil thing. "And I hope your granddaughter is all right."

Even through the pain, he sensed the room's temperature plummet. He glanced at Stoner, surprised, and watched the anger seep from its hiding places and coalesce, pulsing through the old warrior's cultured façade. It had been buried so deeply, he'd forgotten all about it.

"My granddaughter is dead."

Oh, hell. He had to learn to keep his mouth shut. "Bombing civilians is just plain wrong."

"Indeed." Stoner's voice was icy. "As you proved when you participated in the bombing of Patchbourne."

That unnerving chill swept through Faust again. "Patchbourne airfield."

"The airfield is not half a mile from the hospital."

None of this made any sense. "Your granddaughter was at the hospital?"

Stoner shoved his ashtray aside. It clunked against the lamp's base and whirled near the edge of the desk. "My granddaughter was not at the hospital and she was not injured in the bombing raid. *She was assaulted and murdered by a man with no more humanity than a beast.*"

"Oh, my God." It was a prayer and it was all he could say. The rampant rage in Margeaux Hall finally made sense.

Stoner leaned both hands on his desk, cold and white. "I see you do not understand me. Her body was found in the forest less than a mile from here."

His pulse and the pain pounded harder, too loud to think through. Vaguely uncertain, and uncertain why, Faust cocked his head.

Stoner huffed, as if at a stupid student. "Very near to where you were captured."

Understanding finally exploded. "Are you accusing me?"

"I am asking you." Stoner's voice dropped to a whisper.

He forgot the pounding pain, his swimming head, and lurched to his feet. The lovely blue sitting room twisted around him and he grabbed the desk's edge. "No. I did not kill your granddaughter."

Stoner sat still, silent, accusing—no matter what he claimed—contemptuous. His stare never wavered. It tore through what little control Faust commanded and left him defenseless.

Bruckmann rose and stood over Stoner, one hand on the back of the old man's chair. His eyes narrowed in an echo of Stoner's contempt.

"I didn't kill anyone." Words tumbled from him in a torrent. He couldn't stop them any more than he could dam the chattering little Patch with his hands. "Just because I was in the area—other men must have been, they were hunting me—one of them must have—I'd never—"

Stoner finally spoke. "Sergeant Tanyon, return the prisoner to his quarters." He pulled more papers from his desk and bent over them.

As if it didn't matter.

But it did, more than anything else they'd said it mattered that the old man believe him now. "I didn't do it. Please, you can't think—"

But Stoner wasn't listening, although this had to matter to him, as well. Faust froze and the words froze within him. His pulse filled his head, pounding like an icy drum. The old man didn't believe him and that was clear. Had he been believed at all that morning? Maybe they hadn't developed as much of a rapport as he'd thought.

And maybe he couldn't believe the old man any more than he'd been believed himself.

His soul froze at the thought.

"Lieutenant," Tanyon said, "ring up the guardroom and send down two soldiers with rifles."

Bruckmann reached over Stoner's shoulder for the telephone receiver.

He'd been a fool. "Loaded?"

Bruckmann actually paused.

"No," Tanyon said. "They'll do without ammunition."

Stoner did not look up. He flipped to the second page.

The fury coalesced. He'd been a fool. "You bastards."

He stalked to the door. The room still spun. But his own anger, as cold and white as Stoner's, sustained him.

He reached for the doorknob.

"Herr Major."

He paused. He wanted to ignore the cunning old sod and get out of there. But something stopped him. Rather than turn, he glanced over his shoulder as well as he could. Tanyon, behind him with a hand on his holstered Webley, stepped aside, and there was Stoner, watching him gently, again as if nothing had happened. Faust's blood chilled another impossible degree.

Stoner set the papers on his blotter. "Does the name Eduard Best mean anything to you?"

It was so unexpected it cut through his rage. "Best? There was a professor at the University of Munich by that name."

"Yes, he taught economics there prior to 1936. Only now he's on the third floor of this building, two doors down from yourself."

Faust laughed. It sounded and tasted bitter. "Was he supposed to be my contact? I could have warned you about him. He organized Nazi Party rallies on both campuses as early as 1929." He shook his head. "Sorry, Mr. Stoner. I never ran with that crowd."

"Would you know him if you saw him?"

"Maybe. Professors have a lot of standing in the community."

"Would he recognize you?"

"I can't imagine why. I attended the technical university and never took classes from him."

"I see." Stoner returned to his papers.

The dismissal was clear as a slap in the face. Faust turned again for the door, angrier and more confused than ever.

14

afternoon
Margeaux Hall

Stoner didn't lift his eyes from the document in his hand—and he neither knew nor cared what it was—until the door closed. Bruckmann finished speaking to the radioman on duty and cradled the receiver, blowing out his breath in a whoosh.

"For a moment I thought he was going to attack you."

Stoner swiveled his chair about. "For a moment, he was." He didn't smile. "And while I appreciate your devotion, there was no reason for you to leave your post."

The pale young eyes widened. "But, sir—"

"Protecting me is Sergeant Tanyon's job. Yours is to take down what's said in this room."

It required a prolonged stare before Bruckmann looked away. "I'm sure you're right, sir. The look on his face—well, he got to me, that's all. It won't happen again."

Stoner finally glanced at the paper he held. It was the report on the downed Heinkel bombers; he'd concentrated so intently on Faust's responses, he'd read without under-standing a word. He'd tidied his desk by tucking all his notes into the top drawer, because somewhere he'd heard that a clean desk was more impressive than a littered one. His years at Magdalene had confirmed it, turning the fact from a useless bit of trivia to a potential weapon in the war against Faust. Something so simple, so minor, might finally sway that confused man's mind and tip the tide of the interrogation in their favor.

It certainly wasn't going to be his interrogator losing his temper and hurling accusations. Stoner couldn't forgive himself the foolish indulgence, no matter how much the frustrated protector within him appreciated it.

"Jack, what did you think of his reactions?"

Bruckmann flipped through his notes. "I think he's lying to save his precious skin."

"We've now accused him of two hanging offenses. He shrugged off the first but exploded over the second." Stoner leaned back and swung his chair further about. "Unimpressed on the one hand, overly so on the other. What does that say of him?"

"No one could possibly make up a story like the one he told." Bruckmann closed his notebook. "So I tend to believe that. But Harriet—" He swallowed. "He could be the killer."

"He could." Although Faust's astonished and horrified reaction, jaw slack in his triangular cat's face and dark eyes wide, had shaken even Stoner's prejudiced fury. "It could also mean he's grown accustomed to the accusation of espionage and this overreaction is due to the pressure he's feeling."

Bruckmann shrugged. "I don't know, sir. But it's almost time for Herr Best's coffee break."

"So I see." Another task to plague him. Stoner rubbed his eyes. "Do you feel capable of handling it? The message is in the safe, already coded. I'll write up our next report."

"Of course, sir."

After Bruckmann left, Stoner picked up the framed photograph. The two little girls grinned out at him from their floral bower, frozen in happy immortality. If only it were true.

"Goodbye, dear."

15

the same afternoon
Margeaux Hall

When Bruckmann arrived in the guardroom, Eduard Best was already seated before the transmitter-receiver, headphones over his ears and a slender book open in his hands. Corporal Pym, wearing a second pair of headphones aslant over one ear, adjusted the frequency, and Sergeant Tanyon stood behind them both, immovable as the Rock of Gib.

"Ready, Herr Best?"

Best closed his book and set it aside. "As always, I am at your disposal." His voice was dry.

Bruckmann spared a moment to glance at the book's spine. Goethe, of course; Best only read German writers, in translation because that was all Margeaux Hall's library offered. The selection was also limited, so Best, with one of the finest minds in the field of economics, was reduced to reading the same books over and over again. But pity was no good. Bruckmann had a job to perform and he couldn't let such emotions color his behavior.

"Let's do it, then." His focused thoughts finally registered Tanyon's presence. He froze. "Who's guarding—" He bit his tongue. He'd nearly said the name and alerted Best to Faust's presence. "—the other prisoner?"

"I put him back in his quarters for now." Tanyon seemed on the verge of throwing up his hands. "Dr. Harris wants the other one at Patchbourne hospital for x-rays this afternoon, but I can't be in two places at once."

Of course; as the officer in charge, he should have seen the problem. "Issue me a Webley and I'll take over here. As soon as we're finished, I'll return Herr Best to his quarters. You take a couple of soldiers and the other prisoner, and head for Patchbourne."

Tanyon hesitated, staring at him. Bruckmann's ears warmed. The sergeant could show a bit more confidence in him in front of Pym and Best. Of course, since Tanyon had his orders directly from Stoner, reassurances from Bruckmann would not count for much.

"I'll have Corporal Pym with me." Tanyon still didn't budge. "My responsibility, sergeant."

Tanyon finally shrugged. "Suppose you're right, lieutenant. No other way we're going to get everything done around here."

As the door closed behind the sergeant, Pym glanced up from the transmitter-receiver. "We're ready, sir, but the window's closing."

Bruckmann placed the coded message on the table, glancing at the clock. They only had minutes before Best's supposed coffee break was over; his radio contacts with Germany were arranged around his previous schedule at Wadham University and never varied. Bruckmann stepped back and rebuckled his Sam Browne, the holstered revolver bumping his hip. "Hurry, then."

Best stared out the window, apparently indifferent, while his fate was decided for him. Bruckmann again stilled a stab of pity; the man was a spy and deserved whatever happened to him. An ardent Nazi as long ago as 1929, Faust said, but Best had "escaped" from Germany in 1936 along with a thousand other scholars, he claimed to avoid Nazi persecution for his Red politics. Only trouble with that story was, he'd brought a transmitter concealed in his suitcase, which beat any confession.

Now he was allowed walks in Margeaux Hall's inner keep in good weather and some limited use of the library, most of which he scorned. That was all. No wonder he spent so much time staring out windows, even if all he could see from the guardroom was the driveway and front gate.

Best flexed his fingers and began tapping out his initial contact sequence in Morse code. Pym sat behind him, transcribing each letter as it was sent, as well as the answers received from the anonymous German on the other end. Later Bruckmann would compare the two and make certain Best had sent the message properly, without any deletions or additions of his own. Not that he was likely to get brave or rebellious; his life literally depended upon his cooperation.

The Wildflower operation would be so much simpler if they could just do without these Nazi bastards altogether. But they couldn't. An experienced Morse receiver could tell when a different person sent messages, when the sender's "fist" changed, they called it. Only Best could send Best's messages, if they wanted the Germans to swallow them. MI5 had to keep him, although some days it seemed hanging him would be a kindness.

The dits and dahs seemed to go on forever. Bruckmann leaned against the closed door, his eyelids drifting down at the tapping rhythm. The message concerned the bombing raid at Patchbourne, he knew that much. But although he'd typed some of Stoner's notes, he couldn't remember if they were telling the Germans the damage was bad or not. Well, the new Twenty Committee made such calls, of course, and it didn't concern him beyond the work involved.

As Faust should have realized before asking his boss stupid questions. Bruckmann smiled. It would be almost worth the resulting fracas for that pompous, blustering murderer to catch on: the toffs at MI5 and MI6 could only have identified the most highly visible members of Army Group A's staff. Those were the names Stoner had given Faust to convince him of his encompassing knowledge. But the identities of the more junior German officers were just as important, sometimes more so, because they would be the active commanders in the field. And those were the names Faust had given to Stoner. It had been a magnificent bit of deception.

Finally the tapping ceased. Bruckmann opened his eyes as Best removed the headphones and set them on the table beside his book.

"I have finished, Lieutenant Bruckmann."

"Good." Bruckmann took the transcription Pym handed him, folded it together with the original message Best had sent, and slid both into his breast pocket. Faust's devil alone knew when he'd have time to look at them. "Let's get you back to your quarters."

Best turned again to the window. Over his shoulder, Bruckmann spied the old lorry, parked atop the drive. Tanyon and his guard detail would be leaving soon, driving Faust to the Patchbourne hospital for x-rays.

"There is no time for a walk, perhaps?"

The man would choose now to be difficult. "Perhaps when Sergeant Tanyon returns."

Best still didn't move. "I seldom any more have the

pleasure of Major Stoner's company."

"He's busy."

"I object to spending much time in my room."

"We're all busy." That was the bitter truth. And with the headache of Faust added to the Wildflower operation, it would only get worse.

"And I was not taken to an air raid shelter Saturday night." Best's voice trembled. "I was frightened."

"No one asked you to come here and spy on us."

Best finally turned from the window. "I consider myself a soldier in this war, as you do."

"The Geneva Convention disagrees with you." Best would argue all day if he allowed it. Bruckmann dropped one hand to the holstered Webley, as Tanyon sometimes did when escorting Faust. "Come on, let's go."

Best rose. "I am not a brave man, Lieutenant Bruckmann."

"Then you aren't much of a soldier, are you?" He'd have to remember the trick with the Webley. "Lead the way, Corporal Pym."

16

the same afternoon
Margeaux Hall and in transit to Patchbourne

Faust's white anger buoyed him up the stairs and back to the little third-floor bedroom. After the now-expected slam of the bolt behind him and the clumping footsteps diminishing down the corridor, the fury even held up long enough for him to slam his booted toe into the bedstead, which sent a shaft of agony straight to his right side and probably wasn't the smartest thing he'd ever done. But it was almost worth it when the footsteps in the hallway skittered and stopped for a breathless moment.

Two short steps later, when he reached the window, his breath was no more than ragged gasping and the pounding in his right arm was ferocious. He wanted to collapse into the chair, still where he'd left it facing the window, but he'd learned what an unconsidered movement cost him and instead eased onto it sideways, his left arm resting against the ladder back. For one indulgent moment he curled over, letting the agony wash through him, then he forced himself erect.

There was more than a touch of fear beneath the dregs of his cold rage. Those espionage charges were all too plausible, especially if Stoner spoke the truth about Eduard Best. It was incriminating enough to have been captured near Oxford, the city he knew so well and loved. But to have been captured in the vicinity of a confirmed spy he'd possibly known in Germany, well, that could really kick a hole in his boat.

Of course he'd seen Best around campus in Munich.

He'd attended Best's bloody ranting mandatory lectures on his supposed duty to the Fatherland, which in Best's viewpoint meant joining the Nazi Party and beating up Jews and Communists. Needless to say, he'd ignored the message.

But the allegation about Stoner's granddaughter was infuriating and frankly terrifying. Rage again boiled through the pain at the thought. He'd never hurt a woman, but in all fairness he couldn't expect Stoner to know that. It was the sort of thing civilians believed of marauding soldiers, especially enemy ones. It was a charge that could stick. If word reached the village, he'd be lucky to escape lynching; if he did receive a trial, it would be a farce. He could easily hang for this and Stoner would get his revenge—albeit against the wrong man— even if he didn't get his information.

He leaned his shoulder against the chair back. Was that the connection? Was Stoner putting Faust's life in danger as a lever? Would he offer to protect his prisoner from the lynch mob if he cooperated?

He rubbed his face. It was a vile thing to think of anyone. But once thought, it wouldn't go away. Beneath the rage and pain, his fear grew.

The worst of it was, he didn't know if he could even believe Stoner. He'd gone into the interview his usual trusting self, without stopping to consider the old man's possible motivations, and answered every question put to him. If those espionage charges were a lie, then the entire interview had been one big hoist and Stoner had made an utter fool of him. And the more he considered that possibility, the more likely it seemed and the angrier he became.

Behind him, keys rattled and the lock snapped. He turned. Tanyon stood framed in the doorjamb. Although the worst of the sergeant's anger had faded, he still seemed tense, his chin lowered and dark eyes narrowed.

"What now?"

"We're taking you to the hospital for x-rays," Tanyon said. "And I expect you to be on your best behavior for the trip."

"Or what?"

"That attitude won't get you anywhere." Tanyon shifted in place. "We don't have to do this, you know. We could let you take your chances with infection or Dr. Harris."

"You have a point." He did want medical treatment so he could get the hell out of there. "All right, sergeant."

So for the third time that day he descended the eastern stairwell and crossed the ballroom, past the sitting area and now empty typists' desks, this time past Stoner's office, and through the final door at the end of the corridor.

In the vestibule, only the interior wall was solid, an interwoven pattern of brick in shades of brown. The outer walls and the soaring ceiling were iron girders and bare curved glass, naked even of blackout curtains. Against the solid brick wall rose a black wrought-iron stairwell, the banister and balustrade curling grape leaves and arbors. The second level, above the brick wall, opened into a sitting area on the landing, then the stairwell rose alone to the third floor.

Outside the glass a smooth green lawn stretched to the mortared-stone wall. A lorry was parked on the awful macadam lane, which rolled downhill to a wrought-iron double gate, topped with iron spikes.

Summer afternoon sunshine blasted through the glass door's tracery of grapes and vines. The light spilled over the desk where one young soldier with lank brown hair sat behind a switchboard, a newspaper folded open beside it. His angular face, lit from the side, seemed made for smiling. But at the moment he wasn't, guileless green eyes stretched wide as he stared at Faust.

Two other young soldiers stood with their backs to the blaze of light, holding Lee Enfield rifles between him and the exit, eyeing him with what he could only consider trepidation. He took a good look at them in return. Maybe their weapons were loaded. Maybe Tanyon intended them as clubs; his earlier message had been clear enough and Stoner hadn't counter-manded it. It didn't matter yet, but later, should he manage an escape, he wouldn't want to learn the truth across the length of a farmer's field.

Another salvo encircled his ribcage with pain. This time, he welcomed it; it twisted his face and camouflaged the rising excitement he couldn't contain. All he'd said was, *All right, sergeant,* which could be translated as anything. If Tanyon misunderstood him, it was his own fault.

Just as it was his own fault if he'd believed lies.

He didn't glance at the sergeant until he was certain his expression wouldn't incriminate him. "This must be murder to black out."

"Just get in the truck."

The two kids led the way out the glass door. Faust followed with Tanyon, and his Webley revolver, in the rear. The rush of warm sunlight on his face was intoxicating and although he couldn't see the roses, in their formal beds on the wing's other side, he could smell them.

The lorry probably dated from the last war, the canvas over the rear patched in several places. The long wireless antenna attached to the front bumper seemed incongruous, a modern touch on such an old machine. Beyond the lorry, a single soldier stood guard at the gate, Lee Enfield slung over his shoulder.

Faust paused beside the lorry and continued his look around. The main chunk of Margeaux Hall, off to the right with its own gate and gatehouse, seemed to be Stuart baroque despite its French name, with multiple bays and Inigo Jones tracery in the stonework. Stoner's wing was more modern, constructed of brick with wide, generous windows, especially the floor-to-ceiling ones on the ballroom level. There were three floors, which put his quarters on the top one, right under the eaves of the sloped slate roof.

There was a face behind one of the windows on the second floor, about where the guardroom with its rifles and radio would be. He stopped short and stared.

If Stoner had not warned him Eduard Best was on the premises, it was possible he'd never have recognized the man, so great was the change. The face was the same—thin, sharp, intellectual, actually not dissimilar to Stoner's—but the arrogant demeanor he remembered had collapsed into something pinched and starved, as if the face's owner sat and brooded alone in despair.

Good. His wings were clipped, his venom drawn. He would browbeat no more students, and good riddance.

Deliberately Faust broke their mutual stare and turned his back. Tanyon stood watching him, one edge of his mouth curled.

"I take it I go in the rear?"

"You take it right. Peckham, you're in back with me. Norris, you drive."

"Can't, sergeant," the taller and leaner of the two young soldiers said in a broad Northern accent. "Never learned."

Tanyon guffawed. "You a big city boy and you never learned to drive a little truck like this one?"

Norris turned his head as if to spit but stopped himself in time. "Don't need to drive in the city, sergeant. We've got trams and buses for getting around. It's only out here in the sticks where yokels have to fend for themselves."

"Yeah," Tanyon said, "right. All right, Peckham, you drive."

Using his left hand and the built-in step, Faust hoisted himself into the lorry's hot dark interior almost without pain. So he could climb, at least within certain limits. Perhaps the wall wasn't the insurmountable obstacle—literally—it seemed.

He took a seat on the front bench, nearest the cab.

Tanyon and Norris sat between him and the exit. The engine started and they rolled away.

The lorry slowed at the gate. The soldier on duty shouted something Faust didn't catch, and Peckham laughed in answer. Then the wall slid past the opening in the canvas and the soldier on duty swung the spike-topped gate closed behind them.

Faust swayed with Tanyon and Norris as the lorry turned right. Their speed increased. Through the opening, he watched the apple orchard as the ancient trees rolled past. He caught a glimpse of Woodrow on their left, its rows of staked tomatoes extending almost to the rampart at the forest's edge, then it, too, was gone.

For a moment he thought of Jennifer, sitting on Woodrow's rear steps with a shotgun beside her, guarding against the German invader while her sister died in the forest a mile away. He wondered how closely he'd passed Harriet and her killer in the night, whether the girl had been dead or alive by then. If he hadn't been confused and injured, he might have heard her cries; if Jennifer hadn't been guarding against him, she might have gone looking sooner.

"I see you watching everything over there," Tanyon said. "Don't get any ideas."

Faust shook off those thoughts. He couldn't help Jennifer, any more than he could have helped Harriet. Instead, maybe he could allay Tanyon's suspicions and earn an escape attempt later. Casually, he turned from the road to put Tanyon off guard. "Margeaux Hall is a beautiful building. How did Mr. Stoner get such a great headquarters? In Paris, we were in a hotel."

Okay, it wasn't brilliant. It was a start.

Tanyon's eyes narrowed. His antagonism seemed so strong, Faust wondered if he'd answer.

"We got lucky, in a sense," he said finally. "The old squire had just died—liver failure, I think it was—and his son didn't know what to do with the place. When we showed up, he seemed glad to see us."

"The owner lives on premises? In the main wing?"

Tanyon shook his head. "He's in the service. A young man."

"Just his sister." Norris spoke for the first time.

Faust glanced at him. Norris was tall, easily over six feet, and built wiry as a steel cable. In the vestibule he'd been just as frightened as the other kids, but the calm conversation and Tanyon's steady presence seemed to be steadying him.

Tanyon grunted. "She's out of our league."

Faust gave him a wry glance. If that assessment was supposed to include him, he didn't appreciate it. "You mean the blonde on horseback? She's got a lot of legs, doesn't she?"

Norris snickered. Tanyon glanced at them both, one wrinkle between his dark eyes, and looked away.

The lorry bumped on the road. Their three bodies swayed in unison.

Norris leaned forward. "Is it bad?"

Faust blinked. The kid's hatchet face had lurched toward him so suddenly, he'd thought they were about to hit. "Do you mean my injury?"

"Leave him alone, Norris."

"But he's actually been there. And you know we're gonna be."

And in a clear sudden rush Faust understood the fear and staring fascination he inspired within the kids. He had seen combat. He'd braved the front lines, been under fire, and survived; further, he'd been decorated for valor. He represented the sum of their fears as well as their hopes. He was what they longed to be.

An enemy role model? He glanced aside into Tanyon's impassivity, uncertain what to say. He could tell Norris, and through him the rest of the young soldiers, the truth. That would scare the bejeebers out of them and strip their hearts right out. It was what the Nazis would do, and in the interest of winning the war they'd be right. But he couldn't imagine any of the military gentlemen such as his hero, von Rundstedt, doing anything so crass. He had to follow his own role models and heart, and a pox on the Nazis.

"I've been there, too, you know," Tanyon said.

"Yeah. But we lost. And you won't talk about it."

"I don't know if losing has anything to do with it." Faust chose his words with care; to be misunderstood or come across as patronizing would be as bad as Best's browbeating. "The British Army was brave. I've rarely seen better soldiers." He paused. "Do you play cards?"

Norris' eyes widened. "Of course."

"Well, that's what combat is like."

"Like playing cards?" His skepticism was heavy.

"This is why I don't talk about it," Tanyon said. "I don't think you can."

"Okay." He thought again. "You've been on a rifle range?"

"Target shooting? Of course."

"That's easy, isn't it? You kneel, brace the rifle butt against your shoulder, align front and rear sights, squeeze the trigger. You might even hit what you're aiming at."

Norris sniggered again. "Right."

"Well, that's what it's not like. That's slow, careful, deliberate, and the enemy isn't going to let you get away with it. On the front lines, you spot the enemy position and fire as close to it as you can, shooting around the corner in quick bursts, from behind whatever shelter you can find and showing as little of yourself as you can."

He shrugged. "We've trained for that."

"Good. The enemy is behind cover, too. That's where chance comes into it. You hope he eases out for a shot or a look while you're firing."

"I can do that."

"But of course, he's doing the same thing."

Norris looked blank.

"When you ease out for a shot, he's going to be firing at you."

The kid leaned back, flexing his elbows over the edge of the truck bed. "Yeah. I can do that."

"See?" Tanyon said.

Faust sighed, sending a lance of pain across his side, and tried one last time. "It's always hot on a battlefield. It was even hot in Norway. You're sweating, your eyes are stinging, and you're shivering cold, all at the same time. There's smoke drifting past. It's hard to see. It's noisy. The heavy guns are firing behind you and the shells howl as they pass overhead. The tanks are clanking, engines growling. There are planes bombing the enemy positions and sometimes your own. People are shouting and screaming. It's hard to hear your sergeant. But you can hear the bullets. They smack when they hit flesh. They sing past your head. And it stinks. Blood has a particular odor; you never forget it once you smell it. You can also smell gunpowder, and burning, and vomit, and sometimes a soldier has a close call and soils his pants. You're always afraid. I think fear's a good thing. It keeps you looking in the right direction. It keeps you sharp. A good soldier learns to use his fear, so it's just another tool, like his rifle or gas mask."

Somewhere during that soliloquy, something he said hit home through Norris' cockiness. Faust sensed, if not true understanding, then at least recognition, in the young soldier's eyes. For a moment the image he painted with words reflected off Norris and back to himself, and he wondered if the kid would try to tell the others about this conversation. Then the lorry swung left and braked, and Norris looked away.

"You ever soil your pants, sergeant?"

"Wouldn't tell you if I did." Tanyon tossed up the canvas flap. "That's personal, that is." He jumped from the lorry.

120

Norris and Faust followed more slowly. The little shock of hitting the pavement caused another spasm of pain to flash across his ribs and he held onto the lorry until it passed.

The Patchbourne hospital was a four-storey, unadorned white building with rows of windows rising to the flat roof. To the west was the village green and market, with railway tracks to the south. To the east, less than a half mile away beyond a grain field, Faust saw long low metal buildings, complexes of brick ones, empty stretches of concrete, rows of parked Spitfires and Lancasters. The air above rippled in the hot afternoon sunlight. Halfway across the field, in the middle of the yellow grain, gaped a dark hole as if something large had made a hard landing and burned.

"I don't know how long this will take," Tanyon said to Peckham. "You take the lorry back and make yourself useful. I'll call when we're ready."

"Right, sergeant."

Tanyon turned around. His dark eyes were speculative, uncertainty obvious even on his poker face. Faust faced him and kept his chin low.

"I didn't do it." He kept his voice low, too; this was strictly between them. "I didn't kill Mr. Stoner's grand-daughter."

The lorry backed from the lot and drove off, toward the market. Dust swirled around them on the hot pavement, stinging Faust's eyes, then settled at their feet. Tanyon didn't blink. His speculation faded to his usual impassivity, and Faust relaxed. He'd passed muster.

"Huh," Tanyon finally said. "Let's get moving."

Faust followed Norris into the hospital, those boots as usual clumping behind. He felt better already, sort of.

17

The X-rays had been taken several hours ago. But Faust and his two guards still sat in the reception area outside the fourth-floor clinic. To one side of him, Norris glanced through an illustrated magazine, lips moving, rifle propped beside him; on the other, Tanyon maintained his silence, still shooting an occasional glance sideways.

Faust, supporting his injured arm, watched the other patients as one by one they vanished into the clinic's inner recesses, where Dr. Harris and a surgeon held court. They re-emerged clutching jars, bottles, bandages. All of them stared at him, and his clearly German uniform, in passing, their expressions eloquent mixtures of loathing and rage. But none of them met his gaze for long when he stared back. Slowly the line whittled down: a grimy mechanic in R.A.F. blue with a bandage over one eye; a middle-aged man in a suit hobbling with a cane; a screaming child with burns over her face and arm. He didn't return the mother's glare and was relieved when they left.

Finally only one woman and her two children remained, sitting on the room's far side. The woman, tiny and delicate, knitted bright red yarn into a jumper. She looked nowhere near thirty, but her daughter was easily ten, so perhaps she just carried her age well. Her blonde hair was short and stylish, at odds with her flowered cotton dress, and her trim legs curved about her chair as if at a tea party.

Her two children, the boy no more than a sturdy two or three, played with little metal airplanes at her feet. Faust recognized the toys as a Spitfire and a Messerschmitt Bf 109, their R.A.F. roundels and *Luftwaffe* crosses and swastikas clear against their bright silver paint. Repeatedly the daughter, with the Spitfire, shot down the German plane, always casting a sly glance in Faust's direction as she imitated cannon fire through her monotonous coughing. And repeatedly her younger brother spiraled the Messerschmitt down to a grisly death on the tiled floor. Each time it happened, Faust closed his eyes as if in pain—which was true—listened to the giggles and grinned, too.

But finally he turned to Tanyon. "You know, we haven't had lunch—"

He cut off as a loud mechanical moaning began outside, building to a ululating howl within moments. He stiffened, his skin prickling; it was the most eerie noise he'd ever heard. The daughter froze in the middle of hacking and her mother jerked erect, staring into space.

"Air raid." Tanyon glanced at Faust, face deadpan, eyes sardonic. "Good timing."

The mother started up with a wordless cry, shooting Faust a look of pure loathing.

He ignored her and strained his ears. Beneath the droning klaxon there was another drone, steadier and more uniform, not close yet but approaching.

Norris rose, too, dropping his magazine on the floor. His color drained, leaving him grey, eyes wide and staring at the ceiling.

"Wait, Norris. Women and children first."

The clinic nurse, her cropped hair iron grey and her bosom generous beneath her starched white dress, darted from behind the counter, her arms piled with charts and files. "This way, Mrs. Oldfield. Flora, Thompson, down to the shelter."

They herded the children out as Cavanaugh, Dr. Harris, and the surgeon appeared from the clinic's recesses, heaving cardboard cartons.

"All right, Norris. Lead the way and don't get too close to the Oldfields." Tanyon looked at Faust. "You follow and no funny stuff. I'll be right behind you."

The droning was getting closer fast. Faust glanced at the ceiling as if he could see through it to the approaching planes. He wasn't certain just when he'd stood up, but he and Tanyon were both on their feet. "Okay, sergeant."

The others were gone. He obeyed Tanyon's orders and kept his distance; he was just starting to establish a rapport with the sergeant and now was not the time to jeopardize his groundwork. But he couldn't prevent an occasional glance up, just the same, and his pulse quickened through the pain lancing across his side.

The corridor stretched the length of the long building. Ahead, the women and two children, near the end, turned right and vanished. The medical men followed, then Norris was gone, too, and he and Tanyon walked alone, a line of open windows glittering on the left. He heeded his instincts and picked up the pace. The droning beneath the still-shrieking alarm grew steadily louder. Without turning his head, he knew Tanyon had one hand on the Webley. Considering what approached overhead, it seemed the lesser of two evils.

They reached the stairwell and started down. Voices drifted up, clear and frightened. The droning seemed directly overhead and nearly drowned out the howling klaxon. At the first report of ack-ack fire, Faust ducked and slipped on the stairs. Then a second gun fired and a third, the distant bangs merging into a continuous background rumble beneath the droning. He caught his balance and quickened again.

"The hospital is marked?" he called over his shoulder.

"Big red crosses on the roof," Tanyon said. "I helped paint them."

That was assuming the *Luftwaffe* could aim their destructive contraptions. "I feel so much better." He moved faster.

Four flights down, below the basement entry, they overtook the others. The toddler's short legs stumbled on the stairs and his delicate mother's chivvying could not drive him faster. Her dress was rumpled, as if she'd tried to carry him down but couldn't, and her net bag of yarn sat abandoned on the landing. The surgeon was trying to offload his cardboard boxes into Dr. Harris' long arms, but it was obvious it wouldn't work.

Faust slowed, matching the boy's pace even though his heart was trying to escape from his chest. The racket overhead couldn't possibly get louder. Mrs. Oldfield's voice was a shrill wail.

"Norris!" Tanyon yelled. "Get Thompson! Carry him!"

But Norris threw one terrified glance over his shoulder. He shoved past Mrs. Oldfield and her brood, past the nurse and the three medical men trying to rearrange their burdens, and leapt down the last flight of stairs, hitting the ground running. His hands were empty, Faust realized, his rifle gone. Norris vanished within moments.

A metallic scream joined its banshee voice to the relentless droning. Faust flinched. He'd called in air strikes in Poland, Norway, France, and he knew the sound of a bomb dropping when he heard it, even through the building's muffling. There was no one else to do it. He leapt the last few stairs, ignoring Tanyon's shout and the sudden clawing pain in his side, and swept little Thompson into his arms.

The walls convulsed. Plaster crashed and boiled. The lights flickered, brightened, went out, leaving them in utter blackness. Someone screamed. Little arms and legs wrapped about Faust, squeezing him in half, and small hot breaths panted on his neck in rhythm with his pounding pulse. Far ahead, a pale beam of light arched through the darkness, flashed about, fastened on them. Another metallic shriek stormed overhead. Faust wrapped his right arm about Mrs. Oldfield, who had a death-grip on Flora's hand. His left arm supporting the petrified child, he half-dragged, half-ran for the light. The others pounded beside and behind him.

The shrieking was unbearable. Would being underground protect them from a direct hit? He didn't know. He couldn't chance it. He swept Mrs. Oldfield and Flora against the wall and covered them with his body, still supporting Thompson. Tanyon was suddenly beside him, forcing the grey-haired nurse into the same embrace, twining his arm with Faust's. Dr. Harris, the surgeon, and Cavanaugh joined on the other side.

The explosion deafened him and rocked the very ground he stood upon. Debris cascaded down. Something heavy bounced off his shoulders. His knees buckled, piling him and Thompson atop Mrs. Oldfield. Only Tanyon's grip kept him standing. Even the light at the end of the corridor vanished. The little body wrapped about his vibrated like a tuning fork. He counted the seconds—one thousand and one, one thousand and two, one thousand and three—reaching nine before the rumbling diminished to a bearable level and twelve before the last debris clattered atop his shoulders. Then the light flashed again like a homing beacon. Tanyon pulled him up. They staggered through the unbearable racket, coughing in the boiling dust.

The shelter door was open. The wielder of the flashlight, invisible and ghostly behind its beam, lit their way down a flight of steps. Faust stumbled in the Oldfields' wake, Thompson still clutching him like a lamprey. Above them, someone closed the door and the sounds receded.

"It's okay now," he whispered. "We're safe."

"Daddy." Thompson's voice was less than a whimper. Faust barely heard him. He hugged the child tighter.

He stopped at the bottom, cradling Thompson and murmuring to him, straining his ringing ears for the barely audible replies. The hospital basement stretched ahead, a broad open area with supporting columns, lit at regular and distant intervals by small bulbs on the walls. It created a dim shadowy refuge crowded with dim shadowy people. The subdued whispers, all the noise the refugees seemed willing to make, lent the whole an added touch of unreality, like an outer circle of Dante's hell.

His first sweeping glance turned up no one he recognized. It was as if Norris, the doctors, Cavanaugh, Mrs. Oldfield and Flora, even Tanyon had vanished into that realm in the time it took for him to stumble down the stairs.

"Where's your mom?"

"I don't know."

"Let's look for her, okay?"

"Okay."

His murmured reassurances were going unheeded. Thompson clung to him and trembled.

Unfortunately, now the immediate danger was over, his adrenaline receded with the bombers and the pain returned, worse than ever. He had forgotten everything except survival during the explosions and had used his arm without thought. The renewal was agony, and Thompson's leg-lock squeezed his ribcage where the still-embedded shrapnel clawed at him. To top it all a new ache, a dull and ugly one, was just getting started across his shoulders and the back of his neck. His knees and arms shook.

It wouldn't be impressive to faint with the kid in his arms. "Do you want to get down and find your mom?"

Thompson tightened his grip. "No."

"I'm sorry. I have to put you down."

A pause. "Okay."

Faust lowered him to the ground and wished he could collapse rather than kneel beside him. A little hand touched his left one. They clung together.

Although the air was cool, a droplet of sweat fell into his eye. He glanced down. His uniform was plastered with dust. He felt grime on his face and a chill dampness beneath his arms and around his collar. Hot and cold, just as he'd described for Norris. Faust crouched beside Thompson, clamped his right arm against his side, and wiped his forehead and eyes with his left sleeve.

Tanyon appeared from the gloom. "Where did you get off to?"

"Right here." His voice shook in tempo with the rest of him.

Mrs. Oldfield paused at the shadow's edge, her eyes

enormous in a face that seemed white even in the darkness. She scurried forward, grabbed his and Thompson's joined hands, and separated them. "Thank you." Her voice shook, too. But she pulled her son away and stepped between them.

Faust glanced aside. Although he understood, it stung. *They flee from me, that sometime did me seek*— Wyatt knew all about being unappreciated.

But Thompson took one step beside his mother and then stopped. "I have to go now."

Even with the pain, it was worth it. He looked into the grave blue eyes and couldn't repress a smile. "I know."

And after that Thompson didn't seem to know what to say, either. "Bye."

"Goodbye."

He followed his mother into the shadows.

"Can you walk?" Tanyon asked.

He wiped his face again and rose. Everything still hurt. But at least his knees no longer shook. "I think so."

"Come on, then."

They walked side by side down the center of the long room, without consultation seeking the dimmest path where the light from the small bulbs couldn't reach. People sat on packing cases, on folding chairs, on the floor, reading, knitting, huddling. All of them, even the children, cast furtive anxious glances toward the currently-quiet ceiling. Several spotted him. He saw more than one tilt his head toward a neighbor and whisper, then more eyes slid his way. Without speaking, he and Tanyon walked faster. If worse came to worst and the citizenry took the law into their own hands, Tanyon wouldn't be able to protect him. Even if he wanted to.

"Did we find Norris?"

Tanyon huffed. "I'll deal with Norris."

But no one stopped them. They crossed the long room in silence, toward a glow halfway down. Faust began to pant again and the naked cement walls threatened to spin. In this condition, he couldn't protect himself.

The glow proved to be brilliant fluorescent lighting. White dividers blocked off a small relief station beneath the strips, a camp kitchen opposite. Beyond stretched rows of bunk beds, vanishing into an ever-deeper gloom.

All four medics bustled behind the dividers. Faust spied Flora sitting on the examining table, Mrs. Oldfield beside her, and wondered where Thompson was.

"Stick around, sergeant," the surgeon called. "He's next."

"Yes, sir."

They withdrew to the shelter of the kitchen, putting it

between them and the roomful of refugees. Faust smelled soup and his stomach growled.

"People seem to be settling in for the long haul."

Tanyon glanced at him, then resumed his cautious full-circle scrutiny. "Saturday's raid lasted all night."

"All night? Are you serious?"

Another glance.

"I didn't think we had that many bombers, that's all."

"They come in waves about thirty minutes apart. Just as people are catching their breath from the first round, here they come again."

It made sense. "So they're landing, rearming, and taking back off."

"Don't you know your own bomber tactics?"

Faust scowled. "Why should I? I drive tanks."

The next glance was openly sardonic.

"What do you know about your fighter tactics?"

Tanyon huffed. "They come out of the sun."

"Not at night."

Mrs. Oldfield emerged from the relief station, hand in hand with Flora. Her still-wary glance swept over them, standing in the shadows. She averted her eyes. For a moment he thought she would brush past in silence and even though he understood that, too, it still stung. Then Flora paused, forcing her mother to stop beside her.

Only then did Mrs. Oldfield speak. "Thank you again." Her glance, quick as a bullet, included both of them.

Tanyon nodded.

"You're welcome." Faust glanced down at Flora. He'd always liked kids and these two were great. "You, too."

"Are you hurt?" Flora asked. "You keep holding your arm."

"It's not bad. You're not coughing any more."

She shook her head. "Cough syrup."

The surgeon appeared behind her. "Come on in."

"Gotta go," he said to Flora.

She nodded. "See you."

Cavanaugh helped him off with his tunic, shirt, and undervest, then Faust climbed onto the examining table. The surgeon popped two x-ray films onto a light box and flipped it on, brightening the enclosed area even further.

"Are those my ribs?"

"And your shrapnel. Two pieces."

Dr. Harris peered over the surgeon's shoulder at the films. "Deep?"

"Not too bad." He glanced at the grey-haired nurse. "Set up for day surgery under morphine."

She nodded and turned to the cartons they'd lugged downstairs, set on a counter nearby. She and Cavanaugh dug out scalpels, needles, catgut, ointments, and bandages, setting them onto a rolling table covered with a white cloth.

Dr. Harris and the surgeon circled behind him on the examining table. Faust peered over his shoulder as well as he could, more curious than apprehensive.

"Can you move this elbow forward at all?" the surgeon asked.

He dragged his right arm across his chest with his left. The torn flesh at the back of his arm tore further. He suppressed a hiss.

"That's good. Just hold your arms so and lie on your left side. Cavanaugh, give him a hand. Nurse, administer one-eighth grain of morphine. Dr. Harris, will you assist?"

One-eighth grain wasn't enough. It shoved the pain into a defensive posture but didn't defeat it. Faust, on his side on the examining table, felt the scalpel's first slice and tried to stay still.

"I know," the surgeon said. "Sorry. We must restrict painkillers."

"Along with everything else." His voice shook again. He cleared his throat and tried humor. "Cigarettes at a pack per month—that's inhuman."

"Three for prisoners," Dr. Harris said.

"A pack for three months? I won't survive."

"No, three packs per month." Dr. Harris gave him a curious look. "Who told you otherwise?"

Stoner, of course. He clenched his teeth. That was all the proof he needed: he'd been had and he was the biggest fool on the planet.

Cavanaugh lit a fag and stuck it between Faust's lips. With the first puff, something painful tugged at his side, then the surgeon dropped said something into a small glass bowl on the instrument table. It was red and gooey, but sharp metallic edges shone in the bright lighting.

"Part of an airplane skin," the surgeon said, "in case you're interested."

He spoke around the cigarette. "Not the sort of souvenir I'd like to keep close to my heart."

Another painful tug and a second, smaller piece joined the first.

"It feels better already."

"I'm sure it does," Dr. Harris said. "The pressure's out of the wounds. Any sign of infection?"

"A little inflammation, but not bad. Let's wash it out,

pack it with sulfa, and stitch him up, then we'll look more closely at your arm."

Those stitches had to be entirely removed and resewn. He felt that, too.

"You've got to quit using this arm," the surgeon said.

"What exactly happened back there?"

"I didn't tell you?" Dr. Harris said. "There's a six-inch long slice across the back of your arm, right through the muscles. I stitched it up, but you keep ripping the stitches. Each time you do, it gets bigger."

"We'll give you a sling. It'll remind you not to use the arm."

After Cavanaugh had wrapped the last bandage and rebuttoned his shirt for him, the surgeon made him swallow a sleeping pill.

"Sir," Tanyon said, "if the all-clear sounds, I'll have to wake him and return him to Margeaux Hall."

"Not tonight," the surgeon said. "Tonight he stays here and sleeps. Take these first bunks so we can check on him every few hours. And the soup smells ready."

This wasn't so bad. Faust drank thick vegetable soup, sitting on the ground in his shirt sleeves, boots off, beside the first row of bunks. He should have known the English were too practical to panic. Lynch mobs only happened in bad Western novels, the sort Hitler read.

The painkiller was wearing off but the sleeping pill was starting to work; the pain advanced but his mind retreated. He stretched his feet, his legs, his back, rolled his head, and his body responded better than it had all day. And finally he could breathe; the deep burning in his ribs was gone. Even when Tanyon made him take the top bunk and he had to clamber up as best he could, it didn't spoil his elation.

Because it proved that, even with only one usable arm, he could still climb.

18

midnight
the Patchbourne hospital air raid shelter

At some point in the night, Faust drowsed up through foggy layers of sleep. Again he heard that steady droning overhead. It was close enough to wake him but not, he decided, close enough to alarm.

There was someone in the narrow bunk with him. He smiled in his doze. Perhaps sleeping space was rationed, too, with bunks so prized in the shelter that Tanyon or Norris had been forced to share with their prisoner.

But the hair tickling his chin was fine and downy, and it was hair that had tickled his chin before. He opened his eyes as Thompson rolled over in his arms, wide eyes reflecting the first aid station's dimmed lighting.

"They're back," Thompson whispered.

"Yeah. But they're not close."

A distant rumble joined the droning. Either anti-aircraft fire or bombs exploding. Hopefully their aim was better this time around.

"They can't aim very well, can they?"

"No."

"They're bad all around."

"Yes."

He was almost asleep again when Thompson asked, "Are you German?"

He opened his eyes. Again he met that wide childish stare, this time aimed at him.

"Yeah."

Thompson blinked for a minute. "Are you bad, too?"

He started to laugh, then paused. Was he? It wasn't a thought he cared to entertain in the still, close hours of the night, especially in a discussion with a small child. *Faustus, begin thine incantations And try if devils will obey thy hest, Seeing thou has prayed and sacrificed to them.* Marlowe was enough to scare anyone.

Finally he said, "I don't think so. Do you?"

Thompson looked him over for a long serious moment.

"No." He rolled back over.

Within a minute they both slept.

19

morning, Tuesday, 27 August 1940
in transit from Patchbourne hospital

Tanyon's problems began first thing in the morning.

"I told you to go back to the Hall," he said to Peckham outside the hospital.

"This is what I get for trying to be helpful." Peckham was a beefy kid a hair shorter than Norris and a lot thicker through the shoulders, with a bruiser's face and challenging eyes, as if he enjoyed a good rough game of rugby. He stood outside the hospital and gave Tanyon a long-suffering look. "I rang Mrs. Alcock and asked if there was anything she needed at the market while we were here. Saving petrol for the war effort, right? And I was getting cabbages when—" He waved one disgusted hand at the lorry, buried beneath the wall of the hospital.

Tanyon swore, long-windedly and with great imagination.

"That'll teach you to buy cabbages," Faust said. "Ugh." He'd had too much peasant's food as an orphaned kid. If the menu was heading that direction, he was heading elsewhere.

"Don't start," Tanyon said to him. "Peckham, you stay here and salvage the lorry."

"Sergeant, half the wall's in the cab. What if I can't dig it out?"

"Don't come back. Norris, we'll take the train." He turned to Faust. "I am not in a good mood—"

"This I can see for myself."

"—so don't try anything cute."

Tanyon had reason for concern, Faust conceded, meeting

the level warning stare without flinching. Granted, he still hurt in multiple places, including a bruised ache across the nape of his neck and the tops of his shoulders where part of the ceiling had fallen on him during the air raid.

But the deep burning pain among his ribs was gone and at last he could breathe deeply. He'd had a good night's sleep and two rolls for breakfast, his head was finally clear, his body felt responsive beneath the aches and pains, and the sun echoed his enthusiasm in a clear blue sky. Best of all, Norris couldn't find his rifle and Peckham's was buried in the cab of the lorry.

It was going to be a beautiful day.

The train was a local, of course, a crawling beast that took forever to cross the twelve miles between Patchbourne and Patchley Abbey. It didn't offer first-class compartments, so they sat in the coach seats with the other travelers, windows wide to the morning air, and Faust had a perfect view of the countryside. It was as good as a topographic map and he noted the farmhouses and roads along the way. When he noticed Tanyon watching, jaw square and eyebrows lowering, he smiled back.

He still didn't know how many young soldiers were in Stoner's employ, but among the ones he'd met, Peckham seemed the sharpest. But something had convinced Stoner and Tanyon to select Pym for the lance corporal's stripe instead. He'd have to study all these kids a little better. If, of course, he stuck around that long.

At the Patchley Abbey station, Tanyon and Faust waited outside while Norris used the new dial phone inside. When he returned, he shook his head.

"Sorry, sergeant, the car's down. Sloane's working on it."

Tanyon swore again. His vocabulary had real depth, and Faust didn't bother to hide his grin.

"How long?" Tanyon asked when he finally started repeating words.

"Don't know."

"Did you ask?"

"You didn't tell me to."

"Training in initiative will always tell," Faust said. At least he could figure out why Norris hadn't gotten the stripe.

"You're cruising, mate."

"It's a lovely day for a walk."

Tanyon didn't even glance at him. "Norris, pop over to the bakery and ask Mr. Oldfield if we can borrow his car."

"Why can't I stay here with him? I can't drive, in any case."

The sergeant scoffed. "How are you going to guard a prisoner without a weapon?"

"His cutting wit is enough to frighten me," Faust said.

"That's two," Tanyon said, his face reddening. "Move it, Norris. You're on report as it is."

While waiting, Faust shrugged out of the sling and tucked it into his pocket.

"Dr. Harris won't like that," Tanyon said.

"It's cutting into my neck," he lied. He already knew this was going to be his day and he wanted no encumbrances. "I'll put it back on when we get to the Hall. Unless you tell him he'll never know."

Norris returned in a spluttering Austin that seemed held together only by patches of rust, driven by a young man with a pale face, black hair, and tension lines about his mouth. For the third time, Tanyon entertained Faust, this time *sotto voce* and only until the young man stepped from behind the wheel.

"Mr. Oldfield's out making deliveries," Norris said, "so I stopped by the vicarage."

So Tanyon had enough respect for the cloth to shut up when a member thereof put in a personal appearance, despite the more blasphemous word choices he'd already displayed.

"Good morning, Mr. Ashleigh," Tanyon said. "How are you now?"

"Definitely better." The vicar leaned on a stout blackthorn stick, favoring his left foot. He didn't glance at Faust.

"I'm sorry to inconvenience you."

"Whatever I can do for the war effort, sergeant, you know that."

"How did he injure his foot?" Faust asked when they were well on the road. It was only a matter of time; the Austin's engine sounded on its last gasp, missing more often than not.

Tanyon drove, squinting in the brilliant sunshine. Norris, wearing the sergeant's web belt and holstered Webley, sat behind him, Faust in the rear passenger's seat with the driving mirror angled his way. The road ahead wound like a dusty invitation between two drystone walls, chicken runs on one side, measured rows of some low-growing vegetable on the other, the countryside extending over several rises to a forest that broke its southward march only for the little lane. If it was the same forest he'd followed south the night of his capture, then they were close to Margeaux Hall and he was running out of time. But he couldn't believe his gut feeling wouldn't play out.

Fighting his stupid little grin was useless. He heard his heart beating high and clear over the Austin's rattling, and couldn't believe the two Englishmen didn't hear it, too.

"Mr. Ashleigh was an Army chaplain," Norris said. "He stepped on a German mine in France."

"Bumf."

Tanyon grunted. "I wouldn't tell him that."

"But it's nonsense. There haven't been any German mines laid in France since 1918."

Norris opened his mouth but Faust pressed his attack right through him.

"I know we just overran the place, but we didn't take the time to plant mines. We were moving too fast to need them. Right, sergeant?"

In the sudden spellbound quiet, Tanyon's ragged breathing was clear even above the Austin's pitiful engine. Faust listened, his pulse accelerating.

"You son of a bitch. You wait until I stop this car."

As if on cue, the engine quit. Tanyon swore for the fourth time and shifted to neutral. He leaned close to the dash, ear cocked and eyes narrowed, and pressed the starter.

Faust lashed across his body with his left fist and caught Norris unsuspecting on the cheek. The kid hit the side window and ricocheted, but Faust didn't wait to see it. He smashed the rear door open, scrambled across the verge, and rolled over the wall.

The chickens nearest his landing spot squawked and flapped. He grabbed a handful of pebbles from the base of the wall and threw them over the runs. More fowlish outbursts erupted deeper within the property. Then he scuttled forward, crouching beneath the wall's cover, listening hard—and if he didn't know better, he'd swear he heard half of Bach's *Double Violin Concerto* beneath the birds—but he forced himself to concentrate. He couldn't afford to lose another opportunity against the capable sergeant.

They'd stopped on a rise, so Tanyon would have to set the brake before jumping out. And the Austin's doors opened to the rear, so he'd cross behind the car.

Norris he discounted without a second thought.

There: the metallic rattle of the driver's door opening, grating beneath the squawking and the violin's high clear notes. Faust rolled back over the wall and re-crossed the road ahead of the car in a crouching scramble that kept his head below the bonnet. He caught a glimpse of Tanyon's beefy frame as it hefted over the chicken-side wall behind the car, then the birds reacted to Tanyon's arrival. He laughed noiselessly, exultation outstripping the blood in his veins, and rolled over the other wall on the far side of the road.

Keeping his head down, he followed the line toward the

distant forest. Maybe he should head back the way they'd come, to further fool Tanyon. No, then he'd have to contend with Patchley Abbey, and he couldn't hope to slip through or around the village with any speed. Too bad the field was planted with turnips instead of something tall a man could hide in.

It was official. He'd escaped.

At the top of the first rise he paused and peered over the wall. The forlorn Austin stood in the lane, three doors hanging open. Tanyon was clearly visible scrambling deeper into the chicken runs, head swiveling like a hunting hound's and dust puffing about his boots. He looked as if he'd be distracted for awhile.

For a moment Faust didn't see Norris, then movement caught his eye. A lone figure trotted, head down, along the road parallel to his own path and getting closer fast. Faust ducked back behind the wall.

Tanyon was sending Norris to Margeaux Hall to sound the alarm, so much was obvious. Faust had to crawl along under cover; he couldn't hope to keep ahead of a man running on an open road; so Norris would win their race. Tanyon's help would be coming.

But it wouldn't be coming fast. The lorry was buried beneath the hospital wall in Patchbourne, the car he'd never seen was out of commission at the Hall, and there didn't seem to be any other form of transport available, except perhaps the chestnut hunter, so the expected help would be on foot. They might report to Tanyon's position and start the search at the chicken runs, or they might fan out at the Hall and work their way to him. Judging by the terrain, the latter was the better choice; they'd hope to sweep him before their line to Tanyon or into the village.

Bruckmann, being physically more able than Stoner, would be in charge of the manhunt; would he have the sense to extend the search south of the road? He was green as spring growth but he wasn't stupid. Faust would have to assume the search would cover the entire area and he'd meet the searchers head-on. And because he still didn't know how many men were in Stoner's crew, he couldn't assume the searchers would be so widely spaced he could slip between them.

There was only one option: to let Norris get ahead, then break cover and run for the woods, trusting to the lay of the land to hide him from Tanyon. That way, he'd get past Margeaux Hall before the search line formed. If Norris happened to turn around, well, there was nothing he could do about that. It was just the chance he'd have to take.

So he crouched in the wall's lee and listened to Norris' loping footsteps as they passed his hiding place and galloped down the rise's opposite slope. He waited for ten more seconds, then peered over the wall. Yes, Norris was well away and Tanyon still scrambled among the chickens. For a moment longer he hesitated. But he could see no other option. He broke cover and raced across the turnips, slanting away from the wall and road, aiming for the shelter of the forest.

The first few strides hurt almost enough to change his mind. They jolted his arm, and each step's shock ripped through his body and converged on his injured side as if drawn by a magnet. But then he found his pace and got the hang of leaping over the mounded rows. Running settled into a rhythm, like a tank barrage or sweet hard thrusting, and it was suddenly so easy it was good through the pain and he laughed for the sheer joy of using his body again. He accelerated down the slope, glancing at Norris slogging along the road, and forced his own pace up the following rise.

Near the top but before silhouette point he paused, crouching among the plants and turning for a glance. With a shock he saw Tanyon staring beyond the chicken runs, past the Austin forlorn on the road, and right at him. Good thing both rifles had been lost—particularly as he could almost see the steam blowing from the sergeant's ears. But the Webley didn't have the range for such a shot, and even in that infuriated moment, Tanyon didn't bother to draw it.

Faust rose and resumed running, crossing the second rise and descending the next slope. He hadn't expected his only advantage to vanish so rapidly and disappointment made a bitter taste in his mouth. For a moment he considered giving himself up and saving his major effort for a future and hopefully better chance. But he couldn't bring himself to quit so easily. Instead he put his head down and charged up the final rise. At least Tanyon didn't have a radio with him; he couldn't communicate with Margeaux Hall and give the expected search party Faust's new position.

Unless...

He paused at the top of the last rise, the forest dark ahead of him, and turned once again.

Tanyon had not followed him across the field. The sergeant stood at the farmhouse doorway, speaking to a shadowy someone within. Behind the cottage, telephone lines stretched into the distance. And there was a switchboard on Margeaux Hall's front desk and instruments at each duty station.

Including Stoner's.

He lowered his head and galloped into the forest.

20

the same morning
Woodrow and Margeaux Hall

Stoner had not slept well. Months ago, Jennifer and he had transformed Woodrow's vegetable cellar into an air raid shelter, and while it was snug and secure enough, it had seemed empty with only two of them present and the long hours had been a wearisome time indeed. They'd lit a lonely lantern and he'd read Thomas Gray's odes and elegies aloud. But the background droning of aircraft engines and flak bursts had accented each pentameter and Harriet's ghost had never interrupted to request Housman's livelier strains. So Jennifer had blown out the lamp and they'd stretched onto their cots. Stoner had breathed as quietly as he could until her sobs had dwindled into gentle snores. Only then had he relaxed enough for sleep, and every fresh wave of bombers overhead had awakened him. Each time he'd awakened, he'd checked on Jennifer and looked for Harriet, then remembered she was dead and silently raged anew. The all-clear at dawn had found him more exhausted than when he'd settled for sleep.

Even his longing for Harriet hadn't entirely distracted him from his concern over Faust and Tanyon in the Patchbourne hospital's air raid shelter. Not because of the villagers; they were a practical bunch with good sense and humor to match, and would tolerate a German officer in their midst with patience if not aplomb. No, it was Faust who'd kept Stoner's eyes fluttering open at odd, quiet moments through the night—that winsome devil with his expressive face and alert eyes, who would surely seize the first chance offered to misbehave. Tanyon was a good man, experienced and attentive, but Stoner could not suppress a suspicion his sergeant was outclassed. As for Peckham and Norris—well, even with rifles they barely entered the equation.

That morning at Margeaux Hall, the Wildflower work flew thick and fast. A fat dispatch case arrived from Brigadier Marone, containing the requisite disinformation to be transmitted via three of their captive agents, including Bläser's engineering analysis of the mythical "super-Spitfire" supposedly rolling off British factory floors. Stoner and Bruckmann drafted the messages, paying particular attention to the "voice" of each agent, then polished and coded them, double and triple checked their work, and scheduled the transmissions on the Wildflower calendar. The telephone message from Norris, informing them of their delayed return, was like an unexpected if brief holiday.

"You know, I think we're getting faster at this," Bruckmann said. "A month ago—"

And on the beat, Stoner's resistance gave out. He yawned hugely. Bruckmann froze in mid-word, so surprised he didn't even close his mouth.

"Oh, Jack, do forgive me, there's a lad. Those bombing raids are playing havoc with my schedule." He glanced at the phone on his desk. "Perhaps I should ring Mrs. Alcock for a spot of tea."

"Sir, I think we're done for now." Bruckmann gathered the papers into a pile, placing his notes atop the stack. "I'll put these in the safe, then Jennifer and I can type your notes. Why don't you catch a few winks? There's nothing further you can do until Tanyon returns with Faust," he hesitated, "or the police arrive."

The sudden memory of how Harriet had died renewed the ache in his heart. If he knew the details, perhaps the ache wouldn't be so bone-shaking. It couldn't possibly be worse.

"Perhaps you're right. Call me in an hour, otherwise," he let his voice twist into irony, "I won't sleep tonight."

This time his old soldiering instincts won the day and he dropped off immediately, waking at a touch with the drugged feeling of having slept deeply but not for long. Bruckmann stood beside his cot, lips compressed and tension lines about his mouth.

Stoner sat up. "All right, tell me the worst."

"I just took a call from Pamela Alcock." Bruckmann hauled in a deep breath. "She relayed a message from Sergeant Tanyon. Faust is loose."

He'd known the news was sour as soon as he'd seen Bruckmann's expression. But still, it was bad. He kept his voice calm but couldn't prevent his temper from showing. "Damn and blast, Jack, I believe I specifically said I did not want this to happen." He rubbed his eyes. "Did she say how he managed it?"

"It seems to be a somewhat involved story, but I did gather that Mr. Ashleigh's car was stalled out on the road before her house."

"Oh, lovely."

"Perhaps it's not as bad as all that. She also said Sergeant Tanyon had spotted Faust and was taking steps."

Stoner threw back the covers and rolled out of bed, reaching for his shoes. "Well, you'd better get going, hadn't you? And kindly inform our good sergeant I await his report with bated breath."

21

the same morning
at large in the Dark

The forest's sheltering shadows closed over him like a blanket. Faust hesitated again. Which way? He'd instinctively headed for cover, which was fine as far as it went. But now the chase was seriously on and he needed a direction, at least for the short term. After all, finding the coast was the easy part; England was an island; just walk in any direction and sooner or later he'd get wet.

Going straight ahead, deeper into the forest, seemed attractive on first thought. But that was the direction of the expected searchers, and if he wasn't careful he'd run right into them. Doubling back toward Patchley Abbey still wasn't much of a choice; heading south for the Thames would land him in the middle of shipping traffic and populated areas. He could go north into farm country, then east for the coast; or southwest for the upper reaches of the Isis, then south and east beyond the river; or maybe southeast for the Chilterns and go to ground along the escarpment.

But he couldn't hide for long, not in a German uniform. One thing for damned certain: changing into stolen civilian clothing was not an option. He couldn't chance it. If Stoner wasn't lying, he was in enough trouble as it was.

North seemed best, but that meant he had to cross the road and get beyond Bruckmann's expected search line, preferably before it formed. But Tanyon was likely to be in that path. All the sergeant had to do was wait atop the last rise and the entire road would be visible before him. Faust had developed a grudging respect for Tanyon as a straight military man, but he couldn't forget how the sergeant had let him get too close in Margeaux Hall's corridor. He was good, but it was worth a look. Faust turned north in the Dark and slipped through the underbrush back to the road.

But Tanyon was there, on the pavement astride the rise, and that route was blocked. Faust crouched in the brush, eyeing Tanyon's beefy build, the khaki battledress outlining him against the dark trees. Maybe he could go through the man. No, the odds just weren't in his favor. With Norris, he'd had the advantage of surprise. But Tanyon would see him coming as soon as he broke cover. And the sergeant had the Webley again, one hand resting on the unsnapped holster.

Perhaps he could lure Tanyon into the forest—break a branch, make some noise, tease him off his sentinel position and then get past him. Doubtful; Tanyon had been duped once; it wasn't likely to happen again soon.

The forest it would have to be, which meant he didn't have much chance of staying out for long. He resigned himself to a quick capture and again considered giving himself up to protect his injuries. But then he remembered how good it had felt running across the turnip field and his resolve hardened. Okay, so he wouldn't get far. Just being out of his cage for a while and irritating the English would be reward enough. And he'd give them a run for their money while he was at it.

Faust eased back from the road and through the brush, feeling each step before he took it, until he was well away. Then he sprinted toward the southeast and the Chilterns. Perhaps he could put enough distance between himself and Margeaux Hall so the expected search party missed him. After all, how many men could Stoner and Bruckmann possibly command?

22

the same morning
Margeaux Hall and Mrs. Pamela Alcock's chicken farm

Bruckmann roused out the seven men, including Norris, who could be spared for the manhunt, leaving Carmichael as secondary radioman in the guardroom, moving Sloane from the garage to the front gate, and freeing Glover from the switchboard by wheedling Mrs. Wainwright into covering it, which was quite possibly the most distasteful job he'd done since flattering the dragon lady of Brighton. Corporal Pym issued rifles to the detailed soldiers as they shrugged into their gear. Bruckmann, strapping a holstered Webley onto his Sam Browne belt, telephoned RAF Patchbourne and the Army encampment outside Oxford, convincing the duty officers their lives would not be complete unless they committed their reserves to his manhunt. The Army, of course, weren't flying combat missions around the clock and were vastly more sympathetic. Bruckmann received the cheering promise of two engineering companies, about 140 men.

"Send them directly to the site." He gave directions to Pamela Alcock's chicken farm. "You can't miss it; there's a car abandoned in the middle of the road and our sergeant is already there. His name's Tanyon."

"Right-o," the duty officer said. "We'll use it as a field exercise and sharpen these lads up, shall we? Do you want the chap in one piece?"

Bruckmann had no trouble imagining Stoner's response to that question and quailed. "Absolutely. He's important."

"Makes it more difficult but we'll manage. Shall I see you there?"

"On my way now." Bruckmann cradled the receiver and rose. "Damn, we needed this."

"I hate that man." Jennifer slammed over the carriage of her typewriter. "I absolutely hate him."

He checked the Webley's cylinder. It was fully loaded and he returned it to the holster. "I tend to agree."

Steven Wainwright raised his head from the usual bottomless stack of invoices. "Might I be of service?"

Bruckmann paused. The Wainwrights were refugees from the London bombing, advertising agency clerks who seemed perfectly at home in an office. But Steven had shown himself inept with a rifle during Home Guard training. "Someone has to hold the fort here. You two are elected." His glance included Jennifer, then he joined his little command outside—all seven of them.

They awaited him by the lorry in a respectful line, Pym at its head. Bruckmann wondered why he suddenly rated such reverence and then saw the dents and dust covering the vehicle.

"Sweet saints and fairies. What happened here?"

Pym saluted. "That's how Peckham brought it back from Patchbourne, sir."

Peckham remained frozen in a flawless brace.

Of course: the bombing raid. Bruckmann wanted to rip his hair, or better yet Peckham's, but that would hardly inspire the troops. Instead he returned the salute. "All right, corporal. Let's get moving."

When they arrived at the chicken farm, the RAF contingent was already there, a handful of grim sentries in blue with matching shadows beneath their eyes. While they pushed Mr. Ashleigh's poor Austin off the road, six Bedford trucks pulled onto the verge near Tanyon's position atop the rise and gushed forth khaki-clad soldiers in a considerable stream. They formed into perfect phalanxes before their lieutenants and sergeants, and Bruckmann's spirits rose at the disciplined sight. Now there was a chance against the bugger. He left the Austin and strode to meet them as an officer jumped from the cab of the lead truck.

The Army duty officer looked as he'd sounded: a small, dapper man with a millimetrically-aligned mustache and amused green eyes in constant calm motion. His shoulder straps sported the single crown of a major in the Royal Engineers. Bruckmann liked him instantly.

"Alfred Kettering." He returned Bruckmann's salute and

turned to Tanyon. "Well, sergeant, where shall we find your will-o'-the-wisp?"

"South, sir," Tanyon said. "He went into the Dark over there."

"The forest, you mean?" Kettering paused only long enough for Tanyon's nod. "And of course, you held the high ground on this road and stopped him turning north." He glanced about again, then turned to Bruckmann. "Your billet is northeast of this position?"

"Yes, sir."

"You know, you could have moved directly south from there, instead of meeting us. Then we'd have penned him between our forces."

Bruckmann's face warmed. It had been too obvious for him to notice. "I didn't think of it."

Kettering swept his gaze beneath the massive beeches atop the rise, briefly up into the canopy overhead, then south along the Dark's southern marches and across Jerome Owen's turnips. "Would you know if this chap is familiar with the lay of the land round about?"

"I should think so." Bruckmann hesitated but really, there could be no harm in sharing what was, after all, common information. "He studied a year at Oxford."

"Well, he'd have done some hiking then, wouldn't he?" Kettering stroked his mustache. "You know, if he gets up into the forests along the Chilterns, we'll have the devil's own time wrangling him out of there."

The ruddy situation was looking better by the moment. Major Kettering offered the same sort of sturdy competence as Sergeant Tanyon, along with a lot more words and explanations. "He can't climb. His right arm's been injured."

"One wing down, eh? Then we'll pen him before he gets there." Kettering sounded disappointed. "Well, perhaps he'll make a good show of it." He turned to his own sergeant, waiting patiently nearby. "Deploy one company here, Gregson, in a long line south of the road and a bit north of it in case he manages to give us the slip, aiming generally southeast. Same as we did Saturday night." He glanced at Bruckmann. "This wouldn't happen to be the same man, would it?"

"The same." And damn him for a tinker.

"Gets about, doesn't he?" Kettering returned to his sergeant. "I'll take the other company about by road to the far side of Bowdon and start them in a northwest direction from there. You'll drive him before you and we'll nab him."

The sergeant saluted and trotted toward the two companies, formed up and facing their lieutenants along the verge.

Kettering eyed Bruckmann, then flashed him a smile.

"No offense, leftenant, but your force isn't large enough to be effective, you know."

Bruckmann sighed. "Use them."

So his infinitesimal command was broken up and scattered among Kettering's two experienced companies under their capable lieutenants. The handful of exhausted RAF sentries were sent back to their base, finally smiling.

The two engineering companies broke ranks. Half of them piled back into three of the Bedfords; the others formed a long line facing the Dark, jockeying into position about fifteen feet apart within seconds. Kettering treated Bruckmann to a long, considering look, then smiled again. "Why don't you and your sergeant join me in the southern contingent? You can be in for the kill."

A training exercise. Bruckmann swallowed and concentrated on hiding his bitterness. After all, it was painfully obvious, even to himself, that he needed additional training. He saluted. "Yes, sir. Thank you, sir."

23

the same morning
Margeaux Hall

"What a time to run out of carbon paper." Jennifer slammed her desk drawer. "Mr. Wainwright, have you any to spare?"

"How many times must I tell you to call me Steven?" he said. "And no, I'm out, as well."

She ignored his sally. He was a married man and if he argued with his wife, as all the Hall knew and were reminded several times each day, well, that didn't mean she'd be extra nice to him. Besides, he didn't exactly meet her criteria of a man to match Stoner, not with his wispy mustache and wallflower personality. At least he had the sense to pitch his voice low enough so his wife, managing the switchboard in the vestibule, couldn't hear him. Maggie Wainwright would be suspicious enough as it was, with her husband out of her sight for more than five seconds.

"Today is turning into a nightmare." There was such a stack of work beside her typewriter, she'd be lucky to finish before the war ended, much less before Bruckmann returned to do his share. She'd worked twice as hard, trying not to think of Harriet. She'd even succeeded for a few short minutes. Drat that Faust; this was all his fault. And she'd never forgive him if he'd killed Harriet. She'd rip him apart with her own hands.

Wainwright reached for the phone. "Tom Burbank carries carbons at the mercantile, doesn't he?"

"I think so."

When he cradled the phone a minute later he was smiling. "Yes, Mrs. Burbank says they have some."

"Debbie? What's she doing minding the store?" She ran the village switchboard and was busy enough without handling her husband's work, as well.

"I didn't ask." Wainwright pulled on his jacket. "I'll just walk down and get them, shall I?" He smiled again as he left.

Right. Jennifer stared at the pile of shorthand notes beside her typewriter. Just walk down and get them. Straight past Pamela Alcock's chicken farm and the Dark, where all the excitement was underway that might have distracted her from the agony ripping her apart. While she held the fort alone.

Perhaps Harriet had been right, and men had all the fun. She certainly wasn't going to ask Debbie Burbank her opinion and have their conversation spread all over the village. But if only she could speak with Harriet one more time, have her sister back for a long, hard hug, even if she couldn't have her back forever. The ache in her soul rose again but she quelled it ruthlessly. She had a fort to hold and she wasn't going to run away again.

"Oh, you just want to see what's going on," she said to empty air, and reached for her pad. She could at least organize her notes while he was gone.

24

afternoon
at large in the Dark

About noon Faust exited the forest. A blaze of hot sunshine poured across his face and he reveled in its warmth for a luxurious moment, pausing just below the next rise. He'd long ago given up looking for a line of searchers ahead and chalked the mistake up to Bruckmann's inexperience. They were behind him, which meant he had to move fast and cover as much ground as possible to keep them there. If he could get into the woods along the Chilterns, about twenty to twenty-five miles away, then he could lose the initial searchers and possibly make it all the way to the coast. Best yet, although he was winded, neither his arm nor side hurt worse than they had in the morning.

One-armed, he squirmed in his finest infantryman fashion through knee-deep sedge to the rise's peak and peered over the rounded crest. Rolling hills and dales spread below and ahead, a patchwork of planted fields and pastures and tiny forested tracts separated by the ubiquitous drystone walls and the occasional hedge, a purely English vista that made his heart sing. The elevation crept higher to the southeast; in the distance faded the roughened top of the Chiltern escarpment. He started up, then motion caught his eye and he froze.

A man—no, a soldier—hiked up the slope through a field of stubble directly toward him, about a half mile and two drystone walls away, a rifle cradled in his hands. Faust paused. A lone soldier had no business here. But there was a second one, about fifteen feet to the right of the first and also coming in his direction, and another beyond him. A few moments of searching showed him a long line of soldiers stretched directly across his path as if they knew his location to the inch.

Bruckmann organized that? Faust humphed. He hadn't expected such intuition from the young lieutenant, nor such a large contingent at Stoner's disposal. But of course they would have alerted other military installations in the area, which meant the additional troops would have their own officers and sergeants, which meant his opinion of Bruckmann's practical capabilities could remain unimpressed.

But still, it looked bad. The land sloped down in front of him and on both sides, past a wall into an overgrown meadow where sheep grazed; if he went forward or directly to right or left, he would be silhouetted first against the horizon and then against the grassy area outside the wall, and he'd be spotted before he reached cover. He could return to the forest shadows, but he knew without seeing them that an identical line of searchers approached from that direction and he couldn't be sure how near or distant they were. The further back he retreated, the more he cut what little lead he had.

To his left was a hamlet, no more than a few homes but as good as a roadblock. To his right the ground sloped down to a small narrow valley, not much more than an indentation in the topography, then rose on the other side into a much steeper hill where more sheep grazed. Faust visually traced the line of the little valley between the two hills as it curved toward the soldiers ahead. Halfway along its course, a deeper shadow stopped his roving eye. It was a ravine, where rainwater runoff fell from the steep hill beyond into the valley. If he could get into that, he could possibly avoid both lines of searchers. It wasn't much of a chance but it was all the world offered.

He dropped below the crest of the rise and raced downhill.

25

the same afternoon
near the hamlet of Bowdon

At the hill's top, Bruckmann gingerly stepped over the last anthill, paused against the drystone wall and panted for a moment, then hauled himself over to join Kettering. The engineering officer leaned on his elbows atop the artfully arranged squares of flint and stared into space.

"Where the hell has he gotten to?" Bruckmann asked. "We should have run him over by now."

Kettering pointed with his chin. "Right there."

It took some squinting before he saw what Kettering saw. Halfway up the neighboring hill, half a mile distant across another sheep field, a grey-clad form clambered up a shadowy ravine. Bruckmann said one of the rude words he'd learned from Tanyon.

"Squeezed him out like toothpaste from a tube," Kettering said. "Clever chap, that. Most men would have tried to break our ranks."

The hill and ravine surged up at a precipitant slope and Faust's achievement looked impossible. "His right arm is injured. Just yesterday afternoon a surgeon was cutting shrapnel from his side. He can't climb."

Kettering pursed his lips. "Seems to be doing rather well."

He threw out another of Tanyon's choice expressions. "Let's go after him."

But Kettering touched his arm. "Hold hard, leftenant. Let's do this the easy way." He turned to his sergeant, standing nearby. "Gregson, are you live?"

The staff sergeant unslung his Lee Enfield. "Yes, sir."

"Put one across his bows."

The report of the .303 rifle cracked across the hills like the explosion of a metallic whip. Bruckmann couldn't stop himself from flinching. On the steep slope, the grey-clad form ducked, slid partway down the ravine, scrabbled for purchase, came up against a rocky outcrop, and rolled behind it.

The air shivered as the echoes fell away.

"Seen combat, he has." Kettering's voice betrayed no more excitement than if they discussed the weather.

The hillside was still. Then Faust peered about the boulder.

"He's looking right at us."

"Of course, leftenant. We're the only officers out here."

As he watched, Faust swiveled about and peered up the ravine.

Bruckmann stiffened. "What the hell is he doing?"

"Checking his options."

"What options? We've got him." His stomach roiled. "Don't we?"

"Well, he could make a run for it up the ravine, but he knows we'd just send troops ahead by road to cut him off." Kettering straightened as Faust swiveled back. "Come on, man, be reasonable." He held his arms out to the sides, waist high, and stared up the hillside. A half-mile away, Faust stared back.

They were alike, Bruckmann realized. Differences in education and languages aside, Kettering and Faust were twins under the skin: two military minds traversing the same lines of thought, a tactical fraternity that remained closed to him. Bruckmann bit his lip. The theoretical logic of intelligence work he found simple, comfortable, appealing; all this physical maneuvering made him blanch deep inside. Would he ever be able to look at a landscape, the way these two did, and see it as points of cover and fields of fire, lines of advance and retreat, the best place for an ambush or where to set up camp? They knew; Faust and Kettering both knew he was lost.

Kettering he believed he could trust. But Faust was the enemy at best and a murdering one at worst. For such a man to be so conversant with his weaknesses was both unnerving and inexcusable. Problem was, there didn't seem to be much he could do about it.

Halfway up the slope, Faust sagged. He lifted one hand, rose from cover, and started sliding down the ravine. The watching soldiers cheered.

"Bring him in, Gregson." Kettering turned to Bruckmann and smiled. Again. "There, you see? I told you we'd have him home in time for tea."

26

the same afternoon
Margeaux Hall

What to do with Faust?

Stoner sighed and rubbed his eyes. Weariness sapped him, body and soul, like some dark beast dragging him off to its shadowy lair, and he wondered how long he could withstand it. Papers again littered his desk: Bruckmann's reports, typed transcripts of Faust's interrogations, his own notes from Wurlitzer, from observing Faust's behavior, from he couldn't recall what. He pushed them aside. Rubbish, all rubbish.

Behind him at the secretarial station, the scratching pencil ceased. "Ready," Jennifer said, adding, "sorry." She was neither as practiced nor as swift at shorthand as Bruckmann, forcing him to pause occasionally and allow her to catch up.

He swiveled from the desk to give her his best smile, then leaned his head against the chair back and resumed dictation.

"After consideration, my conclusions are as follows. One: if this prisoner is an espionage agent, he is not their most sterling and was recruited on short notice to fill the obvious gaps in the *Abwehr*'s data regarding the military defenses within our shores. Two: if this prisoner is not an espionage agent, then his knowledge of Army Group A's staff implies he is precisely what he, his uniform, and his identification documents all proclaim him to be, a junior staff officer in training, which increases his intelligence value significantly." He paused; the pencil continued scratching.

Personally he could no longer believe Faust was a spy. Despite his obvious qualifications for such an assignment, his other qualities and characteristics—his unfettered, unhidden emotions, his candid conversation, his obvious confusion at the accusation—all spoke against it. The unworldliness described by Wurlitzer was too marked; Faust was a political innocent abroad.

The scratching stopped. "Ready."

"Even in comparison to the German espionage agents already within my acquaintance, whose level of expertise is not particularly impressive, this man is poorly prepared for such a role and the *Abwehr* would have to be desperate indeed to entrust an important mission to such as he. I cannot consider it likely." He paused again.

Criminal folly on the part of Admiral Canaris, head of the *Abwehr*, it would take criminal folly or downright treason on his part to send Faust to England as an agent. Stoner's entire being rebelled against that possibility, finding it even more improbable than Faust being shot down and captured so near Oxford.

"Ready."

"This of course changes the thrust of the interrogation, as we previously discussed. Our original plan in this instance remains fundamentally sound and I intend to psychologically undermine Faust's position as a prisoner of war protected by the Geneva Convention, forcing him to barter military secrets to preserve his life. Within the intense setting of an interrogation, the leverage afforded by such a ruse should be enormous."

The scratching continued, a background whisper to his thoughts.

It would take a stout man indeed to face the prospect of a firing squad without flinching. But the intellectual and conversational maneuvering required to bring that flinching about could fill any number of weeks. Meanwhile, von Rundstedt's Army Group A hovered across the Channel; England, and Jennifer, remained at risk.

There had to be a method of speeding along the process.

"Ready."

"My next step involves increasing the pressure on Faust via all means possible. The forged trial documents you have promised and which I presume are en route should be of material assistance there. Re-establishing a trusting relationship with the prisoner, which seems to have been damaged by my angry accusation, will be more difficult and will require delicate handling. More than ever, I regret my actions."

He'd worked hard to develop an accord with Faust. But the shattered expression on Faust's face when he'd left the sitting room office the final time told Stoner better than any words that his mistake had cut to the soul. He rubbed his eyes, gritty and tired; how he'd heal Faust's suspicion was more than he knew. It was difficult to imagine even this unworldly young man falling for such a line a second time.

"Ready."

"I believe that should do it, my dear." He stretched and swiveled his chair back to the desk. "Can you type it for me, before the last batch of notes? I'm expecting a dispatch case at any moment and that must go through to Brigadier Marone as soon as possible." He pulled forward his tattered stack of notes.

But no pages shuffled behind him. He glanced back. Allison stared into space. Then he blinked, and it was Jennifer, her high forehead furrowed and her eyes downcast, although not at her notes. Such moments had been happening too often lately, as he confused Jennifer with her deceased mother, and as usual, he felt thirty years older with the blink.

"You're not going to say anything about Harriet?" she asked.

Thirty very long years older. "Brigadier Marone is aware of the situation. There is little I could say which he does not already know."

She glanced up. Pain lingered in her glorious hazel eyes, red-rimmed and as tired as he felt. Beneath the pain, he recognized the same rage that simmered within him, and he reached out, squeezing her hand atop the pad.

"Did he do it?" Her voice dropped to a shaky whisper.

He looked away. "I don't know."

She wrapped her other hand atop his. "I don't understand that man. I thought, well, he's a poet, he'll be soft and dreamy. But he's nothing like that."

"There is a sensitive side to him, one that mourns the loss of his friends and wishes to be liked, even under these circumstances. But his flip side is a practical engineer with a trained military eye which misses little."

After a moment she sighed. "I can't believe he didn't do it. And by God, I'll rip his eyes out."

"If he murdered Harriet, I shan't blame you. However, please permit me to obtain the invasion date first."

Her laugh was shaky. But she rose and gathered up her notepad. "Not a moment longer, though." She kissed his cheek, pressing her face to his, and left.

But before he could do more than sort through his notes

to find his conversation with Wurlitzer—there had to be a means of re-establishing rapport with Faust and perhaps the old tutor had said something worthwhile—she was back, two dispatch cases in her hands. "These just arrived."

Neither case felt heavy, which lightened his weary and burdened soul. "Has the courier left yet?"

"No, he's waiting to see if there's a return."

The first case was from Brigadier Marone and contained the documents he'd been expecting: a forged petition bringing suit against one Hans-Joachim Faust for wartime espionage in violation of the Treachery Act of 1940, properly stamped as if it had been filed with the court; plus an equally fake affidavit, supposedly signed by Eduard Best, stating he had been expecting an individual, identity unknown to him, to parachute into the area during the diversion of a bombing raid near the city of Oxford, with the avowed intention of assisting Best with said wartime espionage. They looked impressive, but for some reason Stoner wondered if Faust would be suitably impressed.

"What should I tell the courier?"

"A moment, my dear."

The second dispatch case held smudged and scruffy copies of handwritten notes. For a moment Stoner stared at the pages, nonplussed: two documents, one written in a hard hand with closed loops and large flourishes below the writing line, the other a thin spidery scrawl that reclined across the page as if its writer held his words and himself on a tight rein.

Stoner read a few lines from the first document:

> I did not recognize the man at first and he did not tell me his name. He drove me in his car to a position overlooking the fields before the Aa Canal, showed me the disposition of the German troops bivouacked there, and explained how tired the troops were from the six-week campaign. Then he spoke of the orders the German troops had received—

Recognition dawned. "Ah. It's the reports from those two captains, Brownell and Clarke."

"The courier, Dad."

Excitement rose within him. This now, was fact, and something with which the practical side of Faust would have a difficult time arguing.

"Have him wait, my dear. Turn the radio on for him, put him in the billiard room, give him a bottle of my best whiskey, just do something with him while I read this and prepare a response. Then type that report for Brigadier Marone as fast as ever you can. Oh, and please ring Mrs. Alcock and ask her to make cuppas for us all, please."

Jennifer didn't move. "Are you serious about the whis-key?"

"No, I am not."

"Just checking." She left again.

Stoner read both reports fast and sat back, stunned. Then he read Clarke's report twice more over his tea, taking notes with a trembling hand. He added a few comments of his own while draining the pot, added an urgent request for a new forged document, specified the details he required, then rang for Jennifer and handed her the lot.

"Is the report finished?"

She nodded. "Just now."

"Then can you type this for me immediately? And then send our poor courier on his way at top speed with the originals?"

She turned her wondering gaze from him to the small sheaf in her hands. "Um, yes, I can. But there are two men here to see you."

"Is it important?"

She looked up. "Scotland Yard."

For a moment he had no idea what she meant and couldn't imagine why the police wanted to speak with him. But in a flash he remembered: Harriet was dead; not only dead, but murdered so horribly neither Constable Mercer nor Dr. Harris would describe her injuries to him. Again he wondered if the knowing could possibly be as bad as the not-knowing.

"Well, that's important, isn't it?" He smiled at her with all of his love and pain. "Please send them in."

27

the same afternoon
between Bowdon and Patchley Abbey

When Faust clambered from the ravine's mouth, a handful of soldiers awaited him, led by Tanyon and an equally weathered staff sergeant.

"Gentlemen, such a pleasure." He glanced at Tanyon. "Cooled down yet?"

"Not until you're back in your cage."

"I did warn you it was a lovely day for a walk."

The sergeants fell in on either side. Beneath the pounding pain of his bleeding arm and his bantering façade, Faust felt real resentment. It had felt so good, driving himself across the English countryside, breaking from prison and stretching his body; being outfoxed and trapped so soon, even if he had expected it, was a rough blow. When the rifle shot had blasted behind him, he'd tumbled down half the hillside and ripped his arm trying to stop his fall. Whoever had assisted Bruckmann was someone he wanted to meet, particularly as they were likely to match wits again in the future.

His first glance at the engineering major confirmed his worst expectations. Now it wasn't merely a matter of getting past Bruckmann and Tanyon; with this competent, experienced man waiting on the sidelines, escaping just became that much harder.

"Kettering," the man said and extended his hand.

At second glance, Faust couldn't help but like him. There was a sympathetic and delighted twinkle in his amused green eyes that spoke of action seen in France and gratitude their positions weren't reversed. If escaping was harder, at least he didn't have to worry about being shot *accidentally* in the process.

"Faust." Without thinking he extended his own hand. Fresh pain sliced up the back of his aching arm. His elbow shuddered and collapsed against his side. He gasped and cradled it there. "I'm sorry, it's just not working right now."

"My fault," Kettering said. "I was warned."

Faust glanced at Bruckmann. Damp tendrils of white-blond hair were plastered about the lieutenant's ears beneath his peaked cap, streaks of dirt finger-combed into them. But his pale blue eyes glinted and his smile was satisfied.

"Lieutenant, how are you today?"

"Much better now, thank you."

"I don't doubt it."

Kettering cocked his head and eyed Faust, one vertical line between his brows. "You know, I was picturing someone rather older. But come along now; I promised the leftenant here we'd have you back in time for tea."

Great. All that work, renewed injury to his arm, grime all over him and fresh dirt rubbed into his uniform, and he hadn't even interrupted their schedule. Next time, he'd have to work smarter. He strolled between the two officers and glanced at Bruckmann, glowing beside him. "Do I get tea?"

"If you find you don't," Kettering said, "give me a ring. I'll nip over with a pot and a flask, and you and I can talk shop."

Three Bedford trucks were parked on the road beyond the hamlet; the lorry and additional Bedfords, it seemed, remained near the Austin outside the chicken farm. So they rendezvoused back there, Bruckmann riding in the lead truck's cab, Faust and Kettering amiably chatting in the second. Tanyon rode in the back with some of the men, including their own, while the staff sergeant, Gregson, marched the remainder back through the forest.

When they arrived, Bruckmann made straight for the lorry. "I'll report in."

"It's been a pleasure," Kettering said to Faust.

Faust smiled. Even if Kettering was a serious roadblock in his escape plans, he had to like him. "Wouldn't mind doing it again sometime."

After Kettering left, striding back to his row of Bedfords, Tanyon glared at Faust. "Oh, I heard that, I did. Now get in."

"Poor old lorry." Faust lifted one foot to the step and grabbed left-handed for the supporting side. "It's seen kinder days."

"Ehhh."

"You know, sergeant, I don't think I've ever heard you laugh. Or seen you smile, for that matter."

"I said get in."

Bruckmann appeared beside them, a worry line creased between his pale eyes. "Carmichael's not answering the radio."

"Sounds like a problem," Faust said. When Tanyon glared at him, he hefted himself up.

But before he swung his leg into the lorry, someone screamed. He glanced back.

A stout woman, almost as wide as she was tall, scrambled from the farmhouse toward the line of Bedfords. Various bits of her wobbled in all directions at once. But Faust didn't laugh because her face was twisted and she howled for help. Her hands clawed the air as if it hid an invisible someone's face.

"None of your business," Tanyon said. "Move."

Faust's instincts, including nosiness, told him otherwise. But Tanyon rested one hand on his holstered Webley. Cornered, Faust gritted his teeth and climbed into the lorry, settling on the bench farthest from the exit.

Tanyon and half a dozen young soldiers joined him. Norris sat nearest the exit and shot him a smoldering look. One side of his face was darkened and swelling.

"It was nothing personal," Faust said.

But Norris turned his shoulder.

He sighed and leaned back. More good intentions gone up in smoke. And speaking of smoke, he desperately wanted a cigarette.

Kettering jumped from the lead Bedford's cab and strode to meet the woman. They converged in the middle of the road. She was still screaming. He put his hands on her shoulders and shook her, causing more multi-directional wobbles. Short as she was, she could easily make two of the dapper engineer.

Tanyon's glare cut across his thoughts as the lorry's engine rumbled to life and the bed quivered beneath them. "You can put that bleeding sling back on now."

Oh, very well. Faust yanked it from his pocket. As he slid it over his neck and the lorry pulled from the verge onto the road, he saw Kettering, hands still on the hysterical woman's shoulders, turn and stare after them.

28

the same afternoon
Margeaux Hall

At first glance, Stoner thought Chief Detective Inspector David Hackney looked more like Watson than Holmes. A decade or so younger than himself, Hackney was starting to get stout around the middle and light on top, with a florid face that spoke more of blood pressure than a pub. His brown eyes were small and closely set, above a large nose and greying handlebar mustache. His police sergeant, Axel Arnussen, wasn't much younger, a small slight man who looked as if a good gust of wind could blow him over but with clear grey eyes full of understanding and compassion. They were the sorts of men who would get results, and Stoner welcomed them into his office with all the warmth he could muster.

After the initial courtesies Hackney jumped straight in. "Will you tell us what happened?"

Stoner described the dance on Saturday night and Harriet's insistence upon attending. As he spoke, Hackney's eyes fastened onto his face and refused to let go, rather like the teeth of a bulldog. Beside him, Arnussen rested a pad on his knee and took notes.

"And as usual," Stoner finished, "she got her way."

Hackney grunted, sounding so like Tanyon that Stoner's eyes widened in surprise.

"A girl should be able to get her way occasionally without being murdered for it. The dance was held at the local pub, you said?"

Stoner nodded. "The Abbey Arms, publican Homer Owen."

"Yes, we're staying there while we're in town. Would he be able to tell us who all attended?"

"If he can't, try Beth Mercer, the constable's wife. She's the Patchley Abbey morale officer." The detective's stare was rather threateningly penetrating. Stoner looked down at his desk. "At first I thought Harriet had simply run away for whatever reason, and I asked at RAF Patchbourne of several young pilots if they had seen her. One, a Flight Lieutenant Langley, recalled dancing with her but didn't remember seeing her in the air raid shelter after the alarm sounded."

"So it's possible she snuck off with someone, a pilot, say?"

"I'm afraid so."

"What was she wearing?"

"A bright yellow sprigged muslin with a square-cut neckline and white crocheted collar." Stoner swallowed. She'd been so lovely and the colors had suited her dark hair and clear complexion so well. "It was the same shade as the eye of a daisy."

Hackney's stare softened and Stoner was reminded of a sad-eyed hound. "I need a photograph of her, a recent one I can keep with me while I work."

Stoner dispatched Jennifer on the errand; the courier had just left for London with his report and request. After she left, the only sound in the room was Arnussen's pencil scratching across his notepad. It sounded like Bruckmann, studiously noting down every word said. Stoner found himself glancing over his shoulder, expecting to see his young lieutenant at his post. But of course Bruckmann was still off, trying to catch Faust.

"What sort of establishment is this?" Hackney asked.

Stoner hesitated. It was an indiscreet question but for a good cause. "I'm afraid it's rather hush-hush."

"Can't discuss it, eh?"

"No, I can't."

Hackney and Arnussen glanced at each other. Stoner's understanding stabbed more deeply, and with it an even deeper horror.

"How much did Harriet know about this operation?" Hackney asked.

"Unlike Jennifer, she was never told of it," Stoner said. "How much she figured out or assumed, well, I can't say. She did wander the office a certain amount after school hours." He swallowed his fear; if the Wildflower operation was compromised as well as his granddaughter murdered, his problems had just multiplied and he knew he'd never forgive himself for exposing her to such a danger. "Do you believe she was murdered for what she might know? Is that the sort of crime you're starting to see?"

But Hackney shook his head. "It's the sort of crime I'm afraid of starting to see any day now but haven't yet. This is all supposition."

Stoner closed his eyes and managed a shuddering breath. The possibility had not been removed. If Faust had fooled him and was after all an espionage agent, it was possible he had tortured Harriet to death to learn details of the Wildflower operation. The thought brought cold resolve; the man who killed her would not escape justice.

Jennifer entered and handed Hackney a photo, shooting a concerned glance across the desk. Stoner recognized the black oak frame as the studio photo of both girls he'd had taken in London the previous summer, prior to the outbreak of war. He smiled his approval of her choice.

"It's the most recent photo we have," Jennifer said to Hackney. "It's about a year old. But I don't believe she changed much, except she grew her hair longer."

Hackney stroked the photographic face with his forefinger, a gentle smile lighting his eyes. Stoner's heart warmed. He had little in common with the gruff copper and hadn't yet achieved a psychological meeting, but this appreciation of Harriet they shared. From the look on his face, Hackney believed Harriet's image could tell him what he needed to know if he could only animate her—as if she was important to him, too, and solving her murder was the only thing that mattered. A compassionate Watson questioning him was far preferable to a cold and analytical Holmes.

"Jennifer, how much did Harriet know of this operation?" Stoner asked.

She scoffed. "Nothing and she didn't want to know. Unless it had to do with a film star or a pilot, she wasn't interested."

Nevertheless, a lack of knowledge wouldn't protect her. Stoner sighed. "She did love men so."

Hackney peered over the frame. "Has she ever gone off with a man she didn't know well?"

"No." Stoner tried to work up enough energy for outrage but found the effort beyond him. "I believe I taught her better, at least."

Standing beside Hackney's chair, Jennifer shifted. "Dad, I just don't know. If the man in question was a pilot—"

Hackney and Arnussen exchanged glances. "Lengthens the suspect list a bit," the sergeant said, and returned to his notes.

Again the room fell quiet. Hackney stared at the photo cradled in his hands. Perhaps he'd hold a séance where he sat, willing Harriet to speak. But when Hackney glanced up and smiled at Jennifer, he only asked, "Did she always wear flowers in her hair?"

"Whenever she could." Her voice broke. "Dad, there's still a lot of typing to finish. Excuse me."

"Of course, my dear." But she was halfway across the room before he spoke.

"Axel will talk with her later," Hackney said as the door closed behind her. "He's good with the ladies, he is."

Arnussen didn't glance up from his notes.

"There's something else I must mention." Stoner looked down at his fingers, once long and elegant, now gnarled and translucent as if covered with rice paper. They were the hands of an old man and didn't look like his at all. He wondered if the detective ever had such inapropos thoughts regarding his changing anatomy. "The murderer may already be in custody."

Arnussen looked up. Hackney lifted his chin. "Oh?"

"This operation deals with," Stoner paused, searching for words that would not reveal too much, "interned German citizens."

"Oh?" Hackney said again.

"However, currently we also have a German military officer in residence here. This man was shot down the night of the dance and was captured the Sunday morning following, just as he exited the forest near the farmhouse back door."

Arnussen grimaced. "This could get complicated."

Hackney pursed his lips and leaned back. "Did you confront him, by any chance?"

"I did. I don't know if that's helpful or not." It certainly wasn't going to help the interrogation.

"Don't know whether it matters. How did he react?"

"He vehemently denied any involvement. But possibly he's lying."

"I don't know," Hackney said slowly. "That's more the reaction we'd expect from a man telling the truth. The guilty ones, now, they often slip up and give themselves away when confronted. There was a case in America where the detective told a suspect the victim had been raped, and stabbed, and shot. The suspect came back and denied she'd been shot, and how was he to know that unless he did it himself?"

Stoner paused. The detective displayed no interest in the

man everyone else considered the prime suspect. Was Hackney merely attempting to shift attention away from Faust? "This prisoner didn't ask what happened to her. He merely denied any responsibility."

"Well, it wouldn't make sense, would it?" Hackney said. "Man on the run wouldn't likely stop to assault a woman unless she got in his way, and then he'd just kill her quick and get out."

It was logical. But Stoner realized he didn't want logic. He wanted a salve for his rage and pain, and if that meant vengeance rather than justice, so be it. It was a humiliating moment. He looked back at his hands and tried the last shot to his bow. "It's also possible this man is here as an espionage agent."

"Makes even less sense. Why would a man who's trying to melt into society cause trouble for himself?" Hackney shook his head. "It doesn't feel right. I'll want to speak with him, of course—if that's allowed? Does he speak English at all?"

Stoner drew a deep breath. The longing for revenge remained. But beside it yawned a deep, empty space that could never be filled again. "Of course you may and his English is excellent."

Hackney grunted. "Stands to reason, don't it? If he's maybe here as an agent—"

There was another knock on the door. Jennifer leaned inside. "They're back and they've got him." The telephone in the work area jangled. She withdrew and closed the door, a wordless exclamation hanging in air behind her.

Thank goodness. Stoner blew out his breath. Why hadn't Bruckmann radioed in a report and let him know?

Hackney and Arnussen rose together.

"If you think of anything else," Arnussen said, "you can reach us through Constable Mercer or at the pub. We're setting up headquarters there."

"Thank you," Stoner said. "And if there's anything we can do to assist your investigation, anything at all, please do let us know. We're most anxious."

"Of course."

The door opened again. Jennifer stood framed in the doorway. Her eyes were huge, her skin grey and damp, and she pressed her handkerchief to her mouth. "Dad. Oh, Dad—"

The world fell away from beneath his feet, leaving him dangling unsupported in the midst of a cold and angry world. "My dear, what is it?"

Hackney froze. Arnussen closed his notepad and slid it into his breast pocket, clearing his decks for action.

"Grace." Her voice cracked on the word. "Little Grace Alcock. They just found her. Oh, Dad, he's done it again." She turned to Hackney. "They're looking for you."

Hackney hurried out, leaving the door open. Stoner heard his voice, calm and steady, from the work area.

"I see. Well, I'm glad you're there to take charge, Major Kettering. Keep everyone away from her—yes, her mother especially—and we'll be there as fast as we can."

It could not be real. Stoner reached behind him for his chair and eased into it. This was too horrifying, too morbid, to be allowed; the fact that it was all too real only made it worse.

He looked up as Hackney returned, pausing near the doorway.

"Not again?" Stoner asked.

"I'm afraid so." Hackney glanced at Arnussen. "Her mother just found her, dead in her bedroom. But at least this lets your German officer off the hook."

"I'm afraid it doesn't."

Arnussen, halfway to the door, stopped and turned back around. Hackney stiffened.

"You see, he just escaped by running through Pamela Alcock's chicken farm."

29

the same afternoon
Margeaux Hall

When Faust arrived back at the Hall, the sullen-faced woman sat at the switchboard.

Bruckmann took a deep breath and smiled at her. "Mrs. Wainwright, thanks again for your help."

Her stare, long and smoldering beneath lowered brows, pushed him back a step. "You're here. Finally." Mrs. Wainwright yanked the headphones over her ears, a crease already marking her sculpted dark waves. She swung to the switchboard and crushed a plug into one socket.

Bruckmann retreated further. Even Tanyon's impassivity was wide-eyed. As one, the two men eased away from the desk and escorted Faust through the open door into the ballroom.

"When you find Carmichael," Bruckmann murmured to Tanyon, "slaughter him."

Tanyon nodded.

"Privates are great fricasseed," Faust said. "I learned a recipe in Poland, if you're interested."

Bruckmann ignored him. Tanyon grunted.

The console radio was silent, the sitting area abandoned. The atmosphere in the typists' pool was frigid enough to shatter with an ice pick. The wispy clerk, Wainwright, huddled over a pile of papers, supporting his chin in both hands, his gaze fastened onto the top sheet as if glued there. At the next desk, Jennifer sat with her back to them. Her shoulders were hunched and the ends of her auburn bob cascaded down, hiding her face.

Tanyon and Bruckmann hesitated. Faust stopped between them. His smile slipped at the edges and he found himself staring at the auburn cascade, the lowered head, the neglected typewriter. Delicate blue veins and bones lined the back of her hand, lying atop her desk, but there was strength in the forearm before it vanished into the crumpled sleeve of her pale yellow blouse. If a man stroked the tiny hairs on her skin, how would she respond?

She gasped, one sharp inhalation as if she burst from deep water, and swung her chair about. Her hazel gaze swept over him, stopped, focused. He'd been caught staring again but he couldn't look away. Her face was damp and red choked her eyes, rims and whites. His smile faded further; such a doughty fighter shouldn't cry.

She didn't look away, either, and her focus intensified. Green sparks flashed behind her hazel stare like electricity shimmering through the ballroom, and Faust remembered the woman running from the farmhouse, screaming, her hands clawing empty air. A curious cold sensation began in his stomach and seeped outward until his fingers tingled. Something—no, something else—had happened.

He wanted to offer condolences on her sister. But before he could decide how to phrase it without risking a ferocious snub, Jennifer erupted from her chair like a recoiling mortar and charged him. Faust froze. The chill wrapped all the way around his body, slowed his thoughts, kept him frozen. Surely Bruckmann or Tanyon would deflect her trajectory. But they seemed as shocked as he, not meeting his glance.

Suddenly she was right in front of him, her light floral scent an intimate anomaly. Out of options, he gave ground, backing away from Bruckmann and Tanyon, astonished at the fury twisting her face. Then his heel hit the oak paneling behind him, she hit his chest in front, and her closed fist cracked into his mouth with stunning force.

Tanyon finally moved, gripping her arm and hauling her away. "Miss Stoner, no."

She wrenched in his grasp. Bruckmann shook himself awake and reached for her other arm. But she shoved both of them off. Her fury stayed focused and her stare never left him.

"Murderer!"

Faust kept his back to the wall. He steeled himself for another onslaught—Bruckmann had abandoned them and stood murmuring with Wainwright, and good as Tanyon was, he couldn't hold her alone. But she whirled and ran toward Stoner's office.

The old man stood outside his doorway, two other men behind him. She ran into his arms and he closed them about her. For a gentle moment she was still while something moved in Faust's soul. Then she stepped back, turned, and fixed him with another ferocious glare.

"She was only fifteen. You *murderer.*"

Faust's mouth opened, closed, opened again. No words came out and not a single thought coalesced in his head. The auburn bob had blown back from her heart-shaped face and red blotches flared in her cheeks. Her chest expanded, lifted her breasts, contracted, lowered them, but he couldn't look away from her face. She wasn't beautiful. Her features didn't match, her hairstyle didn't suit, and her name didn't rhyme with anything.

But she was stunning. She left Campaspe in the dust. And she did something to him he didn't understand. Besides assaulting him.

She turned her back, stepped through Stoner's office door, and soundlessly closed it behind her.

His lip felt swollen and a trickle of something warm slipped down his chin. He touched the spot with his grubby left hand. It came away bloody, of course. As usual, her exit broke the spell. He didn't know what to think of that contradictory, aggravating, ferocious woman. But what she'd said had to be addressed.

"I didn't kill anyone!" he yelled into the ballroom's shocked hush.

Tanyon stepped closer, one hand dropping to his Webley. Faust shoved past him. Stoner seemed transfixed, staring with his eyebrows aloof. The two unfamiliar men, a walrus and a grey ghost, watched with interest and made no move to intervene.

"Mr. Stoner, I'm a patient man." Faust forced his voice down. Still it vibrated through the ballroom. "But I don't think anyone is this patient. Will someone please tell me what's going on?"

For the first time, Stoner glanced at the two strangers. The walrus, in his mid-fifties and sporting an absurd handlebar mustache, shook his head.

Faust rolled his eyes. "All right, fine—don't tell me." His voice wasn't so quiet any more. He turned and strode back to Tanyon. "Get me out of here."

"*Herr Major.*"

Finally. He wheeled about. "Sir?"

Stoner had noiselessly crossed half the ballroom while Faust's back was turned. At first glance, icy tingles watered down his rage. From this closer vantage point, Stoner's labored breathing was impossible to miss. His parchment-thin skin seemed grey and his hands trembled. The signs were unmistakable; Faust had seen them, mere days before Father Matthias collapsed at prayers and slipped from Faust's boyhood life. And this was the second time in the past two days Stoner had displayed those symptoms.

If the old geezer had lied to him, it was good riddance.

"Please forgive my granddaughter's behavior." Stoner's stiff voice matched his formal words. But like his hands, it trembled. "She is distraught."

"Really." He touched his lip again, tasted blood and dirt. "This isn't just her way of saying hello?"

"Such sarcasm is unnecessary."

"I disagree. I'm in a madhouse and normal standards of polite communication don't seem to apply."

Stoner lowered his chin and advanced further. A gentle flush of color grew in his face. The puzzle pieces clicked into place and Faust's breath caught: Stoner was an old warrior and he fed off the fight.

"You understand escape attempts are discouraged."

By arguing, he was helping his enemy. If he refused to fight, could he reverse it? He sucked in a deep breath to slow his pulse, but couldn't stop his mouth.

"You're one to talk, Mr. Stoner. You know I have my duty."

Stoner's eyes narrowed. "A reliable authority informs me that, when English officers imprisoned in Germany attempt escape and are recaptured, they are punished with thirty days of solitary confinement."

Again his breath caught. "In that bedroom, I'm already in solitary confinement."

"A point. I do have a punishment cell at my disposal; however, as it is equipped with neither plumbing, ventilation, nor lighting, I consider it inhumane and prefer not to use it."

Faust considered the horrible prospect of stewing in his own juices—literally. That curious cold sensation invaded his stomach and this time he recognized it as raw fear. His experiment, he knew, was over; he'd never been any good at hiding his emotions and Stoner had to know he was nailed. "Decent of you."

Stoner's expression didn't change but something flickered in the background of his keen blue stare. At least he wasn't crowing, which was also decent of him.

"Therefore," he continued, "I believe two weeks' confinement in the guardroom cell are indicated. Sergeant Tanyon, perhaps our Bläser contingency would also be appropriate. Lieutenant Bruckmann, please assist the sergeant in securing the prisoner within his temporary quarters." He turned to the two civilians. "I'll send Dr. Harris along immediately."

It was a rout but Faust didn't care; his skin remained intact and attached, and that conversation would only have gotten uglier. He waited until they were on the stairs before he spoke again. "So what's this contingency?"

Bruckmann and Tanyon walked close to his sides. Even if he took Tanyon out first, he couldn't take them both. Well, maybe if he knocked Bruckmann down the stairs.

"Wait," Tanyon said. "We'll talk in a minute."

The guardroom on the second floor was a long open space, less than a third the size of the ballroom beneath it. On the opposite wall, Lee Enfield rifles were aligned in a vertical case, a stout table and a dozen wooden chairs between them and the door. Two more rifles, both coated with plaster dust, one with a bent barrel, lay on the table, and eight young British Army soldiers sat around it, rising awkwardly as they entered.

On the right-hand wall, another hefty table supported the transmitter-receiver. Carmichael, seated before it as if he'd never left a post in his life, pulled the headphones off one ear and swiveled on his chair to face into the room. At his left elbow, the unbarred window, bordered with rumpled blackout curtains, poured the only light into the room.

At the end of the room farthest from the door, a cell was blocked off by vertical iron bars and a swinging gate. It contained a cot, a blanket, a flimsy table, and one chair, and if they actually locked him up for two weeks in there, he'd be ripping his hair out before tomorrow.

Tanyon pushed him into the room's center, beside the table. The young soldiers scattered and lined the walls, surrounding him. Faust's pulse picked up speed. Stoner's unknown contingency had some ugly possibilities, and he still hadn't countermanded Tanyon's threat of using rifles as clubs.

"Lieutenant, come on in and close the door," Tanyon said. "Sloane's still at the front gate? Whiteside, you watch the door; Reynolds, you listen for the phone; Carmichael, you stay on the radio. And you and I will have a good long talk in a few minutes."

Faust glanced about at the young faces. He'd been there long enough to recognize most of them. Lance Corporal Pym, with his steady grey-eyed stare, stood over the rifles on the table as if to protect them. Tall wiry Norris with his bruised face had wanted to be brave but hadn't managed it. Carmichael at the radio, unconcerned even by Tanyon's promise, his haircut as bad as ever and ragged beneath his canted ear-phones. The switchboard operator from yesterday afternoon, Glover, whose guileless green eyes seemed made for smiling. Ellington with his shorn bullet head and parted lips, uncertainty driving out his usual dreamy expression. And Peckham, who'd proven himself stout enough to unload the hospital wall from the lorry's cab. The other two he didn't know yet, although he assumed the chesty youngster with com-placent brown eyes and weathered skin who planted his back against the closed door was Whiteside. The other, presumably Reynolds since he stood near the phone, was a lanky thin-faced kid with a slack mouth and small close-set eyes who seemed content to hang in the background behind Bruck-mann, letting others make the decisions and take the blame.

They all met his eyes and most returned a hard stare. Ice seeped from his guts into his chest and abdomen, leaving him hot and shivering and cold, like on a battlefield. Maybe he should grab one of the rifles for self-defense. No, they'd be all over him if he went for a weapon. Besides, he still didn't know if they were loaded.

Tanyon hefted one Lee Enfield, not the one with the bent barrel. "Lieutenant, what did you learn from Mr. Wainwright?"

"Grace Alcock." Bruckmann visibly swallowed. "Her mother found her in her bedroom, butchered."

The room seemed to swim around him. "I didn't kill anyone."

What looked like a seaful of skeptical faces swiveled from the sergeant to him. But Tanyon, their centerpiece, braced the rifle butt atop the table and leaned on it. "I know."

They all turned back to the sergeant. Faust blinked and found air. But again, he didn't know what to say.

Bruckmann crossed his arms. "All right, sergeant. We're listening."

"You didn't have time." Tanyon spoke to Faust, as if they were alone in the room. "You weren't in Pamela Alcock's chicken runs for more than a few moments. Then you rolled back over her wall and took off across Jerome Owen's turnip field on the road's other side. I saw you run into the Dark all the way over there. And I know you didn't cross the road again."

"You couldn't see the whole road, sergeant," Norris said. "You can't know that."

"From the top of the rise I could see enough of it. Nobody crossed."

If he'd tried to force a way through Tanyon atop the rise—worse, if he'd succeeded—

"Besides, we caught you outside Bowdon and you had to run most of the way to get there in less than three hours. If you'd taken the time to butcher someone first, you wouldn't have made it so far. So unless there are two homicidal maniacs running around, you aren't it." Tanyon paused and nodded down toward Stoner's office. "They'll figure it out sooner or later."

The hard stares were fading into uncertainty, even Bruckmann's. Faust found more air and started panting, as if he'd run across another field. If he'd grabbed for a weapon—

Tanyon glanced at the rifle in his hand, then meaningfully at him. "You expecting the worst?"

He looked away. Norris and Peckham sniggered. But Pym huffed as if insulted. Bruckmann remained silent, arms still crossed.

"You'll find Mr. Stoner's not like that. He doesn't allow physical stuff, at least not generally. There are only certain situations where he'll turn a blind eye."

"For example?"

Tanyon fingered the rifle. "You'll have to learn from experience."

This time Whiteside and Carmichael joined the snickers.

Faust glanced at Bruckmann; an officer shouldn't allow threats of physical violence. But the lieutenant didn't react, which meant he was on his own.

Bastards.

"So what's the game, sergeant?"

"Take off the sling," Tanyon said.

Well, it was true he'd fight better without it. Faust tugged his arm free and slid the white cloth over his head. "Would you actually use a rifle on an unarmed and injured man?"

"After you smacked one of my boys silly and made me look a fool? Your boots."

He blinked. "What about them?"

"Take them off."

Faust paused. If he gave up his boots, it would be harder to escape again. But Tanyon only gave him a moment to think. He cradled the Lee Enfield and eased closer, knuckles whitening about the stock.

It wouldn't be worth the fight, at least not yet. He propped his right boot on the table's edge, unlacing it left-handed. His fingers fumbled on the knot. They were staring at him again, and he could feel himself reddening as he unlaced the left one.

He kicked off both boots. "Okay, your move."

"The tunic."

This time the snickers rippled through all the grinning youngsters, even Pym. His flush deepened. It was one thing to be stripped and searched upon first capture; that was expected; but this, Stoner's contingency, was public and demeaning. He narrowed his eyes. If he did fight, he'd start with Tanyon. Nobody else mattered.

The sergeant wasn't smiling. He eased even closer. Another step, and he'd be close enough to whip out with the rifle's butt and catch him in the stomach or across the face. "Unless you're willing to be finished, don't even start."

He unbuttoned his tunic. "I resent this."

"Now the shirt."

He peeled it over his head and eased it past the bloody bandage, tossing it, too, on the table. But when Tanyon opened his mouth again, Faust beat him to the punch. "No."

"Lieutenant, I think your invitation to this party should be just about used up."

Faust glared again at Bruckmann. An officer shouldn't permit this, damn it. But Bruckmann stood beside Carmichael and the radio, his face expressionless. For a long moment he didn't move, and the hot blood drained from Faust's face into his socks. Then the lieutenant tilted his head—*them's the breaks, mate*—and Whiteside closed the door behind him.

Tanyon's expression hadn't altered. This, Faust knew, was his last chance. To fight or not to fight? If he did, that swinging rifle would take less than a second to put him retching on the floor. He'd be stripped by force and thrown into the cell. Would the additional misery be worth it, just to make a point?

"I've got my orders." Tanyon's voice was quiet. "We're going to follow them. Do you have to do everything the hard way?"

He stripped, cold with rage. "Bastards."

"That your insult of choice?"

"What do you think?"

"I think I've got a few of my own."

He threw his trousers on the table and stood in the midst of the grinning kids in his shorts and undervest.

"In the cell," Tanyon said.

Damned if he'd admit defeat. He grabbed his tunic, yanked his cigarettes and matches from the breast pocket, and jerked his sling from beneath the pile of clothing. He paused long enough to glare back then stalked into the cell. Tanyon closed it behind him and the lock snapped.

"Blankets on the cot if you get cold," Tanyon said. "Set the cot on fire and you sleep on the floor."

"There are words for people like you and laws against wearing such an ugly face."

Tanyon grunted. "Ellington, run this uniform down to Sally and see if she has time to clean it."

"Do you expect to earn Brownie points?" His hands shook so hard he snapped the first match. He threw it on the floor and tried again.

"You also have to police your area."

"Not for your dear old mama."

"Damn, you've got a mouth on you." Tanyon threw the rifle he held to Norris. "Clean that and put it away. Whiteside, hand me the duty roster. Since our schedule's all shot to criminy," he added over his shoulder, "for some reason I won't name, I'll have to sort out who's actually on duty and who's not."

At least he'd accomplished something. "Get used to it." He inhaled hard and welcomed the nicotine surging into his system. They'd all beaten him: Kettering, Jennifer, Stoner, Bruckmann, Tanyon.

Revenge would have to be explicitly juicy to make up for this.

30

the same afternoon
Pamela Alcock's chicken farm

Hackney smelled death, and another tiny piece of his heart died within him.

It was always the same. Whenever he witnessed the horrors that could be inflicted upon the human anatomy, whenever he considered the possibility that could have been his own sweet wife lying there, or one of his sons, or the cleaning lady down the street, or the greengrocer next block over—whenever he smelled death, he became a little sadder.

Arnussen saw the changes in him, he knew. He and the sergeant had worked together for over twenty years now, advancing together through the ranks, and he knew Arnussen measured every step his heart retreated. It was different for him. The sergeant never seemed to take death personally. He could look a corpse or a murderer in the eye and never miss a meal or a step. He just smiled his little smile, commented on how life did go on, didn't it, and kept going himself as if to prove his point.

But Hackney had never learned to let a case go. He couldn't solve all of them; no one could. And the cases he couldn't solve remained open, in the files and in his mind, framed photographs of the victims crowded atop the bookcase beside his desk, smiling and watching him through the years. And he remembered all their names and their families' tear-streaked faces and how they'd died and where they were buried. And on the anniversaries of their deaths, he visited their graves if he could. And whenever he stood at the grave-side of an unsolved homicide victim, another tiny piece of his heart died.

This girl's bedroom was at the back of the house, casement windows wide open to the cackling chickens in their runs. A soldier stood on the lawn outside, rifle on his shoulder, guarding her death. Kettering had been as good as his word and the crime scene was almost untouched. Only the poor mother had intruded, stumbling from her daughter's bedroom in hysteria, and her fingerprints would be there in any case. Kettering had assured them he'd stopped in horror at the door. It was as close to unspoiled as the police would ever get.

"Not as bad as the other." Arnussen indicated the mush that had once been a young girl's chest. "Not as much bruising on the face, either."

"Still a lot of rage, though. How many times do you think he stabbed her? Twenty, thirty?"

"Something like that."

Hackney forced himself to examine her nude body, the blood splatters on the headboard, the bruising and overkill, and implant all of it into his memory. The only thing he touched was her dark hair spilling over the pillow. Then he straightened.

"Let's get a photographer and a fingerprint expert out here. After they're done, we'll let the doctor in."

"Did you see this?" Arnussen pointed with his pencil toward a bit of bloody rag on the closet floor.

Hackney fumbled a rubber glove from his pocket and put it on, then picked up the bit of cloth. It was a handkerchief, smeared not spattered, and seemed wet with more than blood. "He cleaned himself afterward." He held out a hand; Arnussen, prepared and waiting, gave him a small paper bag. Hackney dropped the handkerchief into it and rolled down the top. "It might be local. Let's see if we can trace it after the lab. boys are through with it."

Arnussen made a note on his ever-present pad.

Hackney scanned the room: the cheaply framed print of Gainsborough's *The Blue Boy* above the headboard, now splat-tered with gore; the feminine undergarments on the floor, kicked halfway beneath the bed and peeping from beneath the disarranged dust ruffle; a violin in an open case in the corner, stamped into splinters. He gestured. "Do you think we might get a boot- or shoeprint from that?"

Arnussen made another note. "The weather's been dry. But we'll see."

"Do you think she was alive to see it happen?"

"Gentlemen."

They swiveled toward the door. A tall man stood framed in the opening with a medical bag in his hand. His grey suit was rumpled as if he'd slept in it.

"Dr. Harris," he said, not entering. "I've read enough Dorothy Sayers and Ellery Queen novels to know what a fingerprint is and how not to leave one. May I come in and see the body *in situ*?"

Arnussen glanced at Hackney and shrugged. Hackney invited the doctor in with a sweep of his arm.

"Thank you." Dr. Harris paused at the bedside. "Grace."

The doctor's taut words swam in pain that sounded personal. Hackney cocked his head. "Did you know her?"

"A patient." Dr. Harris, too, touched her dark hair, Hackney noted. "We took out her tonsils when she was twelve and her inflamed appendix last year. A sickly girl, our little Grace. Was," he added.

"Can you estimate her time of death?" Arnussen said. "Unless you want to excuse yourself for personal involvement."

Without answering, the doctor set his medical bag on the foot of the bed, well away from the blood spatters, and pulled on surgical gloves. Then he moved her eyelids, felt her cheeks, waggled her jaw. "No rigor yet." He shifted her slightly and peered at her back. "But lividity's started." He glanced up at Hackney. "Do you want me to do a temperature test?"

"Please."

He sorted through his bag and produced a rectal thermometer. Hackney turned away, looking out the window at the sentry on the back lawn, now standing at rigid attention. Nearby stood the trim, slender figure of Major Kettering, arms folded across his chest, staring back without blinking.

"Just over ninety-five degrees," Dr. Harris said, "say about two hours."

Arnussen wrote it down.

"Thank you, doctor." Hackney turned from the window and Kettering's glare. "Where do you want us to send her body after the photographer's done?"

Dr. Harris hesitated, glancing down. Hackney followed his gaze to the huddled figure sprawled across the bed, her blue eyes glassy and fixed on nothing. Another bit of his heart died.

"The best autopsy facilities are still at Patchbourne hospital, even though part of the building caved in during our last bombing raid. But you know, I've done some autopsy and surgical photography myself, and my rig's outside. Do you want me to—give it a whirl?"

At least he hadn't said *take a stab at it*. Hackney glanced at Arnussen and decided his sergeant was thinking the same morbid, absurd thought.

"Why not?" Hackney said. "Are you still driving about? Can you get petrol?"

"Motorbike and a medical allowance." Dr. Harris pulled off the gloves, dropped them inside-out into his bag, and removed it from the bed. "I have a covered sidecar for my various equipment, including my horn."

Hackney stared at him, eyebrows up.

"I play in the Patchbourne symphony orchestra, such as it is." Dr. Harris nodded toward the bed. "Grace played second fiddle."

Hackney glanced, not at her, but at her crushed violin. If he could get the boot's owner, he didn't care what his heart did.

While Arnussen directed Dr. Harris' photography, Hackney escaped into the den. A pudding-shaped woman with the same dark hair, now shot through with grey, moaned and tossed on the creaking sofa. Her eyes drifted open as he watched, then closed as if the weight of her lids was too much to lift. Sedated, apparently, and for the best. Questioning and comforting her was a job for Arnussen, he with his cordoned-off heart and gentle smile for the ladies, he who had deliberately never married and never opened himself up for either the pleasure or the pain.

A group of framed photos clustered atop a doily on a small table. One showed a dark-haired girl playing in the string section of a small orchestra. Hackney slid it into his coat pocket and let himself out the front door.

Kettering awaited him on the front lawn, arms still folded. "What do you think?" he asked before Hackney got his mouth open.

"I think we have a serious problem." Hackney glanced about. Most of the soldiers he'd seen on his arrival had vanished, along with all but one of the Bedford trucks. Only a few sentries still formed a perimeter around the chicken farm. "Where did everyone go?"

"I sent most of my men back to our encampment," Kettering said. "But I can and will produce them whenever you like."

"Major, how many men were involved in the search for the German officer today?"

Kettering pursed his lips. "There were a half-dozen RAF men, I believe off-duty sentries, no officer, only a lance-corporal in charge. But they were too fagged to be much use so we sent them back to their base before the search began.

Leftenant Bruckmann had his sergeant and seven men with him. I brought two companies, each with its own lieutenant and non-coms, and my own sergeant. Say about one hundred fifty, sixty men, all told."

Hackney winced. To those men he'd have to add the pilots and villagers from the Saturday night dance and any additional troops and Home Guard units involved in the first manhunt. The suspect list couldn't be longer if the investigation took place in downtown Oxford rather than a quiet village. "We'll need statements from all of them. Then we'll have to correlate them with alibis from Saturday night."

Kettering's intensity faded. "What about Saturday night?"

"This is the second murder, you know."

"Is it?" Kettering stroked his pencil-thin mustache. "And Saturday night was the first time we looked for that jerry. You know, I spoke with the man and even liked him. Who would have thought it?"

Too many people were going to make that assumption. "We don't know he did it and we do have all those other men to account for."

Kettering stared at him again. "You don't think the circumstances—"

"I know too many men, and women too, have been hanged on circumstances that didn't stand up to much scrutiny. But I'd rather it didn't happen on my watch." He sighed under Kettering's intensifying stare. "If he does turn out to be guilty, of course, that's another matter. But we need facts to prove it first."

"Well, you know your job best." Kettering sounded doubtful. "Where does one start looking among all this?"

"With you." Hackney fumbled his own little-used pad and pencil from a pocket. He flicked it open to a blank page and looked up into Kettering's equally blank but rapidly reddening stare. "I don't mean you're under suspicion. But until I know where everyone was, or was supposed to be, I won't be able to determine who wasn't, if you catch my drift. Please just tell me about Saturday night."

"Well. In that case." Kettering again stroked his mustache. "The klaxon went off just before nine thirty Saturday night, but I'd have to look at the duty log for precisely when. We expected to be hit, same as the RAF base eighteen miles to our northeast, so we went into the shelters as the flak gunners got to work. But just after ten, we received word from Civil Defense at least one plane had been brought down and a parachute sighted near Patchbourne. So we organized for the search—"

"The same men as today?" Hackney wrote as fast as he could. He'd never learned shorthand, worse luck.

Kettering paused. "One company was the same, Leftenant Daingerforth's Eleventh Field Company. The other out Saturday night was Leftenant McCoy's 208th. Today the 208th are involved in Colonel Birnbaum's exercises, repelling pretended German invaders from Oxford proper." He removed his peaked cap and wiped his forehead with a handkerchief. "Unless someone has a day pass or is on sick call, those men are currently quite occupied. I suppose it could be called a blessing in disguise for them."

"Was there a third company involved today but not Saturday night?"

He repositioned his cap. "Leftenant Gibbs' 210th. They remained in the air raid shelters, off duty."

"Can that be conclusively proven?"

"Certainly." Kettering's voice was stiff. "Sentries on duty at all exits. No one would have gotten through without authorization and none was forthcoming."

"And you were out Saturday night, as well?"

"I was." Kettering sighed. "I see what you're getting at. You're trying to whittle down the number of men who could possibly be suspected."

"Yes," Hackney said. "Of course, we can't assume anything at this point."

"Meaning?"

"Meaning every man in each of those three units will be asked to account for his movements at the times of both murders."

"You chaps have your work cut out for you. That's about two hundred soldiers." Kettering pursed his lips, then cocked an eyebrow. "I don't suppose our staff could be of assistance here, taking statements and such? Not to imply your lads aren't capable, but it would be a lovely training exercise."

"Any assistance the military can offer will be gratefully accepted," Hackney said. "Like everyone else, we're short-handed."

"Excellent." Kettering paused. "Were you in the first war?"

Hackney heard the machine-gun fire of the Somme in his inner ear. "I was and know all about training exercises in August heat."

Kettering grimaced. "In full field kit, cursing the old bugger responsible for hauling you out—I never thought, back in 1925 when I joined, I'd ever be the old bugger himself. Just goes to show."

It was hard to produce a smile. But he managed. "So on Saturday night, you organized for the search?"

"Yes. We drove to Patchbourne and Bicester, oriented ourselves with the jerry's suspected landing site, and formed up into two long lines, facing each other across country and working toward each other. I thought we'd corner him easily but somehow we missed him." Kettering shrugged. "Most of the jerries shot down lately aren't too keen on running. With the invasion expected any day now, all they're doing is sitting back on their laurels and waiting for von Rundstedt's armies to arrive and rescue them. But this chap seems entirely different. He's serious about getting out of here."

Hackney paused, wondering if Stoner, the ascetic professor, had considered this aspect of his stubborn prisoner.

"I hear on Sunday morning, a girl with a shotgun winkled him out," Kettering said.

"I believe I've met the young lady." She'd certainly handled the German officer roughly enough, as if she thought she owned him.

Kettering clasped his hands behind his back. "You know, back during the American colonial revolution, one of our chaps commented that, even if we defeated all the men on that ungrateful continent, we'd still have to fight the women. I believe there's an Austrian corporal in Berlin who's about to learn the same lesson about Englishwomen."

Again he recalled the swinging fist, the crack as it landed on the German officer's mouth, her utter fearlessness in charging him. "I'll second that."

"Hope I get to meet her someday," Kettering said to thin air. "Lass like that's worth consideration."

Hackney flipped to the next page on his pad. "And today?"

"Oh, well, this morning I took a call directly from Leftenant Bruckmann about ten. We did roughly the same thing, except between that turnip field across the way and the far side of Bowdon. We cornered him in a ravine near there and convinced him to surrender with a three aught three. Seemed a cultured man, educated, witty, that sort." Kettering paused. "I admit I quite liked him. If it wasn't for this ruddy war—"

Hackney cut him off. "Right."

"Then, as we were loading to move out, Mrs. Alcock ran screaming from her house. I came in here, stopping at the door as I told you, and didn't know what to think."

"Very good, sir." Hackney dated the scribbled statement, hoped he'd be able to read his own handwriting later, and flipped the notebook closed. "And again, we appreciate any assistance you can offer."

Kettering took the hint. "You seem to have this under control. I suppose I should get myself and my men back to Port Meadow and start on those statements for you."

As he strode off toward the waiting Bedford, his men scrambling about him, Arnussen and Dr. Harris emerged from the house and Constable Mercer appeared from the chicken runs.

Mercer waved over his shoulder in the general direction of the clucking birds. "There's all sorts of footprints out there in the dirt. I can identify Pamela's from her brogues and Grace's from her smaller shoes, but there's at least three sets of boots I can't sort out. One of them doesn't come any closer to the house than the wall, but the other two march right up onto the lawn and vanish in the grass, one from the road, the other from the Dark."

"Good work, constable." Arnussen wrote it down, of course. "Get on the horn to Patchbourne and Oxford, find someone qualified to make plaster casts of those bootprints. You'll have to stick around until they get here and identify the prints for them."

"Certainly." Mercer disappeared into the house.

"I've rung for an ambulance to pick up Grace," Dr. Harris said. "And I've rung Pamela's sister, who's cook at Margeaux Hall, to come for her. Do you want me to develop these snaps myself or would you rather I give you the film and let your lads take care of it?"

The doctor's slender fingers certainly looked capable. "Can you handle it?"

He nodded. "We have a darkroom in the Patchbourne hospital basement. I do a lot of surgery photos."

"Is there anything you don't do, doctor?"

Dr. Harris glanced back toward the house and its sad occupants. "I don't butcher little girls." He stalked across the lawn toward a motorbike and sidecar parked near the single Bedford truck still hulking on the grass verge.

When he was out of earshot, Arnussen stepped up to Hackney's shoulder. "Well?"

Hackney watched as both vehicles started engines and then bounced onto the road, rolling off toward Patchbourne. "There go at least two possibilities right there."

The engines died in the distance. Arnussen stared at him, one vertical line between his Nordic blue eyes. "I can't forget how the German lost his temper in the Margeaux Hall ballroom."

"And I can't forget how he let a woman corner him against a wall and smack him in the mouth. He didn't even defend himself."

"Why would you suspect Kettering?"

"He was out both times. He's insinuated himself into the investigation, as a lot of clever murderers do. He's also unmarried, or at least not wearing a ring, and interested in meeting the ladies roundabout."

"And Harris?"

"Knew the victim, knows the house and area. Also unmarried. Also being helpful and working his way into the investigation. He's mobile these days when many other men aren't and into every sort of activity imaginable."

Arnussen peered at him sideways. "Is that now a recognized criminal trait? Should I quit the playhouse?"

"No, but it gets him out. A man like that knows what's going on. He could have known when the German officer was loose and arranged the crimes to implicate him. Of course," he added when Arnussen opened his mouth again, "all we have to do is check alibis. These are possibilities, no more."

Arnussen sighed and slid his notepad into his pocket. "And what do your famous instincts tell you?"

"I think, Axel old lad, it takes brass-bound balls to kill one girl in the middle of a bombing raid and another in her own bedroom while her mother's on the grounds tending the chickens."

"Or someone who knows the mother's habits?"

"Or an utter fool."

They stared down the empty road, shoulder to shoulder.

31

evening
Margeaux Hall

"I used to be a sergeant myself." Hackney gestured toward the sofa.

Tanyon perched on the sofa's edge and rested his hands on his knees, dark eyes sliding sideways. Hackney followed his gaze to Stoner, sitting at his desk with the newly arrived dispatch cases before him. Bruckmann sat at the secretarial station, already taking notes. Hackney sighed and swiveled back.

"Can't exactly throw a man out of his own office, can I?" He lowered his voice to a rumble; hopefully it wouldn't carry too far in the room's deathly quiet. "He's got work to do, too. and the sitting area in the ballroom seemed the best place for Sergeant Arnussen to question your men."

Tanyon shrugged, rubbing his blue jaw line. "I suppose we could have put you upstairs in Lieutenant Bruckmann's office, or mine."

But Hackney shook his head. "If this establishment is all that hush-hush, then the less I wander in it, the better. We'll just keep our voices down. Now tell me about Saturday night, starting at the dance."

"I didn't go," Tanyon said. "That swing music, it's for the youngsters. The BBC carried one of those Gilbert and Sullivan musical shows, so I stayed here and listened to it. I kept Carmichael upstairs in the guardroom and Glover at the front gate, and let the others go as it seemed like it would be a quiet night." He rubbed his jaw again. "Little did I know."

"Do you recall where everyone else was?"

"Lieutenant Bruckmann walked to Patchley Abbey, but he stayed back to do some work with the old man and didn't leave until after nine."

Hackney nodded as he wrote. That accorded with what Bruckmann had told him during their interview earlier. The blond lieutenant hadn't even made it halfway to the pub before the klaxon went off, taking shelter in a drainage ditch and returning to Margeaux Hall when the waves of bombers eased. And during the second murder, he'd been in company the entire day.

Tanyon continued. "Miss Harriet went to the dance with Sally Owen—she's the housemaid here—and the Alcocks, butler and cook, joined me. I don't know about Peter Owen, the gardener, but the Wainwrights were in their rooms in the old gatehouse. Alcock and I cracked a window for air, making sure no light showed, but when the wind blew the right way and the music was soft, we could hear them yelling at each other something fierce."

"That happen often?" Hackney asked.

"Seems like every night, recently."

He definitely made a note of that. "And Major and Miss Stoner?"

"Miss Stoner said she was too tired for dancing, even for the war effort. So she and Mr. Stoner went to Woodrow when Lieutenant Bruckmann left for town." Tanyon rubbed his jaw again, his dark bristles rasping. "I'm not sure she likes that music, you know? Miss Harriet used to put flowers in her hair and dance all over the ballroom with my boys, but I never saw Miss Stoner do it."

The ghost of Harriet, wildflowers in her hair and skirt flying, swinging about the desks to Glenn Miller and Louis Armstrong in the arms of a young soldier, lightened the dark office. But the image that replaced it was from the Patchbourne hospital morgue.

"Go on, sergeant."

Tanyon settled deeper into the sofa, his eyes losing focus as he stared at the trellis rug. "The air raid klaxon sounded at about nine thirty. I didn't think we were in much danger. I mean, Margeaux Hall's off the beaten path and nowhere near RAF Patchbourne or any other target. So I stayed where I was, listening to the show, when the Alcocks headed off to the shelter. I heard the Wainwrights arguing in the entry hall on their way downstairs, so I know they went, too. Again, I don't know about old Peter."

"Any idea what they were arguing about?" Hackney threw out the question as casually as he could.

"When they went past, she was saying something about him living in cloud cuckoo-land and being too old for such nonsense." Tanyon grinned. "She gave him what-for, she did."

"Wives do that sometimes. You a married man, sergeant?"

"I am and they do." Tanyon laughed but clipped it off short, glancing aside toward the officers. "My wife Edwina's up Kirkcudbright way, as far from the air raids as she can be, looking after the town kiddies evacuated up north. She wanted to join me when I got this billet, it being such a nice one, but I don't want to risk her down here among the bombs and right in the middle of the invasion when it happens. Besides, I can't imagine I'm going to be here long enough for that. Sooner or later, the brass will put me back into the war, and then where would she be?"

Where, indeed. Where would his own sweet Carolyn be, if the cancer hadn't taken her? "So you stayed in the ballroom when the alarm went off."

"I did. Mr. Oldfield of the local Home Guard rang, shy of ten fifteen, letting us know a parachute had been sighted. He asked if he could use my squad in the search. I told him to keep Pym and half the boys and send the other half back here. I didn't get quite half," Tanyon added ruefully. "He only sent Whiteside and Reynolds and they arrived separately, but I put them to patrolling outside the wall opposite the road and Woodrow. I alerted Mr. Wainwright to guard his household, as he's near the main gate. Then I went to Mr. Stoner, and he and Miss Stoner grabbed their shotguns and watched Woodrow, front and back, as well as their postern gate into the Hall. I took up position out near the road, halfway between Glover at our gate and Mr. Wainwright at the main one. When Lieutenant Bruckmann returned, he took over at our gate and Glover moved back to join Whiteside and Reynolds." He shrugged. "It's been a while since I stood sentry duty. Man winds up doing all sorts of odd jobs on these little posts."

"So there are three gates into Margeaux Hall?"

"That's right—the main entrance, near the gatehouse where the Wainwrights are staying; our own entry, where we keep a sentry posted at all times; and the little postern gate to Woodrow."

"How long were you out there standing guard?"

"All night." Tanyon shrugged again. "I patrolled and made rounds, taking reports from all positions, until Miss Stoner ran up at dawn saying she'd caught a German. I whistled for Glover and Whiteside, and ran to help."

Hackney paused. Perhaps a stroke of luck for his investigation, buried among the sergeant's recital. "So if you made rounds of your sentry posts, you can account for everyone you mentioned between ten thirty Saturday night and dawn Sunday."

"That's right." But then Tanyon paused. "Well."

It figured. "Tell me."

"Carmichael," Tanyon said. "It's these young soldiers we've got, see. They're conscripts with maybe six, eight weeks of training, they barely know how to march and shoot, and I haven't had time enough to work them into a proper unit. They don't understand some things, like how important it is not to leave your duty post."

"That's pretty basic, sergeant."

"Well, I'm going to *basic* Carmichael if I catch him away from his post again. He's our secondary radioman and that's one of our most important positions, but he's snuck away twice I know of. I've given him *basic* both times, once today, so he'd better have the idea now." Tanyon sighed. "On Saturday night, I didn't go inside and check on him. I stopped at the Hall's garage twice, used the lorry's radio to call, and he answered both times. But he might still have snuck away in between and I wouldn't know."

Hackney wrote it all down. Behind him, Stoner murmured to Bruckmann but their words were indistinguishable. Good; whatever they were working on, he didn't need to hear. "And today?"

"Today was a fiasco from start to finish. That German, Major Faust, he's determined to cause as much trouble as he can and he's got a mouth on him that won't quit. I know when he graduated from basic training, there was a sergeant out there blessing the day."

Tanyon described the day's cockeyed events. Hackney grimaced as he scribbled. Fiasco was an appropriate term and Tanyon was lucky Stoner was a forgiving commander; many a sergeant had been broken for lesser evils.

"Faust made some crack about walking from the station to the Hall and I wish we had. I could have tied his hands, sling be blowed, and gagged him, too. Instead, when the car stalled outside Mrs. Alcock's chicken farm, he punched Norris and ducked out before I could set the brake. I saw him jump the wall into her property and heard the birds set up a rumpus, but by the time I got there I couldn't see him anywhere. I should have stopped then and taken a good look about, but I figured he could only be a few seconds ahead of me and so I ran into the chicken runs looking for him. I only stopped to take back the gunbelt and send Norris to the Hall for help. Suddenly I realized the birds weren't fussing, except at me, so I stopped then and looked around, and there he was, in the turnip field on the other side of the road, running for the Dark. That's when I knocked on Mrs. Alcock's door, interrupted her sweeping, and asked her to ring the Hall for me."

Hackney paused, picturing the events in his mind. "How long do you think your German was in Mrs. Alcock's farm?"

"About five seconds, and no more."

Meaning those would be his bootprints out by the wall, near the road. Hackney pretended skepticism. "Had to be longer."

"No, sir." Tanyon shook his head. "You've been to the chicken farm? You saw Jerome Owen's turnip field? Well, I was among those birds for maybe a minute, then I saw him all the way on the other side of that field and running like hell. He stopped just before he would have stood out against the horizon and turned around, looking back at me, then he vanished into the Dark as I knocked on Mrs. Alcock's door."

"He could have crossed back over."

But Tanyon shook his head again. "Soon as I knew Mrs. Alcock would relay the message, I ran up the road to the top of the big rise, where I could see the road for a mile either way. That bottled him up south of me. If he'd crossed the road, I'd have seen him. He didn't cross."

It was too early to scratch anyone from the suspect list. But if Tanyon spoke the truth, he and the German were sliding down the ranks fast.

Hackney leaned forward. "Now, think carefully. Of all the men participating in the search today, which can you speak for? If you had to go under oath in court, which men could you swear never snuck off, even for a moment?"

"To swear to?" Tanyon paused, his lower lip jutting. "I could swear to Lieutenant Bruckmann. Whenever I glanced left, I could see that nearly white hair of his shining in the sun. He's got this trick of removing his cap and smoothing his hair back, and I could see him clear as anything. But I don't think I could swear to anyone else. Our own soldiers were spread out among Major Kettering's men, and I don't know any of them to speak to."

Hackney sighed. Bruckmann had been able to swear to Tanyon, but Pym hadn't known any of the engineering soldiers surrounding him and had shrugged at the question. "Right, sergeant, appreciate your help. I'll see Mr. Wainwright next."

In contrast to Tanyon's reassuring bulk, Wainwright

seemed insubstantial, a slender wiry man in his late thirties with sandy hair curling in wisps above his ears and a mustache not worth cultivating. His eyes, a watery green in the dim light, glanced about as if he'd never seen the room before, not stopping on any object, including Hackney, for any length of time.

"Tell me about Saturday night." Hackney tried to keep his voice level despite the shivery pricking in his thumbs. There was something about this man that put him on guard. But he wasn't certain what.

Wainwright shrugged. "The air raid alarm went off about nine thirty and the wife and I went down into the shelter. Not long after ten, Sergeant Tanyon came in and said a German plane had been shot down. I guarded the main gate all night, even though the damned thing's rusted shut and couldn't be opened if it had to be."

"What were you doing before the alarm?"

"Probably reading the paper." Wainwright snapped his fingers. "No, I'm wrong. I was practicing field-stripping my rifle. I've been assigned a Browning through the Home Guard." Pride and excitement rippled across his expression. "It's just an American gun, of course, but I'm going to work at it until I've gotten it down, just as if it were a Lee Enfield."

Egads; armed with a rifle and fighting with his wife. "That American gun can do a lot of damage and I wouldn't write it off so lightly. What were you and your wife arguing over?" When Wainwright looked away, scowling, Hackney added, "Word like that gets about, you know."

"Gossip, you mean." Wainwright's anger flashed but quickly vanished. "Yes, we fight. Maggie doesn't like it out here and wants to go back to London, where all her friends are."

"Where all the bombs are, you mean."

"That's what I've been telling her. She says they have shelters in London, too, and it's not so bad." Wainwright leaned forward. "But I've lived in London all my life and I'm ready for a change. We can contribute something to the war effort out here, something real that will make a difference, and I can work with the Home Guard and become something besides a bloody useless advertising clerk, hiding behind a desk."

Hackney measured the earnestness in Wainwright's face. Too young for the first war, too old for this one, eager for glory and feeling his life pass without counting for anything. It was a dangerous combination, with or without a rifle. It could have spilled over.

"So you guarded the front gate all night."

Wainwright rolled his eyes.

"That's the sort of thing soldiers do, you know."

"Well, I didn't leave my post." Wainwright rumpled then smoothed his hair, eyes on the trellis rug. "Sergeant Tanyon came by several times to check and I reported all clear each time. Then when the enemy did arrive, it was Miss Stoner who got him." He sighed. "I'd have gotten him, I would."

"Now tell me about today."

He shrugged. "Not a lot to tell. When Lieutenant Bruckmann was leaving to search for the German officer, I volunteered to go with him, but he said someone had to stay here. So I stayed and signed off on invoices, as a bloody useless clerk does."

"Miss Stoner said you walked to Patchley Abbey."

"That's right." Wainwright snapped his fingers again. "We were out of carbon paper and she had Major Stoner's notes to type. So I walked to town and fetched some from the mercantile."

It seemed unlikely he'd actually forgotten. "What route did you take?"

"There's only one, along the road past the Dark and the chicken farm, unless you want to cut across fields and get your boots dirty."

Hackney wrote slowly. His nerves quivered at Wainwright's casual knowledge of available back ways. "What time was this?"

"Don't quite remember. It's a twenty, thirty minute walk to town and I left here about ten thirty, I think. But I'm not sure."

"And what did you see?" Time slowed around Hackney, every moment pressing upon his memory and etching itself there with acid. His instincts, honed by decades of police work, sounded a warning klaxon in his subconscious. Sometimes it turned out to be this simple.

But at the question, Wainwright met his gaze. "I saw a line of trucks, six of them, parked along the road in front of the chicken farm, with our lorry and the vicar's old clunker. A couple of soldiers guarded the trucks and Pamela Alcock stood on her front porch, staring about as if she'd never seen such doings." He grinned. "It was sort of funny, actually."

Raw anger surged. "Her daughter was inside, being butchered. I wouldn't call it funny. Did either the soldiers or Mrs. Alcock see you pass by?"

"I talked with the soldiers." Wainwright's words came in a rush, as if speed could overcome his *faux pas*. "I asked them where everyone was, and they said out searching for the

German."

"And when you returned from town, were they still there?"

He nodded. "The whole trip took about an hour, and the search lasted well into the afternoon."

"So you were back here about eleven thirty?"

Wainwright shrugged. "Something like that."

The intensity of Hackney's internal klaxon eased. But a low hum still vibrated in the back of his soul. Dr. Harris said Grace had died around noon or twelve thirty, but estimating time of death was notoriously chancy and even experienced forensic experts refused to cast such estimates in stone. If Dr. Harris was off by even half an hour and she died nearer eleven thirty, then Wainwright could have killed her, run through the Dark, and arrived back in time to believably claim the alibi. Unless Jennifer remembered the precise time he'd arrived back—and Arnussen, who'd spoken with her, said she hadn't—no one could prove otherwise.

Nothing, then, had changed. He still needed more evidence. But his instincts were trying to tell him something and he needed to figure out what.

There was something about this insubstantial man he didn't like. Or trust.

"Is there anything else you want to mention?" he asked as a final fishing expedition.

To his surprise, Wainwright nodded. "I don't know if this means anything, but when I reached the mercantile in Patchley Abbey, the grocer—that's Tom Burbank—well, he wasn't there. His wife Debbie was running the store and the switchboard both."

"Did she say where he was?"

"Catching a nap." Wainwright clearly didn't believe that one. He rose. "And Dr. Harris wanted a word when we were done." He hesitated. "Are we done?"

"Yes, thank you." Hackney scribbled the last of his longhand notes. When he finished, Dr. Harris stood before him, a white smock over his rumpled grey suit, tie loosened and top button undone.

He held out a manila file. "I wish I could offer service with a smile but I simply don't have it in me tonight. Two autopsy reports and all the photos, both from the crime scene and points of contention—I won't say interest—from the autopsies."

"I can't thank you enough for your assistance, doctor." Hackney accepted the file and waved him to a seat. "Do you have a moment?"

"I can spare a few in exchange for a spot of rest." Dr. Harris slumped back as if for a nap. "Please tell me this is only to ask questions and not a request for additional assistance."

"Actually—"

"Damn."

"—it's both."

Dr. Harris rubbed his high forehead. The skin beneath his eyes was red and puffy. Although Hackney couldn't be certain in the dim light, the whites of his eyes seemed dark. "Better request first before I fall asleep."

"I need blood typing done for the German prisoner and for Mr. Wainwright. I assume you know your own blood type?"

"O positive, secretor. I'm happy to give your lads a sample."

"I hope that won't be necessary." Hackney made a note. "The other two?"

"My nurse will draw them tonight and the Patchbourne technicians can process them tomorrow." Dr. Harris glanced up. "Will that serve?"

"Perfectly. Now can you tell me your movements on Saturday night?"

"I was at the dance, playing my horn along with the gramophone for the entertainment of our gallant troops, when the air raid alarm sounded. My service position is at the Patchbourne hospital so there I went, feeling my way through the dark of the night without a decent driving lamp, braving the dastardly German bombers overhead—"

"Doctor, are you drunk?"

Dr. Harris rubbed his forehead again. "Slightly." A tinge of color climbed his cheeks. "I'm sorry. I hate autopsies, especially on someone I knew and adored. In some ways Grace was the daughter I never had."

"You should have said something." Dr. Harris had stroked Grace's dark hair, volunteered any help he could give. "Someone else could have done that."

"Of course. But I have no means of knowing whether said someone would be as motivated and therefore as thorough." Dr. Harris sat up straighter. "I reported for duty at the Patchbourne hospital at nine forty on Saturday night and was there, assisting with the bombing casualties, until seven the following morning, at which time I came here and stitched up one German prisoner of war. I then found an empty bed and collapsed thereon."

Hackney paused with his pencil poised. "Not therein?"

Dr. Harris smiled wryly. "I didn't bother. Next question?"

"Same for today."

"And it was the same. My duty shift at the Patchbourne hospital officially starts at eight sharp and is supposedly over at five ditto, but in actuality it varies according to the needs of the day. If the clinic isn't busy, I sometimes leave early and check on any patients I may have at the airfield, in the village, or here at Margeaux Hall. Because I carry a small transmitter-receiver in my sidecar, running off the motorcycle's battery, I can gambol about in that irresponsible manner and still be brought to heel should a patient require my services.

"Today was such a day. The clinic was duller than boiled cabbage, even after Saturday night's air raid, so about ten I left it in the care of my esteemed colleagues and performed the final autopsy on Harriet. I then came here to check on the abovementioned German prisoner, who underwent minor surgery yesterday evening and had no business running about the countryside putting himself at risk today. Therefore, I was here when the first reports arrived, although he was not, and I was able to meet you at the farm within minutes of the alarm being sounded."

Hackney wrote it all down. "Where were you at noon today?"

"In the morgue."

He glanced up. A shadow haunted Dr. Harris' eyes. "I assume that can be confirmed?"

"By several people, including two lab technicians and my nurse. The session was also recorded for posterity."

If that were verified, Dr. Harris could be the first man removed from the suspect list. Hackney sighed with relief. The man's grief was utterly believable, which meant one down, over two hundred to go. "Thank you, sir. You may now find some well-earned rest."

Dr. Harris promptly rose. "I think I'll finish the bottle first. Should you wish to join me, I'll be in the infirmary on the first floor. Anyone can direct you."

As Dr. Harris left, Hackney grabbed the roll of ordinance survey maps, obtained from Constable Mercer, from beside his chair. As he approached the desk, the two officers glanced up, Stoner flipping over the papers before him and Bruckmann placing his palm atop his notepad. Hackney stood before them, resting the end of the maps atop the desk and feeling the room's quiet seep into his bones.

"Your German prisoner sounds an interesting man."

Stoner's lips curved. "I assure you, whatever you've heard tonight falls short of the truth."

Hackney nodded. "Perhaps it's time I met him for myself."

32

the same evening
Margeaux Hall

Supper was lukewarm watery bland vegetable soup, mostly cabbage, with dry bread. Faust forced it down without too much gagging, left the dirty dishes on the little table by the cell bars, and settled cross-legged on the cot. One-handed, he draped the blanket across his naked shoulders and lit a cigarette; it seemed a fitting symbol for his still smoldering temper. Besides, there was nothing else to do. Behind the radio, Carmichael sat with his back to him, reading a newspaper beneath the table lamp. Otherwise, the room was empty.

Before he finished the fag, Tanyon returned, grey cloth folded neatly over one arm. He dropped Faust's uniform through the bars onto the chair, rumpling it, and tossed the boots onto the floor.

"Get dressed."

Like hell. He eyed Tanyon through the drifting smoke and took another drag.

"Or I'll haul you downstairs as you are. Miss Stoner's gone home, but Mrs. Wainwright is still working. Of course, she's married, so she might not care. But then, she and her man fight all the time, so she just might."

Carmichael had tugged the headphones off one ear. He chortled. "Do it, sergeant. I dare you."

Night had fallen and the blackout drapes were tugged over the guardroom's lone window. Only the small lamp atop the radio table was lit, throwing its circle across the lower part of Carmichael's face and Tanyon's torso. The larger floor lamp by the rifles was switched off and the remainder of the guard-room took cover behind the shadows lining the walls. Faust knew he was visible only as an outline with a glowing cigarette.

He dragged again. He had one puff left and it was more important than Tanyon. "Mr. Stoner might not approve."

"Don't bet on it."

So Stoner really had authorized Tanyon to use whatever means he considered appropriate. Faust breathed smoke. The earlier tension had dissipated, the audience of young soldiers had vanished, and he knew he had some leeway.

"Face it, mate," Tanyon said. "You have to deal with me."

He took the last drag, held the smoke in as long as he could, stubbed the end out on the metal bedstead, and tossed the butt down the open end of the vertical pipe that supported the springs, the only ashtray available. "Trust me, *Sergeant*," he said with the last of the smoke, "I'm going to."

But he rose before Tanyon actually reached for a rifle, shrugged from the sling, and slipped his mouse-grey shirt over his head. It was clammy, stuck to his skin, and caught on the stiff bandages, but it finally smelled clean. "Is this the pattern? I strip to get into the cell and dress to get out of it?"

"Something like that." Tanyon leaned back against the radio table and stared off into space. "It's the detective from Scotland Yard. He's talked with the rest of us. Now it's your turn."

He buttoned the shirt in silence. Without looking at Tanyon, he asked, "What did you tell him?"

He felt Tanyon's glance like a bullet grazing his skin but pulled on his damp trousers without looking, wishing for his suspenders. Sooner or later their absence was going to cause a scene in the ballroom, whether Tanyon hauled him around in his shorts or not. He could live without that particular exper-ience.

"The truth," Tanyon finally said. "Expect me to lie?"

He picked up his tunic, also clean and damp but with the back still unmended, and glanced over. For a bare second his gaze crossed Tanyon's. Understanding deepened the dark eyes within the deadpan face. Faust whipped aside as if scalded, and didn't need to look to know Tanyon did the same.

This wasn't the relationship he'd have chosen. But it was something. It did include a measure of trust. And revenge would still be juicy. He finished dressing without another word and let Tanyon escort him from the guardroom.

In the corridor, though, he paused. "Lavatory first?"

Tanyon looked at him.

He looked back. "I'm not gonna clean it up."

"Next to the infirmary. Leave the door open."

He complied but took a good look about while he did his business. As he had suspected, the window wasn't barred, only fastened with blackout shutters. He didn't let himself think too much; his elation would show on his face and Tanyon would see it. He just washed his hands and filed the information away. He'd work on a plan later. It would be more entertaining than staring at Carmichael's back.

Most of Stoner's crew seemed to be off duty. He glimpsed Pym and Cavanaugh playing billiards in the little room beside Stoner's office, Whiteside tossing darts and Ellington staring off into space, lips moving. Peckham, Reynolds, and Glover clustered about the radio as the alto singer from Charlie Barnet's band warbled *Good For Nothing Joe*. Someone snickered as he and Tanyon passed by.

Alone in the work area, Mrs. Wainwright typed away. All the drapes were drawn and few lamps burned in the ballroom; the one on her desk illuminated only the bottom half of her face, spotlighting a clenched jaw.

In the airy blue sitting room, Stoner and Bruckmann awaited him with the walrus he'd seen earlier. The stout stranger rose from one of the wingback chairs before the desk, watching Faust's approach with small dark eyes that didn't seem to need to blink. The blackout drapes were drawn here, too, and only the desk lamp was lit, leaving the corners dim and secret.

Behind the desk, for once paper-strewn, Stoner rose, as well. He still looked tired, but a gleam of something intense percolated beneath the age lines and papery skin, setting a warning klaxon clanging in Faust's soul. Whatever it was, it wouldn't do him any good at all.

He brought his heels together. "Mr. Stoner."

"*Herr Major.*" Stoner inclined his head, eyes keen.

No, he hadn't imagined it. The old warrior had a counter-attack underway. Faust sighed, the stitches in his side tugging. He had more than an escape plan to think through.

"This is Chief Inspector Hackney. He is investigating the murders and requests your cooperation. Chief Inspector, this is Major Hans-Joachim Faust."

Bruckmann, pencil ready, started writing.

"How do you do," Faust said. "I didn't kill anyone."

Hackney cocked his head. "Whatever he just called you, I can't pronounce it."

Faust paused. There was a sense of solidity about Hackney, like a force that wouldn't be budged before it was ready, and although his eyes were closely set, they were clever. "My name is Faust. The important part of what he said translates as major."

"Major Faust. That I can manage." Hackney looked openly at the sling. "Hurt bad?"

"Not really." Although it had hurt like hell since his tumble in the ravine.

The sharp brown gaze rose to meet his, a casual movement that didn't seem random. "Will it bear weight?"

The sensation of solidity strengthened. Chief Inspector Hackney knew what he wanted to learn, would make his own judgments, and wouldn't be distracted or forced. Faust answered honestly. "I can't lift the elbow from my side. Whether that's because it won't bear the weight of the arm itself, or because of a limited range of motion from the muscle's injury, I don't know."

"I see." Hackney leaned his head back and looked at Faust for a long considering moment, then laid a hand on the papers atop the desk. "Can you read this map?"

He stepped closer. What he'd taken for papers were actually unrolled topographic maps layered one atop the other. With his left index finger, he traced a contour line until he came to the elevation notation. The line on one side was marked with a higher number, the line on the other side with a lower one. "All right, that's uphill and downhill. This is a river?"

"The Patch," Stoner said. "Little more than a stream."

Likely the chattering one he'd followed his first night in England. "And here's Margeaux Hall and Woodrow." He touched their positions. "And this is the forested area, the Dark? Yes, I can read it."

"Good," Hackney said, "then show me where you went and what you did on Saturday night."

"After I landed?" His split lower lip hurt, and he realized he was chewing it. "I'm afraid that's not as easy as it sounds."

Stoner leaned over the map and drew a small cross in the upper left quadrant with a red pencil. "Will it help orient you if I say a torn and blood-stained parachute was found approximately here?"

"Yes, it does." He traced the distance between his landing point and Woodrow, and glanced at the scale reference. "I didn't get very far, did I?"

"Perhaps it's best to remember you were injured," Stoner said.

Was that sympathy he heard? Surprised, he glanced up. Stoner's eyes were grave and without challenge. A truce had been called, it seemed, for the duration of the investigation if not the war. It was a reassuring thought, but still, Bruckmann was taking notes of the conversation.

He turned back to Hackney. "Please understand. I hadn't slept Friday night and walked all through Saturday night. I left my watch in France, I'm not a good judge of time, I'd been thrown from the plane, and I was disoriented. I'd also hit the back of my head and was dizzy. I knew I was bleeding but didn't know how bad it was. And I may as well mention I was scared out of my wits. I didn't stop to look for landmarks. I decided to head southeast and didn't stop moving until I was caught."

"Which Mr. Stoner says was about dawn?"

"About that." He bent over the map again.

"So you took all night to travel less than twelve miles?"

There was something in Hackney's tone, not quite skepticism but nothing near belief, that made him pause. "I just explained the circumstances."

Hackney didn't shift. His shrewd gaze, measuring and assessing, made Faust straighten.

"All right," Hackney finally said. "Why did you decide to head southeast? That's straight for Margeaux Hall."

Behind the desk, Stoner froze.

Faust ducked his head, found the line of the forest on the map, and traced it south past the road. The Dark extended off the edge of the paper, leaving unanswered the question of just how far it could take him. "We're starting to get into my escape plan, which is sort of a military matter."

Hackney leaned onto the map beside him, his big splayed hand atop the Dark, and treated him to another level stare. "You say you didn't kill anyone and I'm trying to find ways to corroborate your statement. But you have to meet me halfway."

He paused. Hackney seemed trustworthy enough. But Stoner listened, impassive, and Bruckmann's pencil hadn't yet paused.

"I can't do anything about them," Hackney said. "You must decide."

Stoner's keen blue stare didn't waver. Surely he wanted his granddaughter's murderer caught, but he wouldn't jeopardize his duty to assist the process. Hackney was right: cooperation couldn't be a half-hearted venture—which meant everyone was still beating him.

"I knew the Thames was somewhere south of me but I didn't know precisely where. I didn't think I was physically capable of swimming or fording it and knew I couldn't talk my way across a guarded bridge in a German uniform. I didn't want to stumble into a populated area, like downtown Oxford, or into commercial shipping lanes. I didn't want to head so far north I wound up in really cold water and could see no reason to head west. So my choice of directions was sort of limited."

Bruckmann's pencil flew.

"All right, that's clear." Hackney touched the red mark Stoner had drawn on the map. "So you went southeast from here?"

"Roughly, yes. This field slopes to the east and southeast, so I went downhill, exited at the far end, fell over this little cliff in the dark, then followed the Patch downstream." He shifted off his hand and traced the path, from the map's upper left quadrant angling down to where he and Hackney leaned. "When it curved off to the east here, I continued southeast, but then the moon went behind the clouds and I got lost. I don't know where I went. At some point, probably around here, I found the Dark and followed it south, because it was better than running headfirst into a farmhouse or something. Just after dawn, I stumbled out of the Dark about here and Miss Stoner charmed me with her shotgun."

"When you were lost, did you see any houses?" Hackney asked.

He told the honest truth. "That bloody blackout works. I didn't even see the ground most of the time."

"Did you hear any dogs barking? Hear chickens in passing, or cows, or anything of that sort?"

He shook his head. "I never saw or heard the chickens until today."

"You right handed?"

"Um, yes."

Hackney picked up the red pencil Stoner had set aside and handed it to him. "Can you trace your path on the map? When you're not certain, use a dotted line."

When he'd finished, sketching across the thick paper in awkward left-handed strokes, Hackney swapped it for a green pencil. "Now trace in the line from your escape today and tell me about it, too. Start at the car."

With his finger, he traced the road from Margeaux Hall back toward Patchley Abbey, traveling slowly past the Dark and pausing on the far side, where the map showed a small cluster of buildings. "This is the chicken farm?"

"Yes," Stoner said.

On the other side of the road, the field he'd crossed rose and fell in waves, the contour lines closely spaced and rippling toward the southern half of the Dark. He pointed at a spot on the road. "The car stalled out around here." He told them about taking advantage of Tanyon's distraction and Norris' inexperience. With any luck, Stoner would give his sergeant an earful later.

"I jumped over the wall into the chicken farm and threw some pebbles over the birds to make them squawk, then moved to a position opposite the front of the car. When I heard the driver's door open, I rolled back over the wall and crossed the road ahead of the car while the sergeant got out and ran around the back of it. Then I just went over the other wall, here on the far side of the road. I followed it to about here, then took off across the turnips."

Something he said hit home with Hackney. The grave, assessing stare melted at the edges into something a few degrees warmer, not trusting but no longer so distant, and that had to be good. Faust told them of his hurried journey through the southern half of the Dark, flipping to the next map in the pile and shoving the top one aside, finally finding and marking the ravine that had sheltered him, much further south than he thought he'd been. "And they caught me there."

Hackney nodded and gathered his maps. "I have three more things to ask of you. Firstly, I need to borrow your boots."

He blinked. "My boots?"

Hackney didn't glance up, eyes narrowed at the maps he rolled.

"May I ask why?"

"We found some footprints about the chicken farm." He fastened the maps with twine. "I need to have plaster casts made of the soles of your boots to figure out which of them is yours."

He hadn't gone anywhere near the farmhouse, so this was evidence that could possibly clear him. But he'd need his boots to escape. If he lent them to Hackney, there was no telling when he'd get them back.

"Unless you have something planned, *Herr Major,*" Stoner said, "you won't be going outside for a while and the floors are warm enough within."

He sat down and fumbled with the knots, angry heat in his face. The question was, could he outwit Saint George over there while waiting?

"Appreciate it," Hackney said. "Secondly, would you be willing to volunteer a blood sample?"

He tugged off his left boot. "Again, may I ask why?"

"The killer left traces of himself."

"Near the victim?"

"Inside her."

He froze. Anger glinted within Hackney's close-set brown eyes and his jaw seemed welded shut. "Oh. And that tells you something?"

"Some years back, the science boys learned that a person's blood type can sometimes be determined from his other bodily fluids. Do you know your blood type?"

He fumbled with the knot on his right boot. "I think it's O."

"Positive? Negative?"

"I don't know."

"Secretor?"

"I don't know what that means." He handed both boots to Hackney.

The detective tugged a brown paper bag from his coat pocket, dropped the boots into it, and rolled the top down. "The sample? It can't convict you but it might clear you."

"All right."

"And lastly, of course, I'll need to take your fingerprints."

"All right."

He had to stoop and twist to keep his right elbow clamped to his side while Hackney rolled his fingers first on an ink pad, then on a white card divided into ten little squares. As each square was filled with swirling inky lines, surprisingly unsmudged, it bared his soul ever more deeply, this time at a coldly scientific level he couldn't fight. With his fingerprints, and his blood, and his bootprints all filed away, he might never feel comfortable in England again.

When it was over, he straightened and stared at his inky hands. They looked awful, as if he'd leave his fingerprints all over the Hall.

Hackney froze. "No handkerchief?"

"I had one when I arrived, but I lost it somewhere. I haven't seen it since I was captured."

"Actually, it was taken from you on Sunday morning." Stoner rose and handed Faust his own. "It will be returned to you, along with your identification and other belongings, when you leave this establishment."

The little square of white linen was already smeared. Surprised, Faust glanced up. Stoner's hands were also black-ened at the tips. So were Bruckmann's and so, he realized for the first time, were Tanyon's.

"We have to take everyone's fingerprints," Hackney said.

"Oh." His wiping didn't seem to remove much ink from his fingers, but at least he might not leave visible evidence of himself wherever he went. He sighed, the stitches in his side tugging. At least he wasn't the only one looking grubby. "I suppose I don't know much about all this."

"Point in your favor." Hackney wasn't quite smiling, but his lips stretched across his face and his eyes crinkled at the corners. "As the criminals do tend to know these things, often from past experience."

"Oh." He returned the no-longer-white linen to Stoner with murmured thanks. "If there's anything else I can do, please let me know."

Hackney's suspicious face didn't seem capable of beaming, but he at least smiled. "I will." He turned to Stoner. "What we discussed earlier—"

"Yes," Stoner said, his chin lowering.

"—seems a better idea than ever."

"I have implemented it."

"Then I'll be going."

Bruckmann set aside his pencil and half rose.

"No, don't bother, your soldiers can see me off. Gentlemen." Hackney nodded to Stoner and Bruckmann, then aside to Faust, and left with the rolled maps beneath one arm and the paper bag of boots in his hand.

As the door closed behind him, Stoner sank into his chair, his shoulders drooping and his head turning aside. Faust waited, but the old man seemed to have forgotten his presence, staring at the photo frame on his desk as if it was the only important item in the room. With Bruckmann's pencil stilled, silence enveloped them. It was the silence of the countryside, without all the background city noises of vehicles and people and machinery, and it was so deep and penetrating, it wrapped itself about Faust like a second skin, closer than his uniform, and pressed against him with its weight. He glanced at Bruckmann, immersed in reading his notes, and then at Tanyon, who looked back without a flicker of emotion. The silence made him shift his feet, but intruding on the old man's grief seemed even uglier.

Finally Stoner sighed. "I'm afraid my heart isn't in our little game tonight, *Herr Major*."

Faust perched on the edge of the wing chair. "I suppose I should be grateful."

Stoner turned to face him. The motion was slow and creaky, as an old man might move, and his focus seemed distant. Faust plumbed the depths of sorrow in Stoner's eyes and couldn't repress his sympathy. If he was being hoisted again, then the old man was an actor of the highest caliber.

"I suppose I should take advantage of your cooperative mood tonight and press the attack home." Stoner looked down at his inky hands. "But it simply doesn't seem to matter. My superior shall be quite upset with me."

"Only if he's inhuman." The weight of that silence, or the weight of something else, remained beneath their words, as uncomfortable as ever.

Again Stoner glanced up. This time a bare shadow of mirth glimmered within him. "I assure you."

"So I'm not the only one with a lousy boss?" Faust could bear that weight no longer. He leaned forward. "I'm really sorry about your granddaughter, Mr. Stoner. But I didn't kill her."

The old man's expression focused and hardened, as if his anger had been waiting in the room's shadowy corners for some such indiscreet words. Faust's breath caught; despite their bantering, the underlying tension remained, camouflaged by the silence and as tempestuous as ever. He had to keep reminding himself that he couldn't trust this man, no matter how charming he seemed, nor how grieving.

But Stoner's anger faded before Faust could respond, and the grief flooded back. He picked up Harriet's photo, lamplight sliding along the edge of the frame like silver fire, and settled it in his lap, as usual keeping her image to himself. "They won't tell me, you know." His voice sounded small and tired.

Behind Stoner, Bruckmann shot a glance at his boss, then returned to his notes. But he no longer flipped the pages.

"I don't understand," Faust said.

Stoner leaned his head against his chair back and draped one arm about the frame, cupping it in a loose hug with his index finger stroking the curlicued corner. "What happened to her. They won't tell me."

Personally, he wasn't certain he'd want to know. Across the desk, Stoner's focus sharpened, his chin tilting, and Faust knew his reaction had been appropriately read. But instead of renewed rage, Stoner smiled thinly.

"I believe the not-knowing is worse than any possible knowing."

It was a blunt and honest opinion, cutting through the tension and across their desktop battlefield, and it was the most candid thing he'd yet heard the old man say. His next breath came easier. There was some sort of understanding here, in the uncertain relationship they'd hammered out in this sitting room-combat zone, something similar to the argumentative, wary trust he'd found with Tanyon.

"I wish there was something I could do." It was the simple truth.

The ghost of a smile crossed Stoner's narrow lips and his

eyes were grateful. "Good night."

Faust was reaching for the doorknob, Tanyon behind him, when the now expected interruption occurred.

"*Herr Major.*"

The old geezer timed it so well. Faust turned.

Stoner's face was again inscrutable, the moment past. "Thank you for your assistance tonight."

"You're welcome. But don't expect it on a regular basis."

Again the ghostly half-smile, this time accompanied by a glimmer of mirth. "Perhaps not. Good night."

33

the same evening
Margeaux Hall

When the door closed behind Faust and Tanyon, Stoner permitted himself a sighing, unguarded moment with his eyes closed. There were people out there in the wide world, he knew, who considered everyday reality no more than a stage for their performance, people who measured their actions based not upon what was proper and appropriate, but upon what reaction it would produce from those around them. Brigadier Marone was such a man, which was perhaps why they had such a difficult relationship. But personally, Stoner hated such duplicity and despised resorting to it.

Not that all his reactions during his brief conversation with Faust had been dishonest; far from it. He did feel grief and discouragement, and anger toward the murderer, whoever it turned out to be. That last he would have to deal with quickly; if it leaked out in another unguarded moment, it could curdle all their future interrogations.

Certainly he felt disheartened. But perhaps he didn't feel quite so disheartened as all that.

"Jack, my lad, I know you must be exhausted. But do you feel you could manage a spot of extra work tonight?"

He heard a sigh behind him, quickly stilled. "Of course, sir. It's something important, then?"

"Perhaps the most important contribution you can make to the entire interrogation."

He didn't need to look to know when Bruckmann stiffened to sitting attention behind him. Stoner smiled. Oh, to be that age again, but to retain the wisdom earned by his poor grey hairs.

"I'm ready."

He turned then. Bruckmann's eyes, in his tired face, were alive and brimful of repressed excitement.

Stoner chose his words with care. "I want you to update the regulations manuals in the guardroom tonight."

The excitement vanished as if ripped by a stout breeze. "The regulations manuals?"

Stoner smiled his gentlest smile. "I believe you'll understand my instructions perfectly when the time comes."

34

the same evening
Margeaux Hall

Cavanaugh awaited Faust at the infirmary's door and led him to the back, where blackout shutters hid those wonderful windows and provided a backdrop for the examination table. A rubber ball and tourniquet, hypodermic syringe, and glass vial were set out on a white towel atop the instrument table nearby. Cavanaugh helped him strip to the waist and wrapped the tourniquet about his left upper arm.

"Hitch a pew," he said. "You ever done this before?"

Faust scooted onto the examination table. "Oh, yes." Not to say he enjoyed it.

"Dr. Harris!"

In the doorway, Tanyon grunted. "You need supervision to draw blood?"

"A witness." Cavanaugh gave Faust the ball. "Squeeze it a few times. He has to take custody of the sample so we know it's not switched and when the police get the results, they know they're getting the right ones."

Dr. Harris appeared through the inner door. His eyes, usually cheerful and cynical, were streaked with red; either he wasn't sleeping or he was on a binge. Either way, it had to be difficult, keeping up with his usual work, attending to war casualties, and performing autopsies for the police, as well.

"Right." Dr. Harris folded his arms. "Go ahead."

Faust, busy studying Dr. Harris' face, felt the sting as Cavanaugh slid the needle into his arm. He froze and decided not to look down. At the door, the doctor shifted.

"Tell me," Dr. Harris said, "what the hell were you thinking, taking off across country the day after surgery? Did we or did we not instruct you to give your arm time to heal?"

It was an attack from an unexpected quarter and Faust flinched. "It's my duty to attempt escape."

"Right." Dr. Harris met his glare with one of his own. "Let's say, for the point of discussion, you get clean away and even make it all the way back to France. What good are you going to be to anyone with a gaping bloody hole in the back of your arm?"

His anger focused, spilled over, and Faust said the first thing that crossed his mind. "At least it would be a German doctor looking after me."

Oops. He shouldn't have said that. But he'd been taken by surprise and if the man didn't like it, he shouldn't have started the fight. Besides, he could still feel the needle in the crook of his arm.

Dr. Harris tilted his head back. Frost sparkled in his green eyes and lowered the temperature in the infirmary. "And what complaints have you to hurl at your English doctor?"

Time to backpedal. "The medical care has been good and I don't have any complaints. It's the official treatment that's a pain."

He froze again, pulse suddenly accelerating. Stoner's voice echoed in his inner ear: *The medical care I received as a prisoner was rather good. It was the overall treatment that was bad...*

Had he been hoisted again?

But Dr. Harris was still speaking. "I can't do anything about that. But nor can I do anything for your arm if you keep mucking it about."

He'd have to think later. "I was careful."

"Not careful enough. I can see blood caking your bandage from here."

The needle slid from his arm. He and Dr. Harris sighed in unison.

Cavanaugh, hypodermic in one hand and lips curving in a small smile, pressed a wad of gauze against the spot and tugged Faust's arm up. "Hold that in place for me and keep your arm above your head."

Faust glanced at his right arm, plastered against his side, then back at Cavanaugh.

"Makes it difficult, doesn't it." Dr. Harris stepped closer and took the hypo. Faust caught a powerful whiff of alcohol. "You hold that, Cavanaugh, and I'll do this—" separating the vial from the syringe and corking it "—and then we'll stitch up that bloody gaping hole—" glaring at Faust "—again."

He had to look ridiculous with his arm stuck up like a flagpole. But he was tired of taking it and clearly lack of sleep was not the doctor's problem. "Are you drunk?"

Cavanaugh's brown eyes widened and his smile vanished.

It earned him another glare. Dr. Harris dropped the red-filled vial into an envelope and sealed it. "You're the second person tonight to ask me that question and I'll give you the same answer I gave him—not drunk enough." He yanked a pen from his breast pocket, jerked the cap off with his teeth, scribbled across the envelope's seal, then recapped the pen and set it atop the counter. "However, unlike him, I am not asking you to join me for the remainder of my riotous debauchery."

But he would not flinch again, no matter how much the doctor irritated him. "I'm not begging for an invitation." The last time he got drunk was bad enough.

The ugly reminder brought another voice into the room with them, a ghostly voice speaking German and camouflaging steel within coaxing words: *"Come on, come for a ride with papa. We'll be back before dawn. No one will ever know."* But this time, the memory didn't stop there. It unrolled further, as if his internal movie projector finally unstuck. Erhard had paused there and drilled Faust with a cocky stare. *"Besides, you need to remember what we're fighting for."*

Faust shivered. If Erhard had said that, it meant—he didn't know what it meant. Something else to consider.

He quit arguing; the memory of Erhard's perfidy, along with Dr. Harris' stinging rebuke, cut too sharply. Instead, he sat still as Cavanaugh sliced the bandage from his right arm, flaked off the dried blood, and removed the old stitches. Dr. Harris didn't apologize, but he did offer two aspirin before threading his needle, and Faust made certain to thank him, both for the aspirin and for the treatment. By the time Cavanaugh tied off the fresh bandage and Tanyon straightened in the doorway, the temperature in the infirmary had risen a few degrees.

Faust carried his tunic and shirt across the hall into the shadowy guardroom and folded them one-handed atop the worktable. Carmichael still sat at the radio, headphones aslant over his ears, but Whiteside and Peckham had joined him and rose from their chairs near the rifle storage as Tanyon followed Faust into the guardroom.

"You know the drill." Tanyon settled his hands on his

hips. "Trousers."

Carmichael slewed around, grinning and ready for another show. But Faust had too much on his mind and didn't feel like obliging. He removed his trousers without arguing and folded them with the rest of his uniform on the worktable, then grabbed his sling, cigarettes, and matches and turned toward the cell. The cot was stripped, rumpled sheets and blankets lumped atop the pillow. It hadn't been when he'd left.

Tanyon and Peckham followed him through the barred gate. Whiteside stopped at the opening.

Faust paused. Something was going on. Again. "What's this? Sleeping space limited?"

Tanyon removed his web gunbelt with its holstered Webley, and handed them to Whiteside. "I don't expect you to like this. Won't enjoy it myself, but I've got my orders and you know I follow them."

"What orders?" Faust didn't move as Tanyon advanced on him. His pulse picked up speed.

"I have to search you."

His pulse revved like a gunned engine. The English hadn't done this when they'd first captured him. "The hell you do."

Tanyon's voice was quiet, excluding the young soldiers from the conversation. "It's Chief Inspector Hackney's doing. He wants to make certain you can't pick up things when you're out of the cell."

His skin was crawling and he didn't want to give in. "What things?"

"Pocket knives, things like that."

A pang of understanding deflated his first raw anger. "Was that how the two girls were killed?"

"Yep." Tanyon didn't blink. "We have to do this the hard way, too?"

Faust looked again at the cot. He hadn't left it that way; someone had searched the cell in his absence. His stomach roiled. "Just get it over with."

Tanyon pushed him to the wall in a one-armed lean, like a common criminal. Faust tried to ignore the sergeant's touch, patting him all over, sliding beneath his right arm, investigating every crease and fold beneath his shorts, even rumpling his hair, but the big rough hands were too intrusive. He fought the bile and won. But his intensifying rage would not be defeated.

Finally Tanyon stepped back. Faust straightened and steadied his breathing. Privacy lost, he thought irreverently, and privacy regained.

"Is this part of the drill, then?" His voice sounded harsher than he'd intended. "Whenever I go back into my cage, I'm searched?"

Tanyon slammed the cell door and locked it. "Hope you don't think I'm going to enjoy it. No wonder your girl threw her drink in your face."

His rage froze and solidified, and he welcomed it like an old friend, ignoring the ribald kissy noises from Peckham. "Try adding pressure next time. I've known pillows that were more fun than you." He couldn't sit, couldn't stop pacing, circling the cot. "You could at least have made the bed while you were at it."

"You two are dismissed," Tanyon said to Peckham and Whiteside. They didn't move, their grins a matched set. Tanyon ignored them, pulled the Webley from its holster, and threw the web belt into the storage compartment. "No one here is your servant. You can make your own damn' bed."

"It was made. You unmade it; you make it." He slid the sling over his head and settled his arm. It felt better. But his feet continued moving, circling him about the cell.

Tanyon made kissy sounds, too, and locked the weapons cabinet on the Webley. Carmichael curled over the radio table and howled.

"You wait, you bastard."

The sergeant paused in the doorway, Peckham and Whiteside behind him. "You're going to call me that once too often."

"And then what? You're really going to kiss me?"

"In the kisser, mate." Tanyon stalked out, voice trailing behind him. "In the kisser."

Faust grabbed the bars. "Ready when you are, darling. I'll take you any day."

But Tanyon was gone, leaving a vacuum in the room where the argument had been. Faust held onto the bars, panting, his pulse galloping in his ears. Revenge, when it came, was going to feel really good.

Carmichael sat up, his reddened face still split with a huge grin. "You want to watch it there. The sergeant's done some boxing."

Had he, now. Faust eased back. Swinging hard would be a pleasure. "So have I." He sighed. "And I still have to make the damned bed."

Surprisingly, the physical activity calmed him. When he finished, he was able to settle on the cot, crossing his legs and wrapping the blanket about his shoulders. He was more tired than he should be and it was deeper than a physical tiredness, more a sapping of his spirits or an exhaustion of the heart. He lit one of his precious cigarettes and inhaled deeply, letting the nicotine soak through his lungs and into his soul, looking at the fag as he let the smoke drift from his nostrils. This pack wasn't going to last anywhere near a month. The hell with it; when he ran out, he ran out, and that was all.

He still wasn't happy he'd had to give Stoner and Bruckmann his escape plan. They'd use the information against him, as he intended to try again as soon as he got his boots back. If, of course, he ever did. He wouldn't put it past Stoner to confiscate them. But escape was moot for now, and Erhard's last words before their flight had finally surfaced.

"Besides, you need to remember what we're fighting for."

The memory was worse than a physical blow, as if Tanyon actually had slammed a rifle butt into his stomach. Faust must have said something to Erhard to make him respond in such a way. Although Faust still couldn't push through the alcoholic fuzz and remember what they'd talked about all day long, with Erhard's words as a starting point, he could imagine a few possibilities.

Maybe Faust had said what he'd been saying since the fall of France: no matter how poorly prepared the British Expeditionary Force had seemed, when fighting for their homes the English would not be pushovers. If the German Army was going to conquer England, they'd have to grab a foothold on the island and not let themselves be pushed off, no matter how high the casualties, because the English would throw everything possible at them, from the Home Fleet to the Home Guard. There would be no second chance. Erhard, with his pride in German might and confidence in their final victory, would not like that.

Or maybe Faust had detailed the battle plan he'd been typing for the last week, the one with the gaping holes he'd tried to discuss with *Oberst* von Maacht. Maybe he'd pointed out all the reasons that plan couldn't possibly succeed and why it would lead, not to another nation subdued and conquered, but to the slaughter of the German 9th and 16th Armies. Erhard wouldn't like that, either.

Or maybe he'd repeated what he knew Erhard had heard too often in the past—how much Faust had enjoyed his year at Oxford, the intellectual freedom, challenge, stimulation, a deeper companionship than he'd ever known before. Maybe he'd said how much he missed and feared for his two closest friends, how he longed for the war to be over so he could get news of them. Erhard, eager for glory and promotion which would only come with the war's continuation, would resent that.

Maybe he'd spoken of gentle Siegi, so guileless and unprepared for the harsh reality of a cynical world. Maybe he'd reminded Erhard how Siegi's death might have been an accident while cleaning his P-38, how it might have been suicide—or how it might have been murder, committed by one of those men Siegi had seen doing something so unutterable it couldn't be forgotten by day or night. Erhard, who had been closer to Siegi than to any of the others in the orphanage, protecting him from some of those harsh realities he hadn't been equipped to handle, wouldn't like that, either.

Maybe he'd poured out his problems with Ritzi, how the eye-popping sex couldn't make up for her insistence he'd join the Nazi Party if he loved her. Erhard, who'd never kept a girl for more than a month, wouldn't understand that at all.

Maybe he'd said he couldn't remember what they were fighting for because he'd never known what that was. But Erhard, with his disdain for deeper meanings, wouldn't give that a moment's thought.

Maybe he'd said it all, all day long, over and over. If so, Erhard hadn't liked any of it.

His stomach twisted. The cabbage soup would be even less appealing if he sprayed it all over the floor. He glanced about, but Tanyon hadn't thought to provide a bucket. Well, all he could do was his best. If he made a mess, he was aiming it outside of the bars and he wasn't cleaning it up.

He pictured that day in Le Havre so easily. Erhard could always be patient when it got him something, so he'd sit back with the understanding expression he feigned better than any actor, pass the bottle or fill the glass, and let Faust talk, and talk, and talk. Naive as usual, gullible and grateful for someone to listen, Faust would have poured it all out—and without thinking through the consequences, he must have laid his soul bare before the man he should have known would understand the least.

So Erhard had let him talk, and nodded, and looked compassionate, and helped him get so drunk he couldn't even remember what had happened. Then he'd taken Faust along on his bombing run, only offering the one subtle hint of what he'd intended—*you need to remember what we're fighting for*—waited until the thrumming of the engines had lulled him to sleep, strapped him into a parachute, and threw him out as close to Oxford as his flight plan allowed. And Faust wouldn't remember any of that, either, if he hadn't awakened when the opening parachute had brushed across his face.

He could even imagine what Erhard had yelled from the

bomber's belly hatch as he braced against the coaming, one hand cupped about his mouth and a huge grin splitting his face, one short little phrase that summed it all up. *"Tell them about it."*

It hadn't been his idea to bail out over England. He wasn't a traitor or deserter. No, it had been Erhard's final joke, and he'd paid for it with his life when his copilot had watched Faust being tossed out rather than his instruments. He'd crashed their Heinkel into its wingmate. Faust knew he'd be paying for the joke a lot longer—

—because he had Stoner to deal with.

What was Stoner up to? When Faust had first entered his office that evening, the old man had shown definite signs of excitement—the gleam in his eyes, the tilt of his chin, the touch of a smile. It had faded as the not-knowing of his granddaughter's murder dragged him down. But there'd been a glimmering spark, screened but not hidden, and tomorrow he'd be in serious trouble.

On the other hand, Hackney's attitude had been reassuring. The detective had spoken of solid evidence, fingerprints, boot soles, blood tests, alibis, all concrete *things* a man could touch, handle, work with. There was a framework in place within Hackney's soul upon which he would nail the results of his tests and analyses. A man like that wouldn't be content with simply hanging someone—anyone—for the crime, but would insist upon nailing the real perpetrator. And he'd smiled at Faust at the end of their discussion. Faust just wished he knew why.

That left only Stoner's charges of espionage clouding his murky future. Those now seemed vaguely ridiculous, although they'd seemed substantial enough when the old man had first broached them Monday morning. Then, with pain pounding in his mind and out-shouting his common sense, Stoner's logic had seemed relentless and like an idiot he'd foundered before it. Now, in the witching hour of the guardroom cell, with shadows huddled along the walls waiting for him to fall asleep, he realized Stoner's allegations amounted to no more than innuendos and suppositions; there hadn't been a smidgen of real, Hackney-quality evidence in the lot. In broad daylight, he had allowed himself to be buffaloed by a pack of ghosts; in the dark of night, finally he could see clearly.

It was like fighting a chimera, like some grotesque monster of his and Stoner's mutual imagination. Faust loved the world of the mind and its secret language of simile and allegory, interpreted so beautifully by the Elizabethan poets. Sometimes Surrey, Raleigh, and Marlowe were closer friends than those still made of flesh, bone, and blood. But that was also Stoner's world, and Bruckmann's, and he suspected he was outclassed. How could he fight something he couldn't see, something they could see better?

He lit another cigarette from the butt of the first. The nicotine had relaxed him, soaking through his body in waves, like a sedative or the lassitude following sex. But that led to yearning thoughts of Ritzi, her throaty contralto and silken hair, her yielding clasping body beneath his—

—the hair in his imagination was auburn, the face no longer glamorous but plain and pleasant, fresh and everyday, and much as he wanted to test her stupendous grace he had to get those thoughts under control. She had charged him across the ballroom's hardwood floors and her pumps hadn't made a sound. Her scent, light and floral, had tickled his senses and imagination. Jennifer: pinafore? ten or more? *Where Jennifer walks, sound and hope fade—*

He shook his head and blew smoke. Pitiful. He'd better stick with reading the stuff. As Sidney said, *Muses scorn with vulgar brains to dwell.*

Stoner could not have real evidence against him. He was not a spy and therefore evidence of his spying activities could not, in reality, exist. But Stoner did not have to play within the rules of reality. The British military intelligence service was famous the world over for its ruthless cunning. They could manufacture evidence, something as concrete as Hackney's *things,* something an English judge and jury could use to convict and execute him. The fact that the evidence was manufactured—and Faust would tell them so—would make no difference to his ultimate fate.

But was Stoner ruthless enough to hang a man on manufactured evidence? Granted, it wasn't Stoner who would make the decision; it was his superiors. But he had to believe Stoner's beliefs and recommendations—the all-important report from the officer on the spot—would carry a lot of weight when those superiors decided what to do with him.

Faust rumpled his hair, then took a long drag and tapped ash into his makeshift tray. Stoner remained an enigma. Sometimes, when his claws were retracted and his eyes softened to the hue of a summer sky, he was downright charming and Faust couldn't help but like him.

But when he played rough, it was rough indeed. Faust was struck anew by the parallels between his own situation and Stoner's in the first war. It echoed more deeply than the clear differences between medical and physical care. Stoner had spoken of officers who didn't know how to use their authority, and while Tanyon wasn't an officer, he was pushy and getting pushier. Stoner had mentioned poor and rationed food, lack of privacy and leisure activities, no room for exercise—and here he was, almost naked in an open cell, losing weight fast, and ready to rip his hair out with boredom and frustration. Even the comment about an army's best officers being reserved for the front lines found an echo; Stoner was shrewd but no longer physically capable.

It was too much to be a coincidence. Stoner, of all people, had to know how such treatment grated, how it built pressure and resentment until Faust yearned to fight back, putting him in the old warrior's court and at risk of saying more than he should.

But Stoner and his staff had also taken it to the next level; they were measuring everything Faust said and using it against him. He'd told Tanyon he didn't like cabbage, and his next meal was a cabbage-based soup that still had his innards twisting. He admired Stoner's granddaughter and found himself accused of rape and murder. And the cigarette rationing was beyond inhuman.

There could be only one reason for squeezing him so hard: the espionage charges were spurious and he was in the middle of an interrogation, not an investigation. And if that was true, then his earlier fear, that he'd betrayed Army Group A's order of battle under Stoner's gentle ministrations, was also true. He'd been a fool and was close to being a traitor. So far the only thing he'd done right was refraining from telling Stoner about Clarke; damned right that, too, would be used against him.

Faust stubbed out his cigarette. He had to conclude Stoner was as ruthless as he wanted or believed he needed to be.

And Faust had no way of fighting that ruthlessness. There was nothing he could say or do to defend himself. He was at Stoner's mercy and, if he didn't cooperate, he could die. A chill climbed his spine beneath the blanket and rippled from his skin to his core. Did he have the nerve to face the gallows without flinching? He sighed. He didn't even know how he'd react when he ran out of cigarettes.

Round one went to the English, damn it.

35

Stoner assembled his staff—Bruckmann, Jennifer, and Tanyon—in the sitting area of his office, serving drinks and cigarettes from his own ration. After the last two days, he was certain they all needed some little relaxation. He himself felt as if Margeaux Hall's exquisite modern roof had caved in on him while he worked; he wasn't quite certain what had happened, or why, but it had caused a horrid mess and somebody had to clean it up.

"Well," he said, "we've no time for inhibitions or ceremony. I must draft a report for Brigadier Marone and require all the information I can summon. Jennifer, my dear, I realize you've had little contact with Faust, but what you've had has been intensive. You've also typed all our notes and know the circumstances as well as anyone. Your thoughts?"

"I wish I hadn't hit him." She set her wineglass on the table, kicked off her pumps, and tucked her legs about herself in a graceful curl. "I don't like him and I'm almost certain he killed Harriet and Grace, but it will only make this harder." She glanced at Tanyon. "Did I hurt him?"

"Split lip."

"I suppose that's not too bad." She grabbed her wineglass again and turned it in the lamplight. The Médoc flashed like sequined blood. "Every time I see him, he looks as if he's laughing at us. I just couldn't stand it any more, that's all."

"Is he laughing at us?" Stoner turned to Tanyon, sitting

in the farthest wing chair, as if he felt uncomfortable hob-nobbing with the officers. "Sergeant, you've spent the most time in his presence. What do you think?"

Tanyon's poison of choice was straight single malt. He'd drained his shot glass twice without pause, and sat looking at the bottle as if weighing the chances of a third.

"He might be, at that." Tanyon picked up the bottle, glanced at Stoner—who carefully kept any judgmental thoughts far from his mind—and poured anew. "He's always looking around, watching people, looking for mistakes. He sees one, he jumps on it."

"We haven't had time to confer," Stoner said. "Did he make any overt moves whilst in the clinic?"

"Now, that's an odd one." Tanyon paused then drained the whiskey in a gulp. "I could tell he was nervous when the air raid alarm went off, because he kept looking at the ceiling."

"Possibly he's never been in an air raid before." Bruckmann still nursed his first whiskey and soda, his expression uncertain as he peered into its depths.

"Maybe not. But when the bombs started falling, he jumped to protect the women and children."

Jennifer gasped. "He—what?"

Stoner set down his wineglass. "You allowed him to mix with the civilians?"

"Didn't have much choice, sir. The bombs hit so close the stairwell came down on top of us. He scooped up little Thompson Oldfield, covered Mrs. Oldfield and Flora when the walls started falling, and herded them into the shelter."

Jennifer's mouth opened but no sound came out. Her glorious hazel eyes widened and her breath caught in her throat. "He did what? But if he killed—he wouldn't—" She turned to Stoner, her legs uncurling from the sofa and feeling for the floor, as if she needed a new foundation for her unsettled thoughts. "Dad—"

"My dear, no one has ever said he is not a brave man." With all his heart, Stoner wished she hadn't heard the sergeant's words.

She stared at him without comprehension, as if at a stranger who'd said something without any context or meaning. Then she jerked her head and turned to Tanyon. "Was—everyone all right? I've been so busy today, I haven't rung anyone for news."

"Faust was hurt the worst," Tanyon said. "He was struck when the ceiling fell and bruised across the shoulders, but the Oldfields weren't harmed. And Dr. Harris did restitch his arm." The sergeant's mouth twitched. "A second time."

No matter how many times Dr. Harris was inconvenienced, the situation contained no humor. Stoner stared at his sergeant until Tanyon glanced aside. "I still shudder at the possibilities. If he'd wanted a hostage, it would have been a sterling opportunity."

"Gets worse, sir," Tanyon said bluntly. "In the night, when Norris and I changed over, I found Thompson curled up in the bunk with Faust. He'd snuck in when Norris wasn't looking. I chased him off, but I'm sure he came back."

Stoner glanced at Jennifer as her jaw slackened, then a small smile touched her lips and eyes. He grimaced and treated himself to a long swig of the Médoc, settling it on his tongue and inhaling over it to taste the apple and blackcurrant aromas. He'd wanted her to think of Faust as a German and therefore the enemy, a living embodiment of the *Wehrmacht* that destroyed France, Poland, Norway, and the Low Countries, and now stood poised on England's coastline. With this new, gentler image in her mind, she would surely see Stoner's treatment of Faust for the manipulative callousness it was.

It was distasteful for Stoner to shrug off thirty-five years of building his students to tear down this one young man. However, he could trust himself to in turn shrug off the experience and revert to his more usual modes of behavior. For Jennifer to see—worse, to understand—the process, was putting her still-forming character in danger of hardening a part of her soul. And that was more than merely distasteful. It was unacceptable.

"They say children know who they can trust." Bruckmann glanced again into the depths of his whiskey and soda, set it aside, picked it up again. "Is it possible we're overreacting here?"

"No, sir," Tanyon said. "We know he's nice to women and children while someone's looking. We don't know what he's like without an audience."

At least the sergeant, with his years of experience, was cynical enough to foresee the worst.

Stoner cleared his throat. "We can afford no more risks. Was Norris of any assistance at all?"

"No, sir. I may have to prefer charges. He ran when the bombing started."

Stoner again tasted his wine, swirling the softened tannin about his mouth. It was a second-growth 1899, not the best from Woodrow's cellar but certainly nothing to slight. It was too good, honestly, to waste on a staff meeting—and what a staff—but then, what was a man to do? If the wine fit... and bringing charges against Norris would involve additional work for his already overtaxed staff.

"He's young," he said. "Like a good Bordeaux, we'll give him more time to mature. Deal with him yourself, sergeant."

"Yes, sir." Tanyon sounded relieved. "I think he's got the makings of a good enough soldier. But he can't handle Faust right now."

"Perhaps we're all outclassed by him." Stoner sighed and sipped again. "But we won't admit to that, shall we? Jack, your thoughts."

Bruckmann set down his drink, shifted, picked it back up. His eyes remained focused on the trellis rug.

"Come, be honest."

He set the drink down yet again. "I'm starting to admire him."

Jennifer's jaw dropped. "Are you daft?"

So she wasn't thinking as kindly of Faust as all that. Stoner examined Bruckmann's set face. "That's honest. I find certain of his traits to be admirable, myself. What about him has caught your attention?"

"You've gone batty."

Bruckmann glanced at her but set his jaw more firmly. "He's good at all the things I'd like to learn—map reading, lay of the land, personal combat, tactics. He's cultured but not the sort of man people muck about with. He doesn't seem to be afraid of anything and if he is, he's not afraid to admit it."

"All admirable traits," Stoner said, "most of which come via experience and education, and most of which you're likely to acquire in time. What about him has caught your attention as opposed to, say, Major Kettering?"

"Dad—"

"A moment, my dear."

Bruckmann picked up his whiskey, finally sipped it, shuddered, and set it back down. "I don't think I'm acquiring a taste for that, in any case. You know, I saw them together today. Major Kettering had a hundred men at his back but kept his eye on Faust. Faust was alone but didn't seem to notice."

"Now we come to the essence of it." Stoner reached behind his wing chair, fetched a wineglass from the sideboard, and poured more of the Médoc, setting it before Bruckmann. "Try this on for size. Are you speaking of Faust's self-confidence, Jack? It's not so impregnable it can't be shaken."

"I don't think so, sir." Bruckmann sipped the Médoc and popped his eyebrows while he savored it. "Wow. That sort of sucks all the spit from your mouth, doesn't it? Perhaps not only confidence."

"Perhaps not misplaced confidence?" Stoner suggested.

"That's more like it." Bruckmann took a second, longer sip. "There's something behind his confidence."

"Perhaps he's tested his limits and is comfortable with what he's found."

The third drink drained the wineglass. "Perhaps he's learned how to make the most of what's inside his limits."

Stoner glanced at the bottle, then refilled Bruckmann's glass. "Now I know how to uncork your thoughts." He topped up his own, but when he glanced at Jennifer, she shook her head without meeting his eyes. He sighed and set the bottle down; she was listening all too closely. Sooner or later, this would require a discussion, one which would disappoint her with him personally, rather than his assignment or commanding officer. "Jack, how do you suggest I break him?"

She flinched at the word, her eyes closing briefly. Stoner looked away.

"Well." Bruckmann paused for another sip. "Perhaps we should try destroying the basis of his confidence."

Precisely his own thought, after reading Captain Clarke's report: undermine Faust's still-secure position as a loyal and honorable German officer. He'd conveyed as much to Brigadier Marone in the morning's dispatch, which Jennifer had typed. Judging by the dawning horror in her eyes, she now understood those notes in her marrow.

"Any specific ideas, Jack?"

"Not a one." Bruckmann smacked his lips. "Grows on you, doesn't it? I suppose whiskey simply isn't it for me."

More of Margeaux Hall's roof appeared to have fallen, and the mess requiring cleaning seemed even larger. Stoner felt bruised in his soul. He'd received confirmation of his plan. But the cost could prove to be Jennifer's esteem and, even to contribute his best to the defense of England, it could prove too high.

"And here I thought a staff meeting a poor way to use a good Médoc."

But his sally only caught her eye for a brief moment. And after she turned her head, not even the rich garnet glow of the wine could lift his heart again.

As it stood, round one went to the *Wehrmacht*.

36

the same evening
the Abbey Arms in the hamlet of Patchley Abbey

From the amount of khaki crowding the Abbey Arms, Hackney judged the local Home Guard had drilled that night. He wound past farmers with hard begrimed hands, shop-keepers and clerks still trim from their day within doors, all in smart battledress and all with American-made Browning automatic rifles on the floor at their feet. The low-ceiled room was dark and smoky, the air dense with the blackout shutters closed, and a cheerful rumble from those crowding the tables and benches rattled the mismatched prints on the walls.

At first he thought he was the only man in civvies; even Homer Owen, the publican behind the bar, wore khaki. Then he realized the women, too, wore uniforms. Many were in the green coats and skirts, red blouses, and flat green hats of the Women's Voluntary Services. But in one corner half a dozen Women's Land Army girls, their felt hats pushed to the backs of their heads, showed off their loose-fitting fawn breeches and long woolen socks by standing and putting their brogues up on their chairs. For a moment, Hackney let himself be diverted by the sight—not something a man saw every day, that—then he spotted Arnussen. His detective sergeant was seated in the corner behind the girls, his glasses on his nose and two tankards already on the table, one full and one empty. The pile of papers before him was an inch thick.

"I'm ready for it." Hackney had walked from Margeaux Hall, letting Arnussen take the car earlier, and he'd kicked up a thirst. He set the rolled maps on the table, the paper sack containing Faust's boots on the floor, and drained half the pint before sitting down, his attention lingering on the young legs. But it seemed vaguely disloyal to Carolyn, not in her grave a year yet, and here he was, ogling some immodest young things carrying on. He sat and opened his briefcase atop the table, positioning it between himself and the Land Girls, blocking the view.

"I've got the statements from the soldiers at Margeaux Hall and the photos from the first crime scene." Arnussen moved his stack of papers aside and tugged off his specs. "And upstairs I've got the three bootprint plasters from the chicken farm. The fingerprint report and the serology on the hand-kerchief should both be ready tomorrow sometime."

"Good work, Axel." Hackney pulled out the file Dr. Harris had given him. "And here are the autopsy reports and photos from the second crime scene." He piled more papers atop the file. "And the statements from Margeaux Hall's officers and non-coms, the clerks, the nurse, the doctor, and the German prisoner of war." He paused for another slug of dark stout. "Good brew, that. We missed the butler, the gardener, the housemaid, and the cook, so if we're going to assemble a complete picture of where everyone was on Saturday night and Tuesday afternoon, one of us must go back."

"The publican makes his own." Arnussen picked up the stack of statements and sighed. "Can we miss the cook and housemaid? They're women, right? Not likely to be a rapist, either of them."

"I can't say they were directly involved, no." Hackney drained his tankard and dug in his pocket for change. "But the cook is Pamela Alcock's sister and the murdered girl's auntie. If anyone was following Grace or being cheeky, she might know it. And the housemaid was Harriet's close friend, so we can't miss her, either."

Arnussen leaned back. His hand, full of papers, fell into his lap. "Think it's going to be that simple?"

Hackney shook his head, gave the empties and change a hopeful push, and opened Dr. Harris' file. "Are they still serv-ing, do you know?"

"One way to find out." Arnussen slipped his glasses into his pocket, grabbed the tankards and coins, and waded through the sea of khaki toward the bar. The Land Girls cleared a good-natured path for him, then returned to peering over their tankards at the pile of papers sprawling across the table. A pub wasn't the best place for a meeting of this sort and not only the Land Girls were surreptitiously watching them. But at least there wasn't enough light for them to read anything, even if they were too close for discretion, and Hackney reminded himself to keep his voice below the level of the general roar.

The autopsy reports were on top. Hackney skimmed the summaries.

Harriet Stoner, aged seventeen, had been dead for about thirty-six hours before her body was found; lividity was completely established along her back and rigor mortis was just beginning to pass off in her eyelids and jaw. There was serological evidence of sperm within her uterus, but due to the rapid start of decomposition in the August heat, it was impossible to determine whether the sex was consensual. The direct cause of her death was massive trauma to her chest, best interpreted as approximately fifty stab wounds inflicted by a short-bladed knife, sharp on only one side of the blade. In addition, she had been beaten severely about her face, and her nose, jaw, and left cheekbone were fractured. Finally, there was a contusion on the right posterior of her occipital lobe, with dirt and vegetable matter rubbed into it. A single dark brown hair, less than three inches in length and readily identifiable as human, had been found beneath her left index fingernail. It was presumed to have been torn from the head of her attacker and the high degree of pigmentation suggested a perpetrator between thirteen and thirty years of age.

By contrast, Grace Alcock, aged fifteen, had been dead no more than two hours prior to being examined and conclusions could be drawn with much more certainty. Rape in her case was definite and savage, with multiple tears to the vaginal wall. The direct cause of death, again, was a frenzy of stab wounds to the chest, in her case approximately thirty blows, also with a one-sided blade three and one-half to four inches in length. Her nose and left cheekbone were fractured, with moderate to severe bruising over the remainder of her face. She too had been struck on the back of her head, although as this attack had taken place within doors the wound was clean. Trace evidence included blood and tissue beneath all ten fingernails, as well as the sperm in her uterus, analysis of which indicated an attacker with type A+ blood and a secretor.

Hackney forced himself to examine the grisly photos from both crime scenes. When Arnussen returned, a tankard in each hand, he started to set the photos aside with a guilty twinge of relief. But when he glanced up, one of the Land Girls, a pretty imp with red hair braided down her back, straightened and turned away too quickly. Irritated, he flipped the photos face down, and the reports, too, for good measure.

"We're in luck." Arnussen slid into his chair. "One of these ladies is the housemaid at Margeaux Hall and the publican's niece. She's agreed to see what's in the kitchen and then come speak with us while we eat."

Hackney recalled Kettering's American Revolution war story and smiled, his irritation vanishing. "God bless the ladies. We'll never win this war without them." He pushed the photos and reports toward Arnussen. "What do you think?"

Arnussen paused and put on his specs. He glanced through the photos but read the autopsy summaries with a concentration line between his eyes, then removed his glasses and chewed the stem. "Surprise attack. Hit on the head from behind. Overpowered, perhaps stunned, by the facial blows. Then stripped, thrown to the ground or bed, and raped. Then—" He replaced the glasses and squinted again at the reports. "This reads like Jack the Ripper with a pocket knife."

Hackney nodded, shuffled the photos and reports back into the file, and slid it into his briefcase, still open on the table between them. The red-haired Land Girl turned away again, her mouth in a moue, and the one standing next to her dug an elbow in her ribs.

"Tell me about the bootprints."

"Constable Mercer and I looked over the entire chicken farm together after you left for Margeaux Hall, but I didn't find anything he hadn't already." Arnussen folded his glasses and slid them into his breast pocket. "Along with the prints that belonged there, we found three sets that don't, either males or bloody large females. One set had a tread pattern I've never seen before, but it stayed out next to the wall, along the roadway, and never came near the house."

"That supports what the German prisoner told me tonight."

"You've got his boots?"

Hackney handed him the paper sack. Arnussen slipped his glasses back on, drew one of the lace-up ankle boots from the sack, and examined the sole, his head tilting back as he squinted. "I can't say for certain, but they look right." He returned the boot to the sack and the sack to Hackney. "The other two sets had tread patterns like our own army or air force boys' boots, but the wear marks and scuffing are pretty definite and I don't think distinguishing them will be difficult. One set overstrode the German's boots at the wall then ran all over the place among the chicken runs, finally approaching the front door and vanishing in the lawn about the house."

"That would be Sergeant Tanyon," Hackney said. "I'll get

casts made of his boots, too."

"The other set, presumably the killer's, approached from the Dark into the lawn at the back of the house." Arnussen shrugged and chewed his glasses again. "The grass, of course, isn't going to show us anything."

Hackney planted his elbows on the table and leaned. It sank beneath him, but not enough to convince him to back off. "Both girls were nude. What about Harriet's clothing? We found Grace's dress hanging in her closet but I can't find any mention of the sprigged yellow muslin Major Stoner described."

"Constable Mercer and the local Home Guard looked in the Dark but found nothing."

"That would be an awfully large and indiscreet trophy for the killer to take away." Hackney tapped his teeth with his thumbnail. "Doesn't seem likely, does it? Keep after that dress, Axel; there's something wrong there."

"I can't use the Home Guard any more; they're all suspects. How about Kettering? How serious a suspect is he?"

Hackney shrugged. "Check his blood type and make certain he's not A positive, then use him and every soldier he's willing to contribute. The more of them out there looking as a group, the less likely the killer, if he's among them, will take the chance of hiding evidence."

"In a crowd, he'd be seen and have to explain it." Arnussen put on his glasses and made a note. "We'll ring Kettering first thing in the morning."

Hackney drummed his fingers on the tabletop. Years of sloppy drinkers had tattooed it with dark rings, overlapping and crowding each other beneath Arnussen's pad. "The killer's clothes—what about them?"

The sergeant looked up from his notes. "Blood stains, you mean?"

"You might be able to bash a woman about the face without getting more than a spot or two on you, and you could pass that off as your own, from shaving or what-not. But you can't go into a frenzy and stab her until your arm gives out without marking yourself."

"Definitely on the cuff, perhaps splashes on the front." Arnussen made another note. "Or on the back, if he lifted his arm over his head and sprayed himself."

"So what did he do?" Hackney paused. "Did he strip as well, after the assault but before the rape and murder?"

"Must have." Arnussen looked up. "Another handkerchief at the first site, do you think?"

Hackney nodded. "Something like that, which means our killer has used and disposed of two in three days. He can't have an inexhaustible supply."

"We'll get on that tomorrow morning, as well." Arnussen glanced toward the bar. "Here comes chow."

Hackney followed his glance and saw a slender young woman in WVS green and red carrying a tray toward them, sashaying between the tables and circling the Land Army girls, her chin down and eyes averted. He scrabbled the remaining documents into his briefcase, closed it, and moved it to the floor. She set thick sandwiches and steaming bowls of soup on the table, then sat down herself with her back to the room and the tray cradled on her lap.

"Love, I could marry you for this." Arnussen shook out his napkin, then set out his steno pad and grabbed a pencil. Hackney had seen him take notes and eat one-handed many times.

"He's lying." Hackney smiled at her, his heart aching. She looked so forlorn, like all the other grieving friends he'd interviewed through the years. "What's your name?"

"Sally Owen." She smoothed her uniform jacket. "Harriet was me best mate."

About nineteen, Hackney decided, her figure trim in the bulky uniform, with loads of black hair around an oval face worth coming home to. Her eyes, dark but colorless in the pub's low lighting, were puffy and red-rimmed as if she'd been crying, and she rolled the tray in her lap as she spoke.

"You knew Grace, too?" Hackney asked.

"Not as well, her being so much younger. And she spent most of her time practicing her music and I didn't care for it. Me dad, Jerome Owen, that is, he farms the land across the road from Mrs. Alcock's chicken runs. Before I went to the Hall, I lived near there."

"You're now housemaid at Margeaux Hall?" The soup was all vegetable, thick with bits of potatoes and carrots and turnips, and the spicy sauce had a tomato base. Before rationing, the recipe might have included ham or beef.

"Started out as parlor maid two years ago. There were five of us then." Sally shrugged. "But then the old squire died and the new one mostly shut up the house. And then the war came. Now I'm the only one left."

"So what do you do?"

"Cleaning and carrying. Rooms and clothes and dishes and floors. Breakfast in bed and meals in her room for her ladyship the squire's sister," Sally's voice took on a sarcastic edge, "her who can't hack the war effort. Meals to the dining room for the soldiers, then clear up after. I help Mrs. Alcock— she's the cook—put together trays for the prisoners on the third floor, but the soldiers deliver them. And I cleaned the German officer's uniform this afternoon."

Hackney glanced at Arnussen, who looked up from his notes and soup spoon with a smile. He turned back to Sally. "And you volunteer as well?"

She shrugged again. "Just doing me little bit. All my friends joined, so I did, too. Harriet had just joined." She bit her lip. "She hadn't gotten her uniform yet. Her birthday was only two months ago, you know."

Another tiny piece of Hackney's heart died. He set down his sandwich. "How long had you known her?"

"The Stoners moved here last summer from Oxford. Jennifer's closer to my age and she's nice, but she's awfully serious and reads poetry and stuff. So I took up with Harriet. She's—I mean, she was always fun." Sally closed her eyes, her lashes trembling. "Wednesday afternoons—that's my half day—we went to the films in Patchbourne and stopped at a tea shop right near the market. We'd fetch tobacco and cigarettes for the major from his shop, although he won't let us smoke, and we'd collect books and stuff he'd ordered. He hasn't done that for a while now. I guess he's busy, with the war and all." She opened her eyes and blinked a few times. "And he never said a word about her going about with the housemaid—never used the word slumming, not to me nor anyone who's spoke to me. He's got to be the nicest man around."

"Tell me about Saturday night."

"Worst night of me life, it was. I'll never forget it." Sally heaved a deep breath, her green jacket rising and falling. "Mrs. Mercer organized the dance for the soldiers at Margeaux Hall, and the pilots and mechanics at RAF Patchbourne, and she asked all us girls to show so they'd have someone to dance with. Everyone but Jennifer came, and it was fun for a while."

Hackney glanced down at his sandwich. He'd put on forty pounds since the cancer took Carolyn and had probably dined sufficiently. But it was a really good sandwich. "Do you remember anyone who danced with Harriet?"

Sally smiled through her tears. "Harriet was a good dancer and they lined up for her. She mostly danced with the pilots—she wanted to marry a pilot—but saved a few for our own soldiers. The ones from Margeaux Hall, I mean. I saw her dance with Reynolds, and Peckham, and Norris, and I think Pym." She paused, dabbing beneath her eyes. "Yes, I'm sure she danced with Pym, too, although she wouldn't touch Sloane because he's always a bit greasy, and Ellington's clumsy. Glover stayed at the Hall on duty, which is a shame because he's a good dancer and she said she missed him."

The sandwich won. Hackney picked it back up. Before he took a bite, he asked, "And when the air raid alarm went off?"

"That's when I missed her. I looked everywhere, but then Uncle Homer made me go into the shelter, down in the basement, and she wasn't there."

Arnussen set down his spoon and took over while Hackney chewed. "Now, think carefully, Sally. Can you recall who all was in the shelter?"

"It's hard to say, because people were coming and going. At first everyone went down and it was so crowded, it was hard to breathe. But later Uncle Owen took a call from the airfield, saying one of the German planes had been shot down and the Home Guard was called out, so all the men left. Even Mr. Ashleigh, the vicar—he's crippled, but he runs the radio and telephone, relaying messages for the Home Guard."

"And the soldiers from Margeaux Hall?"

"They left with the Home Guard and Mr. Ashleigh."

"All together?"

She shrugged. "I suppose."

"So after the parachute was sighted, there were no men left in the shelter?"

"That's right." She paused. "I mean, until they all got back from the search. But I don't know what time that was."

Hackney sat back and sighed. He'd hoped some of the villagers, at least, had stayed in the air raid shelter and could be written off the suspect list. But it didn't seem that would be. Arnussen picked up his spoon, so he resumed the questioning.

"And after the all-clear sounded? What happened then?"

"I looked everywhere. I supposed she went home when the alarm sounded and was in Woodrow's shelter with Jennifer and the major. But when I got back to the Hall, Jennifer met me on the road and asked where she was. That's when I got scared. She ran into Woodrow and I went to the Hall and looked there, but we couldn't find her." She heaved another breath, her jacket shuddering. "So as soon as the major was free, he called Constable Mercer."

He glanced at Arnussen, who folded his napkin, finished his note, and nodded. Hackney gave Sally his best smile. "I believe that's it, love. If I think of anything else, can I find you at the Hall?"

She nodded and rose, gathering plates and bowls back onto the tray. "It was the German, wasn't it?"

He froze with the tankard at his lips. His sideways glance ran into Arnussen's warning stare. He'd forgotten all about the background rumble of pub chatter, but suddenly it was there again, forcing its way into his awareness, and the red-haired

Land Girl still watched them over her tankard.

"Everyone's saying it had to be him." Sally hefted the tray and straightened. For the first time in the conversation, she seemed uncertain. "Harriet chopped up the moment he arrived, and Grace when he escaped. Everyone's saying we should just go to the Hall and string him up, like they do in those Western movies."

With an effort, Hackney smiled again. "So why don't they?"

She balanced the tray and shrugged. "At the Hall, they're real Army and they've got better weapons than those American guns. And Major Stoner's a nice man, but I think he'd do his duty as he saw it."

The only weapon he'd seen in Margeaux Hall was the Webley service revolver strapped on Tanyon's hip. No matter how good the sergeant was, a handgun wouldn't be a match for one of those American rifles nobody seemed to respect, much less a pub full of them. If a lynch mob called on Stoner, there'd be a blood bath. But it wouldn't be the one the villagers anticipated. Hackney searched for something quelling to say.

"I think he would, too." He nodded about the room. "Make sure you tell everyone that. Don't want anyone hurt, you know."

She nodded. "I have. But I will again."

"And we've got a lot of evidence—good, solid stuff—to sort through before we know who killed those girls."

"Then you don't think it was him?" Her eyebrows contracted.

There had to be something he could say to open the village's eyes without spilling information best kept secret. "Tell me, Sally: you cleaned the German's uniform, right? Was there any blood on it?"

Her eyes widened. She jerked her head in a nod. "His jacket's torn across the back, on the right side, and it's all stained."

"Yes, well, that's where he was wounded." Hackney cupped his hand around his wrist. "Down here on his sleeve, love—was there any blood down here?"

"No." She shook her head. "I mean, there are stains on the lining, inside the sleeve, but that's from his wound again. Right?"

Hackney nodded to Arnussen, as if he'd made an important point. The sergeant dutifully noted it down.

"Thanks again, Sally." He leaned over the table and turned to Arnussen. "What do you think?"

Arnussen cocked an eyebrow. Hackney peered aside.

Sally, her forehead drawn into a pucker, paused at the bar, her arms wrapped around the tray of dirty dishes. She glanced about at the somber roomful of chattering neighbors before she vanished through the kitchen door.

"I think," Arnussen said, "we'd already decided the killer probably stripped, too, and therefore wouldn't have blood on his sleeve for Sally or any other laundress to find."

"No need to tell the whole village that little bit. Major Stoner's got enough to worry over as it is." Hackney drained his second pint. "So where do we go from here?"

"We pool our evidence." Arnussen set his empty tankard beside Hackney's. "I'll set up an incidents room, make a list of the men, military or civilian, who were out Saturday night or Tuesday afternoon, then cross off as many as we can based on blood type, alibi, hair color, boot soles, scratches on his body, and handkerchiefs, in that order." He leaned back in his chair, eyebrows up.

Hackney sighed and shoved the empties aside. Arnussen's plan was sound. But just considering the amount of paper to be sorted through, the cross-referencing to be done, the number of people to be questioned before they could start making sense of the evidence—it all weighed on him like some paper version of Chinese water torture. And besides, gathering all that evidence for Arnussen to cross-reference would take time. He had a nagging suspicion this killer was impatient. Two victims within three days, and only while Major Faust was loose... there was something there, some nebulous clue, but he wasn't certain yet what it was.

"It's all we've got, isn't it? Right, then. We'll start first thing in the morning."

37

midnight
Margeaux Hall

It was five minutes to midnight before Bruckmann finished assisting Stoner—outlining the new battle plan against Faust, drafting and typing the next report for Brigadier Marone, finishing the Médoc—and his head sang a merry tune when he dragged himself into the guardroom. Murky shadows lined the walls and camouflaged the room's depths. The only soldier still on duty, Pym, slouched at the radio table over an open book, propped beneath the table lamp. He glanced up as Bruckmann entered.

"Break time, corporal," Bruckmann said. "I've got to work on the manuals for a while."

Pym slid a red ribbon into place as a marker and closed his book. "I know where Mrs. Alcock keeps the kettle, sir."

"Not for me, thanks. Just take care of yourself for an hour or so." Bruckmann cocked an eyebrow. "If you take a nap, don't oversleep."

"Thanks, lieutenant. See you in a bit."

The shelf above the radio table was crammed with manuals for radio procedures, call signs, maintenance and repair, and, because there was no other convenient place for them, the regulations binders. In a wire basket at the end of the line hulked a pile of battered and unopened manila envelopes, all stamped with the lion, crown, and crossed sabers of the Ministry of Defense.

Bruckmann allowed himself a sigh. Stoner was right;

there were at least a dozen envelopes piled there, probably more. But why had the old man insisted the manuals be updated tonight? It wasn't anywhere near a priority item; to his certain knowledge, no one had consulted the manuals in the three months he and the squad had been attached to the Wildflower operation. These were the regulations covering uniforms, the proper method of saluting, the minimum amounts of meat and vegetables to be served—and Stoner simply didn't run such a tight ship for anyone to bother consulting the bally things.

He sighed again and switched on the large floor lamp, driving the shadows from the Lee Enfields, then tossed the envelopes and binders into a pile on the worktable.

Someone behind him struck a match.

Bruckmann started and spun about. In the match's uncertain wavering light, he saw Faust, sitting cross-legged on the cot in the deepest dark behind the bars of the cell, a blanket draped over his shoulders, touching the tiny flame to the business end of a cigarette. When it glowed, he shook out the match. The shadows surged in and swallowed him up. All Bruckmann could see was a dark silhouette, the smolder of gleaming eyes, and the burning end of the fag.

"Sorry," Faust said. "I didn't mean to startle you."

Bruckmann turned back to the worktable. Otherwise Faust would see his growing excitement. After all, he was near the lamp and much more visible.

"You'll understand," Stoner had said.

He hoped he did.

"I'd forgotten you were in here."

"After today's show?" There was a hard edge to Faust's concise sibilants. "How could you forget?"

"There's been rather a lot going on today." He dragged out a chair and settled behind the manuals. "Are you still angry?"

He glanced over his shoulder in time to see the eyes and cigarette tip glow momentarily brighter.

"Would you be?"

"Well." Bruckmann picked up the top envelope and ripped it open. Inside was a small sheaf of replacement sheets, printed, three-hole punched, and ready for insertion. "Well, yes, I believe I would."

"Well, then, yes, I suppose I am," Faust said.

He pulled out the pages, balled up the envelope, and tossed it toward the wastebasket. "Look, sometimes this is the only time I have to get my own work done. Will the light bother you? I mean, did I wake you?"

"No. I'm too keyed up to sleep."

Bruckmann glanced back, surprised. It required a huge serving of self-confidence to frankly admit a weakness to a known enemy. That was honesty, and deeper than he'd expected. Stoner, of course, was wiser; he must have counted on loneliness and tension, the shame of capture and exposure, to lead Faust to seek company, to want to talk.

He ripped open another envelope. It was time to test that water. "Do you mind if I ask a question?"

The eyes and cigarette glowed again. "I can't promise I'll answer."

"Fair enough." Another envelope. None of them were thick; none contained enough sheets to keep him busy any significant length of time. But if he worked too slowly, Faust might catch on. "Well, look—I was conscripted."

His own eyes were growing accustomed to the shadows crowding the cell. He knew he didn't mistake the shrug that shifted the blanket's silhouette. "I joined before conscription started; otherwise it would be the same here."

"In many ways, I still think like a civilian. Do you know what I mean?"

The cigarette tip glowed. "I've been in the army for five years now. For the first six months, I was beyond useless."

"Then how did you learn map reading, using the lay of the land, tactics, and all that stuff?" He ripped open the last envelope, feeling his face redden. He was working on the assumption Stoner wanted him to measure Faust's emotional temperature and build a relationship, in which case it didn't matter what they discussed. But admitting his weaknesses wasn't as easy as listening to Faust admitting his, and perhaps that question would have been best kept for Kettering or some other English officer. But it was too late to unsay it and he plowed on. "I've been in the army for nine months now and I still don't get any of it."

But Faust didn't laugh. "You're asking how I learned my trade."

Surprised, Bruckmann paused with the papers half out of the envelope. He hadn't even known how to ask the question; Faust was instructing him in semantics, as well. "Well, how did you?"

"I read some of it. Not long after I joined up, several of our younger senior officers published their memoirs and treatises from the first war—Rommel, Guderian, that young-Turk crowd. I studied what they wrote."

He tossed the last empty envelope at the wastebasket and started shuffling the papers into order. In officer's school, he'd tried to read Rommel's book in translation, but hadn't gotten far before treating it rather like the envelopes. "Yes, but did you understand any of it?"

"Not at first. Guderian I had to read three or four times. Rommel was hard to get into, but toward the end of his book he describes mountain warfare in the Carpathians, and that was great reading."

A glance showed teeth gleaming now, as well as eyes. Bruckmann set the papers aside—hopefully they were in the proper order, not that it mattered—and reached for the first binder. Perhaps he'd given up on Rommel's work too soon. "So you learned by reading."

"Some of it. I also badgered the older men, field officers and non-coms, and asked a lot of damn-fool questions."

He couldn't stop a sigh as he flipped through the binder to the first page to be replaced, pulled out the old one, and inserted the new. "I hate doing that."

"I had to get used to it," Faust said. "I didn't like it at first. A couple of real bastards made fun of me in front of the unit and that wasn't pleasant. I learned who to avoid and who was willing to be a mentor. Several of the officers were born teachers, especially my first battalion commander and then my regimental commander in Poland. I learned a lot from them."

Open the binder rings. Old page out. New page in. Flip over a few sheets. Do it again. But smoke rankled the air of the guardroom and he wanted to cough. "I don't mean to pry, but aren't you smoking rather a lot? I mean, cigarettes are rationed."

The tip glowed as if in response. "Yes, I am, and yes, I believe you. But it doesn't matter. See, I'm going to quit."

He froze, then swiveled about for a good long stare. Faust sat unmoving on the cot, legs akimbo like a statue of some ancient god with jeweled eyes glowing in the dark. The blanket bulked about his shoulders, accentuating his outline and the resemblance. The shadowy figure waved its left hand, and the glowing tip of the cigarette swirled through the dark.

"Do you use these things?"

He shook his head.

"I hadn't realized before how vulnerable they make me." Faust took another drag and then extinguished the cigarette. The glow vanished and only his looming outline remained. "Stoner's using them to jerk me around. I can't allow it any more. So I'm quitting."

Bruckmann returned to the binder. Without checking to see where he was, he flipped open the rings and removed whatever page was before him. "I thought quitting was difficult."

"I've heard that, too, but it doesn't matter. When I'm out of cigarettes, I'm out, and nothing's going to change that."

He inserted a page and closed the binder rings. This sort of determined initiative on the part of the prisoner wasn't in their plan.

"That was your idea, wasn't it." The quiet voice was level, making a statement, not asking a question.

He froze but couldn't stop his gaze from darting aside. Faust hadn't moved. The stare directed his way was analytical, not angry, but there wasn't a trace of amusement in the dark liquid eyes.

"Good move." Faust nodded. "Using my weaknesses against me. Low," he added, "but brilliant. You're good at psychology; why worry about map reading?"

"Look—"

"Don't apologize for doing your job." Faust finally moved, shifting on the cot and pulling the blanket more snugly about his shoulders.

Bruckmann forced himself to relax his clenched jaw. "I wasn't going to."

The responding glance was frankly disbelieving and a bit derisive.

He turned his shoulder and thumbed through the pages. There weren't many left. Considering the way the conversation was going, perhaps that was for the best: let the bugger stew in silence again, until he was ready to be more civil. Bruckmann flipped over a few more pages.

"Now it's my turn to ask a question," Faust said. "What's Mr. Stoner's rank?"

The question caught Bruckmann by surprise and he glanced over before he could stop himself. The level stare, this time fully derisive, told him it was too late to back out.

"What makes you think—"

"This is a military installation. He's the commanding officer, not some civilian overseer. I should have caught on sooner." Faust redraped the blanket. "See, I'm still not good at some of this stuff."

He was caught, fair and square. "He's a major. They reinstated him at his reserve rank."

"And he assumed a young major wouldn't be impressed by an old one," Faust said. "He's wrong there."

Again Faust's words surprised him and Bruckmann smiled. So the German had noticed Stoner's innate charm and courteous competence, even through their verbal warfare. "I know what you mean. He's—"

"For as long as he lasts."

It cut through his smile like an electrical shock. Bruckmann froze, his fingertips tingling as he stared at the discarded page in his hand. He crumpled it and threw it atop the stack. It fluttered off the table. "What do you mean? I know he's getting on—"

Faust shook his head. "Twice now I've seen his lips turn blue and his hands shake. Those are classical symptoms of an incipient heart attack."

He ripped the next page out without bothering to open the rings. "You're not a doctor. You can't know."

"I've seen it before. The father superior at the orphanage where I grew up was an old man, the creaky frail kind, and he used to turn blue all the time. Finally one day, when I was about ten, he keeled over with a heart attack at prayers and died. A new man came to take his place, a younger man." Faust paused. "And rougher."

Bruckmann stared at the ripped-out page in his hand, curlicues of paper dangling from its left edge. It was the wrong sheet. Not likely it was anything important. He crumpled it, too, and tossed it aside.

He'd only been at Margeaux Hall for three months and he loved it. It was intriguing, watching the old man sort through a problem, analyzing its various components and compiling a framework for its solution, then sorting through the solution to the nitpicky details, all of which contributed to the plan's ultimate success or failure. Bruckmann had learned a lot from him; as part of Stoner's staff, he felt he was contributing in a real sense to the war effort. And the Médoc had been nothing short of a revelation. Faust was right: what was map reading compared to this?

And there was the purely selfish side to the equation. Bruckmann had served briefly with a Guards regiment prior to his transfer to Margeaux Hall, and he knew as well as the next lieutenant when he was well billeted. Stoner simply refused to stand on military punctiliousness, instead fostering an atmosphere of mutual trust and cooperation with himself at its head but where anyone could speak up, in or out of turn. The work was hard but stimulating; anywhere else it would be hard but dull and possibly brutal, to judge from letters he'd received from friends in other units. Bruckmann had sampled spit-and-polish, foot slogging, endless drill, and knew he never wanted to taste it again. He knew he'd enjoyed his work; with Faust's tutelage, he now understood why.

But should anything happen to Stoner, there was no guessing what would befall the Wildflower operation. Bruckmann didn't kid himself; he didn't know anywhere near enough to be considered even a short-term substitute for his commanding officer. Should Stoner "keel over," as Faust phrased it, he'd be facing a new boss or a new billet. He could find himself again polishing brass and presenting arms and marching marching marching, without having obtained enough experience to earn himself a permanent place in the intelligence community.

And then there was Jennifer. She'd already lost both parents, her grandmother, and her little sister; if Stoner did "keel over," she'd be alone. Although he couldn't imagine her as the love of his life, Bruckmann enjoyed Jennifer's company and respected her ferocious determination. But even if he detested her, no one deserved such a lonely life sentence.

Not even Faust, who was also alone.

He glanced over his shoulder. The gleaming eyes, liquid in the dark, met his gaze across the midnight of the guardroom. At first glance, Faust's expression seemed honestly concerned. But Bruckmann knew he wasn't imagining the satisfaction pulsing beneath the surface.

Faust's words might be honest. But his motives weren't. Bruckmann realized he was trusting his enemy.

"That's a shame, mate," Faust said.

Bruckmann's budding compassion turned cold with reality. Faust was playing with him. And the green little lieutenant who fancied himself a valuable member of the intelligence community was letting him.

With great deliberation, Bruckmann opened the binder rings at random, slid in the last few pages, and snapped it closed. The clacking metal echoed in the guardroom's shadows with the finality of a sealing trap. His fingers fumbled the binder back onto the shelf—his every move was being watched; he could feel it as distinctly as a physical touch—then gathered the discarded sheets and bundled them into one of the envelopes. Mrs. Alcock could use them in the morning to start the kitchen stove fire.

At the door he paused and turned. Faust hadn't moved, huddling in his corner like a cat studying a mouse. His pretended compassion and unconcealable satisfaction had vanished beneath silent rage. Bruckmann's reality chilled further.

He was helping to destroy Faust. And Faust knew it.

He swallowed. "Good night."

Faust struck another match—it even sounded derisive—and lit another cigarette.

Bruckmann fled the guardroom and knew it for an

escape. He paused in the corridor, listening for the laugh he was certain would chase him. But it never came. Finally he tiptoed away, confused and more upset than he could remember ever being before.

38

early morning, Wednesday, 28 August 1940
Margeaux Hall

"He's onto us, sir."

Stoner glanced up from his notes. Bruckmann stood before the desk, one hand resting on the back of the closest wing chair. His uniform was crisp as ever, but fine red lines seeped from the corners of his eyes and his face seemed even paler than normal.

No one would accuse him of being a heartless commanding officer. Stoner lifted the receiver. "Norris, connect me with Mrs. Alcock in the kitchen, if you please... Mrs. Alcock, would you be so kind as to send along two cups of coffee? Lovely. Thank you." He replaced the receiver. "Do forgive me, Jack. I should have warned you of the reverse side of the Médoc's medal."

Bruckmann's smile was pained. He circled the desk, dropped into the secretarial chair, and rubbed his eyes. "I admit I stopped by the infirmary for an aspirin. That stuff packs a wallop. And Faust is a cunning sod. As I said, he knows we're manipulating him."

Stoner sat back, swiveling his chair to face Bruckmann's station. "Beneath his poetry, he's far too analytical not to have realized something so obvious. Anything else of note?"

"He tricked me into admitting your rank," Bruckmann ticked points off on his fingers as he spoke, "he's not a natural soldier, he's angry over the treatment he's receiving, he respects you personally, and he's not above being manipulative himself. Oh, yes, and he's going to quit smoking."

"Is he, now?" It was the most interesting item on his lieutenant's list. "He doesn't like our restrictions, does he? I believe he'll find that task more difficult than he's imagined."

"He says he's prepared for it."

"I doubt that, Jack, very much indeed. When he reaches the end of his supply and the craving hits him, he shall suffer more than he's ever imagined. Please ensure I warn our esteemed sergeant to be prepared for the worst."

Someone knocked softly at the door, then Sally entered with a small tray and set cups of steaming coffee before them. "We made fresh for you, sir."

"Thank you, Sally." Stoner tilted his head. "You are being cautious, lass, aren't you?"

She hugged the tray to her chest and shot him a sidelong look, her dark eyes white-rimmed like those of a frightened filly. Her black hair, usually fluffed about her face, peeped from beneath an old-fashioned white mob cap. "Ain't spending no time with no one I don't know."

When she'd gone, Stoner took a sip. "What else?"

Bruckmann set down his cup, picked it back up, held it beneath his nose, stared at his blank notepad.

"Tell me, Jack."

"Sir, I don't mean to pry, but I must ask." Bruckmann hauled in a deep breath. He seemed partly afraid of his own daring, and partly just afraid. "Have you a heart condition?"

Oho. Stoner sat back. Morning sunshine poured through the two French windows, splashed across his desk, glittered off the white porcelain coffee cup, warmed his face and hands. When he went, hopefully it would be from a pleasant room, rather like this one, and softly, quickly. And not until he saw Jennifer well settled, not to be left alone. "Sergeant Tanyon did say he was observant and always watching for weaknesses. Yes, Jack, I have a heart condition; I believe you'll find most old men do. But I hope he hasn't unnerved you with frightful stories."

Bruckmann examined his cup, picked it up again, set it down untasted. The saucer rattled. "I'm sorry. I don't mean to pry."

"Affection and regard are never misplaced, Jack."

His lieutenant flushed, hopefully with pleasure.

Stoner let the silence deepen as he drained his coffee. He set the cup down and chose his words with care. "All lives are finite. We must simply do the best we can with the time we have."

Bruckmann stared at his barely-tasted cup. "Yes, sir."

"Is that all, then?"

"I believe so."

"And in what condition are our manuals?"

"God alone knows."

Stoner laughed. Bruckmann flashed a wry smile and picked up his cup, this time actually drinking.

"Are we ready to proceed?"

Down went the cup again. "I must sharpen some pencils. I'm sorry."

"Prepare yourself, then, and I'll ring Sally for a clean-up. Then we shall advance once more unto the breach, dear friend, once more." He paused. "Or close the wall up with our English mouths."

Bruckmann snickered over his pencils. Stoner, satisfied with one sally, telephoned for the other.

39

the same morning
Margeaux Hall

Breakfast was more cold cereal, this time *sans* molasses, with two slices of dry toast and lukewarm acidic tea that didn't need a mug to stand straight. Faust sighed and ate it all. With these rations, it was no wonder his trousers didn't fit, when he got the chance to wear them.

When he'd finished, Tanyon brought water and the safety razor—no mirror this time—and watched from the cell's open doorway as Faust washed and shaved. Peckham half-sat on the work table with an air of expectancy, as if awaiting his favorite show.

Faust chose his words with care; it wouldn't do to start the day by irritating the sergeant just when they were starting to get along, sort of. "I appreciate the opportunity to wash, but I'd like a bath and my underwear needs cleaning."

Tanyon grunted. "Have to ask the old man."

So much for thinking they were getting along. He might as well hit back. "Do you mean *Major* Stoner?" Maybe he was getting the hang of this blind, left-handed shaving routine; he hadn't cut himself yet.

But Tanyon didn't glance up from watching his hands. "Yes, I mean Major Stoner. You'll find he prefers mister or professor."

Peckham's glance bounced between them and his grin broadened. At the radio, Glover's eyebrows hiked up his forehead. Granted, Glover hadn't heard Tanyon and him *relating* before.

"I guess he's been a professor a lot longer than he's been an officer."

"Not if you count his reserve service."

"Ow!" The blade dug into the curve of his chin. Faust touched the spot and pulled his fingers away dripping red. "You know, I realize you English are trying to upset me and keep me off balance and all that, but it wouldn't kill you to give me a mirror or let me shave in the lavatory."

Tanyon didn't even blink. Or smile. "Have to talk to the old man about it."

"I'm losing weight."

"We've all lost weight."

"I need my suspenders."

"That ought to be entertaining."

Peckham and Glover sniggered.

"Would it really hurt you to—"

"You have to—"

"I know, I know." He washed the soap and blood from his face and grabbed the thin towel. "Do you ever make decisions for yourself?"

The corner of Tanyon's mouth curled. "Not about you."

Faust buried his face in the towel, pressing it against the cut on his chin. Hell, it wasn't his property. "Servile little beggar, aren't you?"

Tanyon's lip curled further. "I beat you, didn't I?"

It stung worse than the cut. Faust lowered the towel and met the three Englishmen's mockery head-on. "Not yet, you haven't."

"Appreciate the warning." Tanyon nodded to the tray. "Want to hand that to me?"

Faust dropped the towel on it. "No." He turned his back and strode to the cot. He'd stashed his last few cigarettes beneath the pillow before he'd fallen asleep, several hours after Bruckmann's retreat from the guardroom.

When he turned back around, striking a match, Tanyon's mockery had vanished. Peckham and Glover barely breathed.

"No one here is your servant."

Faust hauled in a hard first drag. "Really." He turned his back again. Surprising, how much this mattered to him. But his left hand vibrated when he raised the cigarette for another drag.

He didn't look when small sounds told him someone fetched the tray, nor when the cell door clanged shut and the bolt snapped home. The blackout curtain had been drawn back from the window beside Glover's elbow, and early morning sunlight chased all but the deepest shadows from the guardroom and the cell. One beam sliced across the cot's edge and cut a line up the far wall, brightening the battleship-grey paint almost to silver. The wooden floor numbed his bare feet and his still-damp hands were chilled. If he'd stayed in Paris, where he belonged, he'd be breakfasting in his swank hotel room, a volume of poetry propped before him, while Brandt set out his uniform and buffed his boots. He might have found a way to make up with Ritzi, Erhard might still be alive, his arm wouldn't be aching like a mother, and he'd be in his last two weeks of training as a staff officer. This nightmare would never have happened.

He waited for the nicotine to soak through his system and calm him. But this time, it didn't seem to be working.

Cloth rustled behind him.

"Get dressed," Tanyon said. "The old man wants to see you."

He glanced over his shoulder, sighing smoke. The three Englishmen hadn't moved. His bedraggled and scorched uniform lay in a rumpled heap atop the table, minus his boots, of course. But it gave him no satisfaction. "Are my suspenders in there?"

"You have to—"

"Fine." He threw the still-smoldering butt aside and stalked to the table, easing his arm from the sling. "I'll do that."

Tanyon seemed to swell, like a bullfrog. "Pick that up." His voice actually rose.

Now that was more like it. "Bugger off." Setting the sling aside, Faust pulled on his torn mouse-grey shirt.

When he surfaced, Tanyon still glared. "I thought we had this worked out."

"In your fondest fantasies." As he'd expected, his trousers weren't going to fit securely. He muttered one of his rudest English-language expressions, one he hadn't heard Tanyon use before. Glover made a small sound, not quite a cough, and turned to the radio.

Pink rose from Tanyon's collar and invaded his face. "I hope you aren't expecting any satisfaction from the old man."

"From *Major* Stoner?" He squirmed into his tunic. "I don't expect much of anything in this God-forsaken place."

"Good." The sergeant planted his hands on his web belt. "I'm starting to resent your attitude, mister."

"Good." Faust fastened the top button of his tunic and settled it on his shoulders. "And it's *major,* sergeant. Don't forget it again."

Tanyon's eyes narrowed. Faust smiled. It felt like the first time that morning.

"You ready?"

"Do you have a comb?"

"Not for you."

Peckham sniggered. Glover swiveled around, his eyebrows almost in his hairline.

"Of course not." Faust combed his hair with his fingers and took his time, then eased his arm back into the sling. "Yes, sergeant, I'm ready."

40

the same morning
Margeaux Hall

Faust had studied Rommel's book enough to understand the advantages of a purely offensive campaign. He paused before Stoner's desk long enough to bring his heels together, soundless in his dirty socks, but doubtless the old man got the point without the audible emphasis. "Major Stoner."

"*Herr Major* Faust." Stoner didn't blink, his lined face courteous but without a smile. "Please be seated."

"Thank you, but I prefer to stand. I have something to say."

"Indeed." Stoner eased into his chair, leaned back, and folded his hands on the desktop, as if in prayer. "Fire away."

Until that moment, Faust's anger had carried him along nicely. But Stoner's unexpected anticipation, almost eager in its understated scrutiny, made him pause. Suddenly he felt like a whining schoolboy, sniveling to the headmaster about another student, and the image of himself pointing a finger at Tanyon—"*He did it!*"—flashed through his mind. It blunted the edge off his temper, but still, he had to try. "I resent the way I am treated in this establishment under your care."

"Indeed," Stoner said again. "Anything specific?"

"You want a list of my petty grievances?" His anger flared. "Fine. I resent being forced to shave without a mirror when there are perfectly adequate facilities in the lavatory. I resent the public humiliation of being kept in my skivvies in an open cell. I resent being forced to wear my trousers without suspenders for no good reason. And I absolutely resent the continual implied threat of physical abuse from your watchdog over there." He jerked his head at Tanyon, standing as usual to his right and behind him, out of reach.

"The threat of physical compulsion is necessary," Stoner said, with no more emotion than if discussing the weather, "because you have not shown yourself trustworthy."

That was outrageous. "I what?" But he didn't wait for Stoner. "Soldiers should be able to take care of themselves. And I have never threatened a civilian, even when pushed literally to the wall."

Stoner froze, his eyes narrowing and chilling. So that shot hit home. Good—but Faust couldn't suppress a slight tingle, as if he'd gone too far and verbally stepped over some cautionary line. He tried to focus on that first satisfaction but it faded, leaving only the tingle and his pounding anger behind.

"For which I am grateful," Stoner finally said. "And on principle, I agree with your assessment of soldiers. However, I must work with the troops assigned to me and these lads are under my care. I would be a poor commanding officer were I to allow you to run rampant over them."

He didn't want to admit it, not even to himself. But he could see Stoner's perspective. He dropped that line of attack. "My other concerns?"

Stoner watched him, unmoving, patiently impatient.

The point went to Tanyon; this argument wasn't going far. Damn, but he yearned to shove everything off Stoner's tidy desk, causing an unholy crash-and-smash on the floor, and then bury his fist in that smug English face. Was Stoner, with his field rank and ascetic professorial ways, a soldier or a civilian? Whichever role predominated, beneath both resided an old and fragile man. The thought blunted the edge of Faust's rage.

"My suspenders?" His voice sounded apologetic and he flushed. The situation could become no more humiliating. "I'm losing weight and I need them."

"Those have been taken from you to prevent suicide attempts." Neither fear nor satisfaction peeked through Stoner's usual courteous mien. If he'd divined those enraged thoughts, it didn't show.

No matter how impressive he found the old man's control, that gambit took their conversation in the wrong direction and he'd not be tempted. "But if I'm not allowed my uniform in the cell, why can't I wear the suspenders with the uniform outside of it? I can hardly hang myself in the corridors when your watchdog is breathing down my neck." Even such unassailable logic didn't soften Stoner's ice. "I'm not here for your soldiers' entertainment."

"Why are you here, *Herr Major?*" Stoner's eyebrows lifted.

He wasn't entering that debate, either. "You're changing the subject."

Stoner blinked.

It was, Faust decided, his first victory in their desktop combat. This time, his satisfaction ran too deep to be routed. If he could only fight this battle with words and logic, then that's what he'd do, and go down arguing.

The old man seemed to sense his victory, as well, for after their long mutual stare, he broke eye contact and looked down. Faust automatically followed his direction. A signal flimsy lay beneath Stoner's folded hands. The old warrior's counterattack?

"Well," Stoner said, "you do walk past my female clerks, including my granddaughter, and I also have a responsibility for the public decency. Sergeant, my orders are revised accordingly."

"Yes, sir," Tanyon said.

Faust stopped his relieved sigh but only just in time. "Thank you. And my other concerns?"

Stoner jerked his head up, the usual ice in his blue stare giving way to the steel of his anger. "Perhaps you view this as a game, *Herr Major.* However, we English are fighting for our freedom, our culture, and our lives. Your complaints by comparison are trivial."

He'd pushed too far and his control over the discussion had evaporated. Faust perched on the edge of his usual wing chair, the one on the left. "What can I say? If I'd been shot through the stomach and was bleeding all over your office, it would be trivial compared to that." He pulled out his cigarettes. "But my concerns are real and you know this to be true."

"I believe it is time you broadened your scope." Stoner picked up the signal flimsy and glanced over it. "Why is *Oberst* von Maacht looking for you?"

Only three cigarettes remained in the pack. He shook one out, lit it, and dragged hard. He should have realized how the argument would end, once Stoner's inherent combativeness entered the fray. But still, he'd had his lone victory. "Maybe because I've vanished. Why? Are they sending out the bloodhounds? Have they requested information from you personally?"

"Come, don't be facetious," Stoner said. "If you left no

word, as you intimated during our conversation Monday, then that search was conducted upon the discovery of your absence."

"And look what they found." Faust breathed smoke. Again the nicotine wasn't calming him; maybe that would make quitting easier. "I left my desk in a mess, threw my best uniform into a heap on a chair, and didn't grab a toothbrush on my way out the door. Although I wish I had." He tapped ash into the glass tray on the occasional table between the two wing chairs. "Of course my boss is looking for me. Knowing him, he won't quit until he receives word of my capture. He never quits when he has a chance to be a pain."

"One of our listening posts intercepted this radio communication from Army Group headquarters to all subordinate units, initiating an investigation." Stoner didn't glance down at the flimsy.

Faust sighed smoke. "Von Maacht is an old man, Mr. Stoner, but he's not like you. He's vinegary and bitter and enjoys ripping the stuffing out of young upstarts, especially those of us with a university education. He's probably turned five shades of purple by now and this little misadventure is almost worth it, picturing that without having to see it."

"I'll remind you of that assessment in a few days' time," Stoner said, his voice dry. "However, I did not mean to imply that he initiated an investigation into your whereabouts, but that he initiated an investigation into you."

For a moment it didn't sink in. "Into me?"

"The gentleman appears to doubt your loyalty, *Herr Major.*"

No. That couldn't be true. The blue sitting room faded, leaving reality unpopulated and abandoned. Only he and Stoner remained in a narrow cocoon of icy cold nothingness. "May I see that?"

Stoner pushed the signal flimsy across the desk. "By all means."

From headquarters Army Group A to all subordinate units and CID Paris authorizing immediate apprehension Major Hans-Joachim Faust, current assignment general staff Army Group A, on suspicion of high treason. Subject reported missing Friday evening 2300 hours local time, Paris. Forward applicable information concerning subject's suspected current location and any known movements to this headquarters. Signed Oberst Bruno von Maacht, O1, Army Group A, for General-

feldmarschall Gerd von Rundstedt.

He crumpled the little paper in his fist and rested his forehead against it, elbow braced against the desk. But he refused to acknowledge the slow fear that climbed in a shuddering tremor up his spine. It would show in his eyes and Stoner was too damned good at that game. Rommel; being offensive worked for Rommel. "Well, this is something you haven't tried before."

"I beg your pardon?" Stoner said.

Faust set the crumpled flimsy on the spotless blotter. "That is a forgery."

Stoner's chin withdrew into his chest. "If it doesn't capture the flavor of the original, I hope you'll bear in mind that the young ladies in the signal intelligence office who transcribe and decode these radio communications have not received the rigid Prussian training of *Oberst* von Maacht."

"Actually, I can almost hear the old sourpuss dictating this. He'd enjoy the hell out of it." Faust sat back. "But that just makes it a good forgery."

Stoner returned the flimsy to the geographical center of his blotter and laid his folded hands atop it. His chin tilted and Faust's breath caught; damn it, something else was coming at him.

"You realize that if you do escape and return to German-occupied territory," Stoner said, his voice quiet, "you will learn the truth of this matter."

Faust took a deep drag and refused to think. "That I will. Because I have every intention of doing so."

"Brave words, *Herr Major.*" Stoner's measuring stare never left his face.

"Let me put it another way. Do all captured Germans have so much legal trouble in England, or only misplaced staff officers?"

"Meaning?"

"Meaning this is the third allegation you've laid at my door, which is two too many. Either I'm a really bad person, perhaps a really stupid one to leave myself so legally vulnerable, or you're just looking for methods to apply pressure, which means none of those allegations is true."

He paused for a long drag, watching as a slow flush climbed into Stoner's face. Nice to shove that particular shoe onto the other guy's foot. That reaction, at least, was real and not conjured up by his hopeful imagination.

"You fooled me, didn't you, Mr. Stoner? You treated me kindly, told me a few war stories, established a level of trust between us. Then you took advantage of that trust, and my usual naiveté, and convinced me your powers-that-be suspected me of espionage, that I had to establish my credentials or face prosecution and maybe execution. And like a fool I fell for it." He dragged again. "I just can't believe *Oberst* von Maacht is aware of it yet. He's a smart man but he's far from omniscient.

"You lied to me, too. You told me rationing restricted me to one pack of cigarettes per month. At the hospital Monday, Dr. Harris told me official rationing for prisoners of war is three packs per month." He let that sink in. "By now, even I can't help but wonder what else you've told me isn't true."

Stoner returned his stare. The red drained from his lined face, like a flare dying in a night sky, leaving him still and cold and inflamed. Faust inhaled hard, stubbed out the quarter-inch butt, and held the smoke in his lungs as long as he could. He'd drawn his battle lines and fortified his position; now he had to take Stoner's return fire.

"Allow me to clarify the situation for you, *Herr Major.* Firstly, this," Stoner raised the signal flimsy between two fingers, "is a statement, not an allegation. Should you choose to dismiss it and any significance it may have, that is of course your prerogative. I assure you," he added, his voice sinking, "the British government will take this, and all the evidence both for and against you, into consideration when their legal minds determine the final disposition of your case."

He also wasn't imagining the slow flush climbing his own face. Were those charges real, after all? If so, he'd misread Stoner badly. The situation had seemed so clear last night, in the lurking shadows of the guardroom cell. Now, in the cold glare of daylight, his certainty blurred.

Stoner set the flimsy atop his blotter. "Secondly, the allegation of murder, I am sorry to say, was the overreaction of an old and angry man. That investigation is better left to the expertise of Chief Inspector Hackney, who currently displays a rather compelling lack of interest in you. I must ask you to accept my apology for my hasty and emotional outburst."

As much as he longed to remain on the offensive, only one answer was socially acceptable. "We'll regard it as forgotten."

"I thank you." Despite his words, the steel in Stoner's expression remained as chilling as ever. "Thirdly, although you seem inclined to dismiss the charges of espionage, I assure you further they are perfectly serious and will not vanish so obligingly, certainly not with an apology. Finally, official regulations as to cigarette rationing for prisoners of war shall not be applied until and unless your case has been so decided. While you are under investigation, you remain under my jurisdiction and I may set what regulations I consider most suitable for the circumstances." Stoner folded his hands atop the flimsy. In the office's breathless hush, the onionskin paper rustled, startlingly loud. "Is that clear?"

No sense trying to meet that stare. The white-brick fireplace shimmered in the morning sunlight through the French window and Faust's pulse pounded in his ears. The room tightened around him, hollow and cold. "Perfectly. I apologize for calling you a liar. I didn't understand."

"We shall also regard that as forgotten." Stoner leaned back in his chair. "I hope your injury is less painful this morning, despite your malapropos exercise yesterday."

Faust risked a glance. But not a trace of satisfaction lurked in the old man's cultured face. Maybe his gullibility overwhelmed his common sense even more than usual, but unless this was a magnificent bluff, he'd utterly misjudged Stoner last night. And he'd have to wait until he was back in that cell, with the shadows that had misled him so badly, before he'd have time to think again. *Let waking eyes suffice to wail their scorn,* Daniel had written, *Without the torment of the night's untruth.* "Thank you. It seems much better."

"Excellent. Have you further concerns?"

Can I trust you? But there was no sense asking such a question. For that matter, he might be a fool for asking any of his hundreds of questions, but he threw one out to test the water. "Is Professor Best also under investigation for espionage?"

"The evidence against Eduard Best is too incriminating for further investigation," Stoner said. "He has been questioned concerning his activities and further convicted himself from his own mouth."

A chill shivered over Faust. Stoner's trustworthiness remained in doubt. But if that statement was true, then perhaps the charges against him weren't specious, either. "Is he awaiting execution?"

Stoner tilted his chin. Faust braced himself.

"Not as long as he cooperates."

Even being prepared didn't soften that one. Faust stared into Stoner's gentle blue gaze, as *sans merci* as anything John Keats wrote, horror twisting in the pit of his stomach.

"Are you saying you've turned him? You've turned Professor Best into a double agent?"

Stoner's smile contained no humor. "The prospect of having one's neck stretched tends to encourage most people to cooperate."

That was clear enough.

Faust swallowed bile. "Is it possible for me to hear this from Best himself? I'm serious; that man was a rabid Nazi."

"I assure you that leopard has not changed his spots." Irony edged Stoner's voice. "From your privileged position within the guardroom cell this afternoon, you shall witness his supervised Morse transmission to the Fatherland he serves so faithfully. At that time you may ask him any questions you like."

Stoner seemed serious and it was impossible not to believe him. With an effort, Faust looked away. Beyond the open French window, the old gardener pushed a clacking mower past the flower beds. Only two cigarettes left. Maybe he should save these for when life with Stoner got desperate... no, he had to be tough. He lit one and inhaled deeply.

"I see." It sounded stupid but what else could he say?

"Any further questions?"

He had to admit he'd received a credible if unpalatable answer to his first one. But he still didn't know whether he could believe what he'd been told. His thoughts wobbled, throwing him off-balance, as if he'd stepped onto what he'd thought was trustworthy ground and tripped a land mine, as if overnight Stoner had metamorphosed from a professor to a soldier. He certainly displayed a lot more aggression than charm during this discussion, possibly due to having been called a liar. "No, sir."

Stoner glanced down at his hands, his face expressionless. "Then perhaps this is an appropriate moment to broach a second unpleasant but necessary topic. I must inform you that your friends within these islands are not withstanding investigation particularly well."

The comment was so unexpected it cut through his defensive anger. Munting's wicked grin and Barrington's gentle smile flashed across Faust's memory, as real as if they sat in the next room. "My friends? Why are you investigating my friends?"

"Surely you understood this process would cover your entire background?"

He dragged hard. "I didn't think about it. So what is there about two ordinary Englishmen that's not standing up to scrutiny?"

Stoner leaned back in his chair, pulling his hands into his lap. The signal flimsy, released from their weight, rustled again. "Prior to the opening of hostilities, certain of our landed gentry believed their way of life to be threatened by social democracy. Some few of them further believed National Socialist principles comprised an excellent solution to their problem."

But this topic he could forecast and his temper rose to block it. "If you're talking about George Barrington, you're crazy. He's Welsh and he's gentry, but he's almost fanatically British."

"He was photographed at a meeting of the British Nazi Party in 1934."

"When he was taking advanced courses in sociology." Damned if he'd let them slander Barrington. "He also attended meetings of other political parties—the Communists, Labor, the Tories. He wrote and told me how disgusting it was, but he earned a first at All Souls."

Stoner paused. "Are you aware of his current location?"

If only. "No. I know he's in the RAF and I know he flies Spitfires. But I always sent mail to his father's Regent's Park town home."

Another pause. Stoner seemed to consider his words, lips pursed. "And Peter Munting?"

"Is in the Army, headquartered in London. Barrington and I used to laugh at him, saying if he ever got an office in the City, we'd never get him out of it, and that looks to be prophetic. I sent mail to his Bayswater flat."

"Do you know his post or assignment?"

"No, I don't. Mr. Stoner, we weren't stupid; we knew there was a chance of another war. We took security seriously and didn't share such information." It was true. But it was also true he'd say anything to protect them. If Stoner figured that out—hell, surely he'd already figured it out and was just as wary of believing him as he was of believing Stoner. The layers here could drive a man to drink. Faust ground the heel of his hand into one eye, then the other. He'd smoked most of the fag and didn't remember a single puff. Damn the English.

"Major Munting," Stoner said, his voice quiet, "is in military intelligence."

"Smart as he is, one would hope so." *Is,* Stoner had said: Munting, at least, was alive and well. And he'd been promoted. Faust's heart eased even as his soul quaked. "If you two ever start working together, this war will be over before Christmas."

Stoner smiled, again without humor. "Thank you." He crossed his legs and even his lack of humor faded. "Did Major Munting also enroll in upper-divisional sociology courses?"

He ground out the butt then slid his crumpled pack of Players, with its lone remaining occupant, into his breast pocket. "He's never liked people that much."

"He also attended the British Nazi Party meeting in 1934."

"Knowing him, he took the photos. Besides, he's not landed gentry and he told me his father votes Labor."

Stoner tilted his chin. But this time, Faust beat him to the punch.

"I hate it when you do that."

Confusion rippled across Stoner's face. "I beg your pardon?"

"You have this way of tilting your head and looking me over as if you could measure me for a suit with just your eyes, and I know there's a zinger coming in from outer space I'm going to have to field. I hate it, Mr. Stoner."

What looked like pure merriment flashed in Stoner's blue eyes. Then it vanished beneath his usual assessing stare. The expression came and went so quickly, Faust wasn't certain he'd seen it. Maybe it had been annoyance.

"The current zinger, *Herr Major,* is that Squadron Leader Barrington is stationed at RAF Patchbourne."

Squadron leader; he'd been promoted, too. And *is.* Faust leaned back in the chair and let it soak through him. Munting, in his beloved City office, was safe as anyone else in London. But as a fighter pilot, Barrington had been in aerial combat since April and in constant danger—

—*RAF Patchbourne.* It finally registered and the sitting room again faded around him. He'd stood outside the hospital, stared across a field of ripening grain at the heat-shimmering runways. He'd been less than half a mile from Barrington then and wasn't twelve miles from him now. His stomach contracted. In this instance, proximity accused through implication.

"You can't possibly suspect Barrington of being a traitor. You can't think—"

"—that he is your contact? That perhaps he maintained communication with members of the British Nazi Party, gathering information for your anticipated return?" Stoner leaned back in his chair, head aslant. "Certainly not. Nor would we imagine Major Munting had any intention of misusing his access to classified information. It never crossed our minds."

Faust hitched to the edge of the chair. "If you don't believe anything else I say—" But he caught himself; he wouldn't beg. Not even for Barrington and Munting. Across from him, Stoner stiffened as if affronted.

Faust pushed up from the chair, stalked to the fireplace, and leaned against the pine paneling beside the navy blue mantel. Near his elbow, the little carriage clock ticked away, the second hand jerking forward in busy spurts. It all seemed so civilized. Nothing in the pleasant sitting room gave any indication of the life-and-death battle being waged there. But he was so upset he had no idea of the time the clock tried to tell him.

He had to move his relationship with Stoner forward, past this aggression and these accusations, allegations, statements—whatever the hell he wanted to call them. No matter what he thought of the old geezer, to talk his way out of trouble with the British government he needed Stoner, if not actually on his side, then at least not antagonistic. The worst of it all was, if not for the circumstances, he'd rather like the old man.

He turned from the wall. Bruckmann hadn't even glanced up from his notepad, but Tanyon had swiveled to track Faust, one hand on the Webley, not a flicker of emotion on his poker face. Stoner sat unmoving, hands in his lap.

Faust cleared his throat. "I met Barrington and Munting on my first day in Oxford. I'd just walked from the train station, down near Jericho, lugging my suitcase along the High. It had been a long trip and I was so tired, I thought I'd drop. But when I climbed the stairs to my room, I couldn't get in because there were these two guys standing in front of the door with their backs to me, reading the nameplate and talking about this Faust character. The short one carried on about nothing sensible—I learned in time Munting often does— saying this Faust had to be a great wizard, a metaphysicist who'd move the Carfax Tower to the top of the Bodleian, or some such nonsense."

He paused. Stoner's tense facial muscles relaxed and his back melded into his chair. His eyes softened to that summer-sky blue and the edges of his lips were starting to curve up.

"I cleared my throat, but they ignored me and the short one just kept talking, something he does pretty well. Finally I figured out they knew I was there but were waiting to see what I'd do." Faust touched the cigarette in his pocket, as if it were a magic charm to bring him and his friends luck. "So I cast a spell on them."

Stoner's lips curved further. "Perhaps not the best spell you've ever cast?"

"Oh, it was lousy. All it did was turn them around to stare at me. But I kept casting it, over and over, in different ways and with different words, until finally Barrington got the message, grabbed Munting's arm, and hauled him aside." He shrugged. "We've been friends ever since."

He and Stoner stared at each other. The room stilled around them as the moment he created extended, second by honest second. Rather like Stoner's admission of not-knowing the previous night, it sliced through their desktop combat, dissected out the war, and left two ordinary people talking. Stoner's smile faded. He glanced down at the signal flimsy on his blotter, pulled it toward him—then pushed it aside, off-center and askew.

Encouraging. "Mr. Stoner, Barrington's father is the Earl of Mercia. He has tremendous political influence and knew Hugh Trenchard, so he'd have some pull within the RAF, as well. If Barrington wanted the assignment of defending Oxford, his favorite city on the planet, chances are he'd get it. There's nothing suspicious in that."

He waited, trying not to breathe.

But Stoner pulled the signal flimsy back toward him and centered it on the blotter. "It's not Squadron Leader Barrington's location I find suspicious. It is yours."

Damn. "I told you what happened."

"And I cannot help thinking you have not told all."

Erhard threw me out. He wanted to scream the words at Stoner, just hurl them into the middle of the argument and let the old man make of them what he would. But he had no idea what that would be, what insights Stoner could find within those simple words, and chances were, it would be something he couldn't afford.

Stoner's expression hardened, the steel returning to his eyes. Faust swallowed. He'd taken too long to answer. The moment had passed and could not be recalled. He returned to his chair and sagged into it.

"Well." Stoner glanced down at the signal flimsy. Without looking away, he withdrew his silver cigarette case from his breast pocket, removed one, put it between his lips, then closed the case and returned it to his pocket. It took several seconds for him to locate the lighter in another pocket, and Faust found himself watching the old hands like a hungry cat. Finally Stoner found the lighter and lit the cigarette. His right hand snaked out and tugged the ashtray closer. Just as slowly, he exhaled the first lungful.

Faust squeezed his eyes shut. But he couldn't stop his nostrils from twitching. Low; that was so low.

"This intrigues me, *Herr Major.*" Stoner stared at the signal flimsy. He picked it up, angled it to the light, and exhaled smoke in a long stream. "Does *Oberst* von Maacht have a reason to doubt your loyalty?"

He refused to think about it. But his heart beat faster.

"No."

"No?" Stoner tapped ash. "Judicial standards in Germany are different from English ones, of course. What in National Socialist Germany is considered sufficient to trigger an investigation? Evidence of black marketeering? A denouncement from a Party member? Disagreeing with official policy?"

His entire body tightened, toes curling on the hardwood floor. "I don't know much about legal matters."

Stoner glanced up, a vertical line etched between his eyebrows. Behind his gravity, Faust detected the same percolating intense something he'd noticed last night. The next line, then, contained the essence of the old warrior's counterattack.

"Or merely having English friends?"

English friends he'd missed so much, he'd told everyone about them. His heart beat even faster and his left hand gripped the chair arm. "I don't know."

Again Stoner examined the flimsy. "CID Paris. Do you know if the term refers to the Gestapo?"

Precisely what he'd sworn to not think about. Faust watched the gardener clack the mower past the French window. Stoner, the old bastard, was deliberately torturing him. But he couldn't stop himself from swallowing. "I think so."

He didn't turn. But he could feel Stoner's stare like unfriendly zephyrs on his skin.

"They have a somewhat unsavory reputation, you know."

Oh, yes. He knew. His feet twitched. But for once, he had enough sense to keep his mouth shut.

"Very well." Stoner rose. "I believe we are finished for the day. Sergeant Tanyon, please return the prisoner to his cell."

"Yes, sir."

It was his worst defeat yet. He'd come so close to establishing a true rapport with Stoner, and instead had probably alienated him worse than ever. Faust paused only long enough to give Stoner a half-bow, then padded for the door, his socks noiseless on the hardwood floor. But with his hand on the knob, he paused and glanced back.

Stoner stood behind his desk, his face expressionless.

"Yes, *Herr Major?*"

He shrugged, vaguely disappointed. "Usually I reach this point and you call me back for one final question or comment. I thought I'd check before I left."

But Stoner didn't smile. "Good afternoon."

41

the same morning
Margeaux Hall

When the door closed behind them, Stoner lowered himself into his chair and sighed. His heart double-thumped every few beats, a singular sensation as if something foreign and living had invaded his chest. The taste in his mouth, a curious combination of satisfaction and shame, was perfectly vile.

Serving in the previous war, a simple battalion commander in the trenches that stretched like open wounds across France, had been difficult enough. He'd received orders from his commanding officer, he'd organized his men and material for the attack or the retreat, and he'd given the word at the designated time. He'd thought it the hardest action imaginable to order his men to their deaths; he'd killed them as surely as if he'd been behind the machine guns mowing them down. It had hardly been easier to align his rifle sights on a charging young German and he'd always aimed at the center of a man's mass for a quick, clean kill.

But moving from infantry to intelligence entailed more challenges than moving from the field to a desk. He had to accomplish with words what he'd previously accomplished with force of arms; he had to fight his enemy to a standstill and defeat him without ever leaving his chair. His progress to date seemed quite adequate: Faust was outflanked, outgunned, and demoralized, wary and confused, uncertain what weapon would next be brought to bear.

Stoner could not help but pity him. But on a battlefield,

even one confined to a desktop, pity was out of place. He had Faust dead in his sights and any weakening would allow the target to escape. Was breaking a man's spirit any more cruel than shattering his anatomy? Had he any legitimate reason to not aim for the center of Faust's soul?

"It's time to finish him off." He swiveled his chair. "We have him trapped, you know."

Bruckmann glanced up. "I would be. But who knows what he'll come up with?"

Stoner rose, restless, and paced to the sideboard near the French window. Dappled sunlight drenched the cut crystal decanters and overturned glasses. It was noon, the sun nowhere near the yardarm, but he wanted a stiff drink more than he wanted his next breath. At least it would wipe the horrid taste from his mouth.

"You know, Jack, I feel somewhat unwell."

"Your heart, sir?" Behind him, Bruckmann's voice rose an octave.

"No, just a touch of nausea."

"Something you ate?"

"More likely something I said." Respectability lost. Stoner grabbed a tumbler and poured Scotch neat. "Do forgive me, Jack, but I find this is the most distasteful task I have ever performed." He tossed the whiskey back, rolled it across his tongue, savored its rich fire. Heat swept through him as if he'd swallowed a live flame.

Bruckmann leaned back in his secretarial chair, one putteed ankle crossed over the opposite knee. His eyes were shadowed with tiredness but glittering as if a bit of the whiskey's flame carried over to him, as well.

"You remember your assignment?"

Bruckmann nodded, swift stiff jerks of his head. "Yes, sir."

Stoner set the tumbler aside. He'd finish this task, finish Faust, if it finished him. "Give it about an hour. Then do your best."

42

early afternoon
Margeaux Hall

Bruckmann erupted into the guardroom with all the desperation he could muster, Tanyon on his heels. He unlocked the rifles and live ammunition storage, never letting himself glance at the cell even though he sensed Faust's startled stare like a physical touch.

Beside him, the sergeant grabbed the first rifle on the rack and threw it to Pym, sitting at the radio. Pym dropped his book to catch it.

"What's up, sergeant?" he asked.

"Parachutes sighted over Oxford." Tanyon grabbed the next rifle and hurled it at Reynolds, standing bewildered in the doorway. "I said get the squad up here, now!"

Bruckmann stacked boxes of live cartridges onto the work table. He stole a glance at Faust and saw him shrug.

"Probably your own troops training." In the after-lunch warmth of the cell, Faust had set aside the blanket. He stood in undergarments and sling, leaning his left elbow against the crossbar.

"And we're supposed to be able to tell the difference?" Bruckmann counted the boxes on the table and reached for more.

"There are two easy ways to tell whether those are British or German parachutes."

Tanyon froze, rifle in hand. Bruckmann stared at the boxes in his arms, at the young soldiers clustering open-mouthed in the doorway, then at Faust. He hadn't moved.

"How?"

Faust yawned.

Tanyon slammed the rifle onto the work table and pulled a pack of cigarettes from his pocket. Faust's dark eyes, tired and red-rimmed, fastened onto the pack with the voracity of a starving man. But he said nothing.

After a moment, Tanyon shook one cigarette half from the pack and held it through the bars. Faust reached for the entire pack, but Tanyon withdrew it an inch. The two men stared at each other. Then Faust shrugged, took the single cigarette, and waited. Tanyon put the pack away, produced a lighter, and held the flame steady. Faust lit the cigarette and withdrew two steps.

"British parachutes can be controlled," he said, smoke trailing from his mouth. "German ones can't. If the men in the 'chutes can avoid the trees and buildings, then they're British troops in training. If they land in the trees—" He shrugged again.

It wasn't the reaction he and Stoner had anticipated. "You said two ways."

Faust blew smoke. "Do you hear any shooting?"

Bruckmann smoldered. "Issue the bloody ammunition, sergeant." He stalked from the guardroom, rifle and cartridges in hand. He paused in the doorway amid his soldiers. "Set up a perimeter and pay special attention to the Dark. Anything moves in those trees, shoot it."

Four steps down the corridor, he turned and tiptoed back, easing past Whiteside and Ellington to hide behind Peckham in the doorway. He arrived in time to hear Faust's voice again.

"Are there deer in that forest? I wouldn't mind a spot of venison. It would make a nice change from all this cabbage we've had lately."

Bruckmann's shoulders sagged. It would be immensely satisfying to use his rifle, and the ammunition, on a certain human target. But he'd have to answer to Stoner. Better to avoid temptation. He shoved them into Whiteside's empty hands.

"Put those away after Tanyon issues the all-clear," he said in a whisper, then crept downstairs to report.

43

early afternoon
Margeaux Hall

"No," Stoner said, "oh, no, no, no, that is not a total failure by any means." He paced between his cot and the French window on the room's far side, where he could work up a good stride. "The bit about the parachutes is simply military trivia and of no value whatsoever. But his reaction—" At the window he stopped. Bruckmann stood near the desk, braced almost to attention. "He showed no excitement? No anticipation, nerves, fear, eagerness?"

"He yawned," Bruckmann said bluntly.

He waved a hand and resumed pacing. "That sounds like play acting." The what-not table with its assortment of Dresden china figurines, the watercolor of children fishing, the light pine paneling, all spun past his shoulder in a colorful kaleidoscope, enough to dizzy him. At the cot he turned again. "The cigarette was most important to him?"

Bruckmann hadn't moved. But his chin sank until it almost touched his chest and a vertical line creased his forehead. "Yes, sir."

"A mistake, Jack, a serious tactical error. He should have displayed surprise, at the least, if he truly knows as little of the invasion as he claims." He tapped one fist atop the other and strode back to the French window. Astonishing how the news rejuvenated him. Perhaps the Scotch should take some of the credit; at least that awful taste was gone.

"What, then?" Bruckmann asked.

Stoner jerked to a stop as if he'd hit a brick wall rather than a startling new idea. Ice rippled up his spine and shivered at the base of his skull. He measured his words and chose them with care. "It is possible he saw through our little ruse, although I'm certain it was carried out with verve and enthusiasm. It's also possible—" He broke off, wet his lips, tried again. "Jack, do you believe Faust is serious about escaping?"

"Great Scott, yes."

"Why?" He breathed the word as quietly as a prayer.

"Why, sir?" Bruckmann paused. "I believe he's serious because he shows determination and—"

"No, Jack, that's not my question. Why should he escape?"

Bruckmann shifted. "Is this a rhetorical question?"

"Escape is a dangerous game. I've played it myself and I've known men who died playing it. Faust could have broken his neck in the ravine, Major Kettering's warning shot might have hit him—" he threw out his hands "—Jerome Owen could have taken a pitchfork to him. It's happened."

"But it's his duty."

"His greater duty is to return his services—intact—to his unit. And to accomplish this, all he must do is sit tight and await the invasion." Stoner paced two steps, but the energy had transferred itself from his heels to his head. He halted and let his thoughts fly. "And he'd be safer in a cell than out wandering should the *Wehrmacht* march into town. They won't know him from Adam and his German uniform might not protect him."

"You're thinking—" Bruckmann broke off. "I don't know what you're thinking."

"He knows the very day. Otherwise he would have reacted to our little ruse."

Bruckmann's eyes threatened to pop from his head. "Then why is he so determined to escape?"

"My first guess is the invasion isn't until next spring. If that's true, then he has every reason to remove himself from our tender mercies. He's an intelligent man and he knows he cannot predict the exact moment his nerve will give way." He crossed the room to his desk. "And he doesn't want to hang any more than the next man. It's time to call in the big guns. You said Captain Clarke is stationed at Brighton? I want him here tomorrow."

Bruckmann didn't budge. "Sir, why hasn't Faust told us about that incident?"

"You mean, he's been nice to the dragon, so the dragon

should be nice to him in return?" Stoner sat down and dragged a notepad from his desk. His thoughts were flying too fast for dictation; Jennifer would have to decipher his handwriting again, poor lass. "I'll mention your suggestion to Jack Lewis at Magdalen; it's the sort of incident he likes to put into children's stories. Captain Clarke, Jack. Tomorrow."

44

mid afternoon
Margeaux Hall

Although afternoon had not yet surrendered to evening, the sky outside the guardroom window darkened fast, a pearly nacre shadowing into gun-metal grey. The air in the cell chilled Faust's naked limbs and felt charged, as if with electricity. He shrugged into his blanket and watched Tanyon put the rifles and ammunition away, checking each box of cartridges, chamber, and magazine before locking them into the storage bin.

"False alarm?"

Tanyon grunted. "Major Kettering. Just wish he'd give the rest of us some warning."

"Thanks for the cigarette, in any case."

The look Tanyon gave him was downright evil. "What you said about the parachutes—was it true?"

Faust shrugged. "If I tell a lie, you'll know it."

Tanyon shrugged in turn. "That's true enough."

Faust gave the sergeant his own version of an evil look. "That should have been worth more than one cigarette."

"It wasn't worth one."

At the radio, Pym glanced over his shoulder with a grin. The sight reminded Faust of the afternoon's entertainment.

"So when does *Herr Professor* Best put on his show?"

Tanyon glanced at the clock. "Twenty minutes."

It hurt like hell, worse than all his aches and pains combined. But Faust gritted his teeth and said it. "May I please wear my uniform?"

Tanyon didn't even look at him, but pulled a web belt from the storage cabinet and put it on. "You have to ask the old man."

"When do I see him again?"

"Maybe this evening." A Webley .455 revolver appeared next. Tanyon flipped open the cylinder, slid a moon clip of six rounds into the action, closed and locked the cylinder in place, and dropped the revolver into his holster. The catch snapped.

"That won't do me much good in twenty minutes."

"You should have asked when you had the chance." Tanyon loaded a second revolver and slid it into another holster.

Faust leaned his forehead against the cool metal and considered pounding his head to a pulp. But it would hurt worse to give the sergeant such satisfaction.

"You do this to me and I will never forgive you." It sounded weak even to him.

Tanyon scoffed. "Hope I'm not supposed to be impressed." He grabbed the second holster and strode from the guardroom.

Behind the radio, Pym rolled his lips together. But he didn't hide his eyes and they were laughing.

Faust turned and leaned his back against the bars, wrapping the blanket more closely about his shoulders. He'd lost every argument he'd undertaken, which meant it was time to go on the offensive, which meant he needed his boots, which meant Hackney had better hurry up with them.

Could he trust Stoner? Faust's original assumption—that Stoner was playing him for a sucker—still seemed plausible. But the cold certainty of the previous night had vanished and he no longer knew what was real.

He paced the cell. He'd been so certain he was right, that Stoner had fooled him and the so-called investigation was actually an in-depth interrogation. And once the idea had occurred to him, he hadn't thought about it a second time. But Stoner's rebuttal had been more of an eye-opener than Irish coffee the morning after. Maybe the old man spoke the truth after all.

And he'd come so close to establishing a true rapport with Stoner. The bitter disappointment lingered like an ugly aftertaste. He knew he'd touched the old man with his story, the same way Stoner had touched him with his tale of the attack at Neuve Chapelle. But he'd hesitated, rather than blurt out Erhard's perfidy, and now he'd be second-guessing that, too. Faust let the blanket fall to the floor and stretched as he paced, twisting at the waist to work out the kinks. His side barely hurt any more, unlike his tortured thoughts. Maybe the English had driven him crazy. If his thoughts kept going on that particular carousel, there'd be no *maybe* about it.

Nor, from the quiet of the cell, could he work up much outrage over the investigation of Barrington and Munting. They were good officers and would stand up to any scrutiny. Besides, after Dunkirk, the English needed all the competent officers they could find and couldn't afford to prosecute two excellent ones unless duplicity was certain. Since no duplicity existed, if Stoner and his superiors did decide to press charges against Faust, he'd face them alone, not with Barrington and Munting beside him.

But that signal flimsy was a different matter. Faust picked up the blanket on his return trip and slung it across his shoulders with a by-now practiced motion, dropping a few deep knee bends while he settled it into place. The signal flimsy scared him and he knew why all too well.

He still wasn't sure he could believe it, which made his fear seem as irrational as his circular reasoning. But if it was a forgery, as he'd told Stoner, it was well done, and he found it easier to picture *Oberst* von Maacht dictating that message and alerting the Gestapo in Paris than picturing himself swinging at the end of an English rope.

Logically, the argument could be stripped down to two sentences: The English had no verifiable reason to press charges against him. But the Gestapo did.

Unbidden and unwanted, Clarke surfaced in his memory: a round face that promised to go florid later in life, like—Faust could think of no more apt expression—like a ripening cabbage with a brushed mustache and fierce dark eyes. He'd last seen that face scruffy with beard and dirt and sweat, a cigarette dangling from the corner of its mouth, defiant beneath it all as if being shot and buried by the *Waffen SS* wouldn't be enough to stop its owner.

After the incident at the Aa Canal, Faust had wormed his way into the First Panzer Division's investigation. He'd questioned the German survivors; there'd been no British ones hanging about. He'd examined each dead face, whether it wore British Army khaki or *Wehrmacht* field grey. Clarke's face had not been there, nor Brownell's.

Nor, for that matter, was Greis'. At the time Faust had assumed that Clarke had hauled the *Waffen SS* commander into the forest for a bit of private vengeance and that his body might never be found. Now he couldn't be certain.

Several Lee Enfield rifles scattered about the encampment had convinced the investigators this had been a British raid to rescue the prisoners. The question of how the British had known the prisoners' location had never arisen. After all, Rommel had punched through France like an express train. He'd left so many British and French soldiers in his wake, still fighting inside the German rear lines, that it had been assumed some of those had rallied and carried off the raid. Faust had signed off on the report without a qualm.

He found himself staring at the battleship-grey wall of the cell. No telling how long he'd stood there, lost in thought. He tried a one-handed push-off against the surface, feeling the exertion in his pectorals and arm muscles, but only a touch of pain in his side. It felt good. He did another then reached for a rhythm, remembering the exultation he'd found running across the turnip field. For a few moments he lost himself in the relaxing toil of the workout. Then Pym turned a page. Reality intruded with the rustle. Faust touched his forehead to the wall, pushed off one last time, and resumed pacing.

If Greis had survived the raid but had not stepped forward for the investigation—unconscious from serious injuries, or hiding from Faust, or whatever the reason, or whatever the reason—then there could be some serious meat behind the signal flimsy. As Stoner had implied, he'd have to be ten kinds of fool to return to Germany and face the resulting hornet's nest.

But if he didn't return to Germany, he'd be stuck in England. He'd have to face Stoner's version of reality, true or not. He shuddered, clutching the blanket closer. He'd have to make some sort of deal with the English devil.

Voices spoke in the hall. A swift glance at the clock showed his twenty minutes were up. Faust cursed the sergeant, his ancestry, morality, and face, and scrambled to the cot, in the darkest corner of the cell. The grey blanket, darker than the walls, would do for camouflage. He draped it about his body as closely as he could until only his head emerged. Maybe Best wouldn't notice him; if he did, no reason to advertise his skimpy attire.

Thunder rumbled in the distance as Bruckmann entered the guardroom, a holstered Webley dangling from his Sam Browne belt. Best strutted behind him and the sergeant brought up the rear.

Maybe he shifted on the cot or made some small sound. But suddenly Best halted and twisted to face the cell. Their gazes crossed. The intervening decade fell away and Faust found himself again in the university lecture hall, watching the arrogant pig strut before the lectern like some intellectual parody of Hitler, parroting the same outrageous phrases in the same hoarse chanting voice. He tasted bile. He'd been wrong. Best's venom had not been drawn. Beneath the starveling look remained the same hauteur, and as he tasted its silent lash Faust's skin prickled with heat. At least the guardroom had darkened from the approaching storm, his first bit of luck.

"Perhaps my lectures bore some fruit after all." Best tilted his chin. "But then, you are here, in this home for un-wedded traitors. Perhaps not much fruit?"

It was just like Best to ridicule Stoner's mannerisms, when Stoner was twice the man Best would ever be. "To what are you wedded? Not the Fatherland you swore to serve, obviously."

Best darkened as thunder rumbled, closer this time. "You will address me properly and with due respect."

"You will suck a lemon." He wished he had a cigarette to spare, or pockets in which to slide his hands, or some other means of emphasizing his disrespect, preferably in the most Germanic manner possible.

Pym choked. At Bruckmann's glance, he swung back to the radio console.

Bruckmann set a typewritten sheet on the table before the radio and dragged out a chair, dropping his other hand to the holstered Webley at his side. "*Herr* Best, we're ready."

Best turned his back on Faust and sat, sliding the head-phones over his ears. He massaged his fingers then began tapping the key. Pym, wearing a second set of headphones, took notes beside him.

The first few letters Best tapped out would be the call-up sign; Faust remembered that much from his signals training. And by careful listening, he realized Best repeated those three or four letters several times, pausing between repetitions. Suddenly both Best and Pym leaned over their notepads and began transcribing, which meant someone on the other end was responding. Once they'd completed the call-up ritual, Best began tapping the transmit key in earnest.

As an officer cadet, Faust had learned Morse code. But he'd never used or practiced it and found he could only discern an occasional letter during Best's long transmission. Of course, the message would be coded; perhaps Best himself didn't know what disinformation it contained; and even if Faust could have sorted out the letters, he wouldn't have understood the message.

As a test of Best's loyalty, then, this was a washout. Just watching him tap out Morse code proved nothing; the man could be transmitting a weather report to Berlin, or London, for that matter, as it was impossible to tell who received the communication.

Finally Best sat back and removed the headphones. "I have finished, Lieutenant Bruckmann."

Pym ripped the top sheet from his notepad and handed it to Bruckmann, who folded it together with Best's page and slipped both into his breast pocket. "Let's get you back to your quarters, then."

"What's in that message?" Faust asked.

Best didn't even look at him, but rose and stood next to Bruckmann. Faust sniffed. Tanyon did the ignoring routine with more style.

"Answer the question." Bruckmann dropped his right hand to the Webley on his belt.

Tough guy tactics. Faust nodded his approval. It wasn't likely Best, an intellectual and never a soldier, would know how to respond. When the professor cringed away from Bruckmann, Faust allowed himself a small smile.

"I do not know." But he still wouldn't look toward the cell.

Faust glanced at Bruckmann. "Tell your boss I'm not impressed."

Bruckmann's lips narrowed. "*Herr* Best, you've lived and worked here for how long now?"

"I do not know." Best stared at the far wall, a flush rising from his neck to cover his face. "I do not know today's date. No one tells me such things."

"True," Bruckmann said. "But I've been assigned to Margeaux Hall for three months, and you were here first. So it's been at least that long, right?"

"That is correct."

"How often do you send messages for us?"

Best shrugged. His eyes flashed. "Every few days."

Faust tingled. Courage remained beneath Best's hypocrisy. Was Stoner aware of it? If not, he wasn't sharing.

"And you send whatever we tell you to send?" Bruckmann said.

The flare of emotion died, leaving Best's narrow ascetic face watchful and still. "Yes."

Faust said something—anything—to hide his growing sense of wrongness. "And there's a German on the other end receiving this transmission?"

Best's glare packed hate. "As I am not on the other end, I do not know."

"Logical." Faust shrugged at Bruckmann. "I have to

think about this."

"Think all you want." Bruckmann turned on his heel, hand still on the Webley. "Let's go, *Herr* Best."

As they left the guardroom, Best's voice floated back. "Before you treated me with more respect."

Bruckmann's followed. "I was younger then."

For just a moment, Faust pitied Best. Then the two years of mandatory haranguing flooded into his soul, scraped raw by the unchanged arrogance. Let the Nazi swine stew.

45

mid afternoon
the Abbey Arms and the road to Margeaux Hall

Not even a decent suppertime, and already Hackney
dragged his feet. He'd taken statements from not quite half of
the Patchley Abbey Home Guardsmen, and most gave satisfying alibis for Saturday night and Tuesday. But two of them...
he sighed and opened the pub's door, leaving the rising
thunderstorm for the murky air within.

Inside the otherwise empty room, Arnussen sat at a table
before the open casement windows, specs perched on his nose,
subdued grey light spilling onto the papers piled high before
him and the empty tankard weighing them down. He'd found
an artist's sketchpad somewhere and drawn a chart on the
oversized sheet, ruled columns stretching across the page. He
glanced up as Hackney settled across from him.

"How'd it go among the dragons?" he asked.

"Most of them were villagers." Hackney set his notepad
on the table.

Arnussen treated him to a shrewd glance. "Meaning at
least one might not be."

"You know me too well." He flipped over several pages.
"Tom Burbank runs the general store. On Saturday night, he
knew which men were about him, but the two I've spoken with
couldn't swear to him being there. Now, he's a quiet sort and I
did have to draw him out to get him talking. It's possible, with
all those goings-on, he just didn't have much to say."

"Or it's possible he wasn't in the search group at all, but

off somewhere doing something else." Arnussen sat back. "What about Tuesday?"

"It seems on Tuesday, just before noon, he couldn't keep his eyes open any longer and snuck home for a nap, leaving his wife to run both the store and her switchboard. Monday night his Civil Defense group taught a first aid lesson past his bedtime, and Tuesday night being Home Guard drill, he wanted to be sharp for it."

Arnussen played with his pencil. "That could easily be true."

"Yes, it could, and his wife bears it out. It's also the sort of thing that's almost impossible to prove."

"So do you think he's our dragon?"

"No." Hackney flipped over a few more pages. "But we have to sort him out. Hopefully he'll have the wrong blood type. Then there's the blacksmith, Sullivan Gilbert—"

"You must be joking."

"—whose parents loved light opera and met on an amateur stage. He takes Home Guard and Civil Defense seriously, because he believes it's past time to put these Germans in their place or we'll still be fighting them a hundred years from now. He kept his mouth shut during the search Saturday night, unlike everyone else, he says, so it's possible no one will remember he was there."

Arnussen sighed, it seemed for both of them. "And on Tuesday?"

"He spent the entire day in his smithy. Pamela Alcock donated her car to the local Civil Defense and meant to buy a horse for making deliveries, but the wheels on the old buggy needed fixing. He worked on those all day and no one came calling, so he has no alibi, either."

"Again, we'll wait on his blood type."

Hackney closed his notepad and tossed it onto the table. "What have you got?"

Arnussen turned the sketch pad around. The ruled columns were headed with their winnowing criteria—blood type, alibi, boot soles, hair color, body scratches, hand-kerchiefs. Beneath the headings, in tight cramped writing, the list of names straggled down the sheet. Hackney flipped deeper; the suspect list covered five sheets and fewer than a fifth of them contained any notations within the columns. He sighed. Although he could do this sort of detailed cross-referencing, it wasn't the sort of investigation he handled best, and a tension headache started the slow climb up the back of his neck.

"This doesn't include the Home Guard," Arnussen said

apologetically. "I'll add them at the end. Kettering sent a dispatch rider with the first batch of his soldiers' statements and blood types, and I've gotten this much organized. I've also done sketches of both crime scenes and a rough diagram of Margeaux Hall based upon what little we know of the place—"

"We don't want to know more about it."

"—showing where people were Saturday night." Arnussen turned the pad back around and riffled the pages. "Kettering kept copies of the statements, and he's got his engineering lieutenants drawing diagrams of their search lines from Saturday and Tuesday, with each soldier's name in its proper place. He's also got another company of his soldiers, one that's not implicated in either murder, out searching the forest for Harriet Stoner's yellow dress and possibly another handkerchief." He flipped back a few pages and peered at a note. "The 211th Engineer Park Company. He said they'll take the forest apart and rebuild it if they have to, but if the dress is there, they'll find it."

Hackney laughed. "I feel for that man's subordinates. How many training exercises of this sort will they put up with before they mutiny?"

"Probably more than you or I." Arnussen dragged two typed reports from beneath his pad. "And Patchbourne sent the German prisoner's boots back, as well as these."

Hackney glanced over the first document as thunder rumbled in the distance. It was the serology report, stating the handkerchief found in Grace's bedroom had been wetted with both saliva and blood from a person of type O positive, as well as sperm from a secretor of type A positive.

"He gagged her with it then cleaned himself afterward." And the fingerprint report hadn't even a partial anomalous print to offer from Grace's bedroom, nothing at all on her bedstead or the window casings. "He wiped the room down, too. Damn him."

"Too much to ask for, that would be." Arnussen replaced the reports beneath his pad, hiding the dark circular stains on the tabletop. "It would be too easy if all we had to do was fingerprint the suspects."

"We wouldn't even have to do that. We could finish the first round of elimination based on blood type and alibi, then print only the men we needed." Hackney rubbed his eyes. Between the lowering electrical storm and the pressure inside him, the headache was full-blown. It would be a ruddy awful night, and he had over half the local Home Guardsmen to interview next day, with several days of cross referencing before they even knew where they stood, what additional evidence they'd need, boot sole casts or physical examinations or hair samples. "You know, Axel, I can't help but wonder if there isn't a quicker way of doing this."

Arnussen cocked an eyebrow at him, then pulled the stack of papers closer and resumed working. "What are your famous instincts telling you?"

"I don't know yet." Hackney massaged his neck. "Why would a man rape and murder a little girl?"

"Harriet was seventeen and a young woman." Arnussen wrote an entry, then pulled the top statement from beneath the empty tankard and set it upside down in another, smaller stack.

"Grace wasn't."

Arnussen inserted another notation into his table. "Let's try it another way. We don't know for certain Harriet was raped. What if she willingly snuck away from the dance with someone? Then say he accidentally hurt her and liked the feeling of power it gave him, and he forced that domination to the ultimate degree and killed her. So now he knows how it's done, but when he goes looking for another victim, there isn't a dance scheduled. So he takes whatever offers whether she suits him or not."

Hackney shook his head. "That won't wash, Axel. Whoever it was, he fancied Grace. Otherwise he'd have found a more isolated victim, rather than killing her right under her mother's nose."

"Hm." Arnussen flipped over another report. "Well, it's definitely a crime of power."

"Perhaps he doesn't feel he has any power in his life right now and he's looking for it wherever he can."

Arnussen froze. "A conscript, you mean? Conscription's necessary, you know. As your light opera blacksmith said, if we're going to defeat the Germans once and for all, we've got to mobilize every resource—"

"Are you listening to yourself here?" The headache pounded as thunder stalked the village like a beast of prey. "You said mobilize resources. These are people, not things, but you're talking about using them when they're useful and throwing them away when they're not, even getting them killed."

"But for a necessary end."

Hackney pursed his lips. "Dehumanizing people always comes at a price. And this might be part of that price. Besides, it doesn't have to be a conscript. It could be someone evacuated from London, someone bombed out of his home and everything he's known."

Arnussen tapped his specs higher on his nose. "Perhaps someone whose family burned in the bombing."

"Or someone older, whose son was killed fighting on the continent or left in France as a prisoner." The thunder and headache were rising fast. "War's an ugly thing and it does ugly things to people."

Arnussen pulled his suspect list closer. "Until your instincts give us more information, you won't mind if I keep plugging at this, surely?"

Wind whipped through the open windows. Arnussen grabbed papers and Hackney leapt for the casement handles. The first drops of rain pattered on the street outside. Homer Owen appeared from the kitchen, shrugging into an oilskin.

"Won't be a lot of business tonight." He crossed to the front door. "Let me put the blackout shutters up, gentlemen, then I'll light the lamps for you."

As Homer left, Hackney sat back with a sigh. "Axel, I need to get out."

"I've been watching you massage your neck." Arnussen glanced at the window, splattered with the first fat drops. "You didn't bring a raincoat, did you?"

"Me?" Hackney shrugged. "I won't melt. I'll walk down to Margeaux Hall and give that poor man his boots back."

Owen insisted Hackney wear his greatcoat, so he was buttoned against the weather as he set out. Nevertheless, by the time he reached the chicken farm on the road to Margeaux Hall, the pounding rain dripped from his hat brim down inside the collar of the coat and onto his suit beneath, and when he reached the Dark, he shook himself like a drenched hound.

This was the true scene of the crimes.

He stopped beneath the trees atop the rise, where Sergeant Tanyon had stood guard and prevented Major Faust from crossing the road. If he had crossed, would he have surprised the killer in the forest, stopping the attack on Grace before it began? If Faust hadn't been so disoriented Saturday night, would he have moved faster, interrupted the killer at work, and saved, if not Harriet's body, then perhaps her life?

The dark and dripping branches met overhead, deepening the afternoon twilight almost to night. The beeches and oaks were a physical presence, as if they breathed and whispered secrets he couldn't hear. They'd held their position along this ridge, running north and south like a border guard between Patchley Abbey and Margeaux Hall, for decades or centuries. Surely people had died here before now. Surely young women had been dragged into the forest's depths during medieval or Elizabethan or Georgian days, violated and butch-

281

ered for some man's vanity.

Rain dripped into his eye. The trees swam together. Hackney blinked and glanced about, disoriented as if just awakened. But the trees kept moving. No, not the trees. Two Bedford trucks were parked just below the rise on the road toward Margeaux Hall, sheltered beneath the overhanging branches. A lone sentry stood before them, watching him with expressionless eyes, rifle at the ready.

And soldiers moved among the trees, heads down in the rain, examining the ground, shifting fallen branches and leafy debris, plumbing the forest's hidden soul. Major Kettering had said he'd send his best, most thorough men to take the forest apart and put it back together. He hadn't exaggerated.

It couldn't be Kettering. If the major had been guilty, he'd have sent slackers, soldiers made careless or dispirited by the retreat from Dunkirk. These men had certainly retreated— more than one white bandage flashed among the tree trunks— but they hadn't surrendered.

Indeed, this was the true scene of the crimes. And some nebulous clue hovered on the edge of his thoughts, just beyond his reach. It wasn't the trees, and perhaps it wasn't precisely here. But there was something, some connecting point, that drew all the elements together and would solve the case. Something else, besides the dress, that had to be found.

Hackney glanced down at the canvas grip in his hand, hefted its weight, and started walking as fast as he could for Margeaux Hall.

46

early evening
Margeaux Hall

He ran along the beach with the Baltic stretching to his right, arms pumping in easy rhythm with his strides, shoes sinking into the white dunes and kicking sand into his socks, sweat running down his back and chest. It felt so good to be free again and out of that frigging cell, away from the English and especially Stoner, that he accelerated for the sheer joy of it, angled toward the water and ran through the tail end of the surf, cold northern water lapping over his ankles and sucking his feet down, slowing him until he realized some *thing* was chasing him, Stoner had set it on his trail, and it got closer and closer but he couldn't escape the water and he slowed further, each step shorter and choppier than the last, until finally he—

—of course—

—awoke to find himself tangled in the grey blanket, his body awash with sweat. Thunder rumbled, no longer in the distance but overhead, as loud as artillery rounds shelling his position, and rain splashed against the glass behind the drawn blackout curtains. Again shadows invaded the guardroom, lurking in the corners and camouflaging the room's hard edges. Damned if he'd let them fool him again.

"What in the world were you dreaming over there?" Pym said. "Tossing and turning like you was fighting something."

He almost lifted his right hand to push his hair off his forehead, but remembered in time to use his left. "I dreamed I was running in the surf. There's a place on the Baltic coast called Neukuhren, where I did part of my officer's training, and we used to run and ride along this wide white-sand beach." He sat up in bed and shook off the blanket. "I dream about that beach a lot, for some reason."

"Huh." Pym turned the book's page, beneath the single lamp burning on the radio table. "I moved my mum from Brighton to stay with her sister, my Aunt Bertha, that is, at Holbeach on The Wash. It's a weird place, lots of grey beaches that change shape with the tides, and flat as stale beer. Sometimes I dream about that, the landscape appearing different if I turn my back." He pushed the book closer to the light. "I don't like that dream."

Faust climbed out of bed and stretched. His stomach seemed hollow, and rumbled in rhythm with the thunder. "Did I sleep through dinner?"

"Any minute now." Pym moved a red ribbon into place and closed the book. "Will your friends invade through The Wash?"

He paused but didn't glance over. "How should I know?"

"They think you do."

"I'm not responsible for what they think." He paced to the iron bars, then back to the cot. He wanted a cigarette, but he only had one left and he'd decided to save it for some after-dinner thinking. Maybe he should just go ahead and finish the pack. No, maybe he shouldn't. "What are you reading?"

Pym chuckled. "I'm reading about you."

It took a moment. Then Faust laughed, too. "Goethe or Marlowe?"

The lance corporal paused, as if confused. Then his eyes sharpened and he glanced at the book's spine. "A chap called Christopher Marlowe."

"That's the best version of the Faust legend." He ought to know; he'd read all of them so many times, he'd memorized chunks of each. "And don't get the idea I'm anything like that guy or related to him. It's a legend, like King Arthur and the knights of the Round Table."

"Huh," Pym said again. "So I don't have to worry about you making a deal with the devil and him coming to break you out of here, do I?"

That depended upon which devil came. But at least now he knew why Pym had gotten the lance corporal's stripe rather than Peckham—Pym could use his head for more than a target. "Not likely."

Those boots clumped in the corridor, then Tanyon entered the guardroom, his arms full of field-grey woolen cloth, as usual bundled into a heap like dirty laundry. He paused in the doorway and riveted a suspicious stare at Faust. "Not likely what?"

"Not likely I'm gonna last until dinner time," Faust said. "What's a guy supposed to do for entertainment around here?"

"We could talk about the invasion."

Faust shook his head. "Not even for you, cutie pie."

Pym chuckled. "I wish I could carry on the way you two do it. That's clever, that is."

"It impresses the girls." Faust made kissy sounds.

Tanyon didn't smile. He strode to the cell and dumped the uniform between the bars and onto the table. "Get dressed."

Faust didn't move. "So you can get fresh with me again? Not interested."

"Chief Inspector Hackney is here and wants to see you." Tanyon leaned against the radio table and lit a cigarette. "Why, I can't say. I don't think you're all that pretty, myself. But since the man walked through the most God-awful rainstorm to see you, then he's going to see you." The sergeant blew smoke toward the cell. "What you're wearing when he sees you is your choice."

Bastard. Faust couldn't stop his nostrils from twitching. But for once, he had no trouble keeping his mouth shut. His hands and feet tingled with nerves, as if the order to advance had been given and the enemy resistance would melt away at the approach of his panzers. There could only be one reason for Hackney to be here. To return his boots. And Stoner hadn't confiscated them.

He sorted through his uniform and several possible responses at the same time. In the dim light, perhaps Tanyon hadn't seen the exultation that must have shown on his face. But if he didn't say something appropriately sarcastic, the sergeant would figure out he was up to no good.

"Then it's time for my best party frock." He held up his uniform tunic and poked his hand through the scorched tear over the right shoulder. "This hardly upholds the honor of the *Wehrmacht*." The drifting cigarette smoke was about to eat him alive.

Tanyon dragged again. "You should take better care of things."

Pym chuckled.

"You're easy to impress." Faust pulled on his shirt and trousers, settling his suspenders on his shoulders and popping them at Tanyon. "You people should take better care of me. Then I might treat you better."

"Anything's possible." Tanyon inhaled again, damn it. "But I think you'd still play hard to get."

Pym laughed again.

"He's not that funny." Faust slid into his tunic with a now practiced motion that didn't lift his right elbow from his side. He glanced at Tanyon. "Do you have a comb?"

"Not for you."

Faust rolled his eyes and smoothed his hair with his fingers. "Do you ever change your standard come-back lines?"

Tanyon stubbed out the butt. "Not for you."

"That's funny," Pym said.

"No, he's not." Faust paused long enough to slip his sling, that lone cigarette, and the dwindling book of matches into his inner pocket. "Fine, sergeant. I'm ready."

The rain pounded on the skylight as they fumbled their way down the dark stairwell. It hammered against the row of windows in the grand ballroom, behind the garnet swags, audible even through the radio's rendition of Bob Crosby's *Swingin' on Nothin'* and the click of billiard balls as Cavanaugh and Carmichael played a game. Faust caught himself whistling the tune and stopped. Appalling, how quickly he'd grown accustomed to captivity. It was past time to get out of here.

He silently clicked his bare heels for Stoner, standing behind his desk, then again for Hackney. "Chief Inspector."

Tanyon took up his usual attendant position. Bruckmann, at the secretarial desk, began writing.

"Major Faust." Hackney rose and nodded to him, not exactly smiling but with his eyes crinkling at the corners. Tanyon hadn't exaggerated. The detective was wet through, dripping like a landed walrus onto the floor of the meticulous office, the imprint of his hefty frame darkly impressed into the wingback chair's cloth. He opened a canvas grip and pulled out Faust's ankle boots. "Here you are."

"Thank you." Faust sat and pulled one on, keeping his face bent over his crooked knee as he laced and tied it. Stoner was too good at that game and Faust didn't want to play tonight. "I had a weird dream earlier, about running on the shore of the Baltic, maybe because my feet were cold." He pulled on the other boot. "I realize that's not a lot in the grand scheme of things."

Hackney shrugged and sat in the other chair. "Cold feet aren't pleasant."

"No, they're not." He laced the second boot. "If I'm not being indiscreet, how is the investigation coming?"

"Slowly, slowly. We've got some evidence, but the list of suspects is long and it's going to take us time to sort it all out."

Hackney fixed him with a keen stare from beneath his sopping hair. "Do you know what I mean?"

"You said you had the killer's bootprints and blood type." He ignored what sounded like a rhetorical question and tied his second boot. "And fingerprints? Did you say you have those, too?"

"No. We hoped we did, but we were wrong."

Boots on; that felt better. Faust turned to face Hackney, the occasional table between them. "Am I still a suspect?"

Hackney paused. His stare had not wavered nor lightened. Tension lay beneath the surface of his casual chatter; it hadn't been there the previous night. "That's a difficult question to answer. Understand, your bootprints and blood type are both wrong for the killer."

What a wonderful English non-answer. "Does that mean no?"

"It means I couldn't make a case against you in a British court of law under British rules of evidence. But not everyone understands the science involved in a case like this."

"I'm not certain I do."

"Well, there you are." Hackney nodded as if he'd scored an important point.

"But what does that mean?" Faust asked.

Hackney paused again. His intensity ratcheted up another notch. "It means some people won't believe the evidence. Some people are still going to think you did it, you murdered those girls, no matter what we say to the contrary."

There was some hidden message buried within Hackney's words; the unwavering stare was too pointed for anything else. But Faust had no idea what the message could be.

"Well, don't some people still believe the world is flat?" Faust glanced at Stoner, impassive and listening politely despite the waterlogging of his office. He turned back to Hackney in time to see his chin lower two inches.

"Something like that." Hackney riveted him with his stare. "Do you understand what I'm saying?"

Caution; Hackney must be advising caution. Perhaps he worried about a potential lynch mob should Faust escape and fall into the wrong hands. And perhaps he had a point, but with Stoner's investigation—or interrogation, or whatever—gathering momentum and about to steamroller right over him, he could no longer afford caution.

"Yes. I understand you."

It seemed to satisfy Hackney. "Right, then." He rose; Faust and Stoner followed suit. "I'll get back to my involved investigation and you gentlemen can return to your concerns."

Stoner spoke for the first time. "Sergeant Tanyon, escort the prisoner back to his cell. Chief Inspector Hackney, can I not interest you in spending the night in spare quarters here? The rain has hardly lessened."

Faust clicked his heels for Stoner and Hackney, audibly this time, and half-bowed before leaving the office, those boots clumping behind him.

"What was that all about?" Tanyon asked as they stepped onto the second-floor landing. The rain pounded the skylight above.

"Damned if I know." Faust glanced over his shoulder. In the blacked-out darkness beneath the skylight, Tanyon's bulk loomed a step behind him. He turned down the corridor and eased along it toward the guardroom. "Did you get the impression he was trying to tell me something?"

"I did, at that."

"Any idea what the message might be?"

"Nope. You said you understood it."

"I lied. Couldn't you tell?" Faust paused outside the lavatory. He didn't turn again. His heart thumped so loudly, the man had to hear it. "Here first?" When Tanyon hesitated, he added, "I mean it, I'm not going to clean it up."

Tanyon sighed. "Leave the door open."

"Fine," Faust said, then twisted and slammed his left fist as hard as he could into the pale blob of Tanyon's face.

The sergeant smashed into the wall and bounced off. His body slumped and started to fold. It was Faust's second victory against the English and it felt fabulous. He hit Tanyon again, harder, with a sort of manic desperation—damn it, this had to work—then put his entire weight behind an uppercut to the jaw. Tanyon's head snapped back, hit the wall again, then he slid to the floor in a huddled heap.

"Sergeant?" Pym's voice called from the guardroom down the hall. "Sergeant Tanyon, is that you?"

Faust swept the lavatory door shut behind him and shot the bolt home. He only had seconds. His heart beat light and free, galloping like a horse along a white-sand beach, and he wanted to laugh for sheer exultation.

He crossed the small room in two strides, stepped behind the w.c., unlocked and pushed out the casement window. The blackout shutters bolted from the outside. No time for finesse; he punched them open and ignored the flash of pain across his knuckles. Rain cascaded into the lavatory, soaking him within seconds. It was tingly and wonderful, like a poetic kiss, like the cold Baltic surf. *No man doth mark whereso I ride or go. In lusty leas at liberty I walk—*

He leaned out and looked down. There were bushes below that would break his fall. Without hesitation he stepped out into the rain.

47

Black night engulfed the entry, black as the pit, and rain cascaded down the etched glass in torrents, splashing in rivulets from overhead. Nobody could possibly want to walk in such a gullywasher, no matter what he claimed. Bruckmann made a last appeal to reason. "Chief Inspector Hackney, are you certain I can't talk you into staying the night? It's no problem, I assure you."

Behind the switchboard, Ellington showed as a pale gleam with darker spots for eyes, glancing from him to Hackney and back. At least in the dark, his usual dreamy, open-mouthed expression couldn't embarrass the military.

Hackney smiled, his small eyes crinkling into slits. "You're a lot like my younger son, Lieutenant Bruckmann. Did I mention that?"

A crash, followed by a calling voice, drifted from upstairs. Ellington sucked in a sharp breath.

Bruckmann ignored it, ignored the spasm of horror it generated within his stomach, and forced a smile even if no one could see his expression. No need for Hackney to figure out they had a disaster in the making. "No, sir. In what way am I like your younger son?"

Hackney glanced up the wrought-iron staircase, then tugged down his sodden fedora and buttoned his still-dripping greatcoat. The housemaid, Sally, would murder them all in the morning. "Lovely manners, but sometimes you miss the point."

He slipped a small flashlight from his pocket. "I like walking in the rain. Like a naughty boy, if I don't come home soaked, it's not worth it." A last wave, and he disappeared into the downpour, the beam of his flash wavering then vanishing in the murk.

Bruckmann secured the door. Without pausing to panic, he clattered up the wrought-iron stairs, running as fast as he dared in the next-to-absolute blackness. The small sitting area on the second-floor landing was deserted, the sofa and chairs mere lumps hulking in the shadows like hiding beasts. An even darker gloom enveloped the corridor beyond, a pathway into nowhere, with only a narrow line of light slicing from the cracked-open guardroom door and cutting into the floor and opposite wall.

"Tanyon?" he called into the blackness. "Pym?"

"Lieutenant?" Pym's voice, coming from the guardroom and still at his post. So the disaster at least wasn't total.

Bruckmann hurried forward and shoved open the guardroom door, releasing the light into the corridor. Something moved further along, groaning and stirring among the shadows near the floor.

"Lieutenant?" It sounded like Tanyon's voice, but shaky, as if hung over. "Give me a hand, would you?"

He ran down the corridor and fell over something soft and yielding before he expected to, tumbling into the wall, the soft something, and finally the floor. Whatever it was swore in Tanyon's voice, too.

"What the hell!" Bruckmann scrambled to his hands and knees.

A large hand clamped onto his shoulder and pushed. His elbows nearly buckled. A doorknob rattled, then Tanyon's voice swore again. Bruckmann's eyes were growing accustomed to the dark and he made out a dark hulking form above him lifting a foot.

"Sergeant, what—"

The foot slammed into the door. It was the lavatory, Bruckmann realized, and suddenly the whole farcical situation made a horrible sort of sense. He scrambled the rest of the way up and followed Tanyon into the room, stopping when wetness misted his face.

The window gaped open and the bathroom was empty.

Bruckmann grabbed at the form beside him and connected with an arm. "Faust?"

He sensed rather than saw the nod. "Faust."

"The bastard." Bruckmann turned and ran for the wrought-iron stairs, Tanyon on his heels.

48

early evening
Margeaux Hall

Faust fell into rose bushes, and damn, those thorns bit deep. He smelled sweetness, crushed branches, wet earth. The rain and runoff water from the roof poured over him like a baptism. *Roses have thorns,* Shakespeare wrote, *and silver fountains mud.* He rolled, yanking free, and fell face-first into the sodden grass. For a moment he lay there, drawing a deep lungful of air laden with moisture and the scents of grass and roses. Then he scrambled up and ran for the wall. The row of apple trees, and Woodrow, should be off to his left somewhere and not quite half a mile distant.

It was so dark, with the uncompromising downpour and the blackout, he only knew the trees were above him from the torrent's sudden slowing, and he nearly ran into the wall before he saw it. The branches he'd seen from Stoner's office almost touched the ground. He scrambled about like a drunkard, waving his good arm and staggering in the dark, wetter than it was possible to be. Finally his hand swatted sodden leaves and he grabbed a bough. Faust held on, gasping with exertion and incredulous delight, and climbed.

At the wall's pinnacle he paused and glanced back. A dim glow lit the glass-walled vestibule. A voice cried out in the night. They were already in pursuit. His pulse accelerated. No half-hearted measures this time; he had to get away before Stoner buried him. Faust dropped to the ground outside the wall.

A big dark shape loomed on his right, a tiny crack of light peeping from one window. He paused again, rain sluicing down his face. He had to get away, but the light drew him. Stoner was still in his office; it could only be Jennifer, alone in Woodrow and not minding the blackout. Faust crept closer.

Yep, it was Jennifer. He watched her cross the lamp-dim sitting room, walking past the unlit hearth to the oak dining table on the far wall. She wore a white apron over a pastel-flowered housedress, her auburn hair pulled back from her face into a bump on the nape of her neck. She carried plates and flatware, wine glasses perched atop, and as he watched, she set the table for two.

He was a fool, he knew he was a fool to stand there and observe her domestic tranquility while a glorious chance to escape this fiasco washed away in the rain. But he couldn't look away. Whenever he'd set a table, at the orphanage or while working at the *gasthaus,* it had only been a job to do so people could eat. Somehow this was different.

She smiled as her quick hands arranged the flatware, her generous mouth softened by the lamplight touching her face from below. Perhaps it was the flame's warmth, perhaps it was the changed hairstyle and the way it emphasized her face's lines, or perhaps it was the palpable happiness that lit her from within. But she was again the most beautiful girl in the world, the one he'd seen across Woodrow's garden Sunday morning while he was too stunned to escape her presence before she captured him, heart, body, and soul. The lamplight returned the poetic roses to her cheeks, the coral to her inviting lips, and emphasized the fine dark eyes that would have attracted Wyatt even more than Anne Boleyn's. If only Faust could sweep her away with him—but Wyatt had been there, too, and gave voice to that emotion four hundred years ago. *I leave off therefore, since in a net I seek to hold the wind.*

He'd never lived with a family, just occasionally shared a girlfriend's bed, so if this was normal he had no way of knowing it. But from the way she arranged the napkins within the wine glasses, setting the table seemed less a chore and more a responsibility, a means of taking care of another person and demonstrating her love.

For Stoner. Never for him, and he had to become reconciled to that fact. He was the enemy and the man she believed murdered her little sister, and even if Hackney disproved one of those, the other remained.

Like everything else in his life, this was an utter disaster. He'd found the perfect poetic woman, one who'd taught him the reality of all those love poems he'd read and misunderstood through the years, who'd taught him to know his own heart without ever speaking a word of encouragement or affection to him. And she'd kill him before she ever would. *I now have learned love right, and learned even so, as who by being poisoned doth poison know.*

Should he knock on the door and tell her Stoner would be late for dinner? He grinned without mirth. No, she had that shotgun somewhere. Better not tempt fate, nor her.

Another voice called behind him. Still grinning, he ran south through the rain, leaving all hope behind where Jennifer walked.

49

early evening
Margeaux Hall

Bruckmann scrambled down the dark stairs to the vestibule, Tanyon behind him. Thunder crashed overhead and inside the curious empty spot invading his soul. They had to get Faust back before Stoner realized he was gone; green little lieutenants who failed at such fundamental tasks were surely returned to other, less desirable duties forthwith.

"He's physical," the sergeant said. "He'll try to fight his way through one of the gates. Ellington, where are those flashlights?"

Bruckmann fished his keys from his pocket and unlocked the front entry, hearing Ellington at the desk sorting through the drawers. Amazing, how calm he felt, panic confined to his unfinished edges while mundane activities demanded his center stage. But his pulse was picking up speed in a gentle acceleration like a train on a downhill gradient.

"You check the postern. I'll run down to our gate." No sense bothering with the main gate; it had rusted shut and the iron spikes atop it would emasculate Faust should he try scaling it. "Who's on duty tonight?"

Tanyon pressed a hard round cylinder into his hand. "Whiteside."

Bruckmann pocketed his keys, flicked on the flashlight, and hauled the door open. The rain roared down beyond his nose, spray tingling on his face and making him blink. It sounded like an oncoming freight train. Nothing for it; he sucked in a deep breath and ran into the storm. Without coat or hat, he was drenched in seconds. Faust would pay for this and it was going to feel good. Bruckmann galloped for the front gate.

The cone of light, dancing with his slithering strides, flickered over a dark form huddled in the lee of the wall. He ran to it as it hurried forward.

"Lieutenant?" Whiteside stiffened to attention, ludicrous in a streaming waterproof, rifle vertical on his shoulder.

"As you were." Bruckmann slid to a stop, balancing as the slick ground seemed to move beneath him. "Faust is loose. Has he come this way?"

Whiteside shook his head. "No one's been near, sir."

The postern gate, then. "I realize this means little under the current circumstances, but keep your eyes and ears open and report anything."

Without waiting for an answer, Bruckmann ran north along the mortared-stone wall toward Woodrow, the finger of light flickering across the lawn before him. His heart beat faster, the train's downhill course steepening as it descended into an ugly abyss within him. The ground near the wall, especially the rough, rooty area beneath the apple trees, had slicked into mud, forcing him to potter about while the prisoner escaped. "Sergeant!"

Another beam of light angled through the rain ahead of him. He changed course and accelerated, shining his own light toward it, but his feet shot from beneath him and he sprawled full-length in the slime. He paused long enough to snarl one of Tanyon's choicest expressions, then scrabbled up, grabbed the flashlight, and stumbled on.

"Anything?" he asked when he arrived.

"Nothing, sir." Tanyon paused, as if tacitly acknowledging the inaccuracy of his original assumption, but he didn't apologize for it. "We have to sound the alarm."

He wanted to swear again but there was no point. He couldn't compete with Tanyon there. A flash of lightning flared across the sky, giving him a brief glimpse of himself as he glanced down. This had to be the most bloody impressive way of reporting to his commanding officer—wet, muddy, and disheveled, a God-awful train wreck. Overhead, the thunder crashed.

"I know. Let's get it over with."

50

early evening
Margeaux Hall

The front door gaped open. Stoner paused, Homburg in hand, staring at this irrefutable testament of some breach underway within his defenses, and paradoxically felt relief—at least he wouldn't have to venture forth into that horrendous storm. He waited in the corridor's shadows, out of Ellington's sight, relief fading into a more appropriate anger, and presently was rewarded with the sight of two drenched subordinates, one tall and slender, the other shorter and stouter, silhouetted behind flashlight beams and running hell for leather through the downpour toward the entry.

He waited until they were inside, the door closed behind them, before switching on the overhead light. It was a glass-walled vestibule, of course, and so the pause made no difference regarding his flaunting of the blackout regulations. But the timing was important.

It worked. Ellington jumped like a startled cat, his chair slithering back toward the filing cabinet. Bruckmann and Tanyon whipped about, guilt written over them with a heavy hand. Both were drenched as if by a fire hose. Mud splattered Bruckmann's entire front, from his collar and tie to his puttees, and smears dripped from his nose and forehead. Tanyon's face, although clean, swelled in several places, most noticeably his left cheekbone and eye. Neither met his gaze.

The situation was undoubtedly serious. But Stoner knew he'd treasure the memory of their tableau for the rest of his life—unless, of course, Faust was not recaptured, in which case he would rue it for the same duration.

"I believe, sergeant," he said, "upon analysis of the situation, we'll find that once again you allowed the prisoner to approach too closely."

Tanyon flushed the color of the swag drapes in the ballroom. "I'm sure you're right, sir."

He stared a bit longer. Nobody moved.

"Perhaps, gentlemen," he said after another suitable pause, "I might trouble you to attend to this inconvenient little matter."

They moved, scrambling for the stairs as if joined at the shoulders. Ellington gingerly tucked his chair back beneath the desk.

Stoner flipped off the light and unbuttoned his greatcoat. "In the meantime," he said, more to himself than to any of them, "I must telephone my granddaughter and inform her I shall be late for dinner."

51

early evening
Margeaux Hall

Something trickled down his forehead. Bruckmann paused in the guardroom doorway and swiped at it. A chunk of mud flew from his hand and slid down the molding. Anger colder than the rain tightened his stomach around that empty spot in his middle. It wasn't possible to live down such a scene; it would color his relationship with Stoner forever. Oh, Faust would pay for this.

Tanyon pushed past him and strode to the rifle storage, wet boots squeaking on the floor and leaving little puddles marking each step. More evidence of their fiasco, if any were needed, and if Sally didn't kill them all, she'd certainly want to.

"Pym, call downstairs and get the squad up here," Tanyon said.

Pym's grey eyes grew rounder as he stared. Then understanding dawned and he lifted the telephone receiver. "Faust?"

"Brilliant guess, corporal." Bruckmann reached over Pym's head, grabbed the call signs notebook from the shelf, and flipped through it until he found the right page. He pulled the spare headphones down, plugged them in, switched the transmitter to voice communication mode, swirled the frequency dial to the correct setting, and squeezed the microphone's pressel button as he glanced over the open page. "Wildflower base to Piccolo base. Come in, Piccolo base."

Storm static crackled. "Piccolo base here. Go ahead, Wildflower base."

"Is Piccolo Eight available? Over."

The hissing of the open radio line spread through the guardroom as Pym replaced the telephone receiver. Tanyon hauled Lee Enfields from the rack, the rifles clacking as he aligned them on the work table. Nothing distracted Bruckmann from the cold voice inside him whispering the situation was out of control.

Then Kettering's voice spoke through static that fluctuated with the rumbling thunder. "Piccolo Eight here, Wildflower base. Do you require assistance? Over."

Bruckmann's heart lifted. "Affirmative, Piccolo Eight. Over."

"What's your situation? Over."

Bruckmann paused. "Same damned thing. Over."

If Kettering laughed, he had the decency to keep his finger off the button until he finished. "Where shall we meet your forces? Over." His tenor was calm and dapper as ever.

Bruckmann paused again, his finger off the pressel, and glanced at Tanyon, hauling boxes of live cartridges from the ammunition storage. "Here?"

Tanyon nodded without looking his way.

Bruckmann pressed the button. "Can your forces come to our base? It's a mile further along the road from the chicken farm. Over."

"We'll be there with bells on." Kettering paused in his turn. Thunder rumbled overhead and static burst on the line, punctuating his words like an audible full stop. "Make that raincoats. ETA approximately one hour. Piccolo Eight out."

Bruckmann ripped off the headphones. "Oh, we needed this."

The squad reported for duty, young nervous faces lining the walls. Norris' bruise from Tuesday bloomed several shades of purple. Peckham flexed his shoulders as if itching for a fight but his eyes were not confident. Ellington, torn from the switchboard for the emergency, at least had his mouth closed. Tanyon issued weapons and live ammunition while they pulled on waterproofs and covers.

Pym picked up his book. "I thought he was awful quiet today. Not like him, is it?"

Bruckmann's temper flared. "Just for that, corporal, you can assist the search and get drenched with the rest of us. Carmichael, you're on the radio," he leaned so close he could smell the dinner on the secondary radioman's breath, "and if you leave it for a moment, this time it's official. Am I clear?"

Carmichael's eyes were guileless. If he looked suddenly happy, perhaps it was because he'd stay dry. "Yes, sir."

Bruckmann stepped back and glanced at Tanyon. The sergeant, his face swelling and darkening by the moment, handed him a holstered revolver.

"Right, then," Tanyon said. "Pym, Norris, Glover, Sloane, you four try to find where he went over the wall. Pym, you're in charge. Two of you cover outside the wall, two of you inside. Start at our gate and work in both directions. Use torches and don't be shy about it. Watch for a red signal flare and report back immediately if you see one. Any questions?"

The four glanced at each other. "No, sergeant," Pym said. His face had lengthened dramatically.

"Then get going." Tanyon waited until their footsteps sounded on the staircase. "Ellington, Peckham, Reynolds, you three search in here."

"In here, sergeant?" Peckham asked. "You mean, inside Margeaux Hall?"

Bruckmann froze. No point searching inside unless—
"We don't know that he did escape."

"Exactly, lieutenant."

The line of notebooks beneath his secretarial station, where he always bumped his knees, holding the complete records of the Wildflower operation; Stoner, aged and infirm, alone downstairs with only his personal revolver in the top desk drawer. Their defenses were thin indeed. If Stoner, that sterling diviner of men's hearts, had misjudged Faust and he was after all a spy, then this was the chance he needed to undo all their work.

"Peckham, you check the garage, the stables, and Peter's quarters," Tanyon said. "Reynolds, you check the outside of the building, and Ellington, you've been good lately, you check the inside. Look for wet spots where he might have re-entered. Watch for a red signal flare—well, as best you can. Reynolds, we know he went out through the lavatory window; start at the bushes beneath there and see if you can follow a path to the wall."

Reynolds grinned. "You mean the rose bushes, sergeant?"

Bruckmann glanced at Tanyon. "One bright spot to the evening."

Tanyon's lips curled. "Carmichael, when we leave, turn the light out and open the drapes. Watch for the signal flare. If you see it, it means I'll contact you on the lorry's radio and have you relay a message to Piccolo Eight."

"Yes, sergeant."

"Get going."

They trooped from the guardroom. Carmichael sat at the

radio, poring over the local garrisons' call signs. Bruckmann shook his head. As if Carmichael didn't already know them by heart. But at least he wasn't making Pym's mistake.

"Lieutenant, we might change into dry clothes," Tanyon said.

Bruckmann glanced at the guardroom window. Rain pounded behind the blackout curtain, as hard as ever. "Can you give me one good reason why I should bother?"

Tanyon shrugged and reached for his greatcoat.

52

early evening
Woodrow

The table was set, the pork loin sliced, the roasted potatoes and green beans on the warmer, the Mercurey Burgundy
at the right temperature and ready to open. So when the
telephone rang, Jennifer instinctively knew the message before
she heard it.

"You're going to be late, aren't you."

Stoner paused, the telephone line crackling. In that
moment, she hated herself. She couldn't have phrased that
more callously if she'd tried. After all, she'd prepared this
special supper to help him relax, to slough off some of his
worry and despondency before she hit him with her own concerns. He didn't need for her to add to his burden any more
than necessary.

"We have something of a situation developing here,"
Stoner said.

Her skin tingled. She'd *known* someone stared at her,
had sensed rather than seen motion outside through the im-
perfectly-closed blackout drapes. "And I think I know why.
Dad, he came this way."

"You saw something?"

"I believe so."

"My dear, you must close those drapes properly." He
paused again. "Although perhaps in this case our mutual
touch of carelessness should be applauded as helpful. Thank
you, Jennifer. I shall relay your information."

That helped. But not enough to matter and she still needed to speak with him. "Should I bring you a tray, do you think?"

"In this weather? My dear, it would be soup before it arrived." He sighed through the crackling static. "I'll ask Mrs. Alcock for something. Don't wait up." He disconnected.

Don't wait up, hell. She slammed down the receiver. He did not have to fight the war alone and he would not evade her questions so easily. She ran for the kitchen.

53

early evening
at large near Margeaux Hall

The sign on the road read *Wynant Dairy* in white letters on a dark background, a second, smaller line beneath proclaiming *Delivery Available.* Faust grinned, still buoyed by a delicious sensation of freedom. Cold rain coursed over him in a steady stream. Even if he caught his death and even if that last cigarette in his breast pocket turned to mush, it would be worth it. He slid over the drystone wall into the meadow.

Half a mile away across the field, a farmhouse perched atop a small rise, barns and sheds in clusters behind it and meadows stretching to the looming backdrop of the Dark beyond. Faust followed the line of the wall, keeping it between his movement and the house. Cows in the first barn, liquid eyes peering at him through the gloom, equipment in the next shed, more cows in the next barn—sooner or later he'd run into a farm dog guarding its territory—hay piled to the roof, more equipment—how many cows could even a dairy hold—and finally he found the stable, the smallest building all the way at the back of the property. He closed the door behind himself.

Two dark and unlovely equine heads turned at his entry, large stout cart horses capable of hauling milk all over the district. But this wasn't a beauty pageant and they'd do. Even with his night sight fully developed, he could barely discern the harnesses hanging on one wall, the feed bins along another, and—*yes*—saddles and bridles on a third near a rickety staircase that disappeared into the eaves.

The darker horse slanted its ears back and turned away as he approached, tack in hand. The other leaned over the open half-door and whuffled at him, a wide white blaze gleaming in the dark. No sense making a fight of it, so he chose the second, friendlier horse, tickled the snaffle bit into its mouth, threw the saddle over its back and settled it left-handed, yanked the girth tight, and propped open the outer door. The mare followed him willingly into the rain and stood still while he wedged his boot into the stirrup, toe braced against the girth, and jumped. *I on my horse, and Love on me doth try Our horsemanship—*

But the mare started off toward the front gate and the road before he'd swung his leg all the way over her rump. For a gut-dropping moment he balanced on one foot, left hand tangled in mane and reins, rain pouring over him and equipage moving beneath. The unfriendly horse inside whinnied. Doubtful the sound would carry all the way to the house. He'd better take a moment and sort himself out.

"Brrr." Without thinking, Faust tried to stop the horse in German, then scrabbled atop wet leather when she proved unilingual. He let go the mane and yanked the reins, grabbing with his right hand for the saddle. The mare stopped, jibbing, and he leaned on her neck as he swung his leg over her rump, foot fumbling for the stirrup. But before he found it, she again set off for the front gate, the wrong direction. He pulled her up a second time, and she threw her head back as she stopped.

Something scraped overhead. Startled, Faust glanced up. A sleepy face leaned out of an open second-floor window.

"What the bloomin' blazes you doing with that horse?"

The deliveryman slept over the stable. Great.

There was a stirrup somewhere down there on his right side. But he no longer had time to hunt for it. He clapped his heels to the big mare's flanks and gripped with his calves, tugging her head toward the rear of the farm. The Dark continued south from there, he knew from his perusal of the maps with Stoner and Hackney.

She jibbed again and tried to turn back toward the gate. Faust smacked her rump with the flat of his right hand. Pain flashed across his biceps, radiating all the way down to his fingers and up through his shoulder joint. The mare flattened her ears and leapt into a lumbering gallop, finally headed in the right direction, a rollicking tabletop like a pogo stick multiplied by four.

"Oy! Come back here with that horse!" The voice diminished behind them as the rain and the night closed in, shielding them in a dark cocoon of wet chaos.

54

early evening
between Woodrow and Margeaux Hall

In the garage, Bruckmann automatically went to the passenger's side of the lorry, and noticed Tanyon just as automatically headed for the driver's side. They'd driven out together several times before, and each time the same thing had happened. Perhaps the sergeant showed respect for him, the officer, by doing the menial work of operating the vehicle. But no. It might be the excuse Tanyon gave, but the truth was more brutal. The sergeant maintained control over the situation by putting himself, literally and figuratively, in the driver's seat.

Bruckmann sighed and scrambled into the cab. Tanyon still didn't trust him to handle an emergency. Remembering his own inadequate response to Stoner's silence in the vestibule, he couldn't blame the sergeant. As the officer in charge of the squad, he should have said something rather than standing there like a scolded schoolboy. Next time, he'd take action first and think later.

The vestibule light had been switched off and the night was blacker than Hades. Tanyon worked the lorry around Margeaux Hall and between the flower beds to their gate. Whiteside opened it for them. Tanyon stopped outside, short of the road, setting the hand brake on the slope and killing the engine. They slithered out into the slamming rain as Whiteside closed and locked the gate with himself on the inside.

Bruckmann had taken two steps when the radio

crackled to life behind him. "Wildflower base to Wildflower Two. Come in."

He spun about and dived back into the lorry, grabbing the mike. "Wildflower Two here. Go ahead."

Tanyon hung listening on the driver's side, sheltering beneath the lorry's lip although drowned vermin weren't as wet.

Even through the storm-static, Carmichael's voice sounded rattled. "I just spoke with Wildflower One. Don't have a call-sign here, but *someone* saw movement outside her window a few minutes ago. It's gone now."

Tanyon grunted. "Miss Stoner, he means, outside Woodrow."

Bruckmann shivered and not from his rain-drenched uniform. Hackney had spoken so reassuringly of blood types and bootprints, alibis and evidence, and claimed Faust could not be the murderer. But to know he'd passed so close to Woodrow that Jennifer had seen him through the night's savage rain chilled Bruckmann more than the cold. At least they knew for certain he had, indeed, left Margeaux Hall behind and wasn't stalking their secrets nor Stoner. It meant the old man was on the right track after all, and all Bruckmann had to do was recapture Faust so he could be finished off, which would be the best possible revenge.

He squeezed the pressel. "Understood, Wildflower base. We'll take up the search there. Wildflower Two out." He returned the mike to its stand. "Gather the squad, all right? I'm heading to Woodrow."

Tanyon nodded. Bruckmann galloped through the rain, skating atop the grass along the rising verge parallel to the mortared stone wall. Behind him, the Very gun coughed. A red signal flare fizzled briefly overhead, extinguished within seconds by the torrent. Not likely many of the squad would see that. He ran on.

As he neared Woodrow, his wavering light flashed across the door. Something moved then stilled. His heart jumped into his throat; Hackney could be wrong and Faust might have doubled back. Pulse pounding, Bruckmann paused and steadied the light. Jennifer stepped onto Woodrow's front porch, closing the door behind her. She wore a tweed raincoat and waterproof deerstalker cap, rather like a female Sherlock Holmes, and carried a large iron cooking pot. She locked the door and slithered down to join him.

He took the pot from her, grunting in surprise at its weight. "Jennifer, you shouldn't be out here. We don't know where Faust is—"

"Do you mean Major Faust?" She pocketed her keys, slid the pot from his grip, and started through the rain toward the postern gate at a brisk trot, leaving him standing.

Bloody hell. He ran to catch her up. "Whatever you choose to call him, we don't know where he's gone or what he's up to—"

"He stared at me through the window and moved on, even though the door was unlatched and he could have walked right on in and done whatever he liked." She didn't slow, water coursing down her deerstalker and flying off in droplets through the drumming rain. She sounded irritated, as if Faust had insulted her by not barging in and helping himself. "That man has no more interest in me than the man in the moon that we can't see through the storm." She stopped at the postern and stared at him, the pot cradled in her arms. "You could open the gate for me."

He'd lost, that much was clear, and perhaps Faust had made a wise decision by not engaging in Jennifer's battlefield. Bruckmann slipped a hand into his pocket.

"My keys are gone." He dug in the other trouser pocket, then both patch pockets on his service jacket, then the breast pockets even though he never kept his keys there. "They are; they're gone." Rain dripped beneath his collar, a cold rivulet racing down his spine and making him shiver. "Damn it, I must have dropped them somewhere."

She thrust the pot into his hands again. "Hold this before we drown." She pulled out her keys and opened the postern, grabbed the pot from him and set it on the ground inside the gate, crossed inside, and relocked it. "Go catch that man, Jack, and bring him back safely. Then get yourself into dry clothes before you catch your death." She hefted the pot and trotted uphill toward the Hall, disappearing in the rain and the night.

Bruckmann clenched his teeth. Faust had definitely made the right decision.

He turned. Tanyon jogged toward him through the rain, the flashlight's finger dancing on the ground. But where there should have been seven soldiers, there were only four.

"Who's missing?"

"Ellington, Norris, and Reynolds." Tanyon stepped closer and lowered his voice. "Peckham says old Peter Owen isn't in his quarters."

The gardener. Bruckmann sighed, removed his hat, and pushed his sodden hair back from his forehead. "That old man's an odd duck, always staring and carrying on in Welsh. Can't understand what he's saying, much less thinking." He replaced his cover. "I take it no one has anything to report?"

Tanyon shrugged and turned to the squad. "All right, torches out. He passed near here somewhere. Find a footprint or something to show us which direction to follow."

55

early evening
Margeaux Hall

Rain pounded on the glass roof. Water puddled across the rough brick floor, crisscrossed with frantic footprints. The front desk and switchboard were deserted, but when she flipped on the light, Jennifer saw all incoming calls had been routed to Stoner's office. She turned off the light, set the pot on the floor, shed her coat and hat, and dried her face and the outside of the pot with the kitchen towel she'd thrust beneath its lid.

She couldn't say she liked Faust—no, he was properly called Major Faust and she would not demean him further. Possibly she never would like him. But she could no longer reproach him for doing his duty, nor blame him for attempting to escape the trap being set for him. And now that she knew he hadn't murdered Harriet, she found she could no longer hate him. It was rather reassuring, knowing he'd seen her alone and hadn't kidnapped her as a hostage or something. Although it also irritated her, for reasons perhaps best not examined too closely.

No, she couldn't reproach Major Faust. Her grandfather, however, was another matter.

She slipped into Stoner's office without knocking, the pot heavy in her arms. He glanced up from his scramble of papers, at first blankly, then with concern as she crossed the room and set the pot atop his desk.

"My dear, really, you shouldn't have."

She set the lid aside, then removed the clean dinner plates from the pot and set his desk as a table before he could move his papers. "I made this dinner; you're going to eat it." She unwrapped the napkins protecting the wine glasses. "It may not be as pretty as it was half an hour ago, but it should taste the same." The bottle of Mercurey came next, wrapped in another napkin. "You work on that. It's Burgundy, so it shouldn't be too shaken to drink."

His face relaxed into his charming little-boy smile, his eyes lighting from within. "My dear, as delightful as this is, I rang Mrs. Alcock for dinner."

"And I rang her a moment later. You eat this or nothing. I know you keep a corkscrew in your pocket." She'd packed the food into glass canning jars, and removed the lids as she placed them between the plates, serving spoons upright. Lastly she produced the candles, smiling at his delighted laugh.

"Your lighter, sir."

He poured the wine while she lit the candles, then he switched off the desk lamp. Shadows flooded the sitting room. He said grace, and his thankfulness for "courage and imagination in the face of adversity" made her smile again. But as she served him, the telephone rang.

"Don't you touch that phone." She handed him the glass jar of green beans and lifted the receiver herself. "Constable Mercer." She rolled her eyes. "How are you tonight?"

The static was horrible and the irritation in the constable's voice worse. "Do you have a situation there you should be telling me of?"

Stoner held out a hand, his smile ironic. So much for his uninterrupted dinner. She slapped the receiver into his palm and resumed serving.

"Good evening, Constable Mercer. Well, yes. I'm afraid it's the same circumstance as previously—oh, I see. Yes, I shall direct our searchers accordingly. Thank you." He replaced the receiver. "It seems someone has stolen Caspar Wynant's cart horse and ridden off in the rain toward the Dark."

She couldn't blame him for trying to escape, she reminded herself. But still she wanted to tear her hair. That man—no, *Major Faust* was exasperating enough on foot; mounted, he could cause much more trouble. "And I wanted you to have a quiet evening."

He smiled again. "Then perhaps you would be so kind as to telephone Carmichael and request he inform our searchers of this somewhat unexpected development."

But Carmichael didn't pick up. She replaced the receiver in its cradle and met Stoner's long, assessing stare.

"I believe I know where he's gone, Dad. Eat while it's warm. I'll handle this."

56

evening
at large in the Dark

The Dark slowed the mare's canter to a shambling trot. Her first trotting paces, rough as a truck with shot springs, nearly threw Faust over her neck and only a panicky handful of mane kept him aboard. Rain splattered down from the leaves above and the debris beneath softened the pounding hoofbeats to gentle thuds. He couldn't see more than a few feet ahead; hopefully the mare wouldn't run into a tree or fall over a cliff. He could only trust her to find a path.

He stood in the stirrups and let his knees and ankles take the jolting. He could hear no pursuit, so it seemed the deliveryman hadn't mounted the unfriendly horse and followed him on his midnight trek across the back pastures. But he wasn't comforted. Once before he'd exited this forest and found Kettering's search line directly ahead, as if the engineering major had read his mind and known his path to the inch. Well, that wouldn't happen this time. Kettering's troops had to travel all the way from Oxford, move ahead of him, and then organize their search line. If he could get past the edge of the Dark before they arrived, if he could get far enough ahead to vanish into the countryside, then he stood a chance against Kettering.

And against Stoner.

Faust tightened his legs about the mare's barrel and squeezed harder.

57

evening
Margeaux Hall

Soft footsteps padded down the eastern stairs, feeling their way slowly in the inky dark like some stereotypical thief in the night in a silly dime novel. Jennifer switched on the flashlight she'd borrowed from Stoner, and the beam caught Carmichael full in the face. Even in so little light, his haircut was horrid. He jumped, eyes squeezing closed, and stumbled down two steps before grabbing the handrail. "Who's that?"

She didn't lower the light. "One guess, Carmichael."

"Miss Stoner." His next breath came easier and he started to smile. "Look what you nearly made me—"

She strode for him. His smile vanished and he scrambled back up the stairs. She followed.

"You deserter, you coward, you randy young goat. Slipping off with Sally every chance you get, whenever someone's back is turned—"

Carmichael gave ground backwards down the second-floor corridor. "Now, Miss Stoner, it's not what you're thinking—"

"Do I look like a fool?" Considering how she must appear after her run through the rain, perhaps that wasn't the wisest question to ask. "Don't answer unless you believe you can survive it." She reached past him, opened the guardroom door, and pointed. The light from the radio table lamp poured into the corridor about them.

He edged past her into the guardroom, never turning his

back. "I'm going to marry her, Miss Stoner, honest, but her mother—"

She pushed him into the chair. "Save it for the vicar, or Sergeant Tanyon, or someone who matters. Right now, get on the radio and contact Lieutenant Bruckmann. Tell him we just heard from Constable Mercer and it appears Major Faust stole Caspar Wynant's cart horse and escaped across his back field toward the Dark."

Carmichael grabbed the headphones and settled them aslant over his ears. Then he paused. "You mean you rang up here, looking for me?"

How could he seem so young when he was months older than she? "How else would I know to cut you off on the stairs?"

"Does Major Stoner know?"

She crossed her arms.

"Miss Stoner, Lieutenant Bruckmann said they'd make it official this time—"

"Are you saying you don't deserve it?" But that was real fear in his child-like eyes. "How fast can you make the call?"

He grabbed the microphone. "Wildflower base to Wildflower Two. Come in." When he released the button, a hissing crackle filled the guardroom, impossibly loud. "I'm letting you hear this, too, so you know I'm not lying to you."

"And I am listening, so it had better be right." Not that she'd know if he made a mistake.

"This is Wildflower Three." Tanyon's voice, deeper than Bruckmann's, rumbled through the static. "Go ahead."

Oh, she hated the transmitter-receiver. It wasn't like the typewriter, machinery she could handle and even sort of understand; it was a big, complicated, masculine contraption, with dials and knobs and switches and gauges, the overriding symbol of modern mechanical technology, and just being in the same room made her queasy. But she would not allow Carmichael to see her tremble. She stood silently by, arms crossed and toe tapping an occasional emphasis, keeping her confusion and nerves to herself.

Carmichael spoke with Tanyon, then with someone claiming the unlikely moniker of Piccolo Eight. Finally he set down the microphone. "I'm done, ma'am." He glanced up at her again, eyes wide. "Are you going to tell Major Stoner?"

That haircut was so horrid, his ears seemed lopsided. Even so, his hopeful charm needed a heart of stone to resist. "You stay at your post for the remainder of this evening and we'll see."

"But I promised Sally—"

Exasperation welled within her. "You don't think she's

silly enough to wait outside for you in this storm, do you?"

"She said—"

"Well, trust me, she's not. No woman of sense would be." She sighed. "Granted, if you didn't love her, you'd never have let her cut your hair a second time."

His eyes widened again. "Third."

Jennifer scoffed. "If she catches pneumonia, it's her own silly fault. You mind your business here or I will tell." Without waiting for an answer, she stalked from the guardroom.

58

evening
Margeaux Hall

Despite the situation and despite its disheveled appearance, Stoner found himself enjoying his impromptu meal. Jennifer had clearly put some thought into her cooking, proving yet again she loved him far more than he deserved, and her results compared well with the best meals he'd had in Paris. He finished off one last bit of potato as she returned, easing the door to behind her and slipping into the wingback chair across from him. Despite her gentility, her heightened color, visible even in the candlelight, spoke eloquently of an aroused temper.

If only he could show his love for her in a similar and unmistakable manner. But he feared what she would ask of him would be the one thing he could not do.

"Well?" he asked. "Is the situation under control or should I take a hand?"

She picked up her wineglass and swigged a long draft of the Mercurey. "I think it's under control." Yet her color remained high and her forehead tense.

He finished the potato, applied his napkin, and sat back, thinking only of how much he loved her so it would show in his face. "This was a truly excellent meal, my dear, and I appreciate it more than I can express. However, when I asked you to help out around the shop, I didn't intend for you to assume the role of sergeant-at-arms." He picked up his wine. "Nor that of den mother."

She laughed, her face relaxing. "You know, Dad, they seem so much younger than I am. But they're not."

"In experience, they are." He held out his glass.

She looked at him, puzzled, then chimed her glass against his. The crystal liquid note flowed into the sitting room's corners. They drank together.

"Your dinner is cold," he said.

She set down her glass and rose. "I'll run it down to Mrs. Alcock's kitchen and warm it there. Dad, there's something I must ask you." Her words came out in a rush.

As he'd feared. Stoner sat back and watched as she repacked the cooking pot.

"It's about Faust—I mean, *Major* Faust."

He sighed. It would be cowardly, pretending to not understand her. "We do tend to speak of him with a deplorable lack of respect, don't we?"

She wiped the outside of one glass jar with her towel. "We speak of him as a commodity to be used."

"War is dehumanizing and I'm finding intelligence operations are little different from the front lines in that regard."

Silently she packed away the plates and the papers beneath were revealed, including the unfinished report analyzing how best to shatter a capable and intelligent man's spirit. The project was more natural to him than he wished to admit.

He cleared his throat. "For those inflicting the damage, such dehumanization is sometimes necessary to maintain one's sanity, and I believe it to be so in this instance. The Nazis must be stopped and our coastline is the most logical place for us to draw the line. Breaking Faust will assist this task." He rubbed his tired eyes. "But even when the process is necessary, it is ugly at best. At its worst," he paused, the memory of artillery shells exploding amongst his men all too clear, "it is unspeakable."

She replaced the glass jars in the cooking pot. "When you first spoke of breaking him, I didn't realize what you meant."

"I meant what I said." He pushed the papers aside. He had no choice but to be brutally honest; she would not thank him for any sugar-coating, no matter how unpalatable the medicine nor how shoddy a light it cast upon him personally. "I meant breaking his heart and will, yes, his body and soul, if necessary."

The last glass jar vanished. Her hands moved as deftly as ever. But she did not look at him again and the pain rocked him more deeply than he'd imagined. He'd taught her the principles she attempted to uphold. It was the most horrific irony for his own actions to call those principles into play and even into question. It was rather as if, in attempting to save her from the German invasion, he'd let her down.

"And what will become of him?"

"If I succeed, he will be a broken man for the rest of his life."

"Do you expect to succeed?"

"No. I expect him to remain defiant to the end." Although with the lever of Captain Clarke and collaboration in Stoner's hand, stern defiance would do Faust no good. His Nazi compatriots put the devil in any deal before him.

She bowed her head over the pot. Her hair fell forward and hid her face behind a curtain of dark red-gold, gleaming in the candlelight. "Dad, I want you to give up this assignment."

The pain deepened another impossible degree. "I cannot."

"Explain."

"I am an old man, my dear. I cannot grab a rifle and defend my country's shores from an invading army. Yet I must contribute something to our defense. If the only task I can perform is crushing an enemy officer's resistance, then I must do so." The depth of his need for her to understand frightened him. She was all he had and he could not bear for this disagreement to wedge itself between them. That indeed would give Faust the final victory. "If our neighbors can offer their lives in the Home Guard, the least I can offer is my honor."

"It's not Major Faust you're crushing." She hefted the pot and met his gaze. Surprisingly, her eyes and face were dry. "It's your own humanity. You're not dehumanizing him—just yourself."

She carried the pot to the door, her cold dinner balanced precariously on top. At the threshold she paused. "I love you." Her voice was soft as eiderdown, as soft as the noise she made closing the door behind her.

His old heart threatened to break. He flipped on the table lamp, blew out the candles, and pulled his unfinished report toward him.

He resumed work.

59

evening
the Abbey Arms in Patchley Abbey

He'd accomplished something meaningful and his head-ache had gone, washed away by the delightful pouring rain as sweetly as if by a mother's hand. Hackney slipped inside the Abbey Arms and stripped off Homer Owen's sodden greatcoat, humming *Tea for Two* as he hung it on a hook in the entry. Carolyn had been so delighted the first time she'd heard that, her favorite tune, on the wireless. They'd danced about the parlor and he'd waltzed right to the sofa, pulling her down on top of him and stealing a kiss while she laughed and tickled back, and Arthur had walked in on their silliness and at least pretended teenaged outrage. Hackney laughed as he hung up his dripping hat. As if parents didn't carry on behind their children's backs, or in front of their faces, for that matter, whenever they liked. Little David had learned to laugh at them, but Arthur never had.

Now little David served aboard *HMS Ark Royal,* flying planes in the middle of the ocean, of all things. Arthur was up north at Scapa Flow, doing something hush-hush with sub-marines, and all Hackney had to go home to was a cold, lonely flat in Islington, crowded with Carolyn's favorite bits and bobs of furniture and what-not. The stuff he hadn't been able to crowd in, he'd let go to the dealers on the Tottenham Court Row. Sometimes at night, after he left the pub, he'd take his after-dinner stroll down that way and look at the pieces in the shop windows, then like as not he'd head back to the pub.

How could anyone pick up and go on after something as devastating as Carolyn's cancer? He shook his head, droplets trickling down his forehead, crossed the entry in two long strides, and burst into the pub. Among the few hardy villagers who'd braved the weather for a brew, Arnussen sat at the window table, papers spread before him. He'd worked his way through more of the statements, but many more remained.

Arnussen's face seemed tight, as if pulled back at the edges, and that couldn't be good. Hackney sloshed across the uneven floor and joined him at the table.

"Homer just told me the Home Guard's on alert," Arnussen said. "Faust has escaped again."

The murky pub, the sodden people, even the rumbling thunder seemed to freeze about them. Hackney gasped.

"I just told him not to do that." He leaned onto the table. It tilted beneath him, tumbling statements and the tankard onto the floor. But he didn't look away from Arnussen's sharpening expression. "I told him, it's going to take time to sort all this evidence and prove he didn't kill those girls. I told him to stay put and give us the time."

Arnussen rebalanced the table and snatched up the statements. His foot knocked the tankard and sent it spinning, his intentional action having an unintended consequence. "Did you say that in so many words?"

"He's an enemy officer, Axel. I can't lay him open to a charge of collaboration, now, can I?"

Another swooping scoop, and Arnussen nabbed the tankard, setting it back atop his stack of overturned statements. He leaned forward and lowered his voice. "What's occurred to you about Major Stoner's wandering German?"

Hackney scoffed. "It's not the wandering German who concerns me. He's got the wrong bootprints and blood type, and he can wander right on back to Berlin or wherever he came from for all I care. It's the men out searching for him who will keep me up all night."

Arnussen grabbed his forearm and held on. "Just spell it out."

He'd dripped rainwater all over the suspect chart, ink and words running together as the trees had run together outside the Dark. "Major Faust is the connecting point here. It's his wandering that's setting the murderer off and spurring him to kill. If Major Faust has escaped again, then I'm afraid there's going to be a third murder." It was another intended action with a looming unintended consequence, and Arnussen's growing horror fed his own. "And I don't know how to stop it."

"Use it," Arnussen said without a pause. "Let's ring the Home Guard, Major Kettering, Major Stoner, and put them on alert. If they can keep an eye on some of the suspects, at worst we can narrow down the list and at best we can prevent the killer from striking."

It could work. "Where's your list, Axel?"

"I've been concentrating on blood type eliminations." Arnussen's soft voice hid a razor within its edges. "But I haven't finished and there's at least fifty men." He lifted his eyebrows. "You realize, based upon what we have right now, we can't eliminate Sergeant Tanyon from this list?"

Hackney paused. Of course with Tanyon walking sentry duty on Saturday night, he'd had no alibi for much of his time, but— "I thought Lieutenant Bruckmann could alibi the sergeant for the search on Tuesday."

"After he arrived on the scene, yes, he could." Arnussen straightened his papers. "But before then, we only have Sergeant Tanyon's word that he stood atop the rise and watched the road. He has the right blood type, he has dark hair, and we know his boots approached the house, albeit toward the front door. But once he stepped onto the lawn, he could have gone anywhere, including around back to Grace's open window."

Hackney stared at the tabletop, where old stains formed interlocking circles, connecting points within connecting points. "So what do we make of the boots that approached the house from the Dark?"

Arnussen shrugged. "If Tanyon turns out to be the killer, why must we make anything of them?"

He squeezed the lip of the table. The chill of his wet clothing, or something, made him shiver. "There are too many on the list. How can we find enough people to watch them all?"

"It's what we've got." Arnussen dabbed the suspect chart with his handkerchief. "Let's get to work."

60

evening
Margeaux Hall

Stoner held the receiver to his ear. His heart pounded a slow, intense rhythm, a stuttering engine in the evening of his life. Hackney's deductions and suppositions made frightening sense. "Is there any way we can assist you and counteract the damage we have inadvertently caused?"

The storm static crackled. "Some of your soldiers have the killer's blood type and their alibis aren't straight," Hackney said. "Is it possible to keep them indoors under observation until Major Faust is caught?"

Those young men—boys, really—he'd considered them too young to fight a war. He'd been glad they'd been assigned to his care, far from the front lines and in relative safety, where they could learn their duties with as little danger as possible. For one of them to be the killer, Harriet's killer, was unthinkable. "I'm afraid most of them are already participating in the manhunt."

Hackney paused. "Which are still there?"

"Whiteside and Carmichael."

Paper rustled, audible over the line in a stretch of quiet. "Carmichael's clear but Whiteside isn't, so that's all right. How about Tanyon, Ellington, Norris, Peckham, Pym, and Reynolds? Understand, I don't suspect anyone in particular and don't mean to cast aspersions. But we haven't been able to scientifically eliminate them based upon the evidence we currently have. Can they be recalled?"

His engine stuttered. So many; and the sergeant as well? "I will try."

"Thank you." Hackney paused again. "One more thing. Your clerk, Wainwright. Can an eye be kept on him?"

The door opened. Stoner glanced up.

Jennifer slipped into the office, easing the door to behind her without a sound. Her forced smile seemed more determined than happy. But then her gaze met his and her smile faded as the true meaning of Hackney's warning exploded in Stoner's soul.

"Oh, yes," he said, sudden energy vibrating in his voice, "I can most certainly do something about him. Anything else?"

"That's it."

He replaced the receiver. He'd do anything necessary. It was too late to help Harriet. He would not lose Jennifer, too.

"Dad?" Her voice trembled and even across the dim sitting room he could see her eyes widening. "Is something else wrong?"

He rose and held his hand across the desktop. She hurried to take it and he tugged her behind the desk into Bruckmann's secretarial chair, where he could protect her as he hadn't protected Harriet. With his other hand, he lifted the receiver and dialed upstairs to the guardroom.

But again, Carmichael didn't pick up. Finally Stoner dropped the receiver into its cradle, his rage growing.

"It is time for that young man to learn a bitter lesson." He paused. As usual, there were too many jobs and not enough people. If he kept Jennifer with him and protected her, some other young woman could die. Hackney had assured him Carmichael was clear, but he would not bet Jennifer's safety on that assurance. Stoner hauled open his desk drawer, scrabbled amongst office paraphernalia, and found his old Colt service revolver. He handed it to her butt first. "You have fired this weapon before."

Her glorious hazel eyes widened until they were almost as big as the revolver. "Um, yes, I have."

"Take it, girl, take it." He rose, clasped her shoulders, and tugged her closer. Beneath her flowered housedress, so feminine and fragile, her bones and muscle were solid and strong, stronger than he felt. She'd accused him of being too protective, claimed she was tougher than he'd implied. He'd have to trust her words and not the panic screaming in the background of his soul. He had to be a soldier and trust her to be the same.

Her eyes darkened with confusion and apprehension. But her trust in him shone through undimmed and he loved her more than ever.

"I want you to go upstairs, locate that recalcitrant young hoodlum, return him to his post forthwith, and have him recall our forces to base."

"Recall our forces to base." She repeated it mechanically, as if memorizing the words.

"Precisely." He squeezed her shoulders and chose his words with care. "Chief Inspector Hackney has informed me the murderer may be one of our own soldiers."

She shivered beneath his hands.

"Allow no one near you." He nodded at the revolver in her hand. "Use it if necessary."

Understanding and then anger hardened her expression. She nodded.

"When you have finished, report back to me. You'll find me at the residential wing's front door."

She nodded again. Then her forehead puckered. "Why on earth will you be there?"

He ignored the question. "If I am not there, the door will be unlocked. Wait for me."

She glanced aside. When she turned back, her anger had been replaced with amused affection. "All right, Dad. I will."

He kissed her cheek, standing close to fill his soul with her presence, then grabbed his hat and coat and guided her from the sitting room. "And I love you, as well, despite your negative assessment of my performance during our current assignment."

"On your way, sir." She gave him a gentle push and vanished into the darkness toward the western, wrought-iron stairs.

He hurried in the other direction, toward Margeaux Hall's residential wing.

61

evening
Margeaux Hall

"Carmichael! You miscreant, where have you gone to?"

Jennifer paused at the head of the guardroom corridor. The sofa and chairs in the westward-facing sitting area—the sunset room, they called it—loomed about her like crouching threats. Rain poured over the glass entry behind her but more gently now, as if sobbing rather than screaming. Beneath the drumming, silence stretched into long seconds. Stoner had seemed so calm and yet so frightened, warning her to be careful as he denounced possibly one of their own soldiers. She couldn't stop herself from glancing over her shoulder into the lurking blackness.

Then a toilet flushed. She slumped.

Down the corridor, a door opened crookedly, as if damaged or poorly hung. A shadow stumbled forth, blacker than the blackness about him, arranging his clothing.

"A man steps out just for a moment and look what happens." It was Carmichael's voice and he sounded embarrassed.

She nearly relaxed. But it could be one of their own. *Let no one near you,* Stoner had said. She stiffened again and waited until the lumbering form ducked through the doorway, then followed him into the guardroom's shadows.

Carmichael settled behind the radio as she entered, glancing over his shoulder. His gaze dropped to her hand and his eyes bulged. Oops; she was pointing the revolver at him.

She lowered it.

"Dad is furious."

"Just don't shoot me." Carmichael leaned back away from her as she advanced into the guardroom. "Honest, Miss Stoner, I had to go—"

"Get on the radio and recall our forces to base." She stopped out of his reach, her hand tightening about the revolver's grip. No matter what Stoner said, it was impossible to be frightened of someone with that haircut.

His forehead crinkled. "Recall—"

"—our forces to base. That's what he said."

He turned to the radio. "Whatever you say." He settled the headphones aslant over one ear. "Where'd you get the gat?"

"Dad gave it to me."

"Huh." He flipped a switch and picked up the microphone. "You're scary enough without it. Wildflower base to Wildflower Two. Come in."

It took three tries, while her stomach churned. Then Tanyon's baritone answered.

"Wildflower Three to Wildflower base. Go ahead."

"Wildflower Three, all Wildflower forces are recalled to base on order of Wildflower One. Over."

Static hissed. "Wildflower base, repeat your last transmission. Over."

Carmichael glanced at her. "Wildflower base to Wildflower Three, repeating. All Wildflower forces are recalled to base on order of Wildflower One. Over."

The hissing stretched for seconds. Then, clearer than clear, Bruckmann swore as if he'd never attended a church service in his life. His words were suddenly cut off. She giggled. Carmichael glanced at her and grinned. Perhaps she wasn't as frightening as all that, either.

"Acknowledge, Wildflower Three," Carmichael said.

Tanyon's voice sounded grudging. "Wildflower Three to Wildflower base. Orders acknowledged. Wildflower Three out."

Carmichael removed the headphones. "Satisfied?"

"Perfectly, but you still must answer to Dad. I mean it; he's furious."

He sighed and rattled the headphones on the table. "It's Sally I'm worried about."

"You don't believe she's actually out there in the rain, do you?" Jennifer scoffed. "Sally has more sense."

"She said she would be and she's never let me down before." He glanced sideways, eyes wide and somewhere between charming and scheming. "I just wish someone would check for me, that's all."

No arguing with love. She rolled her eyes. "Where do you two meet?"

"Out by the main entry, behind the gatehouse where there aren't any windows." The words poured from him in a rush. "I'll take what's coming to me, honest, I will. But I don't like to think of Sally out in the rain when I'm not coming."

"I tell you she's not out there. But someone will check."

"Thank you." His eyes gleamed again. "He's seriously angry?"

"Oh, get on with you." She retreated before he could charm her further.

At the top of the eastern stairs she hesitated. Had she actually heard someone behind her, or just rain cascading from the skylight? She froze and listened. But the uneasy tripping of her pulse overwhelmed anything else. She hurried downstairs as fast as she could in the dark, listening for footfalls behind her.

62

evening
Margeaux Hall

Stoner donned his coat and Homburg in the dark corridor, then stepped through the door into Margeaux Hall's residential wing. The formal entry hall stretched about him, dark paneling and staring portraits faceless in the gloom, stairs sweeping past into the rarefied air of the upper floors. Rain splashed against stained glass panels bracketing the bronze-bound oak door, and as he approached, he saw it was unbolted and only on the latch. Someone had exited and hadn't returned.

He paused. He'd given Jennifer his Colt revolver; the only other weapons were the shotguns in Woodrow or the last Lee Enfield in the upstairs guardroom. He should have instructed her to fetch the latter down upon her return. But he hadn't, so any action he took carried a calculated risk. Stoner took a deep breath, ignored his thumping heart, and stepped out, unarmed, into the rain.

It pattered onto his coat and down his collar, no longer the drenching downpour he'd earlier shunned but a steady thrumming that nevertheless hosed his trouser legs, socks, and shoes within steps. He swept the flashlight's arc about, checking the gravel walkway ahead, the windows of the gatehouse, the looming beeches near the road, and the mortared-stone wall stretching to either side and vanishing in the impenetrable night. But nothing moved; no one, it seemed, had lost his reason sufficiently to venture forth in such weather, except Hackney and Faust. Stoner sighed, drips coursing down the back of his neck: and, of course, by necessity his soldiers and himself.

No light showed from the gatehouse windows, not even a chink where he could observe undetected. The Wainwrights, it seemed, took the blackout regulations more seriously than the Stoners. He sighed again, crossed the half-hearted little garden that Mrs. Wainwright half-heartedly cultivated, and knocked on the gatehouse door.

After a moment, Wainwright opened the door a crack, a broad band of light slicing through the night. "Mr. Stoner." He glanced beyond into the dark, as if expecting someone else to materialize. "Is anything wrong?"

So the quarry lay low in its den. "Mr. Wainwright, did anyone inform you Major Faust has again escaped?"

Wainwright shifted. He moved as if to step outside, then paused, glancing at the rain dripping from the flint roof above his dry head. "No, sir, no one's said anything to me. Do you need my assistance?"

If his hair was dry, he hadn't set foot outside. Stoner's next breath came more easily. "You must guard your household. Keep your rifle handy."

Wainwright nodded jerkily, as if an inexperienced puppeteer pulled his head's strings. "I will, sir. Thank you."

"Good night, Mr. Wainwright." Stoner strode back along the path to the Hall, flicking off his flash after a few steps.

The light from the open door vanished behind him.

Stoner stepped off the path into the grass and doubled back, sweeping the little light into the hidden corner behind the gatehouse. It was deserted. He checked the walkway for footprints and found the usual confused scuffles, examined the closed windows of Margeaux Hall, then glanced in passing at the magnificent iron gate, rusted shut and useless.

It hung open by a foot.

He paused. Unreasoning dread drenched him, colder and heavier than the rain. But he was unarmed and cautious courage could too easily become blatant foolhardiness. Instead of investigating, he flicked the torch off and splashed through the puddles back to the residential wing's front door, arriving in time to catch Jennifer, hat and coat on, before she stepped out into the rain.

"There you are." She withdrew and held the door for him.

He followed. "Where was Carmichael?"

"In the loo. Dad, Sally's missing. I just checked her bedroom but she's not there."

His heart gave an odd double-thump then tripped along,

steady enough but too hard and fast. He'd worried so about his surviving granddaughter, he hadn't spared a thought for the housemaid.

"You still have the revolver?"

"Of course."

"Run upstairs and wake the Alcocks. Ask them both to dress and join us here." He took her arm and held her still. "Then run back to the guardroom, fetch the spare Lee Enfield from Carmichael, and ask him to load it for you. Bring both weapons back."

She hesitated. "Are we leaving him unarmed?"

"My dear, should any enemy advance so far into our stronghold, it will matter little whether Carmichael is armed or no."

"It might to Carmichael." She ran.

"Granted." But she'd already gone. He settled to watching the gatehouse through the intervening curtain of rain. Wainwright would not wriggle away and if anyone lurked outside the gate, there they would remain. He could do no more. But even as he stood guard, he knew in his heart it was too late and he'd failed. If Sally died, he was responsible, as if she were one of the soldiers he'd ordered to charge a German machine-gun position twenty-five years before.

63

evening
northwest of Oxford

Without warning, the mare trotted from the forest and trailed to a stop, blowing for breath, her ribcage expanding and contracting between Faust's legs. He sat back, kicked his feet from the stirrups, and stretched his tired thighs and calves.

They were on the crest of a rise, the Dark behind them, another stone wall and more farmland ahead. In the blackout he couldn't discern any houses or other buildings, but it was a good bet somebody lived down that hill somewhere. Rain still drummed down, more gently now, no longer a raging storm but still a determined washing, and it trickled over his face, down his neck, and into his boots. He laughed, incredulous delight bubbling within him. Let it rain; he couldn't possibly get any wetter.

The stars were hidden. Without their guidance, he wasn't certain where he stood on his mental image of the surrounding countryside, stolen from the maps he'd studied with Hackney and Stoner. An unknown landscape spread before him, all reference points hidden by the night and the rain and the blackout, and he had more chance of riding into someone's farmyard than into safety. And he didn't care.

Because the landscape before him was utterly dark. No discreet bursts of light, no little flashlight cones slid across the ground. No line of Kettering's soldiers spread across his path. He laughed again, closing his eyes and lifting his face into the giddy rain. The mare whuffled in answer and shook her wet mane, and he leaned onto her neck and hugged her, the beautiful ugly beast.

He rested his forearm against the mare's neck and peered around. The landscape to right and left looked the same, empty paths stretching between the forest's edge and the drystone wall, both sloping gently downhill. But somewhere to his left and ahead was the city of Oxford with its beloved dreaming spires. Best not to get too close. And one thing was certain: he wouldn't convince this cart horse to jump over that wall.

He shuffled his feet back into the stirrups, shoving himself erect. The mare lifted her head, flicking an ear back. He slapped her neck, turned her to the right, and squeezed his legs, and she sauntered off in the rain. He gritted his teeth. Her faster paces were lousy at best and his legs ached almost as badly as his arm, but Kettering could still be close and he didn't have time to pamper her. He kicked the mare and she trotted, ears slanting at a discontented angle, head lifting toward him. He kicked again, harder, and finally she lumbered into a canter, rollicking along the wet turf beside the wall.

She could slip or stumble, throwing him into a tree or the flint wall. But he had to make time. He wrapped his legs about her table-top girth and held on.

64

evening
the Abbey Arms

Hackney left Arnussen threatening the British Army with the most God-awful ruckus from the civil authorities if Kettering and his two companies weren't recalled to base, and headed upstairs to dry off. He'd already telephoned Constable Mercer and arranged for the elderly bobby to keep an eye on the blacksmith, Sullivan Gilbert. He'd rung Harry Oldfield, the commander of the local Home Guard, to encourage every man with a daughter, wife, sister, female cousin, or neighbor between the ages of ten and forty, to stand over her that night with his American-made rifle, respected or not. He couldn't think of any other calls he should make, anyone else he could protect or eliminate; but in the back of his mind niggled an unnamed worry he couldn't dismiss.

In his room, he stripped off and rubbed himself down with the big terry towel Homer had given him. Determinedly, he kept his back to the mirror, bolted to the inside of the door; himself fifty pounds overweight was not a sight calculated to cheer him, especially not stark.

He'd put on weight when he and Carolyn first married, too, back in naught-eight. He'd been a bobby on the beat then, getting plenty of exercise, but nothing could hold out against her cooking and he'd heard about it from his mates and sergeant. It had taken both he and Carolyn, working together, to slim him back down, and he'd put it all back on once the cancer had taken her.

He sighed and toweled his back. It seemed his entire world had come to an end with her death. Until then, he'd managed his career, his family, his weight, his life. Now he had to wiggle the towel into the creases about his waist and abdomen. He was a farce, a parody of his old self.

The murders of Harriet and Grace weighed on his mind as much as the fat padded his middle. On impulse, he wrapped the towel about himself and went next door to Arnussen's bedroom. The table there was crowded with the bootprints' plaster casts, the photographs from both crime scenes, the rolled-up maps with Faust's routes traced on them, and all their accumulated papers. Behind the plaster casts he found the framed photos of the living girls: a cheap pine frame for Grace, her bow poised over her violin and eyes up, dark hair held back by a light ribbon, sitting among the string section of the Patchbourne symphony orchestra; elegant black oak for the studio portrait of Harriet and Jennifer, the dark and bright heads leaning together, one smooth and serious, the other with flowers on.

Someone might join their ranks that night. His grimaced at the thought. Surely he'd done everything possible, protected everyone he could—but his nagging inner voice would not be silent. He'd missed something. And if the investigation dragged on much longer, he'd miss something else and someone else might die.

The connecting point. There was always the connecting point.

Hackney hurried back to his room, still clutching the photos. He closed the door, set the photos carefully atop the washstand, and dropped the towel in a damp heap on the floor. Clean drawers were in his hand when, clear as anything, Carolyn's rich gay laugh rang in his mind.

For a long moment he stood motionless. He was acting the coward and Carolyn would have been disappointed. Slowly he turned and faced himself in the mirror.

Twenty minutes later, freshly shaved, hair rubbed and combed, wearing a clean shirt and tie, he rejoined Arnussen in the pub.

"Another one, guv?" Homer called from behind his lowered newspaper.

Hackney shook his head. "Thanks, but I've had enough for one night. Got to work now."

Arnussen glanced up from his reams of paper. He adjusted his glasses and stared, a crease between his eyes. "You've had a thought, haven't you?"

Hackney opened a crisp new manila folder atop the interlocking dark rings on the table. The folder contained a blank notepad, the crime scene photos, the autopsy reports, the serology and fingerprint reports, and the photos of the living girls, removed from their frames. "Just a thought, Axel, old lad."

He advanced the lead on his mechanical pencil and began to write.

65

night
Wynant Dairy

What a bloody night.

Bruckmann slouched against the lorry's front fender; hell, he couldn't get any dirtier or wetter. The entire evening had been a complete balls-up. He'd been embarrassed before Stoner, Tanyon, himself, and his entire miniscule command. He was wet through and coated with mud from mucking about in the unspeakable sludge in the dairy's pastures. His little command had vanished, scattered beyond his control during their search. The prisoner was long gone, his keys to a secret military installation were lost—and now Stoner reined him in, as he might call out a useless puppy from a hunting pack.

If Stoner reassigned him in disgust, it would be no surprise. But hopefully not until he'd seen Stoner rip the stuffing from Faust.

"And so ends tonight's big adventure, gentlemen."

"It's not such a loss as all that." Beside him, Kettering seemed fresh and lively as ever, smiling even with rainwater pouring over him. "There's not a lot we can do now in any case except await news of our quarry and get in out of the wet." He clapped Bruckmann's shoulder. "Call me should you need me, leftenant." He strode off into the rain, mounted his motorcycle, revved the engine to life, and rode away.

"There must be some disaster out there, something in this wide, evil world, to cure that man of his never-ending cheerfulness." Bruckmann turned to Tanyon, still hanging half in the lorry's cab and staring at the wet seat. "I don't suppose you've seen my keys?"

Tanyon scoffed. "I can't see my feet in this."

Bruckmann straightened. "We need to round up the squad."

"Not you, sir. You need to report back. I'll go play in the mud." Tanyon paused. "Take the lorry. We'll walk back. We're already wet as can be."

"Good idea, sergeant."

"Sir."

"Except I've lost my keys."

Without a sound, Tanyon handed over his.

"Thank you." Bruckmann waited until Tanyon slogged off through the slop, then dragged himself behind the big horizontal steering wheel. The night couldn't possibly get any worse.

The rain was lifting and the blackness no longer seemed impenetrable. Still he almost ran the lorry into Caspar Wynant's drystone wall en route to the road. Bruckmann stopped in time, danced a few measures between brake and clutch and accelerator to keep the lorry from stalling, then reversed back onto the driveway and shifted to first.

At the road he paused and glanced both ways, but paused again before swinging the big wheel for the left turn. Bright cones from multiple flashlights danced in the next pasture, across from Margeaux Hall's main gate. Such blatant disregard for the blackout regulations couldn't be boasted by anyone short of Stoner. Bruckmann guided the lorry onto the verge and killed the engine.

As he clambered from the cab into the drizzling rain, one flashlight cone angled his way. "Jack? Is that you?" It was Stoner's voice.

"Yes, sir." He leapt the puddle on the side of the road, squelched through sodden grass to the wall, and leaned over. "Is something wrong?"

"Yes, I suppose you could say so." Despite his jocular words, Stoner's voice sounded sad, disembodied without even a silhouette behind the flashlight. The cone of light flickered over a huddled mass on the ground, then shied away like a frightened horse.

The view had been too brief for Bruckmann to understand the shapeless lump. He shot his own flashlight at it. It took a moment's staring to recognize Sally, or what was left of her. He turned his back and leaned against the sharp-edged flint; he needed all the support he could get while he decided what to do with his dinner.

66

dawn
northwest of Oxford

With grey light beginning to tint the world, Faust halted the mare atop a rise. Ahead sprawled the Oxford skyline, spires dreaming in a sea of mist. They'd passed the wall and gates of Blenheim Palace in the rain and hadn't even seen them.

Ten miles; he and the mare had traveled about ten miles in a straight line from the dairy she called home. Not far, considering they'd trotted for hours with few breaks. But so much of their energy had been wasted circling around farms, even that much seemed a considerable achievement. And the mare, blowing beneath him like a steam engine, was spent.

He'd hiked here as a student and his memory returned clear images of farmlands, pastures, and villages. But not all of the residences had been farms. There were rich men's homes up here, with rich men's toys. Including foxhunters.

He let the mare amble while he peered through the grey dawn, senses alert, for signs of equine civilization—manure in a field, a distant nicker, a fence sectioned off for the hunt. Slowly the light rose about them, the rain dwindling to a mist drifting on his skin. Steam rose from the mare's shoulders and flanks, and his anxiety grew with the light. If he stumbled into a farmyard now, on an exhausted cart horse, he wouldn't be able to run from a three-legged cow; a farmer with a pitchfork could reel him in. Perhaps he should hide for the day. But anywhere he hid, people could find. And ten miles was nowhere near far enough from Stoner for safety. No, he had to keep going, tired or not.

Suddenly the mare stopped, threw up her head, and whinnied. He yanked on the reins and cut her off. But from the mist another horse answered, then another.

"Yes." Faust dismounted and led the mare to the wall. In a moment, a horse stepped from the mist as if past a curtain, a tall rangy horse with a cresting neck and dark coat that glowed in the dim light. Other horses, less bold, paused amid the mist's camouflage; their elegant shapes were outlines drawn, grey pencil on grey canvas, with restless heads and hooves.

He stripped the saddle and bridle from the mare, stacking them atop the wall, and turned her loose with a grateful slap. She wouldn't go far from the other horses; someone would find her and return her to Wynant Dairy, Delivery Available on any other day except today. He laughed at his own wit.

All the horses crowded up to the wall, watching with pricked ears, long before he finished. But he selected that first, bold one, slipped over the wall, and caught it by the halter. It was a stallion, he learned when he bent down to fasten the girth. Excitement bubbled within him. Stallions were intrepid rides, just what he needed to cross England without being caught.

He mounted, found his stirrup, and touched his heel to the horse's side. The stallion moved off instantly—no kicking needed here—and they trotted across the field through the mist, the mares trailing behind, the cart horse lumbering along outside the wall. Faust found the stallion's rhythm easily and posted the trot, his confidence growing as he settled into the one-two beat.

A long, low, dark line loomed ahead—the wall bordering the field. Faust squeezed the stallion into a canter and aimed him at the jump. The stallion flicked his ears, crested his neck, picked up speed. The mares scattered. Faust rose in the stirrups and held on with his calves, his heart galloping, too. If this beast balked, he was a goner.

The stallion planted his feet at the wall and thrust into space. Faust crouched over the saddle as he'd practiced all those years ago at Neukuhren. His heart tried to explode from his chest. The wall flashed beneath them and he yelled for sheer triumph. The stallion landed on the other side, bucked once as if in sympathy with his yell, and galloped on into the mist, leaving the mares and the farm behind.

67

dawn, Thursday, 29 August 1940
Wynant Dairy

The rain softened to a drizzle, and Hackney opened the car door before Arnussen killed the engine. To the north, across the road and halfway up the rise, loomed Margeaux Hall. Its imposing mortared wall stretched into the distance, out of view in the day's first lightening. South of the road, a drystone wall edged the dairy's fields, mist floating over the invisible grass as if tethered. One young sentry, his face pale in the pre-dawn greyness, stood a lonely guard at the roadside. A tall slender figure leaned on the wall near him, face in hands. Even in the murky light, Bruckmann's white-blond hair gleamed like a searchlight beneath the peaked cap.

Hackney squelched through the verge's sodden grass, Arnussen behind him.

"Lieutenant Bruckmann."

"Sir." Bruckmann straightened, resting his palms on the flint blocks. From this closer vantage point, Hackney could see the young officer's greatcoat was rumpled, clammy, and soiled. Mud smeared one cheek and his eyes were bloodshot. "She's over here."

They clambered over the wall, leaving the sentry to his lonely vigil. Hackney spotted the motionless lump huddled at the wall's base, several yards to the right. He dragged his flashlight from his pocket and flicked it on.

It was like a repeating nightmare—the naked body and battered face, splayed legs, the smashed wreckage that had once been her chest. Pooled rain mixed with the blood and kept it red. He stared down at Sally for long seconds, Arnussen's flash bolstering his own and bringing the details into shameless clarity. Then, forlorn, he crouched down beside her. Dark hair wrapped about her face into the edge of her mouth and fell into her uncaring eyes. He wanted to brush it back, not that it would do her any good now.

"Has Dr. Harris been sent for?" he asked over his shoulder.

"I don't know, sir. I'll find out." Bruckmann turned away, toward the sentry.

"Ask him to bring his photography gear." Hackney touched her hair, wet and stringy, careful not to disarrange it. He lowered his voice. "It's my fault, Axel."

"Don't see how you arrive at that." Arnussen dropped his voice to match.

He started the detailed examination of her body. "When I called Major Stoner last night, I told him to keep an eye on that clerk of his so's to clear one more suspect from our list. What I should have said was to keep an eye on any potential victims so's to protect them. I had my instructions turned turkey-end over, and for that Sally's dead."

"Surely he understood the situation."

"That doesn't let me off the hook. I've been at this job too long not to know what's important." He crouched lower and shone the light onto her fingernails. They were clean beneath their pale pink polish. "There's got to be a way of drawing this monster into the open, Axel. There's got to be, that's all."

"I'm not turning up any evidence here." Arnussen glanced at the sky. "Rain's letting up, but it's been pouring for hours. Dr. Harris will have the devil's own time determining time of death on this one."

He grunted. "Exactly my point."

They rose together and clicked off their flashes. Hackney glanced at the encroaching mist, motionless above the grass, so thick he'd have to swim through it. Somewhere a cow lowed. The rain had almost stopped, and only a gentle drizzle caressed his hands and face. Outside the wall, Bruckmann leaned on his elbows, a discreet distance away.

"Think that lad's had any sleep this night past?"

Arnussen shook his head. "Not likely, is it."

Clattering footsteps heralded the return of the sentry, the skirts of his greatcoat flapping about his legs and his rifle bouncing across his back as he galloped across the road. His thin face was pinched and tight, eyebrows drawn together as if in concentration. He crashed to attention before Bruckmann and presented arms. Bruckmann returned the salute.

Arnussen chuckled. "Someone's put the fear of God into that one recently."

Bruckmann approached and rested his palms atop the wall. But he didn't look down. "We've sent for Dr. Harris and he knows to bring his gear."

"Good." Hackney lowered his voice to a growling mumble. "What's that soldier's name?"

Arnussen shot him a look. He ignored it.

"Reynolds." Bruckmann, he noticed, caught Arnussen's glance, too. One wrinkle appeared between the lieutenant's eyebrows.

Hackney nodded toward the two sentries, one at each of the residential and military wings' separate gates. "And those two?"

Bruckmann glanced about. "Norris and Sloane."

"I have nothing against Reynolds personally," Hackney said, lowering his voice to barely a whisper, "and I'm not casting aspersions or suspicions toward anyone. But we haven't been able to scientifically eliminate him from our suspect list based upon the evidence we currently have."

"So it would be inappropriate to leave him guarding the remains." Bruckmann nodded. "Should I trade him off with Norris, do you think?"

"Same for Norris," Arnussen said. "Better make it Sloane."

Bruckmann started to move off, then paused. "Sir, may I ask how many of our soldiers are still on your suspect list?"

Hackney hesitated. "Best not ask, lieutenant."

Bruckmann paused again as if he wanted to argue the point, the wrinkle reappearing and deepening between his eyebrows. But he said nothing, merely stared for an unhappy moment then stalked back to where Reynolds waited.

"So what now?" Arnussen stood at his elbow, also watching Bruckmann.

Hackney turned from the living and the dead, feeling unaccountably heavy. Pearly nacre tinged the sky overhead and dusted the mist with powdered opal. More cows bawled in the distance. He breathed deeply of wet earth, crushed grass, old manure, and blood, and shivered in Homer Owen's still-damp greatcoat.

"That lad reminds me of Arthur, the way he asks the damnedest questions." Sally's face, once worth coming home to, was now swollen and marbled, the nose smashed, eyes staring off into nowhere. "Did you say something, Axel?"

"We should start taking statements, don't you think?"

He sighed. "We have to. But I don't think it's going to do any good."

"Don't start that. We'll solve this one yet—"

"Yes, but when?" He flicked on his flashlight and swept the beam over Sally's huddled mass, the vibrant young woman they'd met only two days ago. "Any new evidence has been washed away by the rain. The grass won't give us any footprints, there's nothing beneath her fingernails, and we already know what will show up at autopsy."

"You don't know that."

"The hell we don't." He clicked off the flash and thrust it back into his pocket. "Yes, we'll get there with the long, detailed investigation. But we don't have the manpower to work it fast, there's no one we can call for help, and we're losing girls, three a week. We've wasted enough time." He took a deep breath, letting the dank air and the stench of blood permeate his lungs. "No, I'm wrong. We've wasted too much time and Sally is dead because of it."

Arnussen stared at him, the edges of his mouth lifting in something not quite a smile. "You do have a thought, don't you." It wasn't a question, either.

The plan had exploded fully grown from his head like some neo-modern version of Athena the previous night, while he'd stared at his fat naked self in the mirror. At the time, he'd wondered if he was, after all, too old and used up to make a difference. His self-indulgent hesitation had given the murderer time to destroy another victim. Sally had been sacrificed on the altar of his vanity and self-confidence.

"Just a thought, Axel, old lad. You wait here for Dr. Harris and keep your detailed investigation going. I'm heading to Margeaux Hall for a word with Major Stoner."

68

dawn
northwest of Oxford

The rain stopped at dawn. Faust and the stallion paused for breath within the shelter of a stand of trees. The rise overlooked a field where a distant group of women cultivated some low-growing vegetable crop, bending and straightening in the sloppy mud until his own back ached. He tied the reins to a branch, keeping several trees between the horse and the workers, and sat nearby on a rocky outcrop. Grey mist still tinted the day, the same shade as his uniform, but sunlight pierced the clouds and his spirits lifted to meet it.

His clothes, although still wet, had been getting drier for several hours. It was time for the great experiment. Fingers trembling, he pulled the crumpled Players pack from his inner breast pocket and extracted his last cigarette. It and the matches were damp, but he stuck it between his lips, convinced a match to strike, then held it to the business end of the cigarette until it caught.

The first lungful was sheer ecstasy, something beyond orgasm. He lay back across the rock and stared up at the still-dripping leaves, letting the smoke drift from his nostrils and feeling the nicotine surge through his system. For a moment the leaves spun about him, and he closed his eyes against the dizziness. Then the world settled back down, once more orderly and wonderful—even in the wet, even on the run in England—and he laughed, remembering to keep it quiet so the women wouldn't hear him. The stallion whuffled, just as quietly, as if in answer.

He'd have to wait here until the women were far enough away not to identify his uniform when he rode from shelter. Might as well enjoy it while he could.

69

early morning
Margeaux Hall

Stoner wore uniform.

Bruckmann's flying fingers paused over the typewriter. Glover stood behind the front desk while Stoner, in dapper khaki, wrote something into the logbook and said a few words. Whatever he said caused Glover to sit hurriedly and tuck himself behind the switchboard, eyes wider than ever.

Then Stoner turned and strode up the corridor into the grand ballroom, and the cold in the pit of Bruckmann's stomach solidified into a cannonball at the old man's squared shoulders and stiffer expression.

Stoner never wore uniform unless he visited another military installation. Not because it made him uncomfortable—far from it—but of his two personas, he preferred dressing and being the Oxford don rather than the major commanding Margeaux Hall. Bruckmann considered Stoner's affability, the amused blind eye he turned to military strictures, and knew within the wellspring of his soul that last night, the situation had gone too far for even the old man to tolerate.

He bent over the keyboard and looked busy.

"Jack."

He glanced up as if surprised and rose from behind the desk. "Sir?"

Not a flicker of amusement lit Stoner's icy blue eyes. "While you're working on that report—"

Heat climbed Bruckmann's face. He should have known

he wouldn't fool the old man for a second.

"—please have Carmichael report to my office." Stoner glanced at his watch. "Let's call a staff meeting for eight. Report with Sergeant Tanyon at that time." He strode on.

"Yes, sir," Bruckmann said to his departing back. "Good morning, sir."

The office door closed.

Bruckmann released his held breath in a whoosh. Thankfully neither the Wainwrights nor Jennifer had yet reported for work. It didn't take an Oxford don to figure out what Stoner's so-called staff meeting would entail. He reached for the telephone.

70

early morning
Margeaux Hall

Clarke entered the glass-walled vestibule, peaked cap beneath his elbow. A young soldier sat behind the switchboard, plugging a jack into a socket. The kid's face, angular and good-natured, puckered with confusion, and his guileless green eyes were clouded. How long ago had he been conscripted? Four months, maybe five? Long enough to learn how to handle a rifle and a switchboard, and probably damn all else.

"Good morning, soldier."

"Yes, sir?" The young soldier started to stand, then sat again. "Can I help you?"

Not even four months; three at the most, if he didn't know to remain at his duty post no matter who came through the door. "My name's Clarke. I have orders to report here this morning."

If possible, the kid's face puckered further. "Here?"

Of course, it would be expecting too much for this rear-echelon outpost on the backside of beyond, a good seventy miles from the coast and nowhere near the expected invasion zone, to remember he was coming at all or even have a clue as to why he'd been ordered to report there in the first place. Clarke held his temper but promised himself it wouldn't be for long. If the Germans started invading without him, he'd find the man behind this visit and heave him face-first into his breakfast, which was probably a damned sight better than anything the front-line troops, his own troops, were receiving.

He opened his mouth to speak a modified version of his mind but paused as a lanky second lieutenant entered from the ballroom, a dispatch key in one hand and papers in the other.

"Right on time today." The lieutenant, still with the awkward arms and legs of youth, didn't glance at Clarke. He crossed to the filing cabinet, pulled a dispatch case from the top drawer, unlocked it, stashed the papers inside, then relocked it. Only then did he look up. And pause. "I'm sorry. I thought you were the dispatch courier."

"Not today." Clarke kept his voice carefully gentle.

The lieutenant's pale face reddened. With his white-blond hair and blue eyes, he looked like the national flag on two legs. "May I help you?"

Second time might be lucky. "My name is Clarke. I have orders to report here this morning."

Not a flicker rearranged the lieutenant's searching expression.

Clarke sighed rather than scream. "This is Margeaux Hall?"

Light finally dawned. "Clarke," the lieutenant said, "Captain Clarke. Of course, I'm sorry." He replaced the dispatch case and circled the desk. "You're a bit earlier than we expected, that's all. My name's Bruckmann."

From this closer vantage point, Bruckmann's face seemed paler than even it had a right to. Raw red lines crept in from the edges of his eyes to surround his blue irises. He'd taken the time to shave and change his shirt, but this was a man who hadn't slept last night. Clarke reined in his impatience and temper; there was a story here, after all.

"This way, Captain Clarke."

Clarke followed Bruckmann into the ballroom, past the empty desks to the sitting area. The old-fashioned console radio was closed and silent. Playing cards, leather-bound books, and dirty ashtrays littered the tables. The swags drawn from the line of floor-to-ceiling windows admitted the summer morning's sunlight in all its splendor, and lighted the notepad and handlebar mustache of an overweight civil servant sitting on one sofa, using a briefcase across his knees as a desk while he wrote.

Bruckmann paused. "I must ask you to wait here with Chief Inspector Hackney. The major is busy at the moment and we have a staff meeting at eight, but as soon as he's available I know he's anxious to meet you."

Clarke made no move to sit. "Lieutenant, why am I

here?"

The writer scratched away without seeming to notice them. But Clarke didn't believe that for a moment.

Bruckmann paused again. "You're here to see Major Stoner. Beyond that I can't say."

The name was familiar. "There was a don at Magdalen named Cedric Stoner. Any relation?"

"The same."

Perhaps this wouldn't be a complete waste of time, after all. Clarke gazed out the window at the serene lawn criss-crossed with slanting early morning rays. "Damned clever man, he was reputed to be."

"I assure you, he still is," Bruckmann said, unruffled. "Would it ease the wait if I called for a spot of tea or coffee for you gentlemen?"

The pencil halted.

"Sounds like a yes to me. Thank you, lieutenant, tea would be a kindness." Clarke sat on the other end of the sofa as Bruckmann returned to the work area and lifted the telephone receiver at one desk.

So he had to wait through a staff meeting. Clarke picked up the nearest book and glanced at its spine: *Dr. Faustus,* by Christopher Marlowe. The title jolted him. Before he could rouse any resistance, that wrenching memory of the Aa Canal flooded into the forefront of his mind, reached down his gullet, grabbed his unprepared innards, and twisted them.

He didn't bother to open the book. Even Marlowe's best was a non-starter; the image of Faust in Clarke's imagination had dark hair the color of cocoa, an expressive wedge-shaped face with a high forehead and lively dark eyes, narrowing to a determined chin, and wore a field-grey uniform with the ribbon for the Iron Cross First Class. The best poetry couldn't compete with the still-raw memory of that slender hand shaking out a fag and offering the pack: *"Do you use these things?"*

Clarke tossed the book onto the table, atop *Treasure Island* and *Twelfth Night.* No use fighting. The memory had been triggered and it would dominate his thoughts until it, and he, were spent.

Every detail of that rencontre was etched into his soul with acid. The memory had obtained a life of its own within him and at the slightest provocation would spill across the screen of his mind like a newsreel. Without any effort at all, he tasted the acrid smoke of Faust's strong cigarettes, hefted the gentle weight of the P-38 pistol thrust into his hand, cringed anew at the shame of not even recognizing him.

It was an obsession. He shoved the book across the

table, knocking an overflowing ashtray to the edge. To his left, the pencil never hesitated. But Clarke knew he was being studied. He sat back and crossed his arms. Shame and anger flavored the memory of Faust openly leaning forward to study his Royal Warwickshires regimental flash, the teasing tenor echoing again in his mind. *"Infantry: oh, frag. I'll try using small words."*

Yes, Faust had had some fun with him. They'd both had it coming. And despite all the contempt he'd inflicted on Faust during their joint year at University College, he'd saved all their lives. Clarke could only hope he'd gotten away with the God-awful risk he'd run.

The door opposite the sitting area opened. A young soldier stepped through and closed the door behind himself, his face grey. Even across the room, the red rimming his eyes couldn't be missed.

"That kind of staff meeting, is it?"

Hackney glanced up from his notes for the first time. "Beg pardon?"

"I've had my share of those."

The chief inspector glanced at the young soldier's re-treating figure, then examined Clarke the same way a hungry hound might fasten his attention on a tasty morsel. "Young Carmichael, you mean? Actually, his fiancée was murdered last night."

He couldn't have heard that right. "Murdered?"

"That's why he's upset." Hackney returned to his notes, then nodded at the cluttered table and filthy ashtrays. "The housemaid, she was. Wonder who they'll get to clean for them now?"

Clarke stared at him, too shocked to think.

"But I don't doubt," Hackney rumbled on, adding a few words to his notes, "the staff meeting's going to be all that, and more."

With an effort Clarke turned away, in time to see a sergeant, the only Regular Army veteran he'd seen in Margeaux Hall, clatter down the wrought-iron staircase in the vestibule. Even across the length of the grand ballroom, his magnificent shiner and bruised cheekbone and chin were glaringly obvious.

Yes, there was a story here. And Clarke couldn't wait to hear it.

71

Faust and the stallion trotted along the edge of a field beside a drystone wall. The dawn mists lifted, leaving them nakedly visible in brilliant daylight. But no one approached, no one called out, no fingers pointed their way; so he concentrated on making the best time he could while saving the stallion's strength for a long haul. The stallion had proved himself a magnificent beast, and with each hoofbeat Faust's spirits rose higher until he felt incandescent, like a switched-on light bulb. All it would take was a fuse and he'd go up with a bang.

Judging by the angle of sunlight pouring across their left sides, it was eight or nine o'clock and almost time to take a breather when he spotted a little copse ahead, one field away. The perfect spot. He urged the stallion into a hand gallop. The horse snorted, tossed his head back almost into Faust's face, and surged forward, the soft thudding of his hooves into the turf accelerating to a four-beat cadence. No, he didn't want to let this ride go, not unless he had to; the copse and another rest it would be.

At the base of the wall, the stallion planted his hind feet and leapt, the takeoff pushing Faust over his withers. He gripped with his legs and held on for the seconds they were airborne, nearly yelling again for raw exultation.

"What the—oy!"

The stallion landed, ears slanting back toward the yell

behind them, and shied for the first time. Faust wrapped his legs about the stallion's girth, gripping a handful of mane along with the reins, and risked a glance over his shoulder.

Two British Army soldiers crouched in the lee of the drystone wall, starting up from their huddle about a field transceiver. Faust's glance lasted two seconds at most, but the moment seared into him like a brand—not recent conscripts but tough and seasoned soldiers in crisp battledress, their hard faces slack-jawed. Even as the stallion galloped away, the one on the right threw himself to his knees and reached for the microphone.

Only two of them and their rifles were stacked against the wall behind the transceiver. Faust faced front. If he could gallop beyond their vision before reinforcements arrived—

But the field had sloped downhill and he hadn't seen it clearly from the wall's other side. It swarmed with British Army troops. And most of them were staring at him.

Faust straightened in the saddle, squeezing his legs to get the stallion's attention and tightening the reins to halt him. Several hundred soldiers filled the scenery ahead; the little copse, his intended resting place, also showed movement through the trees; there was even an artillery battery halfway down the hill, big field guns trained in the opposite direction but the crews starting to turn. It looked like training maneuvers, so their rifles would be loaded with blanks. No way he'd make it through their ranks; even if they couldn't shoot him, someone would get close enough to grab him and haul him off the horse.

But there were only two men behind him. He reined the stallion about, his knee then the horse's nose nearly knocking the drystone wall, and drove in his heels. The stallion flattened his ears, chin tucked and mane flying, slewing divots as he dug in.

One hefty lance corporal barred his escape, Lee Enfield pointing up. Blanks, Faust reminded himself, and kicked the stallion. The other soldier yelled into the microphone, words incoherent, his gaze sliding sideways as the stallion's big feet pounded in his direction. But he didn't budge from his post. In his heart, Faust both saluted and cursed him. Too much to ask for a British Army soldier to abandon his post in the heat of combat.

The lance corporal met Faust's stare, face reddening in the sunlight, and also held his ground. He was easily six feet tall, shoulders broad to match. It wasn't likely the horse could jump that high; he was good, but not that good, and horses hadn't been trained to jump through a man rather than over him since the death of knighthood. To signal his intentions and give the corporal something to think about, Faust rose in the stirrups and leaned over the stallion's shoulders, narrowing his eyes against the sun's glare.

As if in answer, the corporal ratcheted a round into his Lee Enfield's chamber. Blanks, just blanks; it didn't matter. Faust squeezed his legs. The stallion accelerated again, jibbing at the bit, forelegs reaching as if to eat the ground before him.

The corporal didn't aim. He fired into the air, his slit-eyed stare never wavering. The bottom dropped from Faust's stomach. That sound—the point-blank explosion of the rifle would panic most horses. Already the first rush of the rifle's whiplash crack reached his ears. The stallion froze, forelegs planting in the dirt and head rearing up. Powerful hindquarters dropped and the saddle fell like a landslide beneath Faust. He frantically braced himself for the sliding stop, scrabbling atop the leather as his crotch lost contact with the saddle. One foot slid from the stirrup. But his legs' death grip held. His arms braced against the stallion's rigid neck and stopped his body before he slammed face-first into the animal's massive skull.

Without taking the time to straighten himself, Faust opened the reins to the left and clapped his legs to the stallion's sides. Momentum still carried the stallion toward the British soldiers, braced hooves driving into the plowed ground. But he took the escape Faust offered. His feet scrabbled, dug in, and hurled them about, parallel to the wall.

Soldiers scrambled up the hill. None of them mattered. The stallion could outstrip any man on foot. Only—and yes, here it came, a motorcycle. The rider, anonymous in leather helmet and bulging goggles, bounced the machine across the rutted rows and angled toward the stallion's racing path. Faust rose in his remaining stirrup and gripped with his other calf, balancing on the stallion's neck like a jockey, and urged him to even greater effort. The stallion, ears flat against the base of his skull, surged forward again. If they could make it to the next drystone wall, he still had a chance.

More soldiers were firing now, Lee Enfields crackling. But most of them were to the stallion's flank and the racket only chased him into greater speed, his body lowering as he raced flat-out for the wall. The motorcyclist revved to follow, slanting alongside as if to cut them off. But the cycle could only go so fast over the plowed rows without its rider losing control. Faust held to his course. The stallion answered the challenge and side by side horse and machine thundered toward the wall. Only fifty feet to go. His mind was clear as he calculated the odds; he still had a chance.

But with thirty feet to go, another British Army soldier rose from behind the wall dead ahead, brandishing a Lee Enfield and yelling like a demon. The stallion hesitated and Faust's heart lurched into his throat. Frantically he tried to sit down. But the stallion's hindquarters had already dropped and the big head suddenly filled the space before him. Faust's body slammed into the top of the stallion's neck, knocking the wind from his lungs and the thoughts from his mind. He launched from the saddle into self-propelled flight. He grabbed for something—anything—to hang onto. But his nerveless hands closed on empty air. The stallion's massive skull smacked into his pelvis in passing. His body whirled in space. Then he crash-landed into the dirt.

For a sickening moment the world kept spinning. Faust squeezed his eyes shut. He tasted dirt and blood and disaster, heard hoofbeats and the roaring engine diminishing away, smelled oil and warm wet earth. His left arm was beneath him. He tried to push himself up. But a heavy weight smashed atop his back, flattened and held him down, and then his right kidney exploded, exploded again and again. No air could fit in his lungs and instead he thrashed, helpless and blind beneath the ballast atop him. Other voices yelled, an excited pandemonium as heavy as the weight on his back.

Then the beating stopped and the weight lifted. The voices dropped to a babble.

"I said that's enough, corporal." The furious tenor sounded directly overhead. "Must I put you on report?"

Another voice, rough but not rebellious, murmured an answer Faust couldn't hear through his own gasping. His head swam and excruciating pain blasted through his every cell. By now he'd be surrounded by a circle of triumphant British Army soldiers. Not a sight he wanted to see, but he pushed himself up anyway. His arm shook beneath him. But he'd manage better with his face out of the dirt, and he forced himself to a sitting position despite the agony drilling down into his right flank.

The tenor spoke again. "Get him up."

Strong arms hauled him to his feet. Faust let them, even leaned on them, before he straightened. He knocked the dirt from his face and opened his streaming eyes.

It was as bad as he'd figured. The troops that had been scattered at exercises across the field now crowded around him. If any were nervous, they hid it well.

"Search him, sergeant." The tenor belonged to a first lieutenant, only a few years older than Bruckmann but as tough and seasoned as the soldiers. He stood with hands on hips, short red-brown hair spiked about his weathered face. His expression was satisfied but his eyes were narrowed, anger smoldering.

Faust cradled his right arm in his left. As the agony in his flank faded to a pounding ache, other pains asserted themselves—bruised soreness across his shoulders, cramping in his tired legs, a new and aroused stabbing in his left hip. But as usual the sharp tearing pain across the back of his right arm demanded the most attention. Maybe he'd ripped the stitches again. Dr. Harris would not be pleased.

From behind, rough hands patted him down, frisked the small of his back and his sides beneath his arms, ran down his legs, slipped his disheveled and no-longer-quite-white sling from his pocket. "Just this, Lieutenant Briggs."

"Naseby, Ginling, Stanley-Smith, you're with me." The lieutenant took the sling and examined it, then slid it into his own pocket. "Bring him and see he doesn't stray. Sergeant, resume exercises." He glanced about at the circle of gloating faces. "Everyone should be quite awake by now." He brushed by Faust and stalked away.

Two of the grinning soldiers guided him in the lieutenant's wake. A third followed behind.

The command tent sat in a hollow on the far side of the copse, several larger tents clustered behind it. One was a cook tent; Faust smelled ham and coffee, and his long-empty stomach rumbled.

The stallion stood outside the opened tent flap, his steaming sides wet with sweat, his beautiful eyes white-rimmed. A soldier held the reins and stared as they approached. Faust paused, but the soldiers kept him moving, ducking him beneath the flap in the lieutenant's wake and into the tent's darkened interior.

Several British Army officers clustered about another field transmitter-receiver at the back. A radioman wearing headphones, his eyes unfocused, scribbled onto a clipboard. The lieutenant advanced three steps, stopped beside the map table, and saluted. A major in the group's center turned and acknowledged.

"Lieutenant Briggs, what in the name of—" For the first time, the major glanced aside at Faust. His eyes doubled in size. "Good heavens."

It was almost funny. But Faust didn't feel like laughing.

"Yes, sir," Briggs said. "That's about the size of it."

The major needed only a second to recover. He turned to his staff, all staring at Faust as if he had three arms. "Are there any German speakers in the battalion?"

No sense being shy. "I speak English," Faust said. His lower lip, originally split by Jennifer's right cross, hurt anew when he spoke. He paused, touched the back of his hand to the pain, and brought it away bloody. "I'm an escaped prisoner of war."

"Your name?"

"Faust."

One eyebrow canted in palpable disbelief. "Faust?"

Faust's temper flared. He'd been doing so well until this strutting popinjay and his assorted minions had gotten in the way. Maybe he could make a break for the stallion standing so handily outside. "That's right. Something wrong with it?"

One of the officers still clustered about the radio took the clipboard from the radioman, glanced over the message they'd received, then offered it to the major, who read it without a word. The disbelief transformed into something cold and disdainful.

"From where did you escape?"

So the message referred to his misplaced self. That sounded like the efficient hand of Major Kettering. Faust gritted his teeth; that man would be the death of him yet. "A place called Margeaux Hall, northeast of Oxford. The nearby village is Patchley Abbey, I think."

The major handed the clipboard back. "Ring them up and see what they want done. Lieutenant Briggs, issue these men live ammunition and take charge of the prisoner." His cold gaze swept over Faust, not missing the way he cradled his right arm. "Hold him outside somewhere."

One of the soldiers pulled back the tent flap. Faust glanced outside, his hope balanced like an elephant on a precipice. But the stallion was gone. It really was over, and the bitter anger brought bile to his throat. He turned to Briggs. "May I have my sling back?"

Briggs stared at him, bleakly, then returned the crumpled dirty scrap of fabric that was his only remaining possession. Faust stepped out of the tent, slipping the sling over his neck and settling his right arm in it as he walked. At least his war couldn't possibly get any worse.

72

early afternoon
Port Meadow, Oxford

The bitterness of recapture dissolved into numbness, like a toothache under anesthesia. But the fury rankled, and the beating and contempt left bruises deeper than the physical. While in Stoner's care, Faust had never felt so vulnerable, not even when Tanyon crowded him with a rifle. At Margeaux Hall there had always been an underlying element of courtesy and respect; this cold disdain made Faust aware of his captivity in a new and personal way.

The constant aroma of everyone else's lunch didn't help.

Lieutenant Briggs' three soldiers wired his hands together before shoving him into the back of a small lorry. He settled into a corner. The bouncing of the shot springs, if the contraption boasted any, kept him awake even after his all-night ride and aggravated his aches further.

When the lorry stopped and the canvas was tossed aside, bright sunlight washed across his face. Faust squinted against the glare. Kettering peered back. They stared at each other, Faust blinking and Kettering strengthening a silence that deepened by the second.

The major finally spoke. "Corporal, is this how you wish to be treated when it's your turn?"

The corporal's expression remained blank. "Sir?"

"Untie him immediately."

So Kettering, despite his *sang-froid* and level voice, was furious. But being forced to rely on someone else's pity only doubled the humiliation.

Faust waited until his captors drove away. "Thank you." Putting real gratitude into his voice was beyond him, but at least he could be civil.

"Think nothing of it." But Kettering's mind seemed elsewhere and his expression remained unforgiving. "This way."

The horses Faust remembered grazing in Port Meadow were gone. The soft mists and magical dreamy mornings he'd experienced, hiking along the Isis and canal, had dissolved like sugar candy into the grim realities of war. A second city, this one constructed of tents, had been erected between the canal and river, and stretched in long lines all the way to Jericho. It was the most massive encampment Faust had ever seen, and as he squelched at Kettering's side through the close-cropped turf, he couldn't stop his head from swiveling like a tourist's. But he attracted as much attention as he gave, and many stares followed the group through the tents to the canal's edge.

Kettering escorted him to a temporary washroom, erected proud of its neighbors, with gleaming ceramics and plumbing.

"Thought you might appreciate a wash-up." Kettering's stiff voice matched his stance. "Should you feel restless, please remember there are sentries at the windows and door." He turned away.

Enough of the sub-zero treatment. Kettering had proven himself a decent human being, and during their previous meeting he'd been witty and chatty. There had to be a reason for the change. Faust twisted the tap, wet his hands, and reached for the soap. "Is something wrong?"

As he scrubbed the grime from his fingernails, he glanced into the mirror, although his grubby image was discouraging at best. Kettering stared at the reflection, chin down and expression uncertain.

"I've spoken with Chief Inspector Hackney," Kettering finally said. "He assures me you aren't the murderer, based upon scientific evidence."

He stole another glance and met Kettering's challenge in the mirror.

"And you want to hear it from me?" He rinsed his hands and face, twisted off the tap, and turned. "Then let me be frank. As I've told everyone since this fiasco began, I didn't kill anyone."

Kettering held their stare. Faust waited, his wet hands dripping. For his self-respect, this was important. He wasn't a criminal and he wanted this decent man to believe him.

"I admit I'm uncertain what to think." Kettering crossed

his arms. His eyes narrowed but did not release Faust from their stare. "I mean, every time you escape, and only when you escape, a woman dies."

His weight sank into his heels, leaving his head unexpectedly light. His stomach tensed, tightened, squirmed. Every time, the man said; *every time.*

"Are you saying another girl has been killed?"

Kettering's eyebrows climbed his forehead. His silence said more than any words.

Faust whirled and retched raw bile into the wash basin.

73

early afternoon
Oxford and Margeaux Hall

The misty morning solidified to palest Alice blue and August heat pounded Port Meadow. Before leaving the encampment, Kettering's soldiers stripped the canvas from the Bedford's back, leaving it open to the sun and rushing air. So in passing Faust had a reminiscent stare at the ancient grey mass of Oxford Castle, the clock and cross of the Carfax Tower, and best of all, a clear view along the High all the way to University's beloved battlemented tower and the inviting dark arch of the entry. That was where it had started, all those years ago; that was where he'd fallen in love with England and where he hadn't learned to shut up about it. Then the truck completed the turn onto Saint Aldates, passing the massive elegance of Tom Tower, and Faust closed his eyes, letting his body sway with the acceleration.

During his year at Oxford, all he'd wanted was a deeper understanding of the poetry he loved, not a shifting of some magnetic pole buried within him. He hadn't asked to be changed so fundamentally; since he had been, he was sorry he'd been such a bore about it that Erhard threw him out of the plane. Faust had to find a way out of this mess.

Before Stoner buried him.

He leaned back against the Bedford's cab. The slanting sun warmed his head, knees, and hands, and dusty air swirled about the truck to caress his cheeks. Even in the sling, his arm throbbed. He ignored it, ignored the yearning hunger for a cigarette, too. He'd had one with Kettering after lunch, he didn't have any more, and he had to get used to it, no matter what his nerves said on the subject. He needed a plan and it had to be good. Faust let the Oxford outskirts roll past unnoticed and concentrated.

Tanyon, Norris, and Peckham took possession of him outside Margeaux Hall's glass vestibule and Kettering's professional soldiers drove away. Tanyon's blackened face, one swollen and one glittering eye, and distinct grumpiness cheered Faust more than the glimpse of his old school and warmed him like the west-leaning sun. But he wasn't tempted by any witticism at the sergeant's expense. He contented himself with meeting Tanyon's stare head on, then turned and led the way into the vestibule where Glover sat at the switchboard, as resentful and unhappy as the rest.

Tanyon and his soldiers were right. The situation had gone too far and he needed to end it. Faust's shoulders relaxed. He'd decided to walk through that door and tell Stoner to file whatever charges he chose. His cooperation was finished. Faust held the trump card. He always had; he just hadn't recognized it for what it was.

Stoner could send his final report to his cold-hearted boss, who would doubtless do, not what was honorable and right, but what was politically expedient—he'd charge Faust with espionage and hold him up as a propaganda tool to bolster the courage of the frightened civilians being bombed across Britain. And he, Faust, would face those outrageous charges with all the dignity he could muster. Meanwhile, no matter what *Oberst* von Maacht personally thought of Faust, as soon as word of his predicament reached Germany, the Nazis would raise a brou-haha. They'd deny the allegations, scream for justice and, most importantly, threaten captured English officers with retribution. Therefore, no matter what verdict capped the trial, Faust's life would be safe. He'd have time to plan a serious escape attempt and make it work, returning to Germany and resuming the staff officer's duties he enjoyed. And he might even get to see the Tower of London from the inside as a bonus.

It was a beautiful plan and he was proud of it. He should have realized sooner that British officers held captive in Germany were hostages to his fate and the English could harm him only at their risk. Faust entered the ballroom with his head held high.

The sitting area was deserted, but Jennifer, Bruckmann, and the Wainwrights sat at their desks. Three of them worked harder than ever. But Jennifer sat hunched over, her chair turned sideways and her wonderful auburn hair falling like a camouflage screen about her face. A partially-typed sheet of paper, rolled into the platen of her typewriter, sat neglected.

Her defeated posture tugged at Faust. He wanted to tell her not to worry, that everything would be all right. Hell, he wanted to push her hair back, tuck her head against his shoulder, and comfort her with his warmth and touch. But before he could speak, Bruckmann pushed between them, forcing his presence upon Faust's attention. It destroyed the moment. The lieutenant wore a savage little smile, his eyes bloodshot and his rage palpable. He knocked on Stoner's door, waited for a word from within, and entered, pulling the door closed and leaving Faust and Tanyon in the ballroom corridor.

Faust leaned against the paneled oak wall, supporting his ripped arm in its sling. Without looking, he could feel the steam emanating from Tanyon. At least something had gone right.

But even with his ear next to the wall, he couldn't discern words from the murmured voices within Stoner's office. Tired of trying, he glanced up and ran straight into Jennifer's unblinking stare. She had uncurled herself and sat up. Although her eyelids were red-rimmed, her wan cheeks were dry. Her generous mouth, folded and pinched as if she held some powerful emotion in check, matched an ugly awareness in her expression and made her seem uncomfortably older. Faust quit breathing; she was so beautiful, he didn't need oxygen. Not even nicotine.

For a crazy moment he wondered if she'd attack him again; for another, if he wanted her to. That experience, with her body so close to his he'd smelled her scent, seemed to have left him with a different sensation than the one she'd intended. But there was neither energy nor aggression in her mien. She seemed empty, like an expensive and elegant Lalique vase sitting on a dusty shelf in a back cupboard. Even though he returned her stare without shame, she neither blinked nor turned away, and his blood warmed at the implied intimacy.

Perhaps, after their respective governments came to their senses and the war ended, perhaps he could find her again. Perhaps then—

He cleared his throat. "Miss Stoner." Speaking first constituted defeat. But surrendering to such a doughty fighter held no dishonor.

Beside him and out of reach, Tanyon watched through slitted eyes, one a fabulous shade of purple. Although his hand rested on the holstered Webley, he didn't interrupt.

She straightened her shoulders. But her stare wavered

not. "Major Faust."

It sounded much nicer than the last name she'd called him. Faust realized he was breathing again. "I'm sorry about your sister and the other girls. But please believe me. I didn't kill them."

She nodded. "I know."

Well, well; something or someone had changed her mind about him, possibly a dowdy overweight chief inspector. Good to know her forceful mind could yield to the logic of Hackney's evidence. Most importantly, she didn't hate him; her glorious hazel eyes were gentle. At the thought, his pulse picked up speed. She was more beautiful than Anne Boleyn, than Campaspe, than Sidney's Stella. *My lips are sweet, inspired with Stella's kiss—*

—but he shouldn't have thought of that. "I'm sorry, just the same."

Sudden energy propelled her to the edge of the chair. He blinked; it happened so fast, it was like waking from a poetic dream.

"I know you have your duty." She spoke in a hurried rush, as if afraid of interruption or losing her nerve. "But can't you hold off escaping for a few days, just until Chief Inspector Hackney catches that animal?" She seemed to misinterpret his hesitation. "He only seems to kill when you've escaped, you know."

Faust glanced at Tanyon. The sergeant listened all too closely, watchful and hooded through his purple bruises. If Faust said the wrong thing to comfort her, it could be taken as collaboration and still get him in trouble with the Nazis. So far he'd dodged that particular accusation and he'd best keep it that way.

"It's going to be okay." But her eyes widened, as if she didn't believe him. "I promise. Everything will be okay."

Before she could respond, the door opened and Bruckmann emerged. "Come on, then."

"Excuse me, please." It was all he had time for, and even those few polite words thinned Bruckmann's already tense lips. Well, to hell with him and his white-haired sensitivities. Faust pushed off the wall and walked to Stoner's office.

He walked fast, head up, feeling a swagger in his step. In a way, he was sorry to bring Stoner's little game to a close. Now that he had a plan and a clear perspective, that game would be played on a more level footing and he'd score a few more points. But in another way, it was a relief. The mounting animosity would end; after the war, when he returned to locate Jennifer, he could find a way to make peace with her grandfather, as well. He could form a rational, mutually respectful relationship with the cleverest and most perceptive man he'd ever met, a man capable of advising him in his developing career as a staff officer. Stranger things had happened.

Faust rounded the corner, took two steps into the sitting room, and slammed to a halt as if he'd smacked into an invisible brick wall.

And Clarke stared back.

74

early afternoon
Margeaux Hall

It was over. It was all over.

And Stoner had won.

Faust's pulse throbbed like a drum in his inner ears. Surely Stoner, ever the proper gentleman, stood behind his desk, surely Bruckmann and Tanyon were behind him somewhere and the sitting room opened before him, its usual airy expanse. But he only saw Clarke, rising from Faust's preferred wingback chair before the desk and turning to face him, calm and courteous as if his presence didn't mean the end of Faust's beautiful plan, of all his hopes, and possibly his life.

Finally the entire, sordid position was clear. Stoner didn't need to submit a report to his lousy boss, no charges would be filed, and the English wouldn't threaten Faust again. They didn't need to. All they had to do was put him in a prisoner of war camp filled with hardened Nazis and tell them of his collaboration, that he'd saved this British officer's life at the expense of several German ones. The Nazis would do the rest. English hands would be clean and British Army officers in Germany would be safe.

If he didn't cooperate with Stoner.

Clarke's round face was anxious, tight as if drawn back by the ears, and his dark eyes were watchful. He barely resembled the arrogant young snob from their University days, and didn't carry much more resemblance to the grimy and determined officer from the Aa Canal. His crisp tailored khaki lent him a professional elegance despite the tense squaring of his shoulders, an irritating reminder of the differences in status and money that had separated them from their first meeting. Since his birth, Clarke's education, career, and position in the world had never been in doubt. Unlike his own, which remained in doubt to this day.

Heat built in Faust's face. He'd never let himself respond to the snobbish arrogance he'd faced during his year at Oxford. At the time, he'd been too awed by the culture such behavior represented, and still under the forgiving spell of Brother Harmonious' teachings. Now, years too late, angry resentment swelled within him. But he contained it and concentrated on one final hope.

Prisoner and serving officer: their situations were reversed and their circle complete. And therefore he still had a last, desperate chance—if Clarke was willing to return his favor.

Faust had no idea how long he stood there, staring at Clarke with wild ideas dithering through his mind. In the room's breathless silence, Clarke's expression grew tighter and his nostrils flared. Clearly he knew the score in the game and this time, it wasn't cricket. Faust stared back across the sitting room, fighting anger and resentment. He had to prepare for combat and could afford no distractions. Surely Clarke expected such a move on Faust's part. Surely Stoner did, too. And Faust had no idea how to play this one.

He forced himself to walk, step after step, into the sitting room. A glance at Stoner showed him standing, of course, behind his desk, unexpectedly wearing a crisp khaki uniform, too, rather than his usual dove grey suit. Complacency underscored the old man's courteous mien, a glittering satisfied intensity not quite camouflaged by his social graces, the opposite of the British Army soldiers Faust had run into earlier. If Faust had ignored those social graces and refused to speak with Stoner from their first meeting, sticking with the name-rank-serial number routine advised during the intelligence lectures he'd mostly slept through, he'd have given Stoner no ammunition to fire against him and perhaps the game wouldn't have advanced to this late stage. Had he inadvertently said something that led Stoner to Clarke?

"I suppose I shouldn't be surprised." His voice sounded rough and he cleared his throat.

Stoner's eyebrows arched. "Perhaps not."

One last unwilling step, and Faust stood before the desk. Without thinking, he'd aimed at his usual wingback chair, on the left side, and Clarke made room for him. Bruckmann circled behind the desk and settled into the secretarial station, and Faust didn't need to look to know Tanyon also took up his customary position.

Jennifer had tried to warn him, with her widened glorious eyes and self-protective posture, that he faced imminent defeat. Or perhaps her concern, like her dinner, had been for Stoner. But one thing was damned certain: she was out of his reach forever because he'd not likely survive the war, and both thoughts were painful wrenches.

What stupid thing had he done that led him to this cliff? He'd been doing so well in his life until he ran into Clarke at the Aa Canal. No, that was unfair. He hadn't done that for Clarke; he'd planned the rescue operation and would have carried it out just the same even if Clarke and Brownell hadn't been there. Those seeds had been sown within him longer ago.

"Clarke, I see you made it." That didn't sound much better. He cleared his throat again. But the lump there refused to budge.

Beneath his polished exterior, Clarke's lowered chin and heightened color signaled his agitation. But he didn't look away. "Thanks to you, yes. We did."

He didn't want to hear this. He wanted to remain angry. But he found he needed to be certain. "Brownell, too? The others?"

Clarke nodded. "All but four."

It corresponded to what he'd learned during the First Panzer Division's investigation. But it was strangely satisfying to hear it from Clarke, as well.

"I'd hoped for the opportunity someday to thank you in person and now I find my gratitude is more than I can express." Although that sort of meaningless platitude was commonly heard, Clarke's words carried heartfelt intent, and Faust thawed at the edges. "It was a damned decent thing to do, much more than we deserved or had any right to expect."

The merest breath emphasized that last phrase. If it contained a hidden message, it wasn't the one Faust wanted to hear. But before he could speak, Clarke continued.

"Did you know I have a wife—"

Oh, hell.

"—and a son?"

Faust's last hope died and the lump in his throat expanded, as if fighting for release. Clarke needed no other excuse. He would not, could not help Faust; he should not endanger his family. His responsibilities as husband and father outweighed any other. A note of panic joined Faust's emotional chorus.

Clarke swallowed. Clearly he understood the ramifications. Knowing that didn't help, either.

"Gentlemen." Stoner gestured to the two wingback chairs, courteous as ever and seemingly unconcerned by the life-and-death power he wielded.

As usual, as if it didn't matter.

Faust's pulse drummed in his ears. He wanted to scream, sling everything off that irritatingly tidy desk, curl up in a ball in the corner, and swear until he turned purple as Tanyon's eye—but they expected him to sit and exchange small talk. All that remained to him was his dignity and those now-useless bloody social graces.

He sat. It felt like his final defeat. "Anyone I know?"

Clarke eased into his chair. His gaze never left Faust's face, as if imprinting the details of this meeting into his memory. "Do you remember the Somerville sisters?"

Though that long-ago friendship hadn't meant much even then, it hurt like another blow. "Cezanne and Cecily. Their father was in the Lords. They used to play tennis with you and Brownell on Saturdays."

For a brief moment, suspicion flared in Clarke's eyes. It was almost funny. "You do remember them."

He wanted to ignore the implied question and let the sod wonder. But such behavior would hurt more than Clarke. Resentment was bad enough; deliberate ugliness wasn't acceptable, even now. "When you and Brownell played singles, sometimes Cezanne would sit and talk with me. Clarke, did you marry both of them? You still haven't told me your wife's name." Although part of him already knew the answer.

A flash of irritation in Clarke's eyes said the omission had been deliberate. If Clarke thought him any sort of competition, that was funnier. "Brownell married Cecily."

"And you got Cezanne." It seemed, not right, but logical. She'd always been kind to him but never more, saving her vivacity and fun for the Englishmen on campus, and Faust had always known she would marry well. But it still stung; damn it, he was as good as any of them. "Congratulations, Clarke. I always thought her a beautiful woman."

An image of Jennifer, ferocious and tender, invaded Faust's thoughts in her usual abrupt manner. He'd lied to himself; there was only one woman he'd ever want to marry, and it hadn't been Cezanne Clarke, née Somerville.

"Thank you." Clarke's voice and face were stiff, which made that the funniest thing he'd said so far. But then he produced a pack of DuMaurier cigarettes from his inner pocket, shook one halfway out, and offered it, and all of Faust's turbulent emotions solidified into a desperate yearning for nicotine. "Do you use these things?"

Some intonation or emphasis lay behind Clarke's facetious words. Faust paused. But he couldn't think through the longing. He took the cigarette, accepted a light, and inhaled hard. "Thank you."

Clarke lit a companionable cigarette with him. Behind the desk, Stoner produced his silver case and did the same.

For the first time, Faust noticed a manila file folder on the desk corner closest to his chair. It wasn't part of Stoner's usual ensemble and seemed jarringly out of place, like a filthy word in a Spenserian sonnet. But before Faust could consider it, Clarke spoke again.

"That's what you said to me at the Aa Canal, you know."

"About the cigarette?" He didn't want to talk about that, either, and hid behind another hard drag. "I don't remember it well."

"I remember it all." Clarke glanced down. Faust followed the gaze to Clarke's left hand, flexed up from the blue padding of the chair arm. The cork-tipped cigarette was gripped so tightly between Clarke's manicured index and middle fingers, the edges were crimping. The textured wool of his khaki uniform sleeve didn't bunch at his elbow and was too finely tailored to ride up his wrist as he lifted the cigarette to his mouth. "I remember every word you said, how you said it, and how you appeared when you did." He paused, a trickle of smoke drifting from his parted lips. "You seemed so collected."

"It was a lie." The DuMaurier tasted wonderful, smooth and elegant as the two Englishmen. But the nicotine didn't seem to be soothing him, no matter the flavor.

Clarke shook his head. "It might have been affected, but it wasn't a lie. You were prepared." He tapped ash. "There at the end, I tried to ask you a question but I didn't phrase it particularly well. Do you remember?"

Surely nothing said so long ago could matter now. Faust shook his head.

"I asked, why are you doing this."

And in a flood, he did remember: dust in the shadows, the shallow valley pouring from their hiding place, the intermixed scents of warm leaves and hot oil, the ugly insult of not being remembered. "That was a crazy question, Clarke. I never hated you—"

Clarke shook his head. "As I said, my meaning wasn't clear. See, I wasn't trying to ask why are you doing this, as in why are you saving my life. I tried to ask why are you doing this, as in why are you doing this rather than something else."

The unanticipated meaning fell between them with the force of an artillery shell. Faust froze, hovering on the edge of an unpoetical, philosophical cliff. It felt like a trap. But no guile showed on Clarke's face, merely honest curiosity. Faust dragged again, glancing at Stoner. The old man remained complaisant, as if they still discussed long-ago Oxford days, but the undisguisable fire behind his eyes belied his intense interest in the subject. This, then, would be at the heart of his attack when it came, and Clarke had merely been encouraged to re-ask his question. Although he knew the score, it wasn't his game.

"Why didn't you go to Greis' commanding officer and report him?" Clarke paused, a gentle crease between his eyebrows. "I don't know what the term would be in German, but every army has a police force and legal officers, a provost marshal, with the authority to bring criminals to trial. Why didn't you report Greis and have charges brought? Surely an accusation of murder would force his removal from the field and prevent him from doing it again?"

A chill climbed Faust's spine, forced higher with each logical word and leaving a trail of uneasy guilt behind, as if he rather than Greis had done something despicable. His own cigarette balanced gingerly between fingers with calluses and cracked nails. Splotchy stains of ground-in soil stiffened the grey wool of his uniform sleeve. In comparison to the Englishmen's tailored and groomed elegance, he had to look a fright. Faust breathed harder. He hadn't expected such insights from Clarke, but the man's mind had never been stodgy.

"I'm a lawyer, you know." Clarke sounded apologetic. "That sort of thing occurs to me. I couldn't understand why you would do something so dangerous when there were other options."

He shouldn't answer at all. In essence, Clarke's candid request differed from Stoner's shrewd game only in its end goal. But while Stoner sought military intelligence, Clarke—although at Stoner's instigation—merely wanted a reckoning for his troubled conscience. Likely it wouldn't matter in the long run. And Faust had to admit an inner voice urged him to justify his actions, an imperative pressure building beside his other emotions.

"Faust?" A definite note of surprise colored Clarke's voice. "You did have other options, didn't you?"

"I did go to his commanding officer." Faust took another drag and glanced at Stoner. The old man sat with negligent ease, but his cigarette burned untouched and the fire behind his eyes smoldered with hesitant glee. Not a sight calculated to cheer him. "He told me I wasn't a true staff officer, not yet, and I should mind my own business until that happy day arrived."

Clarke's jaw clenched, anger tinged with disbelief.

"So I went up the chain of command to the next level. But he refused to take action, too, although he made some noise and whirled about his office in a tizzy." He paused to tap ash. He wanted to stop there; if he went any further in his explanation he'd be giving Stoner more ammunition; but if he did stop there, the blame would not be placed where it should. And again, in the long run this was merely military trivia and unimportant. "I told you Greis and his soldiers were *Waffen SS*, not German Army. No one in the command staff was certain where they stood, whether Army orders outside of combat or maneuvers carried any authority. I needed to report this at Army Group headquarters to find someone with the command weight to stop Greis, and at that time I hadn't yet been posted there and had no time for the trip and ensuing explanations." He shrugged. He'd felt as helpless and trapped then as he was now. "So I did what I had to."

"*Waffen SS*." From the way Clarke said it, from the steady concentration in his expression, he didn't know what it meant. His stare focused even harder on Faust as if to drag a definition from him. "Yes, I remember you using that term. We knew they were something different, some new sort of unit, but no more. Can you explain further?"

"They're not just a different type of unit. Greis' brigade is honestly not part of the German Army, and so," Faust stubbed out his cigarette with angry jerks, "some of our officers were hesitant to enforce their authority."

Clarke paused in his turn. Understanding spread across his face, sharpening his gaze. "Are you saying this *Waffen SS* is a separate and distinct organization? A separate army?" His cigarette had gone out, burned unnoticed to the cork tip; he didn't glance down as he placed it in the ashtray.

Behind the desk, Stoner was motionless as a stalking cat. He'd camouflaged his glee, but his intensity remained.

"Something like that, yes." And let the old geezer make what he liked of it. "The *Waffen SS* doesn't have a command staff and of course can't operate independently, so Greis' brigade was embedded within the front line under the Army command. There are other such *Waffen SS* units out there, although I don't think they're quite as isolated from their own as Greis'."

Clarke shook his head. "Why does Germany need two armies?"

Faust froze. He'd never considered the question before. Something uncomfortable wriggled in his stomach, telling him—no, reminding him, he didn't want to consider it and never had.

But Clarke returned his stare, awaiting an answer. Faust's feet shifted as heat grew in his face. Clarke's head might look like a cabbage with a well-groomed mustache, but a fine mind resided therein. Beyond the French window, new buds touched the rose bushes with splotches of pink and yellow, replacing the blowsy flowers ripped apart by the night's storm. The ancient gardener worked in the closest formal bed, not far from the glass, plying pruning shears to the dead flowers' remains with plodding care. If Faust hadn't fought his way into the technical university, he could have wound up doing just such a job. The heat in his face intensified. He shrugged.

Clarke paused. "Do the Nazis not believe the German Army can do the job they've set it? Or that they won't do it?"

His squirming stomach twisted harder; this was almost as bad as arguing with Stoner, and that still lay ahead of him. He shrugged again.

"Or is it a matter of trust?"

Something snapped. To hell with this. The heat in his face began to fade. He didn't have to take anything from anybody for the Nazis. "Clarke, I don't know." The wriggling in his gut said all three of those suggestions were possibilities. But he still didn't want to consider it.

Judging from Clarke's furrowed forehead, that wasn't an answer he wanted to accept. But after another long mutual stare, he settled back. "So the *Waffen SS* have different standards of behavior and seemingly some political clout, if they're exempt from homicide charges. Are you saying we can expect more murders of this sort? Or something even worse?"

"I don't know." It was probably the only intelligent thing he'd said all day. A lightheaded coldness moved in behind the last of the mortified heat and the sitting room faded around him. Damn it, as usual he'd said too much. He should have left the sods wondering; he didn't owe them anything, either, not even an explanation.

Clarke still stared at him, a gentle crease between his eyebrows although his new understanding remained and strengthened. "I didn't shoot him, you know."

Greis, he meant. A chill invaded the room from nowhere and Faust shivered. If Greis survived, he could be the source of *Oberst* von Maacht's suspicions. He'd thought he could depend on Clarke's rage to handle that problem. At least he had enough sense not to blurt that out before Stoner. "We didn't find his body, so I wasn't sure what to think."

"I brought him back with us."

Faust jerked back, startled. "You—"

"I'm an attorney," Clarke said again, his voice soft. "After the war, Greis will stand trial for murder. There may be some arguments over jurisdiction and problems finding witnesses, but they'll be worked out. And then I'll have the pleasure of witnessing his legal execution."

After the war. Of course Clarke and the British Army staff were aware of the retaliation issue. Faust should have thought of it long ago.

"Would you be willing to testify against him?" Clarke asked.

Faust froze. Another invitation to collaborate and get himself killed, as if Stoner needed any more ammunition. Bloody hell, all he'd done was sit there and react as Clarke hit him with one unexpected line after another, as if he were a verbal boxer flailing against the ropes. It was frustrating.

"After the war, I mean. Will you think about it?"

He rubbed his eyes. "Yes. I will think about it."

Clarke again produced the DuMaurier pack and the matches, and set them on the table beside the ashtray. "I envied you that day, you know."

He couldn't have heard that right. But still Clarke's face showed no guile. "I'm not fishing for a compliment, or at least I don't think I am, but why?"

Color rose into Clarke's face. He didn't look aside. "Ever since school, I've concentrated on establishing my career. I've neglected the things that truly matter—my honor, behavior, ethics. My wife and son."

He picked up his hat and rose, setting off a social chain reaction. Faust stood beside him and wondered what on earth to say. But Clarke continued before he could think of anything appropriate.

"Perhaps I should have read more poetry, or paid more attention to what little I did read." He glanced down at the cigarettes on the table and then turned away, leaving his to-be-burned offerings behind. "I wish I had your courage. But I doubt I ever will." Clarke nodded to Stoner and left.

Faust watched him walk away, an elegant and self-tortured martyr to his privileged youth. In a way, the image was a satisfying one; no one had expected that outcome during their Oxford days. At least his own resentment had faded, leaving an internal emptiness touched with a desperate yearning that made no sense.

Then the office door closed and Clarke was gone. Leaving him alone with Stoner.

75

afternoon
Margeaux Hall

Faust didn't want to turn, didn't want to face Stoner and measure the depth of his intensity. It would only be a camouflage for his satisfaction and it was going to be bloody awful. But such behavior was cowardly—ironic, considering Clarke's parting shot. He prepared for the worst and turned.

But Stoner's lined ascetic face was impassive and grave, devoid of either glee or pity, and his eyes were almost gentle. He waited patiently, standing behind his desk with his fingertips resting atop his spotless blotter. His old-fashioned service dress uniform, well tailored although not to Clarke's pricey standard, sported a gleaming Sam Browne belt and service ribbons providing a brave splash of color on his left breast. His only insignia were his Intelligence Corps badge, on his collar, and his majors' crowns, one on each shoulder tab. Faust found himself staring at those crowns; something was wrong there and he should have realized it sooner.

"Major Stoner." His voice still sounded rough. He cleared his throat again. "I know we have—well, probably a ferocious fight ahead of us. But may I ask a question first?"

Stoner's gravity didn't shift. "Of course."

Faust chose his words with care; if his guess was right, this could be a sensitive subject. "A few days ago, you told me how you were injured and captured in 1915."

"Yes."

"You said you were a major then."

Only a slight stiffening of his shoulders and thinning of his lips escaped Stoner's iron control. But they sufficiently illustrated lingering anger. "Yes."

Twenty-five years without a single promotion: no army treated so capable an officer in such a manner without a reason. A small hollow space formed inside Faust. "Do you believe it was being taken prisoner that interrupted your career?"

For a moment longer Stoner held his gaze, his expression taut and forbidding. Then the old man glanced aside. The tension within the sitting room, built to a pitch during Clarke's visit, shattered at his sigh. Without speaking, he gestured to the wingback chair, waiting until Faust resumed his seat before sitting himself. His eyes remained grave, but his shoulders and face relaxed.

"Remember, *Herr Major,* the military was never intended as my career." Stoner entwined his fingers and leaned his elbows on the desktop, like a professor lecturing a pupil. Again Faust warmed to the old man. "However, to answer what I believe to be your true question, when I returned from captivity in late 1917, I was not reassigned to my unit but transferred sideways to a service position of equal responsibility."

For a field officer, that was a good working definition of one of Dante's outer circles. The tiny vacuum within Faust expanded. "You mean an administrative position."

"Training." The correction was gentle. "I learned it was official governmental policy that, if an officer had once been captured and successfully escaped, he would not be returned to front-line duty as a protection against possible recapture."

There it was, the retaliation issue again. Faust scowled at the fireplace, but paused when his gaze crossed that manila folder on the corner of the desk. It seemed out of place, set casually and temptingly near. It had to be part of the old warrior's counterattack-to-be and damned if he'd oblige.

Perhaps Stoner misinterpreted his silence, for he leaned forward onto the blotter. "I do not pretend to know whether such a policy exists within the German Army. My experience cannot necessarily be compared with your own."

Faust glanced up, surprised. Stoner's earnest expression didn't contradict his gentle eyes. It was one of those honest statements that transcended their desktop battlefield, and as such could only be meant to reassure him.

"Thank you. That's kind." Clarke's cigarettes were at his elbow and Faust nearly reached for them. No, he'd suffered through life *sans* nicotine and he refused to blow through this second pack of relief so quickly. Instead he drew a deep breath and prepared for combat without the crutch. "Well, where do we go from here?"

Stoner's earnestness seeped away. For a moment he seemed sad. But then an implacability entered his expression, that of a warrior taking aim at his chosen target. He leaned back in his chair, examining Faust as if to divine his thoughts through his skull, and his chin tilted.

Faust braced himself.

"I thought we might discuss Plato."

Straight from outer space, that one was. "Plato?"

Stoner's smile this time did not reach his eyes, shrewd and no longer gentle. "All schoolboys learn Plato, do they not?"

"For this schoolboy it's been a few years." He had no idea where this tack could be going. A chill climbed his spine; bad enough knowing in advance he was going to lose, but it was worse not being able to figure out how he'd be trapped.

"Then perhaps only Part Two of the *Apology*." Stoner waited, eyebrows up.

"The sentencing of Socrates." That sounded ominous. Faust stared back, considering. He shouldn't respond; it would only set him up for more grief; but damned if he wasn't interested despite himself. "The prosecution called for the death penalty. Socrates could have bargained for exile or life in prison, promising to keep his mouth shut—" just as he should be doing himself "—but he refused because he believed the unexamined life—"

It hit him just before he said it. His tongue staggered to a halt.

"Socrates believed," Stoner said, his voice quiet and measured, "the unexamined life is not worth living. Viewed from another perspective, it could be said an individual so misguided as not to become intimately aware of his own motivations, relationships, and circumstances has little value, to his native community or to any other."

Fury flashed like an explosion. Faust erupted from the wingback chair, leaned over the desk, froze. Stoner didn't flinch, his gaze as level and penetrating as before. Without looking, Faust knew Tanyon had drawn his Webley. But he didn't care.

Because it didn't matter. Stoner was an old man. Physical aggression remained unthinkable. Even now.

Faust brushed past the file folder on the corner of the desk—whatever it contained, whatever role it played in the old man's attack, he would not touch it—and stalked to the cold fireplace with its navy blue mantelpiece. The carriage clock ticked away, the little hand advancing in abrupt jerks. "You bastard."

"Indeed." Stoner's voice sounded more tired than outraged. "Perhaps, as philosophy has served us so ill, we should turn our attention to literature, specifically your eponymous mythical counterpart."

Another breath, and Faust trusted his temper enough to glance over his shoulder. The motion sent a stab of pain from his biceps to his fingertips. "Major Stoner, if you're going to tell me to belly up and do a deal with this devil, you can save your breath to cool your porridge. I will not betray my homeland."

Stoner hadn't moved. He leaned back in his chair, hands in his lap, chin tilted. His eyes were hooded; the old warrior's battle was well and truly joined.

"You misunderstand me." His voice dropped in pitch and volume. "I intended to point out that you have already done a deal, as you phrased it, with the Nazi devil. This is your opportunity to repent of such black magic and return to the ranks of civilization, as Goethe's Faust did in the second part of his tragedy."

Yeah, but Goethe's Faust wasn't his favorite. "No matter how you phrase it, this is treason and I will not do it." He returned to the wingback chair, past the stupid, irritating folder that just begged him to reach out and pick it up—could Stoner even see it, with the broad-based lamp in the way? The manila was the same shade as the oak desk and its camouflage was flawless. Whatever lay inside it had to be central to Stoner's argument or it wouldn't be there to tempt him.

Faust sat down again. "Plain speaking, then. You English can't risk putting me on trial and executing me for espionage; the Nazis would retaliate against British officers taken captive in France. All I have to worry about is what treatment I'll receive from the other Germans in the prisoner of war camp." He drew a breath and awaited Stoner's return fire.

Stoner's eyebrows hiked halfway up his forehead. He steepled his fingers just beneath his chin. Although his lips widened across his face, it couldn't be called a smile. "Your logic is flawless."

Unexpected but gratifying. "Thank you."

And then the chin tilted. Faust tensed.

"As far as it goes."

He managed not to swear aloud.

Stoner tapped one index finger with the other. "Firstly, the Nazis can only retaliate against actions of which they are aware. The trial before a secret military tribunal of an enemy officer not reported as captured would be unlikely to attract their notice."

The bottom dropped from Faust's stomach. Bile dirtied

the back of his throat and the sitting room faded, leaving him dangling in mid-air. Stoner's cold blue eyes targeted him like a rifleman taking aim across a battlefield.

Inexorably, Stoner's gnarled finger drifted down and tapped his opposite middle finger. "Secondly, even if you are not put on trial or executed, there is no law stating you must be placed within a prisoner of war camp. Your status as an honorable officer has not been ascertained, the circumstances of your capture remain dubious, and my government would be justified in confining you incommunicado within the Tower of London for the duration of the war."

"You didn't report my capture?" His voice shook.

Stoner dropped his hands to his lap. "The International Red Cross provides belligerent nations with postcards for captured enemy officers to send home, notifying their families or commanding officers of their situation. Have you mailed such a postcard, *Herr Major?*"

He was at the mercy of the English government. "This is outrageous."

"In the case of suspected espionage agents, those postcards are generally conspicuous by their absence. As I'm certain you have noticed."

Faust steadied himself. He shouldn't ask, he seriously shouldn't ask. But he needed to understand all the elements of Stoner's trap and besides, the old geezer seemed willing to talk plainly. "Don't take this to mean I'll make a deal, because I won't. But what exactly is it you want to learn from me?"

Stoner still didn't move. But behind their partially lowered lids, his eyes gleamed. "My government desires the details of the invasion, most specifically the scheduled date."

It was too near the truth to be a lucky guess. Faust swallowed and mentally kicked himself when Stoner's glance darted to his throat. "What makes you think I know such classified information? And if I did, what makes you think they'd let me out after dark?"

Stoner scoffed. "On Monday you described your week of misery as a clerk typist, during which *Generalfeldmarschall* von Rundstedt and his senior staff worked eighteen to twenty hours per day. Would you now have me believe they were not drafting the invasion plan?" He tilted his chin. "How many times did you type the plan, *Herr Major?* How well do you know it?" He paused. "What were the questions and concerns you attempted to discuss with *Oberst* von Maacht, the issues he spurned as inconsequential?"

The sitting room wavered around him. He'd been hoisted again, trapped by his own words and naiveté, and the cage of logic the old man had constructed about him fit far too tightly for comfort. There was nothing left for him to do but surrender to the inevitable checkmate. But every defeated nerve within him rebelled at the thought.

He couldn't wrap his brain around it. The outcome he'd considered least likely, those farcical espionage charges, appeared to be the one Stoner was determined to pursue. Faust wanted to fight back, say something, do something besides throw up all over the frigging manila folder. But the trap offered no cracks and he had no leverage. No one escaped from the Tower of London, not even kings or poets. Across the desktop battlefield, Stoner's hooded eyes could not conceal their discreet gleam.

"Major Stoner." Yikes, his voice sounded like he felt. He cleared his throat. "The other night, you told me the not-knowing was worse than any possible knowing."

Stoner froze. His gleam vanished.

Faust hauled in all the air he could hold. "Well, there's something I need to know. Are you English shooting captured spies these days, or hanging them?"

Ten years passed across Stoner's face within seconds. His fire and color drained, leaving him wan and grey, tingeing his lips with blue rouge. The lines deepened beside his eyes and lips, and his jaw slackened, creating wattles on his neck where none had been before. So he didn't like that response; he'd hoped to take a complete victory to his lousy boss. Good; let him feel what it was like to be trapped without an escape. If the old warrior hadn't experienced that sort of defeat since his own capture, it was time for a refresher course.

After a moment Stoner rolled his lips together. *"Herr Major—"*

"Please."

A long and empty moment crept past. Finally Stoner lifted his chin. It seemed to require an effort. "I believe military officers are being given the honor."

A firing squad, then. He'd faced gunfire before. That wouldn't be nearly as bad as standing still while a noose dropped over his head, tucked behind his ear, the manila rope tightening and scratching his neck, a crowd of witnesses standing by—

He shook himself. "Thank you."

"Is that your final answer, then?"

Manila.

He couldn't stand it.

"Oh, *all right.*" Faust grabbed the folder from the desk's corner and waved it in the air. "You knew I couldn't resist, didn't you? Didn't you?"

Stoner actually gaped. "I beg your pardon?"

"You knew, sooner or later, I'd have to look." He propped the thick file in his lap and opened it, revealing a sizeable stack of photos and papers. "You knew—*oh, my God.*"

The top photo was a crisp black-and-white of a dead teenaged girl. She sprawled naked on her back atop a narrow bed, her legs splayed and her eyes staring at nothing from the battered remains of her face. Where her chest should have been was a pockmarked battlefield of savage holes, a glint of white bone visible through the dark gore.

"Herr Major?"

Beneath that one was another of a slightly older girl, also dead. She huddled in a muddy pasture at the base of a dry-stone wall, rainwater puddling in the pounded ravages of her chest. The next, darker photo had been snapped under low-light conditions, and the shadows of trees loomed in the background. But the horrific details were otherwise the same, and the sharp focus revealed the marbling in her face, showing she'd been so for some time.

The turbulence within Faust solidified into cold rage, impossible to control.

"Do you call this civilized?" He scrambled to his feet and slammed the open folder atop the spotless desk. "How dare you speak of German atrocities, outrages, murders. How dare you accuse us?"

Somehow Stoner was on his feet as well, taut and still, his gaze fastened on the top photo. Faust knew at a glance the old man had never seen it before; this wasn't another trap. Stoner touched the photo with a gentle hand, took it by the corner, lifted it. He didn't seem able to look away.

"I did not say all atrocities were committed by Germans. As obviously they are not." His voice remained calm and unhurried.

Tanyon and his Webley be damned. Faust leaned into Stoner's face and jabbed a finger at the photo, stabbing at the image of the slaughtered girl's brutalized chest. "Are you saying Greis is any worse than the butcher who did this? That English crimes are different for some reason, or if Germany is stopped things like this won't matter?"

"Don't be a fool." Stoner's voice sounded tired and sad, belying his words. His eyes grieved. Faust's breath caught in his throat. The old man had known that girl, the one sprawled across her bed, and perhaps he'd mourned with her family. "The nationality of a killer makes little difference to the victim, none at any practical level. The difference lies in the societal response to the crimes." He flipped to the second photo. His breathing rasped, became louder; she had been the housemaid at Margeaux Hall and he'd certainly known her. "Our victims will be given justice." He glanced up. His face, white with rage, held underlying notes of contempt. "Can the same be said for your victims?"

"Mine?" It was a specific and personal insult. Faust lurched back, his fists clenching. "I don't—"

"*You are an accomplice.*" Stoner shouted him down, leaned forward as if chasing him back across the desktop. His hands splayed on either side of the photos, his elbows braced. "The Nazis could not commit their crimes without the German Army's complicity. Sneaking around to foil one atrocity is tantamount to ducking responsibility for the situation as a whole. *You are as guilty as they are.*"

It cut like a whip. Faust opened his mouth. But no words formed. Stoner leaned atop the desk, arms vibrating beneath his weight, glaring. As Faust's shock and shame deepened, the old man's enraged satisfaction mounted, and this time he didn't bother to camouflage it.

Faust closed his mouth. He'd sensed a strange sort of guilt when speaking with Clarke, as if he'd been caught in the act, not Greis. Now it made sense.

Stoner turned away with contempt. His fingers moved to the corner of the photo and lifted it.

Cold whispery zephyrs hissed across Faust's skin, his soul, his thoughts. He wanted to shout a warning. And then he didn't.

The next photo showed Stoner's granddaughter, Harriet.

And the old bastard deserved to know precisely what had been done to her.

No matter what it did to him.

The understanding flared and the decision coalesced within a heartbeat. Faust waited, anticipated, watched, as Stoner flipped over the photo to view the one below. He heard the old man's breathing stop and felt a flash of savage satisfaction.

Let him die.

He watched Stoner examine the third awful photograph, watched as the light dimmed and went out within his eyes. They faded to dullest glass as his lips morphed to a startlingly vivid blue. His breathing did not resume. He stood swaying, a parodied mannequin of his previous shrewd and vibrant self. Then he collapsed into his chair. It clattered and rolled a few inches back.

The noise woke Faust, as if from a nightmare. He couldn't

speak. He could only stare.

This was his doing and his fault. If the old warrior died, then he'd be a murderer. He'd be as guilty as Greis, and Stoner's point would be proven.

Bruckmann's pencil paused. But ever the efficient secretary, he didn't glance up.

Faust found his voice. "Is he breathing?"

"No." Tanyon's single word, harsh and too loud, echoed in the quiet room.

Bruckmann jerked erect and turned.

Faust and Tanyon moved at the same moment. They rounded the desk, one on each side. Faust untangled his right arm from the sling. He couldn't think. He didn't want to think. He just had to do what was right.

They reached Stoner together. As a team, without the need for words, they hoisted him from the chair. Photos and papers rustled, spilled, cascaded to the floor.

Bruckmann stumbled to his feet but stood frozen, gaping. They pushed past him and settled Stoner's motionless form on the floor in the pool of brilliant light from the French window. He felt, looked, handled like a corpse.

"Get the medics," Tanyon said, his voice still harsh. He glanced at Faust. "I never learned it."

Faust nodded. The pulling pain in his right arm mounted. It didn't matter. Stoner had to live and nothing else mattered.

"Hold his head where I place it." He yanked open Stoner's uniform tie, unbuttoned his shirt and coat, adjusted his head and cleared his air passage. Tanyon slid across the hardwood floor and gripped Stoner's head with his knees.

He didn't allow himself to stop and consider what he was doing. Stoner had to live. Faust crouched over the motionless figure, opened its mouth, pinched its nostrils shut, and kissed his enemy, blowing two full breaths into the unresponsive body.

"His chest is moving," Tanyon said. "It's working."

Faust sat up. His head spun. He clasped his right hand atop his left, planted them together on Stoner's chest, and pushed.

His arm ripped. Pain blasted from his biceps to his fingers and all the way to his spine. He ignored it and pushed again. In the background, Bruckmann's voice hammered without intelligible words, panicky and urgent. Faust ignored it, gasped for air, pushed again, and then again.

"Help me count."

"That's four," Tanyon said.

One more push. Faust grabbed Stoner's nose, kissed him again, blew hard twice more. The sitting room wobbled about him. Wet warmth trickled down his arm. None of it mattered. He straightened, found the motionless chest, clasped and planted his hands, and pushed again.

Tanyon counted aloud. "One. Two. Three." Too slow, Faust knew it was too slow, but his body didn't answer his urgent demand for more speed. "Four. Five."

He lifted his hands from the khaki shirt. A red smeary palm print remained behind, evidence of his guilt for Hackney to find. He wobbled above Stoner's face. Something banged behind him and footsteps pounded across the room. Stoner's eyes remained glassy, unresponsive. Faust kissed him again, breathed twice more, pushed himself erect.

Cavanaugh crashed to his knees beside them, clasped his hands, leaned over Stoner, pushed and counted aloud. "One, two—" his voice rose to a shout "—*three*—"

Faust gasped in all the air that would fit in his lungs, planted his lips atop Stoner's, waited.

"—four, *five*." Another shout.

As soon as Cavanaugh paused, Faust breathed twice into Stoner's mouth. He sat back and Cavanaugh pounced again. "One—"

"Don't die." Faust gasped for oxygen, couldn't find it.

"—two—"

"Please don't die."

"—*three*—"

Faust started to lower his face to Stoner's. But the blue eyes moved, fastened onto him, focused. He looked confused. Then he looked affronted.

"Wait," Faust said. "He's alive."

Another hand, a slender and agile one, slipped beneath Faust's arm, fastened onto Stoner's throat. "I've got a pulse," Dr. Harris said. He pushed closer, elbowed Faust aside.

He wasn't dead. Nothing else mattered. Faust crawled away, huddled beside Bruckmann's secretarial station, collapsed with his back against the wall. Through the cordon of Cavanaugh's and Dr. Harris' bodies, he couldn't see Stoner. But a querulous, professorial voice raised and was soothed away. It was enough.

"Where's the stretcher?" Cavanaugh yelled.

Peckham and Sloane brought it, set it beside Stoner, backed away. The cordon of bodies moved, shifted, heaved. Then they lifted the stretcher, this time carrying obvious weight. Dr. Harris glanced at Faust, a clinical and diagnostic glance. Then they carried the stretcher from the sitting room.

Faust wanted to go with them. But his gaze stopped when it crossed a pair of legs, the most beautiful legs in the world, rising into a tweed skirt that could not camouflage the most beautiful woman in the world. Jennifer watched the stretcher pass. But she didn't follow. She watched until the men maneuvered it through the doorway, then turned and looked at him.

The last of the oxygen sucked from the room. Her face was grave, somber, even sad. She knew what he'd done to her beloved grandfather. She had to know. She had to hate him again, she'd never want to see him again, and nothing else mattered.

Jennifer crouched beside him. Her hand touched his, tucked something into his unresponsive fingers. He managed to close them on cloth, linen, soft. He couldn't look away from her face. But he could feel her gift. A handkerchief. She'd given him her handkerchief, and for the first time Faust realized her face was dry and his streamed with tears.

Then Jennifer rose, turned, and ran after the stretcher.

Faust found air. His chest expanded, it seemed for the first time in hours, and his head cleared. The room swirled. He dabbed his eyes, wiped his face, blew his nose.

He'd gone too far. He'd lost his perspective. They all had.

Bruckmann stood near the doorway, staring about like a landed and frightened fish. But Tanyon waited beside the desk, watching Faust. The manila folder, its papers and guilty photos, were scattered on the floor.

Something had to change.

Faust slid his arm back into the sling and pushed to his knees. He scrabbled across the floor, scooped the papers and photos back into the file, set it on the desktop, grabbed the desk's edge, and pulled himself to his feet.

Tanyon watched him, waiting without a word. Faust cradled the folder in his left hand and carried it openly past Bruckmann as he left the sitting room, grabbing Clarke's cigarettes and matches in passing.

In the ballroom he paused. Jennifer of course had gone, that forgotten paper still rolled into the platen of her typewriter. The Wainwrights huddled together at one desk, their hands clasped. They twisted and stared at him. Wainwright stepped in front of his wife, shielding her, his eyes smoldering.

Faust turned left and walked to the eastern stairwell. Those boots clumped behind him.

They took the stairs slowly, one gentle step at a time. It was the best he could manage. By the time they reached the guardroom, Faust's head had cleared and he knew he'd been a fool. No matter how charming or kindly he could be, Stoner was the enemy and he should have let the old warrior die. But he'd rather be a fool than go back and withdraw his rescue, or return to Jennifer the now-grungy handkerchief in his front patch pocket. Something had to change. But not that.

In the guardroom, Faust paused beside the work table and glared at Tanyon; the first change started here. But the sergeant didn't respond, merely waited without speaking. It seemed he agreed. Faust walked into the cell fully clothed, the folder still cradled in his hand. Tanyon closed the gate behind him.

Pym turned from the transmitter-receiver. "Sergeant, Sloane said—"

"Mr. Stoner had a heart attack and collapsed." Tanyon locked the gate and shoved the keys into his pocket. "And I don't know what's going to happen so don't ask. Now ring down to Mrs. Alcock and ask her to make Major Faust here a cup of tea. He performed first aid on Mr. Stoner and kept him alive until the medics arrived." He rapped his knuckles on the work table in passing as he walked from the guardroom.

Pym's jaw dropped. His grey eyes cut sideways toward the cell.

Faust dragged the table into the slant of sunlight spilling through the guardroom window, the legs scraping across the wooden floor. He sat down, opened the folder, flipped the horrific photos over, and began to read as Pym lifted the receiver.

76

late afternoon
Margeaux Hall

When the clock over the radio table had ticked past five, Tanyon returned. "Dr. Harris wants to see you."

Faust glanced up. The guardroom had stayed deserted and quiet. He'd read through Hackney's notes twice, studied the photos and reports, and turned back to the first page again. Only at Tanyon's entrance did he realize how late it was and how badly his arm throbbed. "Yeah, I bet. Thanks." He closed the folder and rose.

"No problem." Tanyon unlocked the gate.

He grimaced. "You don't make a *good* nice person, so don't take it too far."

Tanyon paused with the gate halfway open. "We could go back to playing by the old rules, you know."

"In your fondest fantasies." He ducked out before Tanyon could change his mind, but paused. Pym watched them, brows lowered over his steady grey-eyed stare, as if pondering the changes underway. "Corporal Pym, I'm not trying to give you orders or anything. But no one needs to be looking at this folder." Stoner had seen his granddaughter. Carmichael didn't need to see his fiancée.

Pym glanced at Tanyon, then nodded. "No one will bother it. Including me."

"Thank you." He led the way to the infirmary, those boots clumping behind him. He'd become so used to captivity, the sound was almost reassuring.

Dr. Harris stood at the sink, washing his hands. The back windows were open, a hot breeze whispering through, and the infirmary's inner door stood ajar by an inch. The doctor's clinical eye fastened on Faust as they entered. "Well, you look a tad better. But not much." His voice was pitched low. He flipped off the faucet with his elbow and grabbed a towel. "How do you feel?"

"Like mincemeat." No sense trying to fool a man who knew better.

"I don't doubt it." Dr. Harris poured a glass of water, took a bottle of pills from a cabinet, shook one into his hand, then gave both pill and water to Faust. "We'll start here."

"Thank you." It wasn't an aspirin; in the moment the pill stayed on his tongue before he slugged it down, it tasted far worse. "Damn, that's foul."

"With painkillers, effectiveness is directly related to flavor." Dr. Harris took the glass and set it aside. "Let's have a look at you."

Together they removed his crusted and stained tunic, shirt, and undervest. Then Faust hitched onto the examining table, the breeze drifting across his bare skin, and Dr. Harris began teasing off the blackened bandage. The painkiller had advanced so well, he barely noticed the gauze tugging from the wound, a welcome relief from his previous painful care.

Dr. Harris raised his voice and called over his shoulder. "Miss Stoner?"

The inner door opened. Jennifer slipped through, closed the door behind her, crossed to the sink, and washed her hands, like a professional nurse preparing to assist. This changed everything. A tingle unrelated to the breeze shivered across him, and Faust couldn't stop his questioning glance at Dr. Harris.

"I need for Cavanaugh to watch Mr. Stoner," Dr. Harris said in a discreet murmur. "As a nurse, he's educated and observant, and an unnoticed change in the patient could be fatal at this point. However, I need someone here, as well."

Of course. So he got to sit there, half naked, bloody, and bowed, while the woman he longed to impress took a good look at his ravaged self. The heat in his face had nothing to do with the blistering August sunshine, and he stared at the polished floor while Dr. Harris snipped at the old stitches. She'd turn around any moment now.

It was as bad as he'd feared, her gasp audible across the room. Before he could stop himself, he glanced up. Her widened hazel eyes stared at his chest. The worst of the swelling had gone, but massive bruising, black and purple, covered the right side of his body, criss-crossed with little red stitched-up scabs and smears of crusted blood. Great. Just what he wanted her to see. His life could get no worse if he'd set out to destroy himself deliberately. As Nash said, *Swords may not fight with fate.*

He didn't glance back up. "I try not to look at it."

Her deep breath seemed loud in the quiet room. "Major Faust, I hope you're all right."

She spoke in a murmur, too. If both she and the doctor were whispering, then Stoner had to be resting in the adjoining room. The heat in his face intensified. At least he hadn't spoken much.

"Thank you. I'm fine." What else could he say?

"Actually," Dr. Harris said, "that's what I'd like to discuss." Gentle pressure tugged the old stitches from the back of his arm. "You're not all right, you know."

Even better. "Has something else gone wrong that I don't know about?"

Another tug. "Each time you rip these stitches open, you rip the edges of the wound." A final tug, and Dr. Harris reached past Faust's shoulder, handing an instrument that looked like large blunt tweezers to Jennifer. She set it on the towel atop the instrument table, followed his pointing finger, and handed him a set of small, fierce-looking scissors. "Thank you. And somehow, you always manage to force dirt through the bandage into the wound. Miss Stoner, would you draw me a bit of water?"

She murmured something indistinguishable and glided to the sink.

Damn doctor. "It's not like I'm doing it deliberately."

"Right." The scissors snipped, snipped again, and tugged at his injury. "That's not important, you know. What's important is that sooner or later, the edges of the wound will become too ragged for me to stitch them properly, and then it will become infected." Another snip, then Dr. Harris reached past his shoulder, taking the basin Jennifer handed him. "When that happens, there won't be much I can do for you."

"You mean you'd have to put me in the hospital?" It sounded like an escape attempt in the planning.

"I mean I'll likely have to cut off your arm."

His stomach contracted as if punched. He glared at Dr. Harris over his shoulder. "You're trying to scare me, right?"

Not a trace of humor softened Dr. Harris' concentration lines and he returned Faust's stare with a chilling sobriety. "I'm perfectly serious. And I hate amputations almost as much as autopsies. So if you push it to that point, we'll both be miserable." He shoved Faust's shoulder back around and resumed work.

If he could go back in time, he'd murder Erhard before the plane ever took off and cheerfully accept the consequences. Faust rubbed his eyes, acutely aware of the doctor behind him cleaning the injury and the wonderful woman at his side as she pretended to be busy arranging the instruments. He'd considered her personality forceful, abrupt, ferocious. Nice to know she could be discreet, as well.

His stomach wasn't calming. The thought of permanent mutilation panicked him more than an English firing squad. He could deal with anything else, but not this. Stoner had shown him this fear during their first, seemingly ages-ago interrogation. At the time he'd thought it a distant curiosity and not something he'd have to face within the week. Now he stood face to face with it. And he couldn't let it matter, either.

Hackney's notes made clear what was at stake. Or rather, who.

As the needle slid, barely noticed, into the back of his arm, he snuck a glance at Jennifer. She'd straightened the instruments in orderly rows atop the towel, folded her hands on the table's lip—and stared again at his chest, this time from the corner of her eye. A rosy flush tinged her round cheeks and golden sparks glinted among the brown in the eye he could see. Her breasts rose and fell in quick breaths. Just wonderful. She'd formed a horrified fascination for those bruises and couldn't look away. For the rest of her life, she'd remember him like this.

Dr. Harris tightened the stitches with another tug but no pain. Hopefully the painkiller would last this well through the night. But he couldn't let any of these considerations stop him, either. No matter what she thought of him, no matter what happened, he had to catch the killer tonight.

For her.

77

early evening
Woodrow

That wasn't a boy.

Jennifer leaned against the banister in the dim and silent farmhouse, clutching the laundry basket. She could think of nothing except that man and hadn't since leaving the infirmary. His broad, hard chest, solid muscles that rippled when he moved, tight waist and oh she had to get a grip and not on the ironed shirts. Not on him, either. Right now it might hurt. No matter what else she imagined, she hadn't imagined those awful bruises.

She forced her feet to climb the stairs. One step at a time, up the stairs and beyond this hormone-induced obsession. She'd put the shirts away. Wardrobes. In the bedrooms. *The bedrooms.* No, she would not think of that man in a bedroom. But her mind would not stay blank. The geometric planes of his chest refused to be conjured away, as if he truly were a magician and had cast a spell on her. Heat surged into her face and lovely tingling electrical jolts shivered across her skin. She'd experienced them before but this time was different and much, much worse. She wouldn't allow herself to call it better.

She'd start with Stoner's room. Surely it would bring her to her senses; surely she'd think of him, lying grey and wan in the infirmary while Dr. Harris rang every undamaged hospital in the area trying to find a vacant bed. But the first breath she took across that threshold, redolent with Stoner's clean, subtle, masculine scent, barely touched with a salty sweat tang, blasted another electrical shock through her and she shivered. She'd longed to meet a man who was Stoner's match and this one even smelled the same. The bitter irony of finding that match in an enemy officer could not slow her galloping pulse.

Dr. Harris had warned them for months of Stoner's danger. If it had happened at any other time, Stoner would be dead because Bruckmann, Tanyon, the Wainwrights, and their soldiers all admitted they hadn't known the proper first aid. Neither did she. But the heart attack had happened while that man was in the room. And he'd saved Stoner's life. She'd seen it, heard him begging Stoner not to die. She'd treasure the memory, even if she never saw him again.

With more than usual care, she arranged Stoner's shirts, grey and pale blue and uniform khaki, in his wardrobe. He'd tried to break that man although he hadn't expected to succeed. And thankfully he hadn't. Instead, as she'd warned him, he'd broken himself.

She hurried from Stoner's room to her own and stacked her folded shirts on the shelf, refusing to glance at her bed. There was a law against what she wanted. The government had passed it recently, forbidding Englishwomen giving aid and comfort to enemy soldiers, and whatever else that man was he remained an enemy officer. She could not explore his body, trace the outlines of those rippling muscles, skim the hard tiny circles of his nipples—oh, she had to get this under control. He'd sat on the examining table, his right arm against his side, his left braced out beside him, beside her, as if he'd wanted to wrap it around her and pull her close, and it had taken all her self-control not to step into that inviting circle.

Surely he'd known her thoughts. But he hadn't looked at her, no more than a swift unhappy glance, and then he'd stared at the floor and ignored her utterly. Perhaps he didn't hate her. But he certainly didn't think of her in this same manner, not after Stoner had tried so hard to break him. Not after she'd helped.

And not after she'd slugged him and split his lip.

That magnificent man had stopped and looked at her through the blackout curtains. And then he'd moved on.

She flushed again, grabbed the laundry basket, and burst into Harriet's room. Already its cheerful yellow coziness had an empty feel to it, a bare layer of dust across the dresser and a hollow sound when she opened the wardrobe. Everything was just so awful. If only Harriet were here, to commiserate, gossip, cheer her with her giddiness and laughter—

—there was something on the wardrobe shelf. Jennifer

set the ironed shirts aside, reached into the darkness beneath the swaying line of dresses, and rummaged until her fingers closed on stiff cloth. She pulled out a man's handkerchief, plain and cheap, crumpled into a ball and stiffened with dark, rusty stains. Within a second, she knew what they were and those exciting electrical jolts shuddered into horror.

And there on the rack, right in front of her, hung Harriet's missing dress, the same shade as the eye of a daisy.

78

early evening
Margeaux Hall

Loud voices, quickly hushed, in the corridor outside the guardroom. Faust straightened over Hackney's notes. That had been Bruckmann, but it hadn't been Tanyon who'd hushed him and not many other people in Stoner's command carried such authority. It had to be her. Faust tucked the awful photos to the bottom of the stack, pulled those of the living girls to the top, and closed the folder, rising to his feet.

He expected her to erupt into the guardroom in her usual tempestuous manner. But she paused in the doorway and peered in, as if uncertain of her welcome. Her auburn hair curved about her ear, brushing her jaw line just as he wished to, and her determined chin lowered. "Major Faust."

She was so beautiful. But unlike the cold phantoms of beauty inhabiting the sonnets, she was real, and realistic. "Miss Stoner. I meant to ask earlier, how is your grandfather?"

"Dr. Harris says he's doing better than expected. Thank you for asking." She eased into the guardroom, two soundless steps that echoed within him. Her glorious eyes never looked away from his face. "Sergeant Tanyon tells me you're reading something from Chief Inspector Hackney."

The barest hint of rose invaded her round cheeks. Granted, he was staring. But as usual, he couldn't look away. He'd been blind. Finally he had the right poetic reference. Not Anne Boleyn, not Campaspe, not even Sidney's Stella, but John Skelton's merry Margaret. "I am."

She drew a deep breath. Her breasts rose. Although his body throbbed, threatening to embarrass him, he couldn't look away. *This midsummer flower, Gentle as falcon Or hawk of the tower.* He should have realized it the first time he'd seen her ferocious and tender face.

"Does he say where he'll be this afternoon?"

Faust blinked, and her unbelievable beauty transformed into pleasant and pleasing plainness, her expression vaguely uncertain and hopeful. The guardroom intruded about them, Bruckmann and Tanyon watching poised in the doorway, evening sunlight pouring through the window. Carmichael, silent and white, had relieved Pym an hour ago and sat behind the transceiver as if it could support him in his misery.

"No, he doesn't." Faust caught a breath, too. "I'm sorry, is he missing? Has something—something else happened?"

She hesitated another moment. The poetic rose faded from her cheeks with the vanishing of her spell. Then she drew another deep breath, lifted her chin, and stepped into the guardroom, invading it with her practical presence and not stopping until she stood beside the work table. Bruckmann and Tanyon trailed behind her, the lieutenant uncertain, the sergeant tense. Carmichael swiveled his chair about and watched.

"I've found my sister Harriet's missing dress." Her chin tilted, just as Stoner's did when he threw out one of his unfieldable zingers.

Automatically Faust braced. But although her statement was a zinger, it wasn't like one of Stoner's. Instead of probing for a weakness or pushing him into a corner, she threw out a problem and invited him to help her solve it. She'd considered what Hackney might have given him to read—notes, information, a plan. And then, perceptive as Stoner, she'd figured out what Hackney might have intended—catching the killer.

And here she was, offering her help while asking for his. Rather than inviting him to collaborate, she met him halfway. His pulse picked up speed. He'd intended to track down the killer regardless. But her way was better.

"I see. I gather it was someplace unexpected?"

The last of the roses vanished from her cheeks. "It's hanging in her wardrobe." She dipped a hand into the pocket of her tweed skirt and pulled out a balled-up handkerchief, encrusted with dried blood and nameless other fluids. "This was on the shelf beneath it."

Faust's stomach twisted. Grace's dress had been hanging in her closet with the used and discarded handkerchief on the floor nearby. "Has anyone checked Sally's closet?" She, too, had been found nude.

Tanyon's usual poker face cracked. He turned to Carmichael. "What was she wearing?"

"Her blue dress." Carmichael didn't hesitate, a bitter rage blossoming beneath his white-faced misery. "Her sailor dress."

"The one with the square white collar?" she asked, her voice gentle.

He nodded, two hard bobs of his head. His ragged and uneven hair swayed with the motion. But his eyes, older and tougher than they'd been the day before, permitted no humor.

"I'll know it." She ran from the room, soundless as usual.

Faust's stomach twisted harder. Before he could speak, Tanyon turned to Bruckmann. "She shouldn't go alone."

Without a word, Bruckmann ran after her, footsteps pounding and diminishing down the corridor.

The sergeant glanced at Carmichael, then at Faust. The grim set to his jaw remained, but his eyes were uncertain.

Faust shook his head. "Carmichael's not a suspect."

"I damn well better not be." The last of yesterday's charming and tentative youngster vanished. Carmichael, it seemed, had grown up that morning in Stoner's office.

"Chief Inspector Hackney doesn't work that way," Faust said. "He bases his investigation on the evidence and only eliminates people from his suspect list when he can do it scientifically. In this case, both you and I have the wrong blood type."

The defiance spewed from Carmichael like air from a balloon. He glanced down at his hands in a brief echo of the boy he'd been. "Oh. Sorry, sergeant."

"Sergeant Tanyon, on the other hand, has the right blood type, or the wrong one, depending on how you look at it." He paused, letting Tanyon darken with rising anger. "He also has the same hair color as the killer. But he gave me an alibi on Tuesday and it cuts both ways: I couldn't murder Grace because I couldn't cross the road, and that's because I saw him there. If I didn't have time to kill her, neither did he." Faust paused. He hadn't noticed the tension between the two men until it dissipated. "So the killer isn't in this room."

Hurrying footsteps sounded in the corridor and murmured voices traveled ahead of them.

"Nor is it Lieutenant Bruckmann," Faust said. "He has the wrong blood type and hair color, and he has an alibi for the time of Grace's murder."

Jennifer's low voice was still loud enough to carry. "Did you find your keys?"

Bruckmann answered. "Someone put them on my bedside table."

"Are you certain it wasn't you?" She burst through the doorway, a flush of color in her cheeks as if she'd run all the way from the residential wing.

"I'd used them to unlock the entry only a few minutes before." Bruckmann trailed her, scowling. "I dropped them on the lawn in the rain, and someone found and returned them. But no one's admitting it."

Faust knew nothing of Bruckmann's keys and didn't care to. He watched Jennifer and she smoldered, eyes narrowed. If he'd needed a symbol for her then, he'd look no further than Jack London's dominant primordial beast. His pulse stumbled within him; she was stunning.

"Well?" he asked.

"It's there. The handkerchief, too." She shuddered. "It's still wet and awful. I didn't touch it."

He knew the answer. But he asked the question anyway. "How many people can get inside both Woodrow and Margeaux Hall, find his way about, and put those dresses away in the proper women's wardrobes, all without being seen and noticed?"

"Very damned few." Tanyon turned to Carmichael. "We've got to find Chief Inspector Hackney or Constable Mercer. Call the Abbey Arms again."

When Carmichael cradled the receiver, he shook his head. "Sergeant, you know it's got to be one of our squad. What can we do?"

Hackney had reached the same conclusion, although he'd based it upon the timing of the third murder, which had happened before any of Kettering's troops or the Home Guard even knew their least-favorite German officer had escaped. Faust waited, barely breathing. He needed to take charge of the discussion and guide it in the proper direction. But before he could do that, they had to accept his authority. And there was little he could say to convince them, particularly the sergeant. It would have to be a matter of trust.

Tanyon, Carmichael, and Bruckmann glanced at each other then turned as one. Faust found himself facing four stares, three of them uncertain and skeptical, but the other feminine, steady, and confident. And she mattered most. He suddenly needed air and drew a deep breath.

"Chief Inspector Hackney left this folder—this information, in Stoner's office for me to find. I think he intended for me to sneak it out, hidden under my sling."

He paused. If Jennifer had any inkling of ripping him to shreds, now was the time. But she hitched a seat atop the sturdy work table, spread her tweed skirt about her legs, and waited. She preferred to hear him out rather than blame him for Stoner's collapse. A gentle, hopeful flame flickered to life within Faust. This was a woman worth fighting for.

"I'm convinced Chief Inspector Hackney wants us to draw the killer out and capture him."

"Wait one minute." Tanyon, of course, objected first. "I'm not willing to take any such chance without Mr. Stoner's approval in advance."

Jennifer didn't turn. "He can't be awakened."

That was an unexpected complication and not a welcome one. Faust froze. "Don't tell me. One of Dr. Harris' famous anodyne concoctions?"

She scowled, the expression cute on her wide, heart-shaped face. The flush faded from her cheeks but her anger remained. "He's not going to be available until sometime tomorrow. Do you believe we can wait?"

He spoke the honest truth. His face would show his sincerity. "I don't believe we can. And I can explain why not."

She crossed her legs. "Well, then."

Tanyon and Bruckmann glanced at each other. The lieutenant blew out his cheeks, slumped into a nearby chair, and fingered his white-blond hair back from his face. "All right. We'll listen. For now."

A better reaction than he'd hoped for. "In his notes, Chief Inspector Hackney talks first about the killer's possible motive—why this man is killing, and the related question of why he only kills when I've escaped." Faust pulled the chair from behind his table and sat. "He says originally he thought the killer timed his murders for during my escapes to implicate me. And then he wondered if there was something about me specifically that set the killer off. But when he thought about it, that didn't seem right, especially in regard to the first murder." Damn, that sounded insensitive. Hesitant, he glanced at Jennifer.

She didn't flinch. "You mean Harriet's murder. Please go on."

Ferocious and tender, kind and brave and now tough, as well—Faust shook himself. "Because that doesn't seem right, does it? I mean, at the time of the first murder, I wasn't even here yet. It's true I'd bailed from the plane—" not the right time to explain Erhard's perfidy "—but I was miles away and no one had seen me. I was just some faceless, unknown entity somewhere out there. So whatever it is driving this man to kill, it's not me specifically."

Bruckmann threw out his hands. "Well? What, then?"

"What else happened Saturday night?"

Tanyon crossed his arms over his barrel chest. He still stood, forcing Faust to look up at him. "The air raid."

"The area's first air raid," Faust said. "Or at least, the first since the squad has been here. Am I right?"

Tanyon paused. He and Bruckmann glanced again at each other. But Carmichael nodded. "That's right."

"Well, on the front lines I've called in air strikes, and I've been strafed, and I've fired anti-aircraft guns at attacking planes. But Monday afternoon was my first air raid, and it's different from anything else. It's distant, impersonal, and just as deadly as combat but without the ability to fight back. I felt vulnerable and scared, and I hated it."

For the first time, Bruckmann seemed interested, perhaps despite his better intentions. "Are you saying the air raids are driving this man to kill?"

"The war," Tanyon said.

Faust nodded. "The war itself. During the air raid, the real character of war came home to the killer and it scared him. So he tried to prove it didn't."

"By killing Harriet?" Jennifer straightened and threw back her hair. The flowing red-gold shimmered in the sunlight blazing through the window. "Then why didn't he kill during Monday's air raid?"

"Well." Faust thought a moment. "The inspector didn't address that, but my guess would be the killer couldn't get alone. I mean, he's not likely to kill in front of witnesses." He glanced at Tanyon. "Norris was with us in the hospital air raid shelter, which was packed. How about everyone else?"

Tanyon pursed his lips. "Peckham was in the shelter near the Patchbourne market, and that would be crowded on a summer afternoon."

"All the local farmers would be in town selling their crops, right?"

The sergeant nodded.

Faust turned to Bruckmann. "And the soldiers who were here?"

"Carmichael was on the radio—"

"I was," Carmichael said, "and I didn't leave it."

Bruckmann ran his fingers through his hair, combing it back from his temples. "Sloane was at the front gate, and Glover was on the switchboard." He paused, eyebrows up.

Faust shook his head. "Both Sloane and Glover have the wrong blood types. They're not suspects."

Bruckmann shrugged. "The Alcocks and Wainwrights went down into the cellar with Sally, and the old man walked to Woodrow to be with you." He nodded toward Jennifer, and she nodded back. "I gathered the squad into the ballroom sitting area and had Pym read aloud from the civil defense manual while I kept working. Plan was, if any of the bombers came too close, we could jump into the cellar. But it was never necessary."

"So I'm right."

"It seems so." Bruckmann leaned his head back. "I asked Chief Inspector Hackney this question and didn't get an answer. Now I want one. Who's on the suspect list?"

He'd memorized it. "In alphabetical order—Ellington, Norris, Peckham, Pym, Reynolds, and Whiteside, although Pym's and Ellington's hair might be too light."

Bruckmann and Tanyon both froze, their jaws slack. The six suspects, absent physically, paraded invisibly through the guardroom: Ellington, with his dreamy expression and mental escapes, who might need for some sick fantasy to become real to counter nameless fears; Norris, who wanted to be brave but hadn't managed it, whose teetering self-image could depend upon belying his failure; Peckham, clever and sturdy, able to unload the hospital wall from the lorry's cab and just as able to muscle a woman about to fulfill his needs; Pym, steady and unflappable, perhaps hiding a looming psychological cracking point; Reynolds, content to hover in the background but who might long for more, and more respectful, attention; Whiteside, guarding the front gate in even the worst weather, seemingly taken for granted but somehow maintaining his complacency, as if he had hidden sources of satisfaction.

Bruckmann said one foul phrase and buried the heels of his hands in his bloodshot eyes. "Sorting this out is going to be wonderful."

"But—" Jennifer didn't even glance at the lieutenant. She rubbed her forehead and tried again. "There wasn't an air raid on Tuesday afternoon when Grace was killed."

"Oh, but by then I was here," Faust said, "the big, bad enemy officer, and that changed everything. Now the war was even closer and it had a face." He turned to Tanyon, still standing with his arms crossed. "I bet you told the squad to keep away from me because I'm dangerous. Right?"

Tanyon flushed beneath his bruises. "On Mr. Stoner's orders."

"That's right," Carmichael said. "He said, even with one arm injured, you could still beat us, or worse." He froze, uncertain, as if afraid he'd said too much.

Better not to go there. "The point is, you guys were prepared for the worst and even seemed to expect it. So when I slugged Norris and jumped from the car, suddenly I was no longer under control. The war broke loose, wearing my face, and the killer panicked."

"Which drove him to kill again." Bruckmann nodded sagely, lower lip jutting out. "And the same would hold true for last night."

"So I'm right." Jennifer leaned forward over her clasped hands. "If you just stop escaping until he's caught—"

But Faust shook his head. "Even if by some miracle the war is declared over tonight and I'm sent back to Germany, never to be seen here again, something sooner or later will still frighten him. Remember, he's not afraid of me specifically and his fear doesn't have to be rational. It just has to be something that makes him feel he's lost control, or respect, or something."

She hung her head. The red-gold hair cascaded around her face, hiding her like a camouflage screen. Then she sat back up, her hands pushing her hair behind her ears. "So chances are he's going to kill again."

Tanyon grunted. "Haven't seen any sign he doesn't like it all of a sudden."

"True enough." Bruckmann crossed one ankle over the other knee. "Whatever made Hackney think of such a motive?"

"If I'm reading these notes correctly," Faust said, tapping the folder, "it originally occurred to him when he interviewed Mr. Wainwright on Tuesday night. He said he caught a glimpse then of a man afraid of the war and uncertain how best to confront it. The concept lodged in Hackney's mind, but he says it took him a while to sort it out."

Bruckmann nodded. "Is this all, then? Anything else?"

Faust opened the folder and withdrew the two photos of the living girls. He glanced at Carmichael. "I've never seen Sally, so if this doesn't hold true for her, tell me, okay?" He propped the photos against his sling and held them vertical with his left hand—Grace on the left with her bow poised over her violin, Jennifer and Harriet on the right. "Does anyone notice anything interesting about them?"

His audience stared at the photos. A line creased Bruckmann's forehead first. Then Jennifer grimaced. But it was Tanyon who spoke.

"Their hair."

"That's right," Faust said. "They both had dark hair, worn loosely about their faces." He raised his eyebrows at Carmichael.

The young soldier nodded. "Sally wore her hair a lot like Grace's and it's just as dark."

"That seems an odd coincidence," Jennifer said.

"Chief Inspector Hackney doesn't think it's a coincidence at all," Faust said. "He believes the killer knows exactly what he likes—" he glanced at Jennifer and canted one eyebrow "—as most men do—and he's noticed the girls and women in the neighborhood who fill his bill."

Tanyon's eyes narrowed and cut sideways to Jennifer. "So he's got a prearranged list of victims."

"And even if I don't escape, the next time there's an air raid, or a reported attack, or he doesn't meet Sergeant Tanyon's standards in a training exercise and gets yelled at—" He turned the photos around. It was a wonderful shot of Jennifer, and both Harriet and Grace were pretty, too. "Who knows what will set him off next."

Bruckmann rubbed his eyes again. "So we're supposed to flush this bugger out? Don't suppose he says how?"

"No, he doesn't—"

"—but it's obvious, isn't it?" Jennifer finished for him.

She showed not a trace of fear, only the remains of her smoldering anger and a fighting challenge. His body responded; good thing he was sitting down. Not even Donne's Elegy 19 affected him so strongly. *License my roving hands, and let them go before, behind, between, above, below—*

—but he shouldn't have thought of that. "If we call everyone in the area and warn them to be on the alert, and I do mean everyone—"

Bruckmann jerked erect. He started to speak, shaking his head, as if their joint idea had just occurred to him and he didn't like a word of it.

Her chin lifted and she spoke through his stuttering start. "—and if I'm in Woodrow alone—"

"—and if I'm watching through the window," Faust said, "we can flush the killer out and catch him."

Tanyon finally uncrossed his arms, tossing the cell a cynical glance. He cleared his throat.

"Oh, yeah," Faust said, "there's that part, too. How about if I give my parole and promise not to attempt escape before, say, dawn tomorrow?"

79

late evening
Margeaux Hall

Tanyon escorted him to the lavatory. Most of the squad were off duty, and the frantic strains of Louis Armstrong's *Tiger Rag* drifted up the open stairwells to meet them in the blacked-out corridor. Faust fumbled through the inky shadows, those boots clumping behind him.

"I still think this is a lousy idea." Even without a visible body, the deadpan voice illustrated Tanyon's poker face.

"I wish I had a better one to suggest." His heart pounded in his chest as if it intended to escape and leave the rest of him behind with the English who'd driven him crazy. That part of him, at least, didn't like the plan either.

The sergeant grunted. "Carmichael will stay on the radio, Sloane on the front gate. As soon as the suspects are out hunting for you, I'll put Glover to guarding the residential wing, the Alcocks and Wainwrights and Honoria, and prevent the killer from doubling back."

They'd already discussed this a thousand times, of course. But the sergeant sorted through it again, as if looking for the flaw. Which implied something seemed wrong to him but he wasn't certain what. Faust shook off the thought even though his pulse accelerated. They wouldn't let anything go south.

"Then Lieutenant Bruckmann and I will drive out in the lorry and watch from a distance. As soon as you or Miss Stoner yell, we'll come running."

They paused outside the lavatory. Faust pawed about in the dark, located the knob, pushed the door open, paused. Their location and situation echoed the previous night's events, only without the rain thundering overhead.

Tanyon seemed to notice that, too. His clumsy boots shifted in the dark. "And bugger you if you're double-crossing me."

It was too much to resist.

Faust let go the knob, twisted, and slammed a left across his body into the pale blob of the sergeant's face. It connected, but not solidly. Tanyon grunted, hit the wall, ricocheted, came back. Faust didn't need to see him to know the sergeant was steaming and swinging. He ducked into the lavatory, closed the door, braced it, and laughed as the fist crunched into it rather than him. On the door's far side, the swearing began. Hey, his escape had to look realistic if they were to fool the killer.

But he left the door unbolted; no sense forcing them to repair it again. As he crossed the room, he wriggled from the sling and tucked it into his pocket. Even if he earned Dr. Harris' never-ending ire, he'd need both hands for the job ahead. He just wouldn't spend too much time contemplating possible results. Besides, she was worth it, worth fighting for.

This time, when he jumped from the window, he aimed away from the rose bushes. He didn't need to learn that lesson twice, not even for realism's sake.

80

late evening
Woodrow

Two lines of light peered from the farmhouse's upper windows, one on each side of an outer corner. Faust picked the window on the left. It commanded a sweeping view of the farmyard, its kitchen garden and orchard. The hillside beyond climbed to Margeaux Hall, where discreet flashes of light from the vestibule already showed as the hunt for him, and the killer, got under way.

He climbed the appropriate apple tree and straddled a curving sturdy bough. It sagged beneath his weight, scraping and settling atop the honey-tinted bricks framing the casement window, which opened into a trim, tidy corner bedroom. A single bed stretched along the interior wall with a small nightstand at its head, and a beautiful carved wardrobe and rolltop desk clustered near the two windows. An ornate oil lantern cast a dim glow across the walls from its hook above the opened desk. Tasteful, classical, and evocative of its owner—but the room was empty.

Green apples from the branch above wavered uncomfortably near his head, and soft oblong leaves tickled his ears. It smelled intoxicating, like fresh cider, like his first morning as a captive and the apple-wood fire Stoner had lit for him, just before Jennifer had erupted through the front door and crashed through the last of his resistance.

The more time he spent in her presence, the less certain he became. Okay, she was aggravating, ferocious, tender, brave, tough, and logical, and if he paused long enough to think in depth, he could probably add to the list *ad nauseam*. But while he knew for a fact she was plain and pleasant, no more, sometimes when he saw her, she transformed magically into the most beautiful girl in the world even though she wasn't. He couldn't blame it entirely on lust, although he had to admit a goodly dollop thereof colored his thoughts. Nor was it just some sophomoric extension of long-ago poetry classes. Something clouded his judgment of her in a way he'd never experienced with any other woman before. And not only did he not know what to do about it, he wasn't certain he wanted this particular problem solved, a mystery as piquant as the woman who inspired it.

She entered the bedroom, soundless as ever, and in the gentle glow of the lamplight her spell was cast. In its grip he floundered, helpless, and he reveled in it as she glided across the room to the window and peered through the parted blackout curtains, starting when their gazes meshed. Then she smiled, unlocked the window, and turned the casement handle to open it a few inches.

"Major Faust."

He'd never tire of hearing her say his name. "Miss Stoner."

She smiled. "I'm sorry, but—" She stopped, her perceptive gaze searching his face. "Is there something else I may call you? That sounds so distant and formal."

Surely enough oxygen existed in the farmyard that she couldn't suck all of it from his lungs. But he found he needed several deep breaths before he could answer her. "The Oxford tradition is the unadorned last name."

Her smile deepened. "But your surname carries overtones that we're ignoring right now."

He couldn't look away and her breathless spell tugged him further under water. No one ever called him anything else, or even seemed to understand those overtones of devilish deals. But Cupid's adept cut through his pitiful attempts at magic and enchanted him with ease.

"Your Christian name, Hans. It translates to John, doesn't it?"

Perhaps she'd been caught in her own spell. But Ritzi had never looked at him with such trusting warmth, no matter what he did with her body, and the thought sucked the last of the oxygen from his lungs. Was this how a mother looked at her son, a wife her husband, a sister her brother? If only he knew. "Hans-Joachim. It translates to John-Jacob."

"John-Jacob." She said it slowly, as if savoring something special and delectable. "I like it." Her chin tilted. No use bracing; he'd been vanquished days ago. "I'm Jennifer."

The first time he'd heard her name, he'd considered it tame, unpoetical, like something from a backwater English village lane. Now he knew backwater English village lanes could be among the most titillating and unnerving spots on the planet. Besides, even if he did like sonnets best, who said poetry always had to rhyme?

Earlier in the guardroom, they'd turned one relational corner, talking through the implications of the murder investigation and learning to solve problems together. He had a feeling they'd just turned another, possibly an even more important one.

"Jennifer." He wanted to straddle that branch all night and worship her through the cracked-open casement window. But implications remained within their murder investigation, and with the thought her spell shattered. Damn it, he sat there mooning while a murderer stalked the night. "Jennifer, where's the shotgun?"

She gasped, eyes widening in her plain face. "Oh, good grief. It's downstairs. I'll be right back." Without a sound, she ran from the room.

Okay, so maybe he was truly in love for the first time in his life. Perhaps that was all the excuse he needed for being hare-brained. But it didn't explain why such a practical, capable, collected woman forgot something so drastically important.

Something crashed downstairs. Faust quit breathing.

"Jennifer?" He didn't dare raise his voice. Maybe she'd just dropped something.

His accelerating pulse didn't believe a word of it.

81

late evening
Woodrow

Pain radiated from the back of her head, pounded in her skull, and echoed within her bones. Jennifer tried to push herself upright. But the farmhouse floor canted beneath her, her arms refused to hold her weight, and she sagged back down. Something had moved behind her, barely a whisper of sound that hadn't belonged, before her hand closed on the shotgun's barrel. Then her head had exploded, someone sniggered, and her eyes next focused on the glimmer of moonlight splayed just beyond her nose. Funny, she couldn't remember falling.

Good. Their plan was working. It was just working in the wrong room, and Major Faust—no, John-Jacob, wasn't there to rescue her. Besides, she hadn't told him what she'd needed to tell him, and this could go horribly wrong if he didn't figure it out.

Strong rough hands gripped her from behind and hauled her up. She swayed, tried to reach for the shotgun on the dining table, but her hands didn't want to obey her mind's orders and her fingers refused to close. She squirmed and tried again, but her body was jerked back into something hard. Long arms snaked about her waist and breasts, pinioning her arms and upper body, and held her closer than any man had before.

"Thought you were too good for me, didn't you." A sharp accent whispered in her ear, rougher and deeper than she remembered it. Fingers squeezed her left breast, pinched it, rubbed and scratched with sharp nails. It seemed as if he played with a rubber doll, not her body. "Harriet didn't. She liked it. You will, too, you'll see." The arm about her waist dragged her even closer. Something hard and round pressed between her buttocks. "Know I will."

Fury exploded within her. Jennifer smashed backward with her right elbow, kicked back with both heels, fought to free her arms, opened her mouth to scream. But the hand released her breast and shoved a wad of cheap cloth into her mouth. She gagged, bit down, connected with something soft and fleshy. The hand jerked back but the gag remained.

"Bloody bitch." Something hard slammed into her temple and again pain flared. "Harriet was nice. Sally was, too. But you're going to be like Grace, aren't you." Another blow, and the sitting room reeled. She sagged in his grip. "Well, that's all right. She squirmed, but she just made it better for me." The living cylinder rubbed her bum and throbbed. "Lots better."

She slammed back with her head—she'd find some way to take this murderer down, she'd butcher him and hang his carcass out for the crows—but somehow he ducked, blew in her ear, giggled. Again he pinched her breast, throbbed against her, and a note of panic whispered within her fury. He dragged her toward the stairs.

"Keep fighting, bitch. I like that, too."

The arm about her waist heaved her up two steps. She kicked again. But not too hard this time. Upstairs was the right room. Upstairs was John-Jacob. Smart and brave, he'd figure out the problem even if she hadn't explained it. He'd hold the murderer and she'd kill him.

82

late evening
Woodrow

Strange scuffling noises drifted upstairs. Faust's blood froze. He had to help her. He wriggled his left hand through the partly-opened casement window, twisted awkwardly sideways, grabbed the crank handle, and heaved. But it refused to turn. Shoving harder didn't budge it. Then he saw the glass had wedged against the branch he straddled and it wasn't going to open further. Stoner had mentioned that when he'd told the story of Jennifer cleaning her bedroom windows from the outside—one window would open, the other wouldn't, and he'd chosen the wrong one. He had to climb down and get to the other window, the one that would open.

Footsteps and scuffling bumped up the stairs. A rough whisper, intoxicated with power, drifted ahead. "Do it again, bitch. Just like Harriet, that was."

He tried to wriggle his arm from the casement. It wouldn't budge, either. He was caught and pulling harder didn't help. He turned, twisted, yanked. Cloth ripped. His tunic's turn-back cuff had wrapped over the corner of the glass. He flicked it free, his arm slithered painfully out, and he slid back along the branch to the trunk.

Two dark forms, spooned together as one, stumbled into the room. The glow of the lamp flickered over Jennifer's furious, ferocious face, glinted off her bared teeth and gagged-open mouth, but left a shadow over the face of the tall, wiry man squeezing her. The arms pinioning her writhing body were encased in khaki wool sleeves, free of stripe or device. The hands were big and rough, and one of them wriggled atop her left breast—

—which Faust already considered his own private property, although he had no right. A pounding began in his ears, dull and steady, like an echo of Jennifer's rage—

—beside the bed, the man whirled Jennifer about. The shadow lifted. Norris sniggered, his erection tenting the front of his pants. He tangled his left hand in Jennifer's blouse, hauling her forward as if to kiss her—

—and the pounding turned sharper, quicker, colder. Faust gathered his legs beneath him, rose on the branch, half-crouching, half-balancing, left arm wrapped about the branch above. Green apples bounced against his head. He had to climb down fast and jumping might be quickest, he wasn't all that high—

—Norris smashed his right fist into Jennifer's face. Her limp body fell to the bed. Norris grabbed the strap of his Lee Enfield rifle, slung across his shoulders, then tugged it into his hands and raised it over her face.

Faust's control snapped. They were out of time. He released the branch overhead, ran three slithering crouching steps along the wide bough, jumped, curled over, wrapped his arms about his head, and crashed through the casement window.

Frame and glass shattered, spraying the room in one impossible crawling second. Norris whirled, the Lee Enfield cradled in his hands, the giggling sneer sliding off his face and leaving raw terror. Jennifer pushed herself up, teeth still bared, one hand rising toward her mouth. Faust's boot toe clunked against the window ledge. He fell forward, off balance, face-first into the flying glass shards. He tried to untangle himself. But he stumbled, Norris swung the rifle at his head, and Faust knew he was going down.

"Run!" he yelled.

The wooden stock smashed across the right side of his face. A white flare erupted behind his eyes, obliterating the room about him. The angle of his fall changed. Faust grabbed for support. His hands slid across carved wood. The right one slammed metal, wrapped about a handle, tightened, stopped his fall and ripped the stitches from the back of his arm. Agony seared his right side.

Footsteps scrambled. Someone grunted. It could be her. She needed him. Faust forced his eyes open and fought through the pain. Norris swung the rifle again, the wooden stock growing larger as it came closer. Behind him, Jennifer slid from the bed to her feet. But instead of running, she grabbed a laundry basket beside the door, swung it about, slapped it over Norris' head, and yanked. His body bent backward. The rifle skimmed inches before Faust's face and slammed into the corner of the wardrobe.

Damn, what a woman. Faust scrabbled, boots skidding among the crunching shards. But Norris ducked, hissing between his teeth. The basket slid off his head. He hefted the rifle. Jennifer froze, holding the wicker before her like a shield. Her gaze crossed Faust's, meshed, held.

"Get help." He ignored the slicing pain in his arm and pushed himself off the wardrobe, stumbling toward Norris. At least they had him between them. "For Pete's sake, run!"

She dropped the basket, whirled, and vanished through the doorway without a sound.

Norris let her go. He turned and tried to raise the rifle, finger feeling for the trigger. But Faust ducked aside and charged. His body seemed to move at half-speed. Without warning, Norris doubled the rifle about and swung it, a hard fast blow that whipped across Faust's jaw and sent him spinning. His knees hit the floor, smaller pains slicing into his shins. His shoulder thumped into the bedsprings and his body sagged beside the mattress, refusing to heed his demands for action. He needed cover. Hell, he needed a weapon. But nothing was close and he didn't need to look to know Norris would strike again. Faust wrapped his arms about his head and curled into a ball.

The first blow slammed, by chance or design, into the exposed back of his right arm. Agony exploded like a mortar round, as if shrapnel sprayed through his body. A red flare erupted among the remnants of the white one behind his closed eyes. His elbow convulsed against his side. A voice that sounded like his own cried out.

"You're not that bloody tough." Norris' voice sounded right overhead. "I could have taken you any time. So much for the invincible German Army."

Faust couldn't see, could barely move. Pain pulsed across half his body, even through the lingering effects of the painkiller. He reached out blindly, grabbed rough woolen cloth, tried to yank the tall body off balance. But another mortar round exploded inside his head and blew his thoughts away.

83

late evening
outside Woodrow

Get help, the man said. Jennifer's feet skidded down the stairs without any conscious intervention from her. Another thud, a loud one. Run, he'd said.

And leave him defenseless behind.

She could run back upstairs with the shotgun and blow that murderer full of pellets. But they'd spray throughout the room and half would hit John-Jacob. She could swing it, slam Norris from behind, give him a taste of his own blood-soaked medicine. And if he saw her first, he could take it away from her and use it on them both.

She wanted to scream, sob, rant. She wanted to run back upstairs and help him. But her feet knew better. They kept moving. They flew past Stoner's dust-covered study, rounded into the sitting room, crossed the kitchen. Her hand reached out, snagged her keyring in passing. Her other hand twisted the knob, threw open the back door, and her feet leapt out into the night.

She raced around the corner of the farmhouse. Overhead, the blackout curtains had been ripped from the smashed window and lamplight spilled over the gnarled apple tree like a flickering flame, tendrils seeping across the ground before her heedless feet and lapping at the looming tree trunks. She ran past them. At the base of the hill, where the macadam lane emptied through the military wing's gate, a wash of moonlight showed the blacktop empty. Bruckmann and Tanyon still arranged the nonsuspects within Margeaux Hall; the lorry, bringing the cavalry to their rescue, hadn't arrived.

She and John-Jacob were on their own.

"Jack!" She doubled about and ran for the postern gate. Norris didn't carry keys; if she could get through, she could find help, find someone to save *him* the way he'd saved her grandfather. "Sergeant Tanyon! *Jack!*"

Footsteps pounded behind her. She didn't slow, didn't glance. It could only be Norris; John-Jacob would be stumbling after those blows. She swerved between the trunks, screaming as she ran. He already knew where she was and she refused to hide.

She slammed into the postern, inserted the key, fumbled. It jammed. The footsteps pounded closer, heavy breathing like a hateful steam engine approaching. The key wouldn't turn. To hell with getting help. She'd kill him with her bare hands.

She whirled, screaming wordless anger. Norris was right there, right behind her. His hands were almost to her throat. She ignored them, reached past them, fastened her own upon his face and ground her thumbnails into his eyes.

He recoiled, shouting something foul. She held on. His grasping hands missed her throat, wrapped about her wrists, yanked. She dug deeper, still screaming her rage, threw her weight against his body and forced him back beneath the trees. Down the hill an engine growled, rumbled, died, then someone else shouted: Sergeant Tanyon's baritone, aroused and closing.

Norris gasped. He pulled back. She screamed one final challenge, let go his bleeding slippery face, and wrapped her fists in his uniform collar. Bruckmann and Tanyon would be here soon. If she just held on—

Norris threw a panicked glance down the hill, turned back to her. He drew back his fist.

Something big and dark and magnificent dropped from the branch overhead. John-Jacob landed behind Norris, whipped a grey-clad arm about that loathsome neck, and yanked. For a moment they wobbled, all three teetering on the sloping ground in a frenetic dance. Suddenly she understood John-Jacob's intention. But it was too late to let go. They fell into a sprawling heap, John-Jacob on the bottom.

84

Bruckmann scrambled from the lorry and chased after Tanyon, sliding in the muck beneath the apple trees at the base of the hill. She sounded as if someone was skinning her alive. Entwined forms clustered outside the postern gate, lurching back toward the orchard, stumbling in a writhing dance. Then they all crumpled, falling as if mowed down by a machine gun. The smallest figure, the one on top, screamed again, drew back a fist, and pounded the next one down.

Bruckmann dug into the slope and galloped past Tanyon. The wash of moonlight darkened. Surely after a blistering hot day, they wouldn't be cursed with clouds at night? But the last of the dimming glow faded and vanished.

One of the faceless figures whipped aside, throwing Jennifer into a crumpling heap and racing away. It could only be the killer. The running man cut across the farmyard, ran blindly through the kitchen garden, swarmed up the Roman rampart, and vanished into the Dark.

Jennifer rolled over and rose to a crouch beside the still-motionless third. Bruckmann slowed. That third form huddled as if it would never move again. His blood chilled. If Faust died before he told what he knew of the invasion—green intelligence lieutenants had been broken for less. Much less.

"Jennifer?"

She turned. Her pale face blurred in the darkness. "It's Norris! Get him!"

Tanyon thundered past, ripped through the garden, took the rampart in one leap, and vanished.

Faust stirred. He grabbed the hand Jennifer offered him and pulled himself to a sitting position, even if he did wobble once there. Satisfied, Bruckmann ran on, following Tanyon's path. If it truly was Norris, with his long legs and wiry build, they'd have the devil's own time catching him, and no deal to be had.

85

late evening
Woodrow

The pounding footsteps diminished in the night. The moon reappeared and brilliant moonlight again bathed the hillside. For a breathless moment silver silence descended. Then a cricket sang, another answered, and some semblance of reality returned to the glistening night. Jennifer gasped, her breath rasping in a throat dry and sore. Had Norris choked her, after all? She couldn't remember. Her throat ached, her head, face, legs, breast. She felt ravaged, and the thought of that murderer getting away boiled her blood. But the chase had passed beyond her reach and she could do no more, no matter how much she wished otherwise.

John-Jacob dragged his feet beneath him and rocked, as if about to fall over from the weight of those broad shoulders. His head would fit perfectly in the crook of her neck and they could give each other aid and comfort beneath the apple trees, breaking the law together all night. But he grabbed her hand and tugged, his feet shuffling and his hot gaze trailing after the chase. What in the world was he thinking? She scrambled to her feet, fought his bulk, and heaved him upright. He leaned, staggered, and his entire weight descended on her shoulder. Her knees buckled. It was heavenly, inexplicably exciting—but then he staggered off in pursuit, across the path tracked through her poor little garden. John-Jacob scrambled up the rampart and vanished in the Dark.

Proving even magnificent men could be utter fools upon

occasion. Just like Stoner.

She ran back into the farmhouse. Her shotgun still lay in a pool of moonlight on the dining table, cold and deadly. It was loaded but boasted neither magazine nor cylinder, and Norris might double back, seeking the lorry for a quicker escape. One shot wouldn't nearly satisfy her.

The shells were in the sideboard, and she propped the shotgun beneath her arm as she scrabbled in the drawer. Napkins, napkin rings, tablecloth, doilies, odd trinkets, all spilled onto the floor as she dug into the back. The tips of her fingers closed on a stiffened cardboard box that rattled as she tugged it closer. It slid, balked, turned aside. She exclaimed wordlessly and adjusted her grip. Suddenly it slithered to the front. One-handed, she gathered it up and straightened. The box collapsed, and tumbling, rolling shells cascaded across the farmhouse floor.

Bloody hell. Jennifer fell to her knees, scrabbling for the little cylinders. In the dim moonlight, they flashed and vanished in all directions. She gathered one, two, several, but her nerveless fingers dropped those she held as fast as she grabbed new ones. It was maddening and not to be borne, and she screamed her frustration to the night.

This was getting her nowhere. She forced herself calm, set the shotgun beside her, and slid her forearms across the floor, rolling the shells toward her spread knees and skirt. They bumped her skin, aligned with her bones, and without effort she scooped a double handful into her pocket. Leaving the rest, she ran back outside, jumping off the front porch into the rutted rows of her garden.

Silver moonlight spilled across the wavering greenery and the stark wound of crushed, trampled plants. The crickets had fallen silent but in the apple boughs behind her, a nightjar sang its alien trilling churr. In the Dark ahead, something rustled through the discarded trash of autumns past, approaching fast. She raised the shotgun to her shoulder and peered along the sights.

Let him come.

86

late evening
in the Dark, outside Woodrow, and at the Alcock chicken farm

He had to be crazy.

No other reason for his behavior. He'd gone crazy, Stoner had applied too much pressure and shoved him right over the brink, and here he was, staggering through a forest alone, not even trying to escape but trailing after a chase that had left him so far behind, he couldn't even hear their footsteps. Faust staggered to a stop, leaned his back against the nearest tree, and let it support him while he gasped for breath. He glanced back; he hadn't traveled far enough to lose sight of the forest's edge. Pitiful.

The chase was in Bruckmann's and Tanyon's hands now and he couldn't help further, no matter how much he wanted to be in on the capture. Besides, some small and evil man (a Nazi, surely) had climbed into his skull and whaled away at his brain with a miniature sledgehammer. His knees stung, his arm raged, and when the last of the painkiller wore off, the rest of his aches and pains would pipe in. Damn it, somebody else could take the next hit. Faust pushed off the tree and stumbled back along his zigzag path, scuffing through leafy debris and stumbling over roots and fallen branches. No matter how he tried to reason with himself, his sullenness refused to lessen, as if he'd quit something important. Hopefully one of those impervious Englishmen would be hurt as badly before the night ended.

In the distance, Jennifer's voice shouted, wordless and

enraged.

A cold, horrified knot tangled his throat. He stumbled faster. They'd left her alone—no, to be truthful, he had. If Norris beat Bruckmann and Tanyon off, gave them the slip, doubled back, she was vulnerable. If anything happened to her, it was his fault. His chest tightened. He forced his feet faster through the debris, gasping for breath like a drowning man.

Without warning the trees ended. He found himself bathed in gentle fluid moonlight, took the next step before he remembered, and fell over that frigging rampart. Again the forest fooled him, just as it had Sunday morning at his initial capture. It felt as if the ground opened beneath him but he threw his weight back and slid down the slope on his caboose.

A rifleman stood in the kitchen garden, awash in moonlight. The barrel aligned on him was so steady, its black mouth was round, neither foreshortened nor wavering. Faust rolled. The plants provided the only cover; if he tried to scramble back into the forest—

—not a rifleman. It was a shotgun-toting, ferocious, aggravating woman in a tweed skirt, and after scaring ten years off his life, she lowered the barrel and ran toward him. Faust collapsed back against the rampart, swearing. In German; even crazy he hadn't lost all his manners.

Jennifer fell to her knees beside him. "You silly fool, I nearly shot you."

She would not blame him for this. On second thought, she still held the shotgun; she could blame him for anything she wanted. "You screamed."

"Of course I screamed. He's getting away and I'm furious."

He peered at her sideways. Mistake. The glistening moonlight spilled across her stunningly beautiful face, gentler than lamplight, cool rather than warm, inviting and intoxicating. He fell headfirst into it.

Without thinking he lifted his hand toward her. Damnation, he really had lost his mind; she might not hate him, but for him to imagine any sort of bond growing between them could only be moonlit lunacy. At least in the dark she couldn't see the flush that warmed his face. He pulled his hand back.

But she gripped it in both of hers and held on. Her palms were soft and her fingers entwined about his. Surprised, he heaved himself upright, curled his legs, and suddenly his face leaned toward hers, barely a kiss away.

He was seconds from losing control. And it was wrong.

Even if by some miracle she did reciprocate his desire, with a killer on the loose and more than half of Stoner's squad out searching for Faust, now was not an appropriate time and the rampart was nowhere near an appropriate place. He jerked his gaze aside, panting. Somewhere nearby, a nightjar chirred and a cricket answered. The moon escaped the clouds. Its cool light flooded over him, spilling down the farmyard to the apple orchard, the mortared-stone wall, the macadam lane joining the backwater country road—

—and the parked lorry.

His pulse picked up speed.

"He's going to get away, isn't he?" Her voice was anguished.

Faust hauled in a deep breath flooded with the heady aroma of crushed herbs, basil and thyme and parsley. Her gentle floral scent rushed beneath like a counterpoint. "Give me a hand."

She rose beside him, fluid as the moonlight. Her grip on his hand changed and she tugged him to his feet. For a moment he thought she'd tuck herself beneath his left shoulder and support his weight; the thought shivered up his spine; but then she released him and drew back, clasping the shotgun to her torso. "You've got a plan."

He forced his feet to move, bumping past staked squash and over rows of lettuce. "Can you drive?"

She waded through the sea of plants as if through a river. "The lorry? Heavens, no."

Figured. "Can you follow directions?"

"Well." She paused, negotiating the last row of beans and erupting into the full moonlight. "Of course I can. Why? Can't you drive?"

"Not with one arm." The way his right arm screamed at him, if he tried to turn a steering wheel, he'd pass out. He stumbled faster.

"Oh." She trotted beside him. His footsteps crunched over gravel, whispered through grass, but hers remained soundless. The downslope ended and the rise began, the lorry ahead beneath the last apple tree. "Yes. Of course I can."

That was reassuring.

He hauled open the passenger door. But this was England, not Germany, and of course the cab was reversed. He'd opened the driver's side. Great, this would be an interesting drive. "What I'll ask you to do isn't more complicated than a typewriter. Go on, get in."

Jennifer swarmed inside and scooted to the center without ever losing her grip on the shotgun. Her stupendous grace made it look easy. But he had to grab the big horizontal steering wheel and drag himself up, gritting his teeth at the onrushing pain and twisting to close the door with his left hand.

He tested the stick and pedals, accelerator, brake, and clutch. Backwards, but otherwise the same, and comforting in a solid, mechanical way. It even smelled right, oil, petrol, lubricated warm metal, and the polished windshield glistened in the night's silver flood. The radio, a modern and recent add-on, hung beneath the dash, handy for both driver and passenger. At sight of it, Faust froze. He'd given his parole and couldn't even consider calling Germany, although it would solve his long-term problem with a few choice words. The possibility caught his breath. But Norris had swung a fist and smashed Jennifer to the bed. He breathed faster. To hell with the radio. He'd find another way, without violating his parole.

He stepped on the brake. "Reach down and grab that lever—yeah, the one in the middle—and pull it as hard as you can."

She glanced at him, her glorious eyes glinting liquid fire in the moonlight. He shivered. But she grabbed the brake lever with both hands and heaved. It gave with a jerk, tumbling her back in the seat. The lorry rocked on the slope and the pressure against the brake pedal intensified.

"Perfect." He eased off and the lorry started down the hill, gathering speed. If it refused to start, they'd never get it turned onto the road and it would make a spectacular mess of the dairy's drystone wall. He held his breath, pumped the accelerator, and gave the starter a solid push. The engine revved, pulsed, started with a heartening roar. He turned the headlights on; the shuttered beams slid across the macadam before them.

"When I tell you to, push the stick toward me, then force it up toward the dashboard. Okay?"

"Toward you, then up." She didn't sound all that certain. "Got it."

"There are grooves within the gearbox that guide the stick into position. It's no harder than setting a tab stop on a typewriter." They were nearing the end of the macadam. "Ready?"

She slid closer. Her scent washed over him. "Ready."

He engaged the clutch. "Do it."

She shifted. The transmission jolted into first gear, he released the clutch and fed in some gas, and the engine rumbled. The lorry bounced across the last few yards of the macadam lane. Left-handed, Faust horsed the steering wheel to the right. It barely budged.

"Where are you going?" she said. "The road's over there."

As if he couldn't see that. He needed more speed to turn the stiff steering wheel, but the lorry had already rolled into the intersection and the drystone wall loomed ever closer beyond the hood. He braced his feet outside the pedals and hauled with his whole aching body, grunting with the strain. The front left tire bounced off the far edge of the road as the lorry swung in a slow cumbersome arc. Damn it, they were going to hit, and adding his right arm to the effort only shot piercing agony across his side.

Then Jennifer dived beneath his arm. She grabbed the spoke beside his grip and heaved, throwing her weight in with his. Her body pressed against his chest, her hair brushed his cheek, and her scent cut through the heavier notes of oil and warm metal, tantalizing and intoxicating. No wonder he'd run mad. But the lorry responded. Its arc tightened. The front fender scraped along the flint blocks with a harsh metallic rasp, brilliant orange sparks spraying the night. Then the sound ceased, the sparks vanished, the lorry angled away from the drystone wall, the tire jolted back onto the road, and suddenly they were slanting back toward Woodrow's kitchen garden, a pool of greenery in the dim headlights.

He abandoned the steering wheel to her tender mercies, engaged the clutch and accelerator, slipped his left hand beneath her body without letting himself imagine what part of her his arm brushed, and shifted up. The lorry jerked forward, the engine note dropped a level, she scooted back across the seat, and he horsed the steering wheel about. The lorry settled into the middle of the road and picked up speed.

"Sorry. I'm not trying to get fresh." No matter how much he wanted to.

The last of the kitchen garden rolled past on their right side, the drystone wall on their left. The shadows of the Dark folded over them. The dim headlights wavered across the road as the lorry growled up the slope.

Faust chose his words with care. "I can't let our adventure tonight change anything, you know. I can't let your grandfather break me."

She didn't hesitate. "I know you have your duty, just as we have ours."

Which wasn't precisely the same as agreeing with him. "All I want to do is catch Norris so I can escape and go home without getting killed."

The lorry crested the rise and descended into ever-deeper shadows. Looming oaks reached gnarled fingers across the road. On its downward slope, the lorry ducked beneath their grasp and eluded them, but each time it seemed they'd be caught in an unbreakable grip.

"Which of us are you trying to convince?" Her whisper was all but inaudible beneath the engine's rumbling.

Aggravating, infuriating, outrageous—and despite his yearning to settle the score with Norris, despite the pain that pounded against his resolve, Faust wanted her more than he'd ever wanted a woman before. He longed to stretch out with her in the Dark's soft leafy debris, roll her over, pin her arms above her head, and love her 'til her ears rang—and it would never happen.

"That's not the impression I wanted to give." He hadn't meant to sound so petulant. But he needed distance before his yearning for her overwhelmed his control, and perhaps it was for the best.

She braced against the dashboard. The road curved left and climbed, flickering in the wavering headlights, and Faust tugged on the wheel as he accelerated. The engine roughened and growled. From his deepest depths, he knew distance between them was the last thing he wanted. But wishing wouldn't change anything.

"I know." She looked away.

Ahead, the road escaped the trees' dominion and moonlight spread over its liberated ribbon, hemmed on either side by the darker lines of drystone walls. The rows of turnips began on the left, the chicken runs on the right. An ugly twisting started in his stomach and the pounding in his head intensified. He shouldn't have snapped at her. But he didn't dare apologize. Or look at her.

"We don't know where Norris will exit the forest," he said. "I'm presuming he'll run in a straight line, trying to put distance between him and pursuit, but once out of the forest he'll look for a place to hide or a means of getting away permanently. It's our job to intercept him before he can." The lorry topped the last rise. Faust shifted to neutral and pressed the brake, letting the vehicle roll to the verge and stopping it short of the wall. "So we need to hide close enough to the forest to see what's happening, but far enough away so we can run and intercept Norris wherever he comes out."

"The barn." Her voice was decided. But the distance remained. "There's a loft high enough to see over the chicken runs."

He set the handbrake, killing the engine and lights. "The barn it is."

They scrambled over the wall and she raced past the

runs, leading the way. The shotgun danced beneath her arm and her feet whispered from dirt to trampled lawn. The chickens they passed squawked, flapped, then settled into an uneasy truce behind them. Faust staggered in her wake. Focusing needed too much concentration, his stomach became more unsteady by the step, and the overwhelming fowl stench smothered him like a feather pillow.

They skirted the frame house and ran toward the looming dark mass of the barn. The ends of the chicken runs opened long corridors to the right, the forest's edge beyond an imposing black boundary with empty depths beneath. Nothing seemed to stir except the sleepy birds. His eyes watered and his stomach squirmed harder.

Jennifer vanished in the barn's shadow. By the time he leaned against the rough outer wall, her face peered from the loft overhead.

"Can you see anything?" A convulsive shudder engulfed him. He gritted his teeth and closed his eyes.

Her voice murmured, softer than the nightjar. "No, not—yes. Yes, there he is." She sucked in a breath. "We did it."

Not yet, they hadn't, and if he didn't pull himself together, they wouldn't. Faust straightened. "Where?"

In the distance, chickens squawked and flapped. The noise rippled toward them, a wave of avian panic in the night. His mind cleared and his breathing steadied through the pounding pain. Combat approached.

"The next to last corridor between the runs." She sounded breathless. "He's coming fast."

Faust eased to the corridor's end but stayed within the shadows. A racing figure approached, spreading the wave of feathered panic with its steps. Perhaps Norris had slowed, but if so, it wasn't by much. His path intersected the wall of the barn; he'd have to turn, north or south, to pass it. North, away from the road, would be the quickest route to a real escape. Faust poised on the balls of his feet. The pulsing pain in his head and arm, his twisting stomach, all seemed to fade into the background, freeing him to fight. When Norris committed to a new path, so would he.

The nearest chickens panicked, an outburst of wings and noise. The dark form erupted from the corridor, angled north, and accelerated, footsteps squelching in the grass. His breathing whooped like a bellows.

The last of the pain faded away. Faust leapt to intercept. He cut across the barn's shadow in three bounds and sprang into the moonlight, reaching for Norris' pumping arm. In the distance, the chickens panicked again. Bruckmann and Tanyon were on their way.

Norris glanced toward him. A ragged gasp hissed beneath the squawking. He spun north, twisting away.

Faust dived after him. His right shoulder crunched into Norris' twisting side. Agony exploded and slammed Faust like a shock wave, redoubled for the reprieve. His body convulsed. But he wrapped both arms around Norris and held on as the farmyard whirled about them.

They slammed into the ground. His arm spasmed, retracted, folded against his side as if taking cover. His stomach heaved. A voice that sounded like his shouted. Beneath him, Norris thrashed. Clawing nails tore at Faust's remaining grip and one boot crunched into his thigh. The explosion intensified. He closed his fist amidst Norris' uniform buttons and held on. The second wave of squawking was approaching fast.

Then Norris scrambled aside. Faust slid off and thumped into the grass, only his fingers tangled in khaki wool binding them together. Norris gathered himself like a runner at the start, twisting toward Faust and drawing back his left fist. He paused and glanced up, eyes widening.

Jennifer dropped the shotgun beside Faust and landed on Norris' back like a Fury. Her arm wrapped around his throat, her fist crashed down on his skull, and her knees slammed into his flanks, driving him into a floundering heap on the ground. She screamed her rage, smashed him again, then lifted his head by his hair and crunched him face-first into the barnyard. Norris cried out, writhing beneath her, but his boots skidded sideways as she slammed her knees into him again.

Faust untangled his arm, grabbed the shotgun, and rolled aside. Another thunk resounded, echoing from the barn's wall and from the inside of his head. The barnyard kept spinning, whirling drunkenly about him. His stomach heaved. Hell, she didn't need his help any more. As Bruckmann barreled into the fight, chickens screaming behind him, Faust rolled to his knees and retched himself empty.

87

night
at the Alcock chicken farm and outside Margeaux Hall

The barnyard pump worked smoothly. Faust rinsed his grungy mouth, held his head beneath the spurting water, then splashed more across his aching face. The cool shock eased the pounding and braced his wobbly knees like a tonic. His interior seemed empty and light, like a balloon that would float away if he took off his boots. He leaned atop the pump, curled over it, and let the relief soak through him. Maybe he'd survive the night, after all.

At the barnyard's edge, Tanyon and Bruckmann hauled Norris to his feet, his arms bound behind him. The bastard hadn't quit protesting yet: he hadn't hurt anyone, he'd been protecting Miss Stoner from the German murderer, he'd practically been caught in the act, what further proof did they want? Standing at the pump, Faust could no longer discern the words. But he could still hear that bloody whiny voice and it grated almost as badly.

As usual, he didn't hear her approach. But when he opened his eyes, her brogues waited nearby, those delicious legs rising into her tweed skirt. Her soft voice cut through Norris' incessant protests without effort. "John-Jacob?"

At least he knew enough not to look up, into her face in the bewitching moonlight. "I'm okay." He dug in his pocket, found the handkerchief she'd given him, and smeared away the drips.

Fingers as feather-light as her step stroked his wet hair

behind his ear and traced down his aching jaw line. "Your poor face."

Her touch coursed through him like another cold-water shower, leaving a hot glow in its wake. Before he could stop himself, he glanced up. The moonlight did the rest. Her eyes, fine and dark in the silver gleam, peered at the bruises he'd earned in her service with gentle concern, and her fingers whispered back up along his jaw line, infinitely slowly. Neither her tousled hair nor the darkening lump on her left cheek detracted a whit from her incandescence. Nor did they seem to concern her.

While his injuries did. Just like Skelton's merry Margaret. *Gentle as falcon Or hawk of the tower; With solace and gladness—*

His heart swelled within him. If he tugged her close, held her against him, touched her lips with his, how would she react? If her desire steamed, too—and he'd never had to wonder about a woman before—she'd kiss him back and tangle her fingers in his hair. But if this was merely gratitude, she'd give him a good smack.

Her gaze lifted from his jaw line and meshed with his. Her expression deepened, mysterious and piquant, leaving him unenlightened. He wasn't certain he wanted to risk it. But his body started to lean toward her—

—and it was just as wrong now as it had been earlier. He straightened and, with more resolve than he'd known he possessed, removed his face from her touch.

With a jerk, she slid her hands behind her, like a scolded schoolgirl. "Sorry."

"It's not that I don't appreciate it." He hesitated; she'd turned away at his first word. "Or like it."

"It's inappropriate. I know. It's just—" Her breath rasped. "I can't help but feel some responsibility for your situation. I know it's not truly my fault." She faced him again. Her chin had firmed in her moment aside and her eyebrows were level. "But I've helped put you here."

So this was gratitude. Faust shoved the damp handkerchief into his pocket, unaccountably irritated. "Your loyalty should be clear."

In the silver moonlight, her eyes flared with something akin to anger. As usual, she didn't hesitate. "So should yours."

He stiffened. Whatever impression he'd given her, it wasn't the one he'd aimed at. And she took after her grandfather too much, at least during an argument. Before he could say so, Bruckmann scuffed across the grass and joined them.

The lieutenant jerked his head toward Norris, still

431

babbling to Tanyon. "He swears he didn't do it. He swears we've caught the wrong man." His voice wavered.

The sergeant's dark glance cut Faust's way, then turned aside as if burned.

Jennifer hauled in a sharp breath.

"Don't bother arguing with him. Just turn him over to Chief Inspector Hackney. His investigation will sort things out." Faust paused. Her fists clenched and she glared across the farmyard as if taking aim. "Besides, I saw him hit Jennifer before he knew I was watching. That's hardly protective."

She glanced over her shoulder, one swift grateful second of eye contact. Then she too turned away.

Bruckmann popped his eyebrows. "That's what we'll do." He returned to his duties.

After a moment, Jennifer scooped up the shotgun from beside the pump and followed him.

Faust's empty stomach clenched. He'd succeeded in putting distance between them. Now he wished he could take it back. More importantly, he wished he'd chanced that kiss. Then he'd know for certain whether it would be worthwhile seeking her out after the war.

Or whether he'd just get smacked.

Bruckmann drove and Jennifer rode in the lorry's cab, while Faust slumped in the back with the sergeant and his prisoner. At least Norris fell silent in his presence, but the kid's hot accusing stare, perhaps a touch calculating around the edges, never left him.

His body rocked as the lorry swung uphill onto Margeaux Hall's macadam lane. The orchard and the mortared stone wall rolled past the opened canvas backing, then the rocking stopped and the engine died. Before Sloane could close the gate, another car, driving without lights, swung onto the macadam and parked. Hackney scrambled out and trotted up the slope, followed more slowly by Arnussen and Constable Mercer. Even in the dim moonlight, eagerness glittered on the inspector's jowled face.

"We've been watching from the dairy and saw you drive out." Hackney leaned over the tailgate and swept a flashlight beam into the lorry's back. "Norris."

Faust squenched his eyes shut. Time for round two.

"It wasn't me." Norris leaned away from Tanyon's restraining grip, as if closer proximity to the chief inspector would bolster his argument. He jerked his head at Faust. "It was him. We practically caught him in the act. What more d'you want?"

Behind the cone of light, Hackney's jaw shifted. "Well, it

might help if he had the right blood type. It can't be him, you know."

"It has to be." Norris straightened, all innocent astonishment. "None of us would do a thing like that."

Faust froze. He'd thrown out the racial accusation to Stoner and been scoffed at. But Norris seemed to expect them to believe it.

He climbed from the lorry, ignored the pain flashing from the movement, and slipped past Hackney into the cool welcome of the night. The lawn opened about him, stretching down to the wall and up the slope to the looming black bulk of Margeaux Hall, and his consciousness seemed to expand to fill the space. The moon overhead, nearly full, drowned out the closest stars. Its flooding light bathed the building and the huge spreading beeches dotting the lawn, glittering off the glass vestibule and soothing his soul. It smelled clean, cleaner than he did, like a newborn world, like a new start. *If all the world and love were young, And truth in every shepherd's tongue—*

From all sides, crickets sang their monotonous chords, and from the apple orchard behind him the nightjar answered with its strange chirring sound, more like a machine than a bird. He lit one of Clarke's cigarettes and added nicotine to the dreamy mix, standing in the moonlight and smoking without thought for long minutes. No wonder so many poets wrote of the nighttime orb and Diana's beauty. A bomber's moon, Erhard had called it, and laughed. If it lit the targeted landscape this well, he could understand why.

He wasn't crazy. He knew that. He wasn't crazy and his loyalty remained intact despite Stoner's onslaught. The murderer had been caught, the local ladies were safe, he'd fulfilled his unsought responsibilities, and now he could escape and return to Germany, to the staff officer's position he'd earned and where he was determined to excel. Everything else could wait. And included in that waiting list was Jennifer, with her tender ferocity, tantalizing lips, and stunningly beautiful soul camouflaged beneath a pleasantly plain face. He dragged hard. Perhaps by the end of the war he'd be over this infatuation. Perhaps not. But he'd have to wait for the world to recover its own sanity to find out.

He hadn't yet found an answer to Stoner's accusation, that Faust and the German Army were accomplices to the Nazis' crimes. The heat of that shameful moment, emphasized by the memory of Stoner's white, enraged face, briefly ruffled his enforced tranquility. But he shook it off. It, too, could wait. And the resumption of peace and order might be enough to answer the accusation for him.

He flipped the butt away and turned. In the car at the macadam lane's foot, Norris sat in the back beside Mercer, Arnussen behind the wheel. Tanyon hunched in the lorry's cab, bent over the radio. The other three clustered halfway down the slope, Bruckmann and Hackney still talking. Jennifer stared past them and watched him. As usual, his blood warmed to her living poetry. But this time he examined the sensation without passion, seeking beyond his earlier assumption that he'd fallen finally, truly in love. He found that somewhere between his lust and his liking lurked a desperate yearning, too shy to put itself forward. He'd never encountered it before. If that was love, at least, like Donne's, it was a reasoning and patient love. *When I am gone, dream me some happiness.*

Faust turned away and strode uphill to the lorry. No matter how beautiful she was, patient his love would have to be.

He arrived as Tanyon returned the microphone to its stand, muttering.

"Something wrong, sergeant?"

Tanyon gave him a long, thoughtful look. "Carmichael's not answering the radio."

"I thought you'd cured him of that."

"So did I." Tanyon horsed himself from behind the wheel and closed the lorry's door with a frustrated shove. "I'm going to check on him." He nodded toward Hackney, Bruckmann, and Jennifer. "Let them know where I've gone, will you?"

Faust leaned against the lorry, letting his aching muscles relax. Bed sounded attractive. "Sure."

The sergeant hiked up the slope to the Hall. A minute later, an engine started and the policemen's car rolled onto the road, accelerating toward the Dark. Bruckmann and Jennifer approached along the macadam lane, Pym and Sloane trudging behind them. Reynolds swung the big gate closed and took a sentry's stand before it.

"Time to wrap this up." Bruckmann hauled open the lorry's door, fumbled about on the floorboard, and produced a Very gun, a flare ready up the spout. He aimed at the sky and pulled the trigger. The white phosphorus exploded, spraying brilliant sparks among the stars as if competing against them. Then he tossed the flare gun onto the seat and stepped back. "Sloane, put the lorry away then you're off duty. Pym, wait here for the rest of the squad and then report to—" He broke off and glanced about, a puzzled line between his eyebrows.

"He went up to the Hall." No need to mention why; Tanyon would tell Bruckmann and Pym if he wanted them to know.

The lieutenant's face cleared. "Well, when the squad's complete, find him and report, corporal."

"Yes, sir."

Sloane slammed the driver's door and the engine rumbled to life. Faust pushed himself erect, even if it did hurt like something foul, and the lorry crawled away, following the lane around the darkened Hall and vanishing beyond the glass. The rumbling died in the distance.

When Faust turned up the hill, Bruckmann stepped into his path. The lieutenant's usual sharp smugness had been wiped away, leaving a young man who looked several years older, more humble and more thoughtful.

"Major Faust, thank you for your help tonight."

It wasn't said quietly and Pym swiveled, watching them both as if again reassessing the situation. Jennifer's face glowed in the moonlight. Faust's breathing deepened and slowed despite the pounding pain. He hadn't expected such a gesture from the lieutenant, which made it even more valuable.

Then a report cracked through the night. Another. Faust stiffened, his sharpening stare meshing with Bruckmann's and his pain fading into the background. Around them, the darkness seemed to crystallize. The silence was brittle as glass, as if the night would shatter if any of them moved. The sound had been muffled but not distant, sharp and echoing. A small-caliber weapon, probably a pistol. Fired inside Margeaux Hall.

Where Carmichael hadn't answered the radio.

"Wait here." Bruckmann galloped up the slope.

"Lieutenant, no—" But Faust was too late and the racing figure didn't stop, pounding footsteps diminishing up the slope. Moments later Bruckmann vanished through the vestibule door.

"Was that a gunshot?" Pym asked.

"Two of them." Faust thought fast, the cool clarity of combat wiping him empty of all else. Bruckmann galloped headlong into an unknown and possibly dangerous situation, where Tanyon had already vanished. They needed to reconnoiter and they needed cover. But on this side of the Hall, if they wanted to observe undetected, the only cover was the slope of the hill; the spreading beeches were too distant to help. And he couldn't leave Jennifer unprotected. "Come on. But please stay behind me."

No one argued. Faust circled the hillside, pistol-shot distance from the Hall. Small sounds trailing his path gave away Pym's presence; Jennifer, of course, was noiseless. The night held its breath, even his pain and the crickets falling silent, and the stars overhead shone frozen and pitiless.

Part way around, the glass vestibule lit with a dim glow. Faust dropped to a crouch, his hand in the grass supporting his weight. A glance showed Pym and Jennifer huddled close behind him. She cradled the shotgun, and Pym held his Lee Enfield ready.

The glow didn't fill the vestibule but slanted through the door from the ballroom, the shadows distorted and moving. Faust circled further around the hillside, moving sideways in a slow crouching glide, until he peered up the slope, through the glass door, and through the ballroom doorway beyond.

A tall, lean silhouette stood ten feet on the far side of that doorway, the light breaking around it and haloing Bruckmann's white-blond hair in passing. A voice—no, two voices were audible, but muffled by the building into a wordless, unidentifiable jumble. With the lieutenant in the way, he couldn't be certain. But the light seemed to come from Stoner's open office door and someone had to be standing there, speaking with Bruckmann.

"What's going on?" Pym's voice was barely a breath in Faust's ear.

He shook his head. "I don't know."

From within the Hall, Bruckmann's voice rose to a muffled shout. Another report cracked through the night. Bruckmann wobbled. Jennifer gasped, a small hand gripping Faust's left shoulder, and a horrified shock shivered through him, reigniting his pain. Then the lieutenant crumpled onto the ballroom's hardwood floor.

Eduard Best stood revealed. In one hand he held an evil-looking revolver, in the other a sheaf of papers. His stare followed Bruckmann down, satisfied and as pitiless as the uncaring stars. Then he turned and vanished into Stoner's office without a backward glance.

88

night
Margeaux Hall

Faust tugged the shotgun from Jennifer's unresisting fingers. Without a word, he scrambled up the slope toward the Hall.

He wasn't certain what to do, wasn't even certain what to think—Best was German and Faust's loyalties should be clear no matter how muddled his brain, so why he'd grabbed the shotgun, he didn't totally understand. But instinct carried him beyond his pain, in a crouching run to the glass door. A final glance showed Bruckmann huddled and unmoving, far enough inside the ballroom to make a rescue hazardous, a dark pool spreading around his head. The light from Stoner's office held steady, not quivering with motion. Faust opened the vestibule door, slid noiselessly inside, held it open for Pym and Jennifer, then closed it behind them.

Jennifer took one unthinking step toward Bruckmann. Faust grabbed her arm and tugged her into the shelter of the brick wall beside the ballroom doorway, his glance inviting Pym to follow.

"You saw who that was?" Faust whispered as quietly as he could.

They both nodded. Pym's eyes were wider than Faust had ever seen them, his inexperience showing.

"Who is there?" It was Best's voice, calling from the ballroom.

Jennifer froze, her back pressed against the bricks.

Damn, they must have made some noise. Faust touched his left index finger to his lips and waited until they both nodded a second time. He pointed at Pym, pointed up the black wrought-iron staircase beside them, then along the west-east axis of the military wing in an echo of the upstairs corridor, then down. Holding his hands upright, he slammed the palms toward each other without touching. Taking Best between them was workable, if Pym could use the upper hallway and the eastern stairs to reach the ballroom's far side.

Pym seemed to understand, or at least his tension eased. He nodded again and slipped up the stairs, vanishing into the blackout.

"I know someone is there." Cautious footsteps approached the doorway.

The thought of Best's pitiless face confronting Jennifer sent a shiver up Faust's spine. He had to protect her. A long step brought him close enough to whisper near her cheek. "Stay here while I distract him, okay?"

Her eyes focused on his lips, watching them as he spoke. But her expression showed no understanding. She stared at his mouth as if mesmerized, her own curving lips parted and quivering with unspoken words, and it could be the last chance he ever had to answer that question.

Faust bent and caressed her lips with his. He was ready to move fast if she swung. But she returned the tender pressure and her weight leaned against his chest. For one surging moment he vanished into the kiss, the gentlest and yet the most intense he'd ever known.

Then Best spoke again. *"Ist es der Verräter?"*

Faust froze, the blood stopping in his veins. Jennifer drew back and the kiss died between them. He couldn't breathe, that despicable word hanging over him like an axe. The world seemed to tumble about him, realigning itself in some manner he still couldn't understand. Then Jennifer's expression firmed. Her hands moved, clothing rustled, and he glanced down as she slid a stash of shotgun shells into each of his front patch pockets. She drew back into the shadows beneath the wrought-iron staircase, freeing him to fight.

Another cautious footstep in the ballroom, someone inching closer. They were out of time. Hopefully she'd listen to his request for prudence rather than her natural ferocity. He cradled the shotgun across his body and doubled about the doorjamb into the ballroom.

Best jolted to a stop. He hadn't moved far from Stoner's office doorway. The light from the desk lamp spilled about him, silhouetted his slender frame, and glinted off the Colt revolver dangling in his hand. He lifted the pistol; Faust made sure he was just as quick with the shotgun, despite the slicing pain that convulsed along his arm. When Best paused, the revolver barrel not quite aligned for the shot, Faust paused as well, ensuring the standoff.

"You called me a traitor." He spoke in German. Best's English had seemed reasonably fluent but he could risk no misunderstanding.

Best eased back a step. Tension radiated from his taut muscles and backward-leaning, defensive stance. The light from Stoner's desk lamp spilled about him.

"You are here."

Faust stepped into the ballroom, circling right to avoid Bruckmann's motionless form without glancing down. He could do nothing for the lieutenant, dead or alive. "So are you."

"I have made my choice." Another step back. One more and Best would be close enough to duck into Stoner's office. But he paused. His chin tilted. "Is it too late to change your mind?"

The parody of Stoner's most aggravating mannerism boiled inside Faust and their standoff set his teeth on edge. It wasn't equal: if the pig jumped for cover, at this range the shotgun would pepper but not kill him, while a well-aimed shot from the revolver could be fatal. Faust needed to end this or find cover himself until Pym came down the eastern stairwell. The metal desks were somewhere to his right. They'd slow although not stop a bullet and were the best he had available. He eased further into the ballroom, feeling the extent of each step with his foot before following with his body. Within three steps, his toe scuffed cloth—the scatter rugs beneath the desks, protecting the hardwood floors. "Why don't you speak plainly, for once?"

"I'm returning to Germany."

Faust froze in mid-step.

"If you like, you may come, too."

It was a lie. It had to be, Faust hadn't managed more than fifteen or twenty miles during his best escape attempt, and if that wimp thought he'd get further than a real soldier, even an injured and aching one, well, it just showed how little he knew. But Faust's pulse accelerated, belying his thoughts. "What?" His voice sounded breathless.

Best paused, staring across the ballroom as if to read Faust's desires through his skull. Then he uncoiled. He let the revolver drop to his side. "I've radioed and a plane is coming to pick me up. There will be room for two." His voice softened. "Don't you want to go home?"

More than anything. By all the poets, more than any-thing he yearned to return to the life Erhard had ripped from him, to his career and books and abandoned Agfa camera. Perhaps Stoner was wrong, perhaps he wouldn't lose his position as a staff officer, perhaps it would be as if this outrageous misadventure had never happened. He wanted to put it all behind him, forget all of it except Jennifer—

—Jennifer, who stood in the vestibule and who hadn't slugged him when he'd kissed her. Best would have to walk past her to leave Margeaux Hall. He wouldn't leave any living witnesses.

Faust brought up the shotgun; he hadn't realized he'd lowered it. Best backed away fast, the revolver swinging up and his face twisting into an ugly mask. At the ballroom's far end, a door opened and someone moved, a gentle wash of moonlight spreading across the floor almost to Faust's feet. It had to be Pym, it was past time he arrived, and Faust whirled and ducked behind the closest desk.

But the report that chased him wasn't deep enough for a Lee Enfield three aught three and the bullet crashed through the desk beside him, slicing an exit wound with jagged curling edges in the metal. That was someone shooting to kill and aiming at him. Faust hurled himself across the hardwood floor, rolled to his belly, and peered beneath the bottom of the desk, his breath rasping into his lungs.

The old gardener stood in the open doorway at the corridor's end. He held an equally ancient single-shot rifle in his hands, and he giggled as he jammed another round into the breech. When he looked up, his gaze traveled across the line of desks as if seeking Faust through the metal cordon. He lifted the rifle to his shoulder and stepped into the ballroom.

That door lead into the residential wing, where Glover stood guard for the people who lived here. He had to assume Glover was down, as well as Bruckmann, Carmichael, and probably Tanyon. These two were ripping through Stoner's command without mercy. He also had to assume they'd rip through him, Pym, and Jennifer, if they got the chance.

Which meant Best had probably lied about the plane, too. The pig had intended to trick him into lowering the shot-gun—and he nearly had.

Faust gritted his teeth, gathering his feet beneath him. He hid behind the row of metal desks closest to the vestibule, with another row between him and the two gunmen. The desks stretched across the short side of the long room, between Bruckmann's huddled body and the floor-to-ceiling windows along the southern wall. The garnet swags were drawn together and that side of the ballroom lay in deep shadow. The distant light of Stoner's desk lamp, halfway down the room, spilled through the open door and broke into a confused jumble among the desks. Moonlight glowed from the opened doors to the residential wing and the vestibule behind him. It didn't reach his cover. Unlikely Best or the gardener could see him. But movement, especially in the open areas between the desks, could catch their eyes.

He could make a break for the vestibule. But drawing their attention toward Jennifer didn't appeal. Nor did the prospect of turning his back on these gunmen; if the gardener would willingly shoot at him without warning, he'd be just as willing to drill Faust from the rear. Besides, he'd be silhouetted by the moonlight while crossing through the doorway. No, the vestibule was out.

Another option was to press the firefight. To do so, he'd have to get close enough for the shotgun to be effective. To engage the gardener, he'd have to charge across the open area to the sofas and chairs, avoiding Best's fire from Stoner's office doorway, where he'd taken cover. For most of the advance, Faust would be hidden by the darkness, but he'd have to cross the area touched by the desk lamp, and again his motion would draw their eyes.

Or he could keep them distracted until Pym arrived. But the lance corporal was already overdue and that worried him. No way of knowing how many of Stoner's captives had escaped and found weapons. If Pym had run into more of them upstairs, possibly he was no longer coming at all. There'd been no sound of a shot, but he could have been taken hostage or ambushed and sandbagged.

Faust risked another glance. On the ballroom's far side, the gardener disdained cover and stalked him openly, rifle to his shoulder. Rather than approach head-on, though, he angled his steps toward the windows, circling the ballroom's outer edges. If Faust did nothing, they'd take him between them. Already the gardener controlled the far end of the sitting area.

An infantry attack it would have to be.

The glow of moonlight at the opposite ends of the ballroom faded, the random clouds working in his favor. He'd get no better opportunity. Faust ducked between desks, diving for the cover of the ones ahead. He flinched as both weapons fired.

89

night
Margeaux Hall

She couldn't leave Faust again.

Not after that kiss. Not after that exquisite moment that roiled her insides, sizzled all the nerves in her body, and clarified their situation in her soul. She'd found Stoner's match. She wanted that man, and after the war she intended to have him. And if Eduard Best and Peter Owen thought otherwise, she'd have to convince them of her claim's priority.

How was the problem.

Jennifer peered around the doorjamb and into the ballroom. The moon had vanished behind a small bank of clouds, hiding her in shadows, but in the glass vestibule she felt naked. If anything did happen to Faust—God forbid—she'd have no choice but to sneak upstairs to hide, and who knew what was going on up there.

The shadows across the ballroom's floor shifted. Best eased from Stoner's office doorway, following Peter's example and stalking Faust openly. After two steps he froze, then aimed Stoner's Colt revolver toward the desks and fired once. Beyond the sitting area, Peter also fired. The bullets whanged as they scored metal.

Her fingers wrapped about the doorjamb and tightened. Perhaps she should sneak upstairs for Carmichael's Lee Enfield. Whatever was going on upstairs couldn't possibly be worse than helplessly watching this.

Peter giggled, a high screechy old-man sound that shivered up her spine. He broke open the rifle, inserted another round, and snapped the bolt home. His stare never left the desks as he settled the rifle stock against his shoulder and resumed stalking her chosen target.

Or she could sneak out the glass door, run back to Woodrow for the other shotgun, or down to the main gate for Reynolds' Lee Enfield, or find the other squad members and bring help. But by the time she returned, it could be too late.

No, she couldn't leave him again.

But she had to do something.

Best took another cautious step away from Stoner's office. The Colt revolver swung along the line of desks, swung back.

She eased further around the doorjamb. Bruckmann lay in a pool of blood. The light from Stoner's desk lamp didn't reach his motionless form. The Webley revolver strapped to his hip formed a visible bump. One quick dash, and she could grab it and join Faust behind the desks.

One quick dash. Right in front of Best.

She hauled in a deep breath. But before she could take the first step, Best glanced over. His eyes seemed to see in the dark, cutting through the shadows and staring right at her. No—the shadows had gone. Moonlight poured through the glass walls and silhouetted her against the doorjamb.

Best swung the revolver toward her. She whipped back around the doorjamb as the Colt fired, a single sharp crack, followed within a second by the solid blast of the shotgun. Her heart leapt—Faust still lived, hidden in the tangle of desks.

But the shotgun's blast was followed by the higher report of Peter's rifle, and she could no longer be certain of that fact.

90

night
Margeaux Hall

Aggravating, ferocious, headstrong—Faust recoiled behind the desk, shotgun braced against his hip. The expected rifle bullet screamed through metal, not close. The sharp tang of cordite choked his lungs, sharper than cigarette smoke and not nearly as satisfying. Damp heat scorched his face. He squirmed between the desks, ignoring the slicing pain in his arm, and peered through the crouching shadows of furniture legs and rolling chairs. Moonlight flooded the vestibule but the doorway was again empty. No dark pool stained the brick floor, and no huddled, motionless form beyond Bruckmann's stopped his pulse. She'd taken cover and hopefully wouldn't try such a crazy stunt again. But now they knew she hid there. If Faust went down, she'd be next.

Cold fear drenched his clenched stomach and he shivered through the sweat. He couldn't let that happen.

Without looking down, Faust broke open the shotgun, inserted another shell, and eased it closed. He rolled to his left side, squirmed to his knees, and peered between desks toward the far end of the ballroom. Best, in Stoner's office, had proved himself a lousy shot. Besides, if he'd fired twice at Tanyon, once at Bruckmann, once at Faust, and once at Jennifer, the six-shot revolver had just about used all its ammunition and Best wouldn't likely carry spare Colt rounds rolling about his empty prisoner's pockets.

But that damned gardener was another matter. Faust

peered over the desk and scanned the distant edges of the ballroom. There—almost at the windows, in one of the darkest corners behind the farthest sofa, was the steady purposeful motion of a stalking hunter. The two gunmen had to be working together. They seemed intent on taking him in a crossfire, so perhaps he could use their strategy against them. If he pressed Best to waste his last round and then charged across the ballroom, he could use the closest sofa as cover and take down the gardener, then deal with Best at his leisure. He gathered his feet beneath him, easing back along the line of desks toward Stoner's office. As soon as the moonbeams darkened again, he'd charge.

The distant stalking motion ceased. A moment later, the gardener fired, the rifle's muzzle flash momentarily lighting the corner and flaring across the gleeful lined face. Faust ducked behind the desk. But it wasn't aimed at him, nor at where he'd been, more toward Bruckmann's huddled form but higher and closer to the vestibule. Faust's heart lurched into his throat. Surely she wouldn't—not again—

He couldn't take the chance. He couldn't leave her unguarded until Best fired that last shot. He'd have to draw it to himself. Faust rose to his knees behind the desk, tucking the shotgun into his right shoulder and aligning the barrel at where he'd last seen that stalking hunter. He couldn't really injure the gardener from this distance, but he could teach the old man some respect before dealing with Best. He'd fired the first shot from the hip, which explained why he hadn't hit anything. Now he needed accuracy and damn it, this was going to hurt.

Faust gritted his teeth and pulled the trigger.

The shotgun's solid blast echoed in the ballroom, flooding the desk area with choking gunpowder, and the recoil kicked his injured shoulder like a mule. A shockwave of agony flashed along his arm. His elbow convulsed down against his side, dragging the stock lower and jerking the barrel toward the ceiling. White fireworks exploded behind his eyes. In the corner, movement flashed, not cautiously, and the gardener ducked behind the farthest sofa.

Something else moved near Stoner's office doorway. Faust forced his eyes to focus despite the pain, forced his hands to break open the shotgun and insert another shell. Best stood framed against the desk lamp's light, the revolver's barrel panning the ballroom. For a second Faust froze, his breath catching. Even knowing Best was a lousy shot didn't make this easy. Maybe it would be safest to stand inside the shadow Best aimed at—but then Best and the revolver swung toward the vestibule.

Yep, she had. The ballroom suddenly chilled, tingling shivers whispering across his overheated face. Faust snapped the shotgun closed with the loudest clack he could manage. Best glanced over, glanced back, and aimed at the vestibule.

Pig. Faust scrambled to his feet and slammed his boot into the closest office chair. It spun from behind the desk, smashed into the next desk over, and clattered away, whirling in a slowing circle. His descending heel caught on the scatter rug. He stumbled back, sat hard on another desk, and let himself slide down to the floor. Papers scattered, whispered, floated down, and something hard thunked down beside him.

Best jerked back around, aimed at the moving chair, and fired. Faust raised the shotgun, but before he drew a bead, Best ducked back into Stoner's office, followed seconds later by a metallic click and then another, as if he'd tried to fire twice more and the barrel snapped home on nothing. A heartening sound. Faust scrambled up and gathered himself for the sprint.

Motion to his left whipped his head around before he'd stepped beyond the first desk. A graceful soundless form, silhouetted by the glow behind her, dashed through the moonbeams toward Bruckmann's motionless huddle. That would be too inviting a target for the gardener to resist. Faust braced the shotgun and fired again toward the far corner, just as the muzzle flash leapt from behind the sofa. Jennifer jumped back and paused in full view, her head swiveling from the corner to Bruckmann, then swiftly to the desks. Her glance crossed his without meshing, as if she didn't see him, instead tracking the chair as it slowed to a stop.

Best stepped around the doorjamb, aiming the Colt revolver at Jennifer. If he'd found ammunition—and in the guardroom Tanyon had flipped open the cylinder of a Webley revolver, slid in a pre-loaded moon clip of six rounds, and closed and locked the cylinder in place. The entire operation had taken mere seconds and Faust had only heard two clicks, just like the ones he'd heard a moment ago from Stoner's office.

Time slipped out of joint, like an arm from a shoulder socket, like a ball bearing from a Panzer track. Jennifer froze. In the wash of light from the desk lamp, Best's finger curved in a hard edge around the revolver's trigger. Cold glints flashed from his pitiless eye. Metal clicked from the far corner; the gardener had reloaded and the opportunity was gone. The hell with the moonlight.

"Jennifer, run!" Faust scrambled between desks and

charged, not the far corner, but Best. His boots thumped on the hardwood floor.

Her head and Best's jerked around. She gasped, then whirled and ran, vanishing into the vestibule. Best ducked back into Stoner's office, his arm swinging the revolver around the doorjamb. Any moment now the gardener would fire. Shy of the desk lamp's pool, Faust twisted, let his thigh slam into the last desk as a brake, and wrenched himself down behind it. He crouched, slipped sideways to the next desk along, vacating the spot where he'd last been seen. The rifle cracked, followed by the revolver's sharper report. Both shots whanged into the desk Faust had just left.

In the sudden silence, the gardener's shrill giggle seemed obscene.

Faust panted as if he'd run a mile. His shaking fingers reloaded the shotgun. That had been too close. He had to find a way to end this or they'd both die—him when he made a mistake or the enemy gunmen trapped him, Jennifer a minute later.

Cautiously he scanned the ballroom's far end. The gardener ran in a crouching rush, back toward the still-open door to the residential wing. Something had changed his plans. Faust cast about the shadows for clues and froze.

The pool of moonlight at the foot of the eastern stairwell rippled. It could be some accomplice of Best's—but the gardener's sudden retreat implied otherwise. Faust's pulse accelerated. Near the residential wing's doorway, the rushing gardener halted and lifted the rifle.

"Pym, take cover!" Faust changed desks again. If he could keep Best firing at the wrong one, they could waste this moon clip, too. "It's the damned gardener. Kill him if you can!"

The moonlit pool warped then stilled as boots thudded from the stairs to the floor. The gardener fired toward the stairwell, gunpowder smoke silhouetted in the muzzle flash. Cordite rolled over the desks. Faust shivered beneath his sweat. Then the gardener ducked through the residential wing's door, leaving it open behind him.

"Pym?" Faust said.

"I'm all right." The corporal called from behind the wall hiding the stairwell, at a right angle to the residential wing's doorway. From there, he wouldn't have a good line at the gardener, but the gardener wouldn't get a good shot at him, either. "Major?"

"Yeah, I'm okay." If he could get his breathing under control, he'd be even better.

"Major Faust?" That was Best's voice, calling from

Stoner's office. He spoke in German and his voice wavered. "This is a mistake. It's all a mistake. I can't control that crazy Welshman. He's a nationalist, he's mad, you see he's mad."

Yeah, right, just as Norris hadn't hurt anyone. "You tried to shoot me." Without thinking, Faust spoke in German, too.

"I thought you were trying to shoot me." The words tumbled out rapidly, as if a verbal dam had burst. "But we must leave now. Otherwise the plane will be gone before we reach the landing spot."

Faust quit breathing. He'd assumed Best had lied about the plane. If he hadn't, if there really was a means of getting home, best yet if Jennifer had the sense to slip upstairs and hide—

Could he trust Best? For crying out cats, Stoner had driven him crazy with that routine and he wasn't climbing back aboard the carousel. He had to make a decision and stick with it.

"Where's the landing spot?"

Best didn't hesitate. "I'll show you."

So much for trust. And hadn't he been through that routine with Erhard? *Come for a ride with papa—*

But if there existed the slightest chance of getting back home without Jennifer being killed—

"We must leave now or it will be too late."

Something about Best's tone of voice, an intense desperation hovering short of panic, sounded utterly believable. Best wanted out of here as much as Faust did. Surely a man smart enough to be a university professor wasn't stupid enough to think he could just walk through the gate and escape. Surely he knew if he didn't have a plane coming to fetch him, he faced recapture and retribution within hours.

Maybe Best hadn't lied about the plane.

Hope surged through Faust, rushing from his heart to his fingertips. He eased back on his heels and risked a swift glance about the ballroom. Not a moonbeam rippled. Jennifer, he knew, didn't understand German; he didn't know about Pym. But he knew the steady lance corporal well enough to know he wouldn't step aside and let Faust run away. To escape, he'd have to either kill Pym or give him the slip. Faust grimaced. If he shot Pym and then learned Best had lied—it would be Faust's head on the chopping block, not Best's—

—and maybe that was the plan.

Hell. He wasn't going to shoot Pym, any more than he'd shoot Jennifer, and that was flat. But if he could get away—

Making a final decision would be so much simpler if he knew he could trust Best. Or not.

"Major Faust?" Best's voice quivered. "We must hurry. Don't you want to go home?"

More than anything. But he hadn't yet found an answer to Stoner's accusation. He didn't know if *Oberst* von Maacht had or hadn't set the Gestapo to investigate him. And he didn't know if the *Waffen SS* had figured out his role in Clarke's raid.

Hell, hell, hell. Around the ballroom, the moonlight glistened, an unbroken stream, across the brick floor in the vestibule where Jennifer hid. In the stillness, he almost imagined he heard her speaking, a low voice without words at the edge of his soul. Or was it his conscience? He'd promised not to attempt escape before dawn. But when offered a chance like this—

He'd held his position for too long. Faust eased across the open stretch of floor and ducked behind the last desk in the line, the one farthest from Stoner's office. He had to think.

And then the floor-to-ceiling window behind him shattered. His thinking time was over.

91

night
Margeaux Hall

She'd been a fool.

Harriet, now, she'd have known what to do immediately. But then Harriet had always looked to the future, to aviation and movies, not to the poetic past. She'd not have hesitated to command modern technology to solve a problem.

Faust and Best shouted at each other in the embattled ballroom. Jennifer ignored the harsh German syllables she didn't understand. Crouching behind the vestibule's reception desk, out of sight from the combat zone, she plugged a jack into the switchboard, lifted the receiver, and waited, her pulse thudding in her ears. Over the instrument, the burring ring seemed excruciatingly loud, but no answering ring came from the ballroom nor from upstairs. So even if she hadn't gotten the proper line, at least she hadn't gotten a perfectly wrong one, warning Best and old Peter of her plan. At worst she'd awaken Debbie Burbank at the mercantile and the entire village would hear of it.

The voice that answered, though, was masculine and hesitant. "Wainwright residence."

She'd done it properly. A silly flush of delight surged through her, followed by a stronger pulse of hope. "Mr. Wainwright—"

She got no further.

"Miss Stoner, for pity's sake, what's going on?" Steven Wainwright's voice rose an octave. "I can hear shooting—"

Best's voice shouted from the ballroom, quick breathless words in German, and after a moment Faust answered more slowly. Jennifer closed her other ear with a fingertip.

"Mr. Wainwright, please listen. I can't speak loudly."

His verbal flow paused. "I can't hear you."

Oh, if only there were someone else. But no one was closer than the gate and no telephone there, and she had no idea of the situation upstairs, if anyone was even there to pick up. Anyone alive. The advertising agency clerk with the wallflower personality, who'd barely nicked a target during rifle practice, represented her only hope. Granted, if she could get him close enough, she could grab his Browning and use it herself.

"It's Peter Owen. He's a traitor." She thought fast. It would take too long to tell the truth. "He and Eduard Best are trying to murder Major Faust before he can tell us anything about the invasion—Mr. Wainwright, can you hear me?" Her nervous hand refused to stay still. She pulled open the desk drawer beside her and rummaged inside. There had to be something she could use as a weapon.

"Yes." His voice wavered. "Yes." A deep breath shuddered over the line. "What can I do?"

Logbooks in a hanging folder, a tin of cookies, one of Norris' comic books, a flashlight, another. Rubbish, just rubbish. "Grab your rifle, load it, and run to the residential wing. Peter's in the entryway, firing through the door. For pity's sake, stop him!"

"Yes." Another deep breath. Jennifer gripped the open drawer, the sharp edge digging into her palm. She had to be patient. But they were running out of time. "Yes, all right. I'm coming."

The line went dead. She crawled from beneath the desk, cradled the receiver, and scrambled to her feet, racing to the doorway and peering around the doorjamb. Best yelled more German words from Stoner's office. He sounded part desperate, part frightened, and utterly anxious. If she hadn't hated him so much, she might have pitied him.

Faust didn't answer, the silence stretching into long, painful seconds. From her vantage point, her back pressed against the brick wall beside the row of coat hooks, she tried to pierce the desk area's shadows. He hid there somewhere, fighting for their lives, injured and brave and magnificent, and perhaps she should after all run upstairs for Carmichael's Lee Enfield, or down to Reynolds at the gate—

At the end of the row of desks, the floor-to-ceiling window convulsed. Glass shattered. The garnet swags billowed, roiled, tumbled in a graceful slow-motion flutter of dark material, falling entwined with a thousand tinkling shards to the floor. Peter Owen stood framed in the sudden wash of moonlight, stepping back from the falling glass with the rifle rising to his shoulder. He giggled as the curtain rod clattered on the hardwood floor, through the last of the falling shards.

And she'd sent Wainwright to the residential wing.

No time to run upstairs now. Jennifer ran to the desk, yanked open the drawer, and snatched her chosen weapon. As clouds swept the moonlight from the vestibule, she raced out into the night.

92

night
Margeaux Hall

Faust dived for cover that didn't exist. The glass shards were still falling, raining down atop the spreading curtains and the hardwood floor. A rush of moonlight and fresh air swept into his dark corner of the ballroom, carrying the gardener's shrill giggle with it. The desks wouldn't stop a bullet, he'd seen the proof, but they were all he had, and he scrambled behind one as the rifle cracked. At this range—

The whanging hit ahead of him, the bullet zinging past just as he'd described for Norris long days ago. The gardener had lead the shot and overestimated Faust's speed; it wouldn't likely happen again. Faust tucked his feet beneath him. This time he *was* in the shadow drawing Best's fire, and nothing shielded his hiding spot from Stoner's office door.

Pym's voice shouted. Sudden footsteps pounded. Faust risked a glance. Pym galloped from the eastern stairwell through the swath of moonlight toward the sitting area, his rifle clutched across his chest, screaming a wordless, ancient battle cry.

It was the best possible distraction and flawlessly timed. Faust straightened, the shotgun braced against his hip. The gardener stood framed in the shattered window, traced with silver moonlight, the bolt open on his rifle. He glanced up, the grin sliding from his face, jaw slacking.

No time to aim. Faust fired. Just as he did, the gardener whipped aside. Not a clean shot, then, but hopefully he at least sprayed his target and gave the bastard something to consider.

Faust raced away from the window, back toward the vestibule and Stoner's office. Tense spots tingled between his shoulder blades and on his chest, as if targets were painted there, and pain sliced through his arm with each step. Best fired, the revolver's flat crack overshadowed by the harsh metallic whiplash of Pym's Lee Enfield, and another bullet zinged past. Surely the gardener had reloaded by now. Faust set his feet on the polished wood. His boots skidded, stopping his legs as his body's momentum carried him forward. He twisted in mid-air—damn it, this was going to really hurt—and landed on his right side, his arm beneath him.

Agony exploded, white-hot and ferocious. But he was ready and pushed through it, forcing his body into a tangled roll that carried him beyond the middle desk in the line. Behind him, the gardener fired again. Metal screamed overhead.

Again the desk only covered him from the gardener's view; his back remained vulnerable to the office doorway and with the broken window, the amount of moonlight in the ballroom had doubled. Best didn't have to expose more than his hand and the revolver to try the shot. Pym's position, somewhere in the chairs and sofas of the sitting area, wasn't much help. And not likely they'd get away with a distraction again.

Maybe he should have remained near the window and traded shots with the gardener. At close range, he might have survived the rifle while the shotgun would finish anyone. As it was, he might as well have stayed in the guardroom cell and awaited Stoner's firing squad.

93

night
Margeaux Hall

If she ran straight out, screaming for Wainwright, she wouldn't survive the stupidity. But that magnificent man had shown her how to hide in the nap of the hill, and once out the door, Jennifer scrambled down the slope toward the gate. Odd, the lawn seemed rougher than in daylight, more likely to trip her feet. But she didn't slow her pace; if she broke her neck tumbling downhill, well, when her lifeless body hit the gate, Reynolds might figure out something was wrong. Surely the shooting should have attracted somebody's attention.

Reynolds. The squad. Jennifer paused and glanced back. She'd crossed a third of the lawn. From this angle, the dim glow of Stoner's desk lamp lit the shattered window from within, silhouetting old Peter's wiry frame but not illuminating his face nor clothing. He was just an anonymous man firing a rifle through the window. The squad had to be watching. They simply couldn't understand what was happening.

Like good soldiers, they awaited orders. And the orders would have to be hers.

She crouched in the lawn, shielding the flashlight with her body and aiming it downhill, toward the distant black spikes of the gate. No one stood in sight. But Reynolds had to be there, standing his lonely sentry duty, and probably the others huddled in the wall's shelter, too. Her fingers fumbled in the darkness, feeling for the button. Behind her, old Peter's voice drifted on the moonlight, muttering his incomprehensible

Welsh. Finally she found the button, switched it on, paused, then switched it off.

She waited long seconds. But nothing moved in the moonlight.

Bloody hell. Now was not the time to learn that those kids, despite their training and Lee Enfields, were truly cowards. She flipped on the flashlight again, fingers trembling on the button. More firing erupted from the ballroom, startlingly loud on the night air. She jumped, sending the cone of light scrambling across the lawn toward the residential wing, before she steadied its aim toward the gate. Off. On. Off.

Something moved at the foot of the hill. A distant silhouette separated itself from the black line of the mortared stone wall, another, a third, all taking hesitant steps toward her. She had to hurry them. She repeated the signal, faster and faster, and her heart leapt as they sped up the slope toward her. Now she had a real weapon to her hand.

Across the lawn near the main entry, another man hesitated, black and featureless in the night. He cradled another rifle across his chest. It could only be Wainwright. She flashed the light in his direction, on, off, on, off. He hesitated for another long moment, then galloped toward her, the rifle swinging like a baton.

She glanced back toward the Hall. Her breath caught. Old Peter eased away from the window's glow, into the camouflaging shadows. He peered about the lawn, examining the sloping hillside behind him. His sweeping glance touched on the three soldiers scrambling up the slope, still distant and not yet a threat; he looked past her without a pause, as if he didn't see her, and his head didn't turn toward the residential wing, where Wainwright was comfortingly closer. She held her breath as Peter hung on his heel. Then another round of gunfire erupted within the Hall, the deep heady boom of the Lee Enfield followed by the sharp crack of the Colt revolver, and Peter swung back to the window. He stepped closer and raised the rifle to his shoulder.

Her heart stopped.

Jennifer flipped on the flash and spotlighted the grizzled head from behind.

94

night
Margeaux Hall

He'd found his last possible cover and it wouldn't hold for long. Faust slithered across the hardwood floor into the kneehole of the desk closest to Stoner's office, tucking his legs in like a pretzel. His pulse pounded, his arm and head pounded harder, and his breathing rasped as if he'd never draw oxygen again. The smothering, choking cloud of cordite caught in his throat. Sweat soaked him beneath his uniform, as if he'd been dipped in a bath. It was crazy, surviving Erhard's practical joke and Stoner's ruthless assault, only to die at the hands of a scheming professor and a gardener. But he had nothing left to hide in but the shadows.

It was only a matter of time. Faust gritted his teeth. He had no intention of dying alone. One of those two was going with him. He'd at least give Pym an even chance. The lance corporal had proven his mettle, trading fire with Best and keeping him bottled up in Stoner's office. He could be trusted to finish the job. And while Faust loathed Best with all his heart, it was that damned gardener he wanted.

Faust peered over his shoulder. Behind the shattered window, the gardener had stepped back. Although the moonlight had dimmed, making details indiscernible, he seemed to be looking down the hillside toward the gate. But if Reynolds and the rest of the squad hadn't interfered by now, they'd not likely suddenly find courage. With Stoner, Bruckmann, and Tanyon down, and with Pym cut off, they drifted without a leader. No, he was alone.

At least Jennifer had kept her head down and hadn't died first. Perhaps she'd learned caution and snuck away, through the postern gate and out of this madness. If so, she might yet survive.

From the sitting area, Pym's Lee Enfield thundered, followed a second later by the sharper crack of the revolver. Somewhere in the darkness around Faust, a bullet scored metal, not close. The gardener stepped back to the window. The dim glow of the desk lamp flashed from his bared teeth. He raised the rifle to his shoulder.

It was time. Faust's breathing steadied. Maybe dying wouldn't be so bad. He wasn't certain he believed in Brother Harmonious' heaven, and it was too late to chant a Hail Mary. But there had to be some payoff for all the hours he'd spent on his knees as a child. He gathered his feet beneath him, ready for his final charge.

Before he could break cover, a circle of light haloed the gardener's head from behind. It looked like a spotlight, bathing an actor on a darkened stage. The gardener whipped around. His gaze swept the slope and halted, facing into the little cone of light—a flashlight? For pity's sake—and then he aligned the rifle back along the beam.

Faust's adrenaline surged. The ballroom seemed to fade about him and time again slowed to a trickle. A flashlight. There could be only one person holding the damned thing. And she was about to pay the price for her fearlessness.

He scrambled from beneath the desk. His boot clunked against a nearby chair and it spun away. He stumbled, staggered, fell to his knees with a crash, lost his balance and floundered on his left side as panic gripped him. The revolver cracked, cracked again, bullets whining nearby, and Pym's Lee Enfield boomed.

More rifles fired outside, a harsh report like a second Lee Enfield followed a moment later by another, closer one. The gardener ducked. Then he ran, sudden pounding footsteps diminishing in the night. Outside, the deep-throated rifles boomed again. The cone of light vanished.

So much for his satisfying vengeance. Rage flared through Faust, white-hot then suddenly cold and still. The ballroom seemed to tumble around him again, as if realigning reality. Then the topsy-turvy world righted itself and he understood his mistake. He didn't need the gardener. The score he needed to settle was older and uglier.

Faust rolled from beneath the desk. He jumped to his feet, in plain view, tucked the shotgun into his shoulder, and aligned the sights.

Best curved about the doorjamb, starting to aim the revolver toward the sitting area. He froze. In the desk lamp's glow, the rippling of his throat and the widening of his eyes seemed highlighted, clear and unmistakable.

Outside, the rifles fell silent. A voice, young and frightened, started speaking, quickly hushed by a woman's firm command. The silence stretched, painfully thin, as Faust stared down the shotgun's steady barrel into the eyes of his target. Then in the distance, a cricket sang, its inhuman, mechanical voice trilling in the moonlight and drilling into Faust's soul. Suddenly he was frightened, too. He'd done everything else wrong, screwed up everything else in his life. If that plane actually existed—

Best's chin lifted, as if he sensed Faust's dilemma. "You do not wish to go home?"

—if it wasn't a figment of Best's imagination—

"We must hurry or it will leave without us."

—or an outright lie—

"Put down the revolver." His voice sounded harsh, rasping from a throat too dry to speak, as inhuman as the cricket.

Best's stare solidified, like ice. "When you lower the shotgun."

Understanding flared, haloed as if by a symbolic flashlight. There it was, the answer to Clarke's question: *Why does Germany need two armies?*

But Clarke hadn't asked that question any more precisely than his first one. Germany didn't need two armies. The Nazis needed their own army, to maintain their standoff against the *Wehrmacht*. Any lowering of weapons on either side gave away the advantage.

Only trouble was, nobody had warned the German Army they were in a standoff. They were being blindsided.

Which meant he couldn't trust the Nazis.

Which meant he couldn't trust Best.

Which his soul had already known, which was why he'd grabbed Jennifer's shotgun to protect the English against another German whom he should have trusted.

As Wyatt said, *The friendly foe, with his double face, Say he is gentle and courteous.*

Along the aligned sights of the shotgun, Best swallowed again. "There will be room for both of us."

Faust pulled the trigger.

95

Faust paused in the infirmary doorway. Dr. Harris stood at the counter, washing his hands. The runoff water swirled pink into the white ceramic basin, and red stains smeared to rust across the front of his smock. His grey suit seemed rumpled, as if he'd slept in it, and the bags beneath his bloodshot eyes would have held all the supplies in the infirmary. He glanced over his shoulder.

"Through there." Dr. Harris nodded toward the inner door. He paused and dropped his voice to a murmur. "I know you must speak with him. But try to remember what you did for him yesterday, and please be brief."

So much had happened since Stoner's collapse, it felt like forever. "I'll try."

The back ward contained six beds aligned beneath open casement windows. Two of the beds were rumpled but empty, Tanyon and Glover gone in the first ambulance. The linens of one bed were smeared with shades of rust, bold finger-painting on an untidy canvas. On the other bed, the stains were on the pillow. Closest to the door, Carmichael lay still, a pristine bandage wrapped about his head. His eyes didn't quite focus, but he smiled as Faust touched his shin in passing.

In the last bed, Stoner was propped up on pillows, several typed sheets of paper arranged in ordered rows on the sheet draped over his knees. Grave and gentle, he watched Faust approach with his usual clarity, and he gestured to the wooden chair beside the bed with a steady hand weak.

"I can't believe Dr. Harris is letting you work." Faust eased into the chair; moving fast hurt much worse than moving slowly.

Stoner's eyebrows quirked. "I didn't ask permission." His voice sounded thin, like that of an old and tired man, but didn't quaver. When he gripped and gently shook Faust's forearm, strength remained within his gnarled fingers. "My dear Major Faust, thank you so much for protecting my grand-daughter."

Not *Herr Major.* Faust couldn't prevent a wince. His career was over. The German Army, rightly or wrongly, would never trust him again. And he couldn't return to Germany until the Nazis were defeated and removed from power; once they realized their star triple agent had quit reporting, they'd want to know why.

The last thing he'd wanted to do last night was touch Best's corpse. The shotgun pattern had sprayed his chest, removing chunks of it, and what remained reminded Faust nauseatingly of the murdered girls' photos. But it had been his execution and his responsibility, and he'd forced himself to start the search with the shredded pockets on the shredded chest.

In one front pants pocket, he'd found a keyring; upstairs in Best's quarters, they'd found a book of Schiller's poems with a hollow spot carved into its pages. When Pym told him Best only read German writers, the same books over and over, it made sense. The old gardener, Peter Owen, had found Bruckmann's keys the night of Faust's last escape, made copies, and smuggled them to Best in the book, proving they'd been communicating in that manner for some time. Best had called Owen a nationalist, a Welshman who wanted to see Wales separated from the English union and independent, like Eire. He'd made a deal with the devil to fight for it. Faust wasn't willing to do the same.

He shifted on the hard wooden chair. "Mr. Stoner, don't take this the wrong way—"

Stoner's eyebrows curved into twin question marks.

"—but next time there's trouble, I'm going to stand behind that woman, not in front of her. She's ferocious."

Stoner smiled. "She'll do." He shifted on the pillows, and his gaze dropped to the papers in his lap. "I understand I also owe you gratitude for saving my own life. You know, I thought I'd prepared myself for the inevitable. I found, when the time came, I wasn't at all ready to die." He squeezed Faust's forearm then let go. "Thank you."

There was only one thing he could say, of course. "I'm glad I could help."

The casement windows gave a clear view through the apple trees to Woodrow. Boards had been nailed across Jennifer's shattered bedroom window, but Major Kettering had promised to repair it properly.

"I'd manufactured so many layers of deceit to keep you guessing." Stoner glanced up. The layers were gone, swept away like their desktop battlefield, and the old man's eyes softened to a gentle summer-sky blue. "Jennifer was right, you know. I nearly destroyed myself while you maintained your humanity to the end."

The honesty in their mutual gaze, Faust knew, would never be breached again. "She usually is."

But not when it had counted the most. Beside the radio table in the guardroom, near the small pool of Carmichael's drying blood, they'd found a half-typed sheet of paper, curled as if it had been left rolled in the platen for hours—the unfinished report Jennifer had abandoned during Stoner's heart attack. Enough had been completed for Best to understand Faust's role at the Aa Canal, even if he hadn't been able to decipher Stoner's spiky handwritten notes by the typewriter. The settings on the radio hinted Best had transmitted the report to Germany.

She'd cried, guilty tears streaking her horrified face. But Faust had shrugged. He'd made his decision when he pulled the trigger.

The old man's smile flashed, quick, appreciative, and pained. "The signal flimsy, of course, was a forgery, and I congratulate you on your perspicacity." He sighed. "It's rather humiliating. The *coup de grace* was delivered by our carelessness and enemy action, and all our cleverness counts for naught."

"Actually, your cleverness saved my life."

Stoner froze. "I don't understand."

"You and Clarke taught me to distrust the Nazis, more than I already did, I mean, which is why I didn't go with Best. For a while there, I was sorely tempted." A disquieting thought. Best had already transmitted the report when he'd tried to convince Faust to return to Germany. If Faust had gone, it would have been to face a savage retribution from the Nazis, and the delivery of such a traitor would have cemented Best's position even though he'd abandoned his mission in England. Faust shook the curled, grimy, bloodstained paper from among the clean ones on Stoner's lap. The typewriter ribbon had seen hard use, but the letters were crisp enough to read. "So the gratitude isn't all one-sided."

"I see." Stoner sagged against the pillows as if tired. But when Faust stirred, the old man again gripped his forearm, holding him still. "However, it's not sufficient to counteract the harm we've done to you. Perhaps we should turn back the clock."

Faust folded the report and tucked it into his breast pocket. It would remind him of what he'd escaped, and of her. "It's my turn to not understand, Mr. Stoner."

"Well, you know, in government offices, nothing is official until a report is filed."

A tone insinuating—no, downright sly colored Stoner's voice, as if he intended to not file that report. If he didn't, then his lousy boss wouldn't know what had happened at Margeaux Hall. Stoner offered him a shield. Although it wouldn't be enough to allow Faust to retire into a prisoner of war camp and wait out the war with honor, it would at least protect him from the necessity of bartering military secrets for his life. He wouldn't have to make a deal with the English government, nor any other devil. Not even the Nazis.

For a hungry moment his hope surged. Treason tasted ugly, he'd found, and not likely it would improve. But only for a moment. "I appreciate this more than I can say. But I'm sticking with my decision. I want to defeat the Nazis. Germany needs a government the rest of the world can trust."

He drew a shuddering breath. Stoner's eyes were wary, his hope balanced. Not a sound came from Carmichael's bed, nor from the outer office where Dr. Harris supposedly worked.

"I don't believe there's going to be an invasion, at least not with the plan I typed."

There. He'd said it. He was officially a traitor. But unlike old Peter Owen, who'd made a deal with Best to support an evil he didn't understand, Faust understood the evil and knew he couldn't support it.

Still, it tasted foul. Stoner's expression, rather than lighting with glee, faded to a sad compassion that hurt almost as badly as Faust's arm.

"Will you tell Lieutenant Bruckmann what you know?" The old man's voice was indescribably gentle, as if he spoke to a pain-wracked child.

His last chance to back out. Faust didn't allow himself to consider it. "Yes."

Stoner's hand tightened on his forearm. "Thank you, Major Faust."

The conversation had lasted long enough. Stoner's color, not robust when he'd entered, had faded to grey. Faust returned the pressure and headed for the door. In the farthest bed, Carmichael's eyes were squeezed shut, tears leaking from the corners and a wide, silly grin on his face. Faust touched the kid's shin again as he left.

Jennifer slipped through the doorway, so close her scent reached him through the strong infirmary cleanser. Her coral lips barely curved into a smile and a flush of purest rose darkened her alabaster cheeks. Her glance, mysterious and gorgeous, quicker than a bullet, aimed at his center of mass and struck deep in his heart. Perhaps his nascent career was over. His life wasn't. Instead of yearning for her from Germany, fighting a war he hated and which could only encourage her to hate him, now he could work to undermine her resistance from within.

He hadn't even known she'd entered the infirmary. He needed to bell that kitty; with her silent step, it was too easy for a man to lose track of her.

She paused, blocking the door and forcing him to pause, too. Before he could back away to give her room, as a gentleman should, she touched his uniformed chest, freezing him in place.

"Major Faust."

For a moment it stung; he'd offended her somehow. Then she glanced sideways, toward Dr. Harris, leaning against the counter with his arms crossed. Their cautious intimacy, it seemed, was not for general conversation.

"Miss Stoner."

Her quick smile lit with gratitude. Then she rolled her lips together and her glorious eyes turned sad. If she magically became any more beautiful, Helen of Troy would have to be knocked off her pedestal to make room.

"Can you ever forgive me?"

Nuts to that. But that didn't seem the right thing to say. Instead, he glanced down. Her palm—and he knew its softness—rested, ironically enough, atop the red, white, and black ribbon of the Iron Cross that no longer carried any meaning.

He slipped his hand beneath hers and brought her fingers to his lips. Her light floral scent flooded through him like a gift. He kissed the air atop the back of her hand, just his breath stirring the tiny hairs there. She shivered, her breath catching, and her pupils dilated.

"Never," he assured her.

She froze, jaw slackening. But he couldn't control his grin and she jerked her hand free. The roses spread across her face, Wyatt's and Surrey's banner of love. His breath caught, too.

From his bed, Stoner rumbled.

She brushed past Faust before he could move and sashayed past the line of cots. But beyond her, Stoner's watchful expression was jaundiced. Faust turned and left the ward.

Dr. Harris hadn't moved. His glance, clinical and cold, swept over Faust and pinned him to the door. "By God, you look as if I don't know how to care for a patient at all."

Great. Just great. She didn't need to hear this. Faust closed the door and leaned against it.

"You've ripped those bloody stitches again, haven't you? Major Stoner has a heart attack, Sergeant Tanyon takes two in the torso, Glover and Carmichael get their heads cracked, Lieutenant Bruckmann's temple sliced open—"

Faust shuddered, his silly grin vanishing. The lieutenant's head wound had bled more than the two rifle bullets that took down old Peter Owen. But Bruckmann's wound was shallow, and even now he stalked the ballroom, a bandage wrapped about his head, swearing fluently as he directed Kettering's engineers in the repairs to Margeaux Hall.

Inexperienced lieutenants were easy to kill. Bruckmann had been lucky. But even at close range, Best had been a lousy shot.

"—well—" Dr. Harris paused. And sighed. "I'll have no choice but to stitch you back up, I suppose." The thought dampened any pity he'd started to feel. "And this time, it's not going to be your arm I'll put in a sling—"

"What would you have done?" Faust asked.

"—they've put you back in the third-floor bedroom, right? I'll send Cavanaugh along as soon as he can be spared and I warn you, I'll be right behind him—"

"That's not an answer."

"How the devil would I know?" Dr. Harris threw out his hands. "How could anyone know, until the situation was upon him?" He dug into the pocket of his smock, strode to Faust, and held out his hand. "Before he left in the ambulance, Sergeant Tanyon asked me to give this to you."

It was a comb. His fist closed about it. The tines bit into his palm.

Seemed he'd made more English friends than he'd realized. Erhard wouldn't have understood that, either. "Yeah, I'm back upstairs. I'll wait there."

In the sunset room at the corridor's end, Bruckmann and Kettering stood together. The bandage around the lieutenant's head sported rusty stains and it tilted over one eye, like something from a pirate ship's crew. Kettering pointed toward the lower floor, his smile gleaming in the morning sunshine but his words too low to carry. His uniform and mustache were as dapper as ever. Beyond them, scaffolding soared along the vestibule's glass walls. Two soldiers and Wainwright stood at the top, bolting pine panels to the girders. Margeaux Hall would finally honor the blackout regulations.

Let them work; it was his turn to rest. Faust turned the other way, toward the eastern stairwell. But something felt wrong. For a moment he didn't understand it. Then he realized—for the first time that week, he walked unguarded.

He missed the clumping boots behind him.

And her silent step at his side.

-30-

About the Author

Hi, I'm Gunnar Grey. I write books. I'm a historian, political junkie, target shooter, and retired adventurer and equestrian. I read avidly and post reviews or at least ratings for most of the books I read. Occasionally my poor husband surfaces from beneath a pile of paperbacks, gasping for air... but I shouldn't bore you with personal issues.

In addition, I format ebooks, including MS Word docs for Smashwords. If you need an ebook formatted or want to meet my references, check out my blog, Mysteries and Histories.

I live in Humble, Texas, just north of Houston, with four parakeets, the aforementioned husband (who's even more entertaining than the birds), an orange betta fish with no manners, a fig tree, the lawn from the bad place, three armloads of potted plants, and a coffee maker that's likely the most important item we own.

If you enjoyed this book...

Trophies

A psychological mystery from the acclaimed author of Deal with the Devil

TROPHIES
J. GUNNAR GREY

Chapter One

current time

Three neat entry wounds drilled through the silk of Aunt Edith's blouse, stiffened and blackened by crusted blood. The underlying color was unrecognizable. I only knew it was supposed to be green because she wore it during our unfriendly dinner the previous evening and I remembered. Lying on the sidewalk with her legs crumpled beneath her, she seemed even tinier than normal, like a toy that had been roughly played with and then pitched aside.

I dropped to my knees beside her. Her eyes were wide, staring at the dawn breaking beyond the storefronts, and her mouth gaped. She was such a private person, so contained, elegant, brilliant as gold beside the base metals of the rest of us. Death seemed an exposure, a stripping of her secrets. A humiliation.

I reached out to stroke the drifting black and silver tendrils of her hair into place. But a hand snatched my wrist and twisted it aside. I jerked my head up—

—the picture window of the Carr Gallery, just overhead, was splattered with something dark. More of it sprayed the polished maple door, the brass railing and handle and mail slot. A small hole in the door, at waist level, had been marked with chalk—

—more dark stains, lit obliquely by the dawn light, trickled down the red brick, dripped from one concrete step to the next, painted the sidewalk. I suddenly realized I could smell it—

—I ignored the background *crump* of artillery fire and panned the rifle's scope along the enemy emplacement, atop the ridge overlooking our sandbagged trench. Beneath the camouflage netting and wilting tree branches I made out one big field gun with its muzzle recoiling, another, a third—

—the enemy spotter stood contemptuously in full view, binoculars to his eyes, gazing off to my left but sweeping this way. The rangefinder showed the distance at eight hundred meters. I set the elevation turret and aligned the sight's upper chevron on his center of mass, drifting aside by one hash mark to compensate for the gentle flow of air across my right cheek. Binocular lenses flashed sunsparks. His lips moved as I took up the initial pressure on the trigger—

—flashback with visual, auditory, tactile, and olfactory hallucinations. Hadn't happened in months. It was impossible to prevent it, stop it, tone it down, or predict its arrival. But we were intimate enemies, my flashback and I, and I knew its script. I clenched every muscle I possessed, including my eyes, and froze in place, ignoring it all. It's how I'd taught myself to respond when the city street morphed into a battlefield without warning, and so far it had prevented anyone from locking me up. I was even able to fool most acquaintances into thinking I was still sane.

But nothing blocked the sights, sounds, or other manifestations. Machine gun fire hammered into the nonexistent sandbags, thuds echoing in my bones, and the dust and acrid gunpowder caught at the back of my throat. Someone screamed, a long shrill sound that climbed higher in pitch and volume, scraping across my nerves. The enemy guns chattered again and a fire of agony spurted across my back. Wavery, sick-feeling blackness rushed in behind the pain. I refused to wobble. I ignored the war zone and the adrenaline tearing me apart, and waited for the screaming in my damaged memory to stop. For several more seconds it dragged on, a horrible rising shriek, but finally it cut out in its usual abrupt manner, as if someone hit a neurological mute button.

The flashback lost. It couldn't control my actions nor force me to betray my internal damage to the civilians. I wanted to collapse with relief. I refused to do that, too.

Ambient city noises resumed. There were lots of voices around, both live ones and the scratchy overlay of radio transmissions, and in the distance someone called my name. Even with my eyes squeezed tight, popping emergency lights strobed across my retinas. I still smelled the blood.

I failed Aunt Edith. Everything inside me wrenched. I failed her and now she's dead. That particular fear, of failing someone important, always followed the flashback. Knowing it was coming never prevented the reaction. I wouldn't show that, either.

Only when I knew I was back in real time did I open my eyes.

Dawn and Boston had returned. The battlefield was gone, replaced by the street of upscale shops, converted from historic red-brick row houses. Picture windows with discreet painted logos and black wrought-iron bars alternated with concrete steps rising to entries, each landing decorated with trees or flowers in wooden barrels. Blood painted the steps and façade of the Carr Gallery, Aunt Edith lay dead and hidden beside the entryway stairs, and there on her other side was a doughy face like something a baker played with before rolling it out. Its expression was outraged and the hand attached to the equally doughy body still gripped my wrist, our arms crossing above Aunt Edith's neck.

"Don't muck up my crime scene, man," he said in pure Brooklynese.

Ice clogged my veins. My field of vision constricted until all I could see was his face before me. I could control my physical behavior during the flashback and even my awareness, once I realized its game was on; I couldn't chain the emotions, nor the adrenaline. The muscles I'd released tautened again. Flight wasn't an option, but pounding something was. "She's not a crime scene."

He glanced down, as if only then realizing Aunt Edith was, or had been, human. "She is now."

I went for him. But strong arms hauled me back and away.

One of the live voices sniggered in my ear. "What a

circus."

No sense fighting. It wasn't the policemen restraining me nor the crime scene technician I wanted to pound. I wanted the spotter, the one that got away during the war. If I could find the murderer who'd dossed down my Aunt Edith, he'd do, as well.

"Charles!"

That was my cousin Patricia's voice, piercing the enshrouding mental fog. I ignored the hands gripping me and peered over my shoulder. She stood alone, makeup smeared and lipstick chewed off, in the midst of the curious bystanders behind a strip of yellow tape. Flimsy as it looked, that tape represented the boundaries of the permissible and therefore was sufficient to stop her. Had they put that up behind me? I couldn't remember seeing it, much less ducking beneath it.

Patty seemed safe, so I turned back to Aunt Edith and eased from the policemen's holds. But a man stepped between the crime scene technician and me—between Aunt Edith and me. "Mr. Ellandun?"

I looked around him and didn't bother being subtle about it. Aunt Edith stared back, the heavy emptiness of the dead replacing her usual honest and level gaze, neither judgmental nor compassionate, with something blank. One of her pumps had fallen off and a chalk circle had been drawn around it. A bit of trash; the most amazing woman I'd ever met, and she'd been tossed aside like a bit of trash. It was beyond wrong. It was obscene.

"It's captain, actually," I said. "Captain Charles Ellandun."

He kept speaking, but as usual, Aunt Edith dominated the scene without trying. Only now it wasn't her elegant vivacity accomplishing that feat, but its absence. She had been the Rock of Gibraltar in my life since I'd been eleven and meeting her had been the watershed moment of my watershed year. She'd always been vital, compelling, more alive than the city itself. It was impossible for her to be dead.

Her skirt was the same as last night, as well, woven wool in the Hunter tartan plaid, the one she'd worn the day I first met her. Likely she'd returned to the art gallery directly after dinner, then. She still wore her wedding ring, as usual her only jewelry. There was no sign of her purse.

"Captain?" It was the man who'd stepped between us, a plainclothes detective in a button-down shirt and dark slacks.

Pounding him wouldn't help, either. I forced myself to look at him. I even remembered his question, although I was too distracted to focus. "Yes, I own several handguns."

"And were you in the war?" His voice was professional, beautifully modulated, and easy to listen to, even at that moment.

Even if he was an irritant.

"Yes." Was I ever.

The long, drawn-out *skrip* of a closing zipper demolished all my good intentions. The doughy crime scene technician slowly sealed the body bag. The shadow of the canvas flaps fluttered across her blank eyes. Then she vanished inside.

The air left my lungs as if I no longer needed oxygen, either. Again tunnel vision narrowed my field of focus, this time to the gurney as it rumbled past. The technician's hand rested atop the lumpy canvas.

I yearned to go for him again and fought the flashback-induced impulse. Although the battlefield had vanished into the scattered recesses of my mind, the subconscious, primal scream of combat still goaded me. Then I caught up with what the irritant standing beside me had just said in his elegant tenor.

Where were you last night.

I stared at him while the implications of that question soaked into the corners of my damaged brain. How long that took, while we locked eyes and assessed each other, I don't know; accurately measuring time has never been one of my finer accomplishments. But the details of his perfect face—expensively styled bronze-toned hair rippling above his ears, brown eyes steady and suspicious, smooth tan that had nothing to do with working outside, not a trace of stubble on the square jaw—left an after-image on my retinas like the strobing emergency lights. How could he stand being so damned perfect? It didn't matter whether pounding him would help or not. I went for him instead.

Again hands hauled me back. And suddenly cousin Patricia was between us, grabbing handfuls of my sport shirt and shaking me, or at least it. "Charles, for God's sake, what is *wrong* with you?"

I nearly told her, nearly reminded her of my diagnosis, but couldn't see the point even if I was an Ellandun and lived for the fight. The gurney and the moment were gone and the bloody adrenaline finally snapped. I shuddered beneath her clenched fists as the aftereffects kicked in. From the way her already wide green eyes were stretching wider, she felt it, too.

"Charles?" This time, her voice was less than a whisper and it broke in the middle of my name.

If I could have stopped the shaking, to protect Patty I would have done it. I'd failed her, too, and again I closed my eyes. Whatever showed in my all-too-transparent face, she didn't need to see it.

Because I'd tried to tackle a plainclothes police detective, Boston's finest slung me into the back of a squad car to cool down, one of an armload of emergency vehicles scattered about the street. They closed the doors, too, and how the July heat that rapidly built up inside that car was supposed to help me cool down, I cannot imagine. The interior stank from the stale fast-food wrappers littering the floorboards and the stain of something I didn't want to identify on the part of the seat I avoided.

I'd put up with all of it if I could have Aunt Edith back. She couldn't possibly be dead.

Outside the patrol car and a few yards away, Patricia and Brother Perfect chatted like old friends, her eyes sliding sideways to check on me every minute or so, his never leaving her damp and smudged face. He'd positioned her so she couldn't see the blood. Her mousy brown hair strained back in a knot that looked painted on, but then so did her jeans, and with her streamlined figure, I'm certain the average male never noticed the hair. To give him credit, Brother Perfect's gaze didn't drop, not even to her green cotton camp shirt, halfway unbuttoned from the bottom and tied in a knot above her belt buckle. Perhaps the stained handkerchief she used to rearrange the sad remnants of her makeup put him off.

Finally she walked away, ducked beneath the yellow crime-scene tape, and waited outside the perimeter, staring at me in the back of the squad car with her lower lip between her teeth. Brother Perfect watched her until their eyes met for a brief glance, and then he turned, opened the squad car door, and slid into the front passenger seat.

To give him further credit, he didn't bother scolding me. "You say you have several guns. Tell me about them."

I rubbed my eyes. "I own an M-16, a Mauser sniper's rifle—"

"Handguns, Captain. Tell me about your handguns."

To hell with him. I moved over until I breathed the outside air. "I have a Colt .45, two old Walther nine millimeters and two new ones—"

"What's the smallest bore handgun you own?"

The question threw me until I realized the holes in Aunt Edith's lungs had been small. "The nine millimeters."

"No twenty-two?" he asked. "Nothing smaller than a nine?"

"No," I said.

He stared at me for a long moment. The shakes had diminished as the adrenaline ebbed away, leaving me taut and intensely aware, and the skeptical curl of his lip made his opinion of my veracity perfectly clear. Again my temper began heating—there was something about him that made that a delightful process—but I swore this time I'd hang onto my self-control.

"I've kept records," I said. "And my LTC Class A and FID are both in order. You're welcome to check them."

"Thank you." The tone of his voice left no doubt he'd do so whether I volunteered them or not. "Are you carrying now?"

"No." But I intended to rectify that as soon as possible.

"So where were you last night?"

"At home." I gave him the address of my condo on the waterfront, north of Burroughs Wharf and well away from the tourist congestion at the Aquarium and Rowe's Wharf. He didn't write anything down; perhaps he had a photographic memory. "I had dinner with Aunt Edith around seven, got home around nine thirty or a bit after, and stayed in."

She had tried to persuade me to be sociable and forgiving, get involved with her latest bloody art show, see the family while everyone was in town as if I had a particle of interest whatsoever in them. The remembrance of how little encouragement I had given her during that, our final conversation, set my insides squirming.

"Can anyone confirm that?"

I hadn't even checked email. "No."

That internal squirming had a distinctly frigid tinge to it now. He'd gun for motive next; wasn't that how they did it on those stupid cop shows?

But he surprised me by motioning me out of the car. He leaned atop the hood, his perfect face strobed by the popping emergency lights so that he seemed dipped in blood then wiped clean, over and over again. I knew that image would stay in my nightmares for a long time to come. Something else to appreciate about the man.

"Don't leave town," he said, and walked away.

***

Shakedown

McKittrick Canyon
Guadalupe Mountains National Park
Culberson County, far West Texas

"Captain Kelly Bonham? Here he is," said the SUV's driver, punctuating his words with a full stop by slamming the vehicle's door. "Your rescue dog."

Yeah. Right. Bonnie rubbed her hands on her fatigue pants. Silly to feel nervous over a dog. It wasn't like she'd accepted a blind date or anything outrageous. Dogs generally liked her, and the more she saw of dogs, the more she preferred them to every single man she knew. But still her palms itched, as if she'd done something stupid and expected to regret it.

Through the tinted side windows, all she could see was a dark outline sitting stiffly upright in the rear seat. It seemed to be staring at her. *Sure, great. Make me even more nervous.*

The driver trudged around the SUV's front, a Texas Rangers ball cap tugged down crookedly over his eyes. His lopsided grin tucked up his cheek on one side, leaving the other side of his face serious, and he set a clipboard and two stuffed file folders on the hood in passing.

"His name's Pojo," the driver said. "That's Papa Oscar Juliet Oscar. He's a registered German Shepherd but not suitable for showing." He popped open the rear door and held it for her with a flourish.

Bonnie wiped her hands again and leaned over.

From the shadows, the most incredible pair of eyes stared back at her. Not the usual canine brown or black—but amber, gleaming pools of expensive, honey-toned Baltic amber, the sort of thing usually seen strung into a rich woman's necklace. Wary, thoughtful eyes, staring without blinking as if weighing her in the balance.

A shock rippled along Bonnie's spine. This wasn't a dog that would wash her face, chase a ball, roll over for a tummy rub. This was a dog that made his own decisions. And he was making one right now.

Without looking away, he yawned, showing off an impressive collection of huge, glistening teeth, a dark mouth, and an amazingly long tongue. His jaws stretched so wide, her head started to spin at the cavernous space opening before her. Then he snapped his jaws closed, teeth clacking.

And looked away. As if she no longer existed.

Oh, crap. Had she ever made a mistake.

Something in her chest plummeted to her abdomen and she swallowed. But her dry throat refused to cooperate. "He's a bomb sniffer, right?" *As opposed to something trained to chew my limbs off, one by one.*

"An explosives detection dog, retired." The driver leaned in past her, hooked on a leash, and unsnapped the red nylon harness from the seatbelt. "Come on, Pojo."

For a moment the brute didn't move, but actually leaned away from the leash's gentle tug. Maybe he thought it was all a mistake, too. Maybe he'd refuse to even get out of the SUV, and a cowardly sort of relief washed through her. When he reluctantly turned and jumped from the back seat to the ground, lithe and graceful as a cat, Bonnie shivered. He didn't look back at her.

"He's what's called a blue Shepherd." The driver rambled on, as if nothing had happened. "See how his lips and nose are dark grey instead of black? It's a genetic dilution and considered a fault. They're born with blue eyes, too, but those change as the puppies get older."

Pojo stalked away, head down, sniffing at the scrubby mountain grass. He turned and in the slanting evening sunlight, the washed-out hue of his mask and saddle became more obvious against his clear tan ruff and brindled hindquarters. Along his level back, several chunks of shorter fur rippled as he circled around them at the end of the leash.

Still ignoring her.

"So he was injured? Badly?"

"Not him, no. He and his handler were sniffing out a minefield near Khost, and the handler stumbled over a tripwire. One of them bounding anti-personnel mines." He rubbed the back of his neck and ducked his head. "Cut the handler in half, but Pojo only caught a few bits of stray shrapnel."

So the dog had seen his handler killed. That sounded like trauma and not a good thing at all. People went round the bend from less. One of her team members suffered from post-traumatic stress disorder. The first time he'd flashed back, he'd had screaming fits in the hospital loud enough to be heard in the next hall over. He'd rolled out of bed, taking the bed with him. He'd had to be sat on and medicated.

One clear ray of golden sunlight splashed across Pojo, backlighting him and darkening that grey to charcoal. Then he stepped past it, nose cutting through tufts of grass and snuffling loudly. What happened when a war dog flashed back? Considering those teeth, did she want to stick around and find out?

The driver held out the leash. She didn't want to take it. The brute on the leash's end twisted her about somewhere deep inside. But already the red nylon was winding around her legs. If she didn't take it, Pojo was going to tie them together, and the driver was too much a Southern country boy for her taste. She slipped her hand through the loop and stepped away.

Time to shake her down, boys.

The twist inside her tightened at the thought. In the days of sail, a newly-built ship, with a new crew and a new captain, would take a short, noncombatant cruise first thing off the stocks. The captain would feel out the ship's behavior, the officers would sort out the crew, and the crew would learn their duties. A shakedown cruise, it was called.

She was going to shake it down with a dog that had more teeth than the law allowed, a dog with a brain that might or might not be in fully functional condition. A dog that clearly wasn't impressed by her at all.

He still hadn't looked at her since jumping from the SUV.

The driver unloaded a giant bag of expensive dog food, carried it through her open cabin door, and reappeared without it. He scribbled a note on the clipboard's paper, scratched an X beside one line, and held it out. "Sign on the line, and he's yours."

Decision time.

That twisting rebelled, and panic spiraled up into her throat, closing it off. She couldn't do this, didn't want to do this. She was an electronics technician, an intelligence officer—not a dog handler or canine psychologist. This beast needed a specialist, someone who could help him adjust to civilian life. Someone who'd know when the time was right to cut short the experiment and put him down.

As if he read her thought, Pojo lifted his head from the lawn and glared at her, amber eyes gleaming. Like a dog possessed by something evil, something that wanted to rip her heart out and play chew-toy with it.

Or a dog who'd branded her a coward at first sight.

She'd proved during the war that she wasn't a coward. To the team, to her commanding officer, to herself. No need to prove it to a possibly crazy dog.

Then again, it's entirely possible he's not. Not crazy, that is. And that would make her—

Bonnie pushed the leash up her wrist, grabbed the clipboard and pen, and signed.

The driver started shuffling papers. "I set his records on your kitchen counter. Here's a receipt—" he handed it over, "—and congratulations on your newest family member."

Yeah. Right. So much for the family tree.

***

Thanks for reading! Dingbat Publishing strives to bring you quality entertainment that doesn't take itself too seriously. I mean honestly, with a name like that, our books have to be good or we're going to be laughed at. Or maybe both.

If you enjoyed this book, the best thing you can do is buy a million more copies and give them to all your friends... erm, leave a review on the readers' website of your preference. All authors love feedback and we take reviews from readers like you seriously. And if you believe that, then feel free to buy a million more copies and give them to all your once and future friends. Not to mention the past ones who will never speak to you again.

Oh, and c'mon over to ours, while you're at it:
www.DingbatPublishing.Weebly.com

Who knows what other books you'll find there?

Cheers,

Gunnar Grey,
Publisher, Author, and Chief Dingbat

δ

Dingbat Publishing

www.ingramcontent.com/pod-product-compliance
Lightning Source LLC
Chambersburg PA
CBHW070828260626
47170CB00007B/2295